W9-BUD-495

NOTE WORTHY

RILEY REDGATE

AMULET BOOKS
NEW YORK

NOTE
WORTHY

PUBLISHER'S NOTE: This is a work of fiction. Names, characters, places, and incidents are either the product of the author's imagination or used fictitiously, and any resemblance to actual persons, living or dead, business establishments, events, or locales is entirely coincidental.

Cataloging-in-Publication Data has been applied
for and may be obtained from the Library of Congress.
ISBN: 978-1-4197-2373-5

Book design by Maria T. Middleton and Alyssa Nassner

Published in 2017 by Amulet Books, an imprint of ABRAMS.

Printed and bound in the United States
10 9 8 7 6 5 4 3 2 1

ABRAMS The Art of Books
115 West 18th Street, New York, NY 10011
abramsbooks.com

for Marlene Hoirup, who gave music to my life

for Terry Hicks, who gave life to my music

and for Benjamin Locke, who taught

me what it means to give it all back

ALLEGRETTO

MONDAY MORNING WAS THE WORST POSSIBLE TIME to have an existential crisis, I decided on a Monday morning, while having an existential crisis.

Ideal crisis hours were obviously Friday afternoons, because you had a full weekend afterward to turn back into a person. You could get away with Saturday if you were efficient about it. Mondays, though—on Mondays, you had to size up the tsunami of work that loomed in the near distance and cobble together a survival strategy. There was no time for the crisis cycle: 1) teary breakdown, 2) self-indulgent wallowing, 3) questioning whether life had meaning, and 4) limping toward recovery. Four nifty stages. Like the water cycle, but soul-crushing.

I scanned the list posted on the stage door for the sixth time, hoping my eyesight had mysteriously failed me the first five times. Nope. No magical appearance of a callback for Jordan Sun, junior. I was a reject, like last year, and the year before.

I moved away from the stage door with dreamy slowness. My fellow rejects and I drifted down the hall, unspeaking. Katie Woods wore a hollow, shocked expression, as if she'd just seen somebody get mauled by a bear. Ash Crawford moved with the dangerous tension of someone who itched to smash a set of plates against a wall.

All normal. At the Kensington-Blaine Academy for the Performing Arts, half the students would have slit throats for parts in shows, dance pieces, and symphonic ensembles—anything to polish that NYU or Juilliard application to the blinding gleam the admissions officers wanted. Kensington loved its hyphenated adjectives: college-preparatory, cross-curricular, objective-oriented. "Low-stress" was not one of them. Every few days, you heard some kid crying and hyperventilating in the library bathroom. I, like any reasonable person, saved the crying and hyperventilating for my dorm.

Another failed audition. I could already hear my mom releasing the frustrated sigh that spoke more clearly than words: *This place wasn't meant for you.*

Familiar anxieties seeped in: that I should be back in San Francisco, working, making myself useful to my parents. That being here was a vanity project. That, as always, I didn't belong.

There was something alienating about being on scholarship, a tense mixture of gratefulness and otherness. *You're talented*, the money said, *and we want you here*. Still, it had the tang of *You were, are, and always will be different*. I was from a different world than most Kensington kids—I'd never been the Victorian two-story in western Massachusetts or the charming Georgian in the DC suburb. I was a cramped apartment in an anonymous brick building with a dripping air conditioner, stationed deep in the guts of the West Coast, and I'd landed here by some freak combination of providence and ambition. And I never forgot it.

I exited the cool depths of Palmer Hall onto a landscape of

deep green and blissful blue. Ahead, marble steps broadened, rolling down to the theater quad's long parabola of grass. To the left and right, Douglass Hall and Burgess Hall flanked the quad, twin sandstone buildings that glowed gold with noon. Nestled in the far north of New York State, a long drive from anything but fields and forest, Kensington in early autumn was the sort of beautiful that begged for attention.

Hot wind fluttered through the quad, dry heat that brought goosebumps rippling up my arms. I stood still, my too-small sneakers warming in the sunshine, as a stream of traffic maneuvered its way around me, confident hands fitting Ray-Bans over squinting eyes, shoulders shrugging off layers to soak in the heat. Neatly layered hair cascaded over even tans. Highlights snatched the sun and tossed back an angry gleam.

Over the banister, a line of backpacks wriggled up-campus toward the dining hall. I stayed put. I never skipped meals at school, but something had gone wrong with my stomach. Namely, it didn't seem to be there anymore, and wherever it had gone, my heart and lungs and the rest of my vital organs had danced merrily after it. Holding the full interior of my body was the dull roar of a single thought: *Fix this.*

I rocked forward on the balls of my feet like a racer before the starting gun. I tried to take steady breaths. All this excess energy, all this drive to get something done, and nowhere to funnel it. Zero options. I would have kidnapped the cast and deported them to Slovenia, but I didn't have sixteen thousand dollars for plane tickets. I would have sabotaged the light board and blackmailed the department into giving me a part, but I wasn't an asshole. I would have bribed the director with my eternal love, but she was Reese Garrison, dean of the School of Theater, and I couldn't think of anything that probably meant less to her than my affection.

I squinted back up at Palmer Hall, its peaks and crevices blacked out against that signature blue sky. Reese had posted the list only twenty minutes ago. If I caught her in her office, maybe I could wring some audition feedback out of the endless supply of needle-sharp comments that constituted conversations with her.

Given her entire personality, I didn't know why I was so sure that Reese, at the heart of everything, wanted us to do well. Maybe it was because she respected wanting something, and there was nothing I did better than want.

With a squeak of rubber on marble, I turned on my heel and walked back inside.

♫

Like all the offices on the top floor of Palmer Hall, Reese's was sterilized white and too bright for comfort, small lights gleaming down from on high. At best, it gave off the atmosphere of a hospital room. At worst, an interrogation chamber from a 1970s cop movie.

Behind a cluttered desk, Reese adjusted her silver-gray frames. Her lined eyes glowed up at me, amplified by thick glass. The lady had a way of making everyone feel the height of your average garden gnome, even those of us who stood five foot ten. She never got less terrifying, but you could get used to it, in the way that when you watch the same horror movie repeatedly, the jump scares start to lose their sting.

"I hope," she said, "that you're not here to ask me to reconsider."

"Heh, like that would work." It came out before I realized what I was saying, and as Reese's lips thinned, my life flashed before my eyes. It seemed shorter and more boring than I would've preferred. "Sorry!" I added. "Sorry, sorry."

I spent half my life whipping up apologies on behalf of my mouth, which I considered to be kind of separate from me as a person. I, Jordan Sun, valued levelheadedness, and also other human beings. Jordan Sun's Mouth did not care about either of these things. All it wanted was to be quick on the uptake, and the only people it behaved around were my parents. You had to be completely unhinged, borderline masochistic, to sass my mom and dad.

But the same went for Reese. Maybe I'd gotten too familiar—I'd known her from my first day at Kensington, first as a teacher and now as a housemother. The old housemother of Burgess Hall, the frighteningly ancient Mrs. Overgard, had gotten around to retiring at last, which meant that Reese lived three doors down from me this year, tasked with overseeing the dorm. This was a bit like living three doors down from a swarm of enraged hornets. Her definition of "quiet hours" was "if I hear music even one second after 11:00 p.m., I will personally rend to pieces everyone you love."

Reese let me wallow in a long moment of sheer terror. Then her small, sharp mouth assembled a toothy smile. "You're right," she said. "I don't reconsider. But I do take bribes in the amount of eight million dollars, unmarked bills."

Before I could laugh, or even register that Reese Garrison had made an actual joke, she asked, "What's your question?"

I glanced around her office, hunting down an inspired way to phrase this. Nothing in here was inspirational.

"Spit it out, Jordan." Reese folded her hands on her desk. The collection of bracelets around her wrists rattled.

"Sorry, right," I said. "I wondered if I could ask for audition feedback. Since you—" I cut myself off. Don't accuse. Step carefully. "Since I haven't had success in casting, so far, I figured it was a me thing."

"A 'you thing'?"

"A pattern in my auditions, I mean."

Reese picked up a pen, spinning it between her nimble fingers. Tiredness passed across her face, a startling little specter of an emotion. She was so expressive, Reese, expressive and flexible—an ex-dancer who had floated on- and off-Broadway for twenty years. "As with everyone, it's a combination of things," she said. "Mostly, the parts just haven't fit. I don't need to tell you, do I? You've heard the lines. Subjective industry. Case-by-case basis."

"Sorry, but—mostly?" I repeated, picking at the single weak spot in the spiel.

"What?"

"You said, *mostly*, the parts just didn't fit me."

One thin eyebrow rose. "And you're sure you *want* to hear what I might have to say."

It wasn't a question. She was steeling herself. I waited.

Race, whispered something in the back of my head. Kensington's race-blind casting policy was meant to give everyone the same shot at a lead part, but I couldn't quite shut off the voice that said, *Of course you, Jordan Mingyan Sun, aren't getting cast as a lead, when the leads are named Annabeth Campbell, Janie Wallace, and Cassandra Snyder*. Or was it my height? The fact that I was taller than half the guys I read with during auditions?

Still, it didn't explain why she hadn't cast me in the ensemble. *Freshmen* got cast in the ensemble.

Reese set down her pen. "Then let me be frank, because this is something you'll want to consider when you're auditioning for college programs: Your singing voice is difficult to reconcile with musical theater. Firstly, there's a timbre to it—and I'm not saying this couldn't be trained out, but it's a harshness, almost an inattentiveness to the text. Like a rock singer, not an actor."

I blinked rapidly. Thoughts about race and stature evaporated with a twinge of embarrassment. "Wh—you mean my pronunciation?"

"That's part of it. It also affects your physicality." She gestured at me. "Your eyes close; you shift and sway; your hands move with the notes instead of with intention. Those tics are a challenge to eliminate."

"I can do it," I said at once. "I'll fix it. If—"

She lifted a hand. I broke off.

"Again," she said, "that's subject to change. Unfortunately, what won't change for the foreseeable future is the number of roles that fit your range. It's just so deep." She took her glasses off, massaging thc bridge of her nose with her sharp fingertips. Wisps of her dark hair escaped over her forehead. "You've got a unique sound, Jordan; you don't hear many voices like yours, and I mean that genuinely. But musical theater will be a tough pursuit for a girl who's more comfortable singing the G below middle C than the one above."

For once, words wouldn't come. Instead, a horrible memory of eighth grade arrived, a middle school choir concert built of white button-ups, an array of bright lights, and a clutter of anxious feet on the bleachers. Our choir director had made every girl sing soprano. My voice had cracked down half an octave at the peak of the song, an ugly bray among the sweet whistle of the other kids' voices, and laughter had popped across the stage. My cheeks had gone as hot as sweat.

Of course this was why. Being an Alto 2 in the musical theater world is sort of like being a vulture in the wild: You have a spot in the ecosystem, but nobody's falling over themselves to express their appreciation. In this particular show, even the so-called alto ensemble parts sang up to a high F-sharp, which seemed like some sort of sadistic joke. For those unfamiliar with vocal ranges: Find a dog whistle and blow it, try to sing that note, and the resulting gurgling shriek will probably sound like my attempt to sing a high F-sharp.

"The last thing I want to be is a naysayer," Reese said, slipping her glasses back on. I bit back a skeptical noise. Naysaying was basically the woman's job description. The arts world, Kensington wanted to teach us, was brutal, so everything here was "no": no's at auditions, no's from our teachers, no, no, no, until we accumulated elephant-thick skin, until we made ourselves better.

"But," she went on, "remember. It's the greatest strength to know your weaknesses. It just means you have a question to answer: How hard will you work to get what you want? And that's the heart of it: from your career, from your time here, from everything, really—what do you want?"

I stayed quiet.

The world, I thought. *The whole world, gathered up in my arms.*

♫

Nothing kills productivity faster than feeling helpless. That night, I sat at my usual table in the corner of the Burgess common room. My hands were fixed to my laptop, which whirred frantically under my palms in the computer equivalent of death throes. The library had slim MacBook Pros to lend out short-term, but for long-term loans like mine, they apparently leased equipment dating to sometime in the Cretaceous Period.

I pressed my hands closer to the computer, absorbing its warmth. The common room was always a few degrees too cold, a perfect studying atmosphere. Even the thermostats at Kensington knew the philosophy. Don't get too comfortable. Stay on your toes.

The evening burrowed into night. Stacks of books shrank around everyone else, vanishing from the scattering of cherry tables at teardrop windows, but my work went untouched. I stared up at the brass chandeliers and out the window at the star-strewn country sky. I stared at the seat beside me, which had belonged to Michael every night last year. He'd sat with a hunch that gave him pronounced knots in his shoulders; beneath my fingers they'd felt like stone beads worked deep into bands of muscle. His hands dwarfed his pet brand of mechanical pencil: Pentel Sharp P200, sleek, black, reliable.

In the opposite corner, Sahana Malakar, ranked first in our class, was highlighting her notes. By the gas-jet fire in the hearth, Will Teagle was mouthing lines to himself, brow knitted. These were the kids I'd been comparing myself to for two years already. Kensington was divided into five disciplines—Theater, Music, Film, Visual Arts, and Dance—and the five schools hardly ever mixed, so although we had 1,500 students, Kensington could feel insular, even isolating. We lived with the kids in our discipline, went to every class with them, and spent our free hours on projects with them. "Full immersion in your craft," Admissions bragged, "and with your partners in learning!"

As my time trickled away, my brain supplied me with the usual helpful spiral of consequences: *If you don't finish this essay, you won't have time for your English reading, and you'll never catch up, and by next week you'll still be on page 200 when everyone else has finished the book, and O'Neill will look at you across the table with his bushy eyebrows doing that knowing waggling thing, and he'll realize everything you're saying is bullshit, and you'll end up with a B, and your class rank will slip, and goodbye Harvard or Columbia, goodbye to your parents being proud of anything you—*

I managed to cram in about two paragraphs around the thoughts, as they spiraled into *Why do you bother?* and *You're never going to make it* and *Give up, give up, give up.*

Finally, mercifully, my phone interrupted. Cheerful music sliced through the common-room ambiance.

The housemaster, Mr. Rollins, squat and well-postured in an armchair across the room, looked up from the play he was annotating. A few studiers shot me disgruntled glances. I mouthed an apology and stuffed notebooks and laptop into my backpack, yanking the stuck zipper so that it chewed black teeth together in an uneven zigzag. I slipped out the door.

The halls of Burgess were a maze of corkboard, colored nametags taped to doors, and embossed silver numbers. 113. 114. 115. I dashed to 119, locked myself in, and took a deep breath before hitting *accept*. "Hey, Mom."

I delayed the audition talk as long as possible, but I couldn't put it off forever. My mother took the news about as well as I thought she would: with a wandering string of Chinese and a lecture that whipped into life like a tornado.

My parents tracked my school performance like baseball nuts tracked the World Series. I never told people about it. A fun side effect of being Chinese is that people assume this about you already. It felt weirdly diminishing to admit it about myself, as if it simplified me to just another overachieving Asian kid with one of *those* moms, even if I was in fact Asian and did have one of those moms.

I weathered her tirade for a few minutes, cradling my phone between my ear and my shoulder. "Okay," I murmured halfway through one of her sentences, not thinking. She broke off.

"Don't 'okay,'" she said. "It's always 'okay' this, 'okay' that. Don't 'okay' me. How about you explain why this keeps happening?" A disbelieving laugh. "It's every single audition since you've gone to that place! It's not just singing. Why don't they put you on the, those, the regular plays?" I imagined the agitated fluttering of her hand as she tried to grab the words, put them in the right order. Mom's English tended to fracture when she didn't give herself time to breathe.

"Because," I said tiredly, "mainstage straight plays always have, like, eight-person casts, and the parts always go to seniors."

"I don't know, Jordan. I just don't know. All we get is bad news. What do you expect us to think, ah?"

"Mainstages aren't everything," I insisted. "I can find a student-led show in October. And my GPA's fine, and everything else is fine, it's just . . ." *that you've trained yourself to sniff out my weak spots.* The sentence I could never finish. Even this much talking back was pushing it. My mother and I had the sort of relationship that operated the most smoothly in silence.

She heaved her knowing sigh. I could picture the slow stream of air between her lips, her mouth framed by deep, tired creases. The sound punctured me.

Silence spread across my room. I'd been one of twenty Burgess residents to draw a single this year. It was twice the size of my room at home. Everything I owned stretched thinly across the space, making it look like an empty model room you might find, three-walled, sitting in the middle of a furniture store. I'd pinned my two posters, *Les Misérables* and *Hamilton*, as far apart as possible, thinking that it might make the white cinderblocks look busier. It hadn't worked.

The only thing I had in numbers were books. They lined up single-file on the shelves, quietly keeping me company. It was impossible to feel alone in a room full of favorite books. I had the sense that they knew me personally, that they'd read me cover to cover as I'd read them.

My mother had always been aggressive about getting me to read, scouring garage sales and libraries for free novels, plays, or biographies. She'd always wanted me to learn more. Do more. Be more. She spent her life hoping for my way up and out.

"I'm sorry," I said, my voice tiny, and for a horrible second, I thought I was going to cry. She never knew what to do with that.

I searched the photos I'd tacked to the corkboard above my desk, trying to distill reassurance out of the patchwork of familiar faces. Near the top hung my best friends in San Francisco, the four of us, arms slung around each other's shoulders. Shanice pandered to the camera, pulling that picture-perfect sun-white grin. Jenna had her eyes crossed and her tongue stuck out, and to the left, Maria and I were in the middle of hysterical laughter, both of us shaded brown by the end of the summer.

I took a stabilizing breath. "How's . . ." I started, tentative. "How's Dad?"

"Fine. We're fine." She sounded weary. I didn't reply. If they'd been fighting, she wouldn't have told me, anyway. And what did it change, for me to know whether they were in a peace period or a war period?

"I need to make dinner," Mom said, her voice softening. "Bye. Talk soon, okay?"

"Yeah, I—"

Click.

I dropped my phone, my whole body heavy. At least it wasn't ever anger with my mom—just anxiety, a nerve-shredding worry on my behalf that made me feel inadequate like nothing else could. Every time I dropped the ball, it made visible cracks in her exterior.

It felt like my parents had been gearing up their entire lives for next fall, my college application season. Last year, I'd read a one-man show for Experimental Playwriting in which a man decides over the course of forty-five minutes whether to press a button that will instantly kill somebody across the world, a random person, in exchange for ten million dollars. If you'd handed my parents that button and told them the reward was my admission to Harvard, I swear to God they would've pressed it without a second thought.

And if you asked them why? "Because it's Harvard." Conversation over.

In a way, I was lucky that they banked on name recognition. Their faith in the arts as a legitimate career path hovered around zero, so if Kensington hadn't been nicknamed "the Harvard of the Arts" by everyone from *USA Today* to the *New Yorker*, the odds of my going here also would've hovered around zero, scholarship or not. I was fourteen when I convinced my parents to let me apply to Kensington, and—when I got the full ride—to come here. I'd cajoled them into it every step of the way. But they would never be happy until I was the *best*. Here, you were more likely to have several extra limbs than be the best at anything.

I slid off my bed and measured my breaths. *Stop thinking about college—stop thinking at all—give your brain a rest.* It was always busy in my skull, always noisy, a honking metropolis of detours and preoccupations.

I hunched over my desk, studying my corkboard. There hung a creased picture of my dad and me, his knees leaning crookedly in his wheelchair, one of my hands set on his shoulders. Beside it was a shot of my mother standing on our building's crumbling stoop, stern and stately, wearing a summer dress with a red and green print. The pictures were three years old. They seemed to be from a separate lifetime. Before Kensington, before the fighting, before Michael, a mirror reflecting a mirror reflecting a mirror, every layer of difference adding a degree of warp.

The corner of a stray picture glinted to the side, snagged behind a family photo. I swiveled it into sight and yanked my fingers back. The image of Michael's face made something clench in my chest. His dark eyes peered out at me accusingly.

Why did I even have that? I could've sworn I'd put all those pictures in the garbage, where he belonged.

The flare of hurt withered into disgust. Three months, and I was still circling the carcass of our relationship like an obsessive buzzard. The worst thing about breakups was the narcissism that trailed after them, the absolute swallowing self-centeredness. Every movie about heartbreak had turned into my biopic. Every sentence about aloneness, every song lyric about longing, had morphed into a personal attack.

I snatched the photo down, crumpled it, and chucked it across the room at the trash can. It missed, landing beneath the open window. The dark ridges of the balled-up photo shone. Outside, a yellowing harvest moon was rising over the treetops.

I approached the window, flicked the scrap of glossy paper into place, and gazed through the glass at the moon. For a second I lost myself in the sight. For a second I could breathe clearly, the first instant of clarity since that morning.

Kensington was beautiful through everything. When I didn't have anything else, I had this castle in the countryside, this oasis, this prize I'd snared. Some days it was a diamond, and I almost couldn't understand how lucky I was to have stumbled upon it. And other days it was a living thing, trying desperately to free itself from me.

2

"WHAT AN IMPERTINENT THING IS A YOUNG GIRL bred in a nunnery!" Lydia jabbed an accusatory finger at me as she approached. "How full of questions! Prithee no more, Hellena; I have told thee more than thou understand'st already." Lydia Humphreys, my ex-roommate, had a football-helmet-shaped bob of platinum blonde hair and a voice that bounced off the amphitheater steps like a solid object.

I flashed a coy smile and sauntered backward. "The more's my grief. I would fain know as much as you, which makes me so inquisitive. Nor is it enough to know you are a lover, when . . ." I grimaced and rewound. "To know you are a lover, when . . . *shit*."

"Should I start again?" Lydia said, drifting out of character.

"I don't think it'll help. I'm so sorry, I should know these."

She waved it off. "It's a short scene. We have until Friday."

"Yeah. I'll get it together. Sorry."

"Really, it's fine," Lydia said. I hunted her freckled face for a trace of displeasure and came up empty. She looked mild and unbothered, but then again, she always looked mild and unbothered. Lydia had grown up with her grandparents and inherited all of her grandmother's mild, unbothered facial expressions. When she took the stage, her face full of life and outrage, she was unrecognizable.

I drifted into a sitting position on the rough stone of the amphitheater stage, eyeing the graduated rings that rippled up and out from us. Weeks at Kensington-Blaine all followed the same trajectory, a sine curve of stress that peaked on Wednesday afternoons. You got the sense, Wednesdays, that even if the Gods of Time came down from on high and magically inserted eighty-two extra hours into that evening, finishing your work would be a stretch. But I needed to find time somewhere to memorize this, get it into my muscles. If you had to think about your lines, you weren't doing it right.

This past weekend's audition had put a permanent twist in my focus. Since my conversation with Reese, whenever I talked, I resented my voice. What did you do with a problem you couldn't solve?

I could tell that Lydia wanted to ask what was wrong, but she stayed quiet, tentative. This was fair. We hadn't had a real conversation since freshman year, which was absolutely my fault, since I'd turned into that apocryphal girl who gets a boyfriend and vanishes into the ether. I wasn't proud of it.

I rubbed the heels of my palms into the seams of my closed eyes, exhausted. Suggesting we rehearse here had been a terrible idea. I saw Michael everywhere in the amphitheater. As last year had dwindled toward summer, we'd snuck out every other night, ducking up the quad fastened at the hands, and we'd always wound up on this stage, a stone circle that glowed like a second moon. We stayed until our voices buckled and our eyelids drooped, because soon he was going to graduate, and it'd be NYU for him and junior year for me. Soon there'd be no more secret hours to steal. Now, there was his ghost at the edge of the stage, six foot two of burning presence as I remembered him: a muscular knot of motion. Watching him move was like watching a firework twist up into the evening before it bursts.

Lydia broke the silence. "I'm sorry you didn't get cast."

I glanced up at her. I'd forgotten how blunt Lydia was, in a way that was never cruel, never for selfish satisfaction. It was so you knew she was always what she appeared to be. She could take a scalpel to a conversation, work it down to the bone, spot your fractures before you could describe them to her.

She smoothed the edge of her skirt. Splashes of pink on white. Lilly Pulitzer, a Humphreys family favorite. "It really is subjective," she said. "Seeing how Reese chooses people is actually very eye-opening." Lydia was assistant-directing the show, which seemed like a brave move. I would never have subjected myself to that quantity of Reese Garrison.

"For real," I said. "What's she looking for?"

"It's different for every part. Way fewer guys audition for the musical, so for guys' parts she's basically like, okay, which of these people can actually sing a high A and sound good? Whereas for girls, there's another whole checklist of stuff."

"God, maybe that's why Michael got leads three years in a row," I said, and instantly hated myself for bringing him up. It was a weird compulsion, like picking at a scab.

"Well," Lydia said, "he was also great. At everything."

"Yeah, I know." Michael could pull on a persona like a well-fitted costume piece. Accents especially—teachers sat up straighter when he did them, taken aback even after twenty years of teaching. He had a flamboyant Italian character he'd nicknamed Angelo and a simpering Frenchman I'd dubbed Pierre; he used to tug them out over the tables at dinner. And he did such a pitch-perfect Dublin accent, burbling out the corner of his mouth, that it was obvious he'd spent three summers in a row there, badgering all the Dubliners to speak more slowly so he could slip their words into his pockets.

His favorite was the noir detective, all flattened and nasal and fast-spoken in a transatlantic twang. Last year, he'd watched about six noir films in a row and then considered himself an expert. He whipped up vaguely hard-boiled-sounding lines about kids and teachers, dragging us into his made-up worlds. "Reese Garrison was a dame whose legs went ahhhn 'til next Tewsday," he'd drawl over my shoulder as I tried to write. "I gave 'er my essay, and she gave me three bullets, one for every danglin' modifier . . ."

And I'd groan, or I'd laugh. Or—mostly—I'd let him distract me. "It rained that summah," I'd drawl back in my smokiest femme fatale voice, playing along. "It rained 'til my conscience felt damn neah clean again." Then he'd reach forward and mess with my computer, and I'd swat at his hands until he'd take my wrists and pull me in, everything else forgotten. Characters abandoned. There we'd be in private closeness, silent all of a sudden and real.

I could still text him. I could break the three-month silence.

The second the thought came, I stood. *Get over this.* "Okay," I said, yanking the folded script pages out of my back pocket. They were an inked, highlighted disaster. I had notes annotating my notes. "Can we maybe run lines?"

"Sure," Lydia said, tucking her phone away. Instantly, I felt selfish for asking her to stay, but before I could offer her an exit strategy, she started the scene. "What an impertinent thing is a young girl bred in a—"

Noise spilled into the amphitheater. Lydia broke off, and we looked up. A group of vaguely familiar-looking boys was jolting down the steps, a herd of pastel shorts and tank tops. They caught sight of us and faltered but didn't stop. Soon they were pooling around the front of the stage, and a pair of them jogged forward.

"Hey there, ladies," said one of them, dark-haired, with even eyebrows that winged out over hazel eyes. He was unreasonably tall and unreasonably good-looking, and he'd also said the phrase, "Hey there, ladies," which obliterated any potential interest with the merciless speed of a plummeting guillotine blade.

"Are you leaving soon?" said the other boy, a redhead who was a more acceptable sort of tall, and whose words sounded so bored it was a miracle he'd mustered up the interest to open his mouth.

"Actually, we're in the middle of a rehearsal," Lydia said, the picture of neutrality.

"Like, just the two of you?" Tall looked at Taller and laughed. "Okay . . . uh, when's your big important rehearsal gonna be over?"

Lydia's lips pressed together almost imperceptibly. The Grandma Humphreys equivalent of taking out a shotgun. As my cheeks filled with heat, I remembered, suddenly, where I'd seen these guys: onstage, at their concerts. They were the New York Minuets, Kensington's douchiest a cappella group. This was an impressive title to hold, since the Kensington a cappella scene was a shade or two less friendly than the mafia, and a shade or two more exclusive. I wondered if the exclusive vibe was something they manufactured on purpose, or if they just fundamentally lacked the ability to befriend people who didn't spend all their time singing nonsense syllables.

"Don't you guys have music buildings to practice in?" I asked.

"Don't *you* have a theater to use?" said Taller, adjusting his perfect hair.

"Yes," I said. "You're standing in the middle of it."

Tall lifted his freckle-spattered hands. "Okay, calm down."

"I am calm," I said, thinking that there was no faster way to enrage a calm person than by telling them to calm down. These music guys had some nerve, anyway, trying to boot us out of a space specifically built for the School of Theater.

To be fair, near the back of their group was a kid I vaguely recognized from the theater school. Even though it was dominated by music kids, a cappella was technically extracurricular. Anyone in any discipline could audition for the half-dozen groups, and as a result, a cappella had become one of the few things that tied Kensington's five schools together (the others being the newspaper and a universal disdain for the administration). Even Visual Arts kids, who hardly ever stepped off the Northwest quad, could be spotted at a cappella concerts, begrudgingly jamming along to some remixed version of a pop song by Justine Gray or Sam Samuelson. The fall Sharpshooters concert was like our version of a Homecoming game—the guys' octet was our oldest group, and, if possible, even cultier than the rest of them.

Behind these two, the rest of the New York Minuets aimed questioning looks at me, murmuring to each other in an inaudible rumble. Tall glanced up at Taller, looking for guidance.

"Look," Taller said to me, in a *clearly-you-don't-understand-the-gravity-of-the-situation* sort of voice. "We have a competition we're preparing for. So if you could just—"

"You mean the one in December?" Lydia said flatly. "Three months from now?"

Taller looked at her. He seemed to have lost the ability to speak. Lydia's blue eyes were flinty beneath the blunt line of her bangs.

We'd gotten a bottomless pit's worth of e-mails about the competition. Aural Fixation, an a cappella group made famous by competition-style reality TV, was visiting Kensington right before winter break. Since their latest lineup had a couple of Kensington alumni, they'd be picking one of our a cappella groups to open for them during the European leg of their international tour over winter break. This, hilariously, meant two straight weeks of sold-out stadiums in London and Rome and Madrid and Lisbon. For concerts that consisted of people pretending to be musical instruments. Unreal.

There was no logical reason for a cappella to have exploded like this. It was the geekiest thing in the world, filled with terrible pun names and obscenely technical singing. It'd been born out of barbershop quartets and doo-wop, for God's sake. Its DNA was filled with strains of undiluted nerd.

Taller found his voice. "See? Even you've heard about it," he said, dripping condescension.

Lydia and I traded a disbelieving look. Even us! Mere plebeians!

"So," he continued. "You get why we need to practice."

"Right," I said. "In this space, specifically. Because there isn't an entire campus's worth of space just on the other side of those steps."

"Right," he agreed, and flashed a brilliant smile. I narrowed my eyes at his perfect teeth.

Lydia and I stood in deadlocked silence across from Tall and Taller. For a minute, I was determined to stand there until the natural world eroded me to dust, but then my eyes fell to the other Minuets' hopeful faces, and guilt crept into me. Maybe Tall and Taller weren't the nicest human beings, but these other kids just wanted to get on with rehearsal. There *were* more campus spaces for two people than sixteen, and anyway, at this point, it seemed like the options were to back down or waste another half-hour testing out new ways to explain the words "go away."

I sighed and relented. "Come on, Lydia. Let's find somewhere else."

There was a smugness to the way Taller said "Thanks" that made it sound distinctly like "I win." Although, to be fair, his entire persona oozed "I win." This kid was really leaning into the Kensington type. When people heard "Kensington-Blaine," they envisioned an alarmingly specific person: He was a third-generation legacy from New England with great bone structure; he was a he, because the school hadn't gone coed until 1985; he was white, with a name like Oliver or Henry or Phineus; and his trust fund was roughly the size of Iceland's GDP. With Kensington's aggressive diversity initiatives, though, the type was transforming, blurring out of boxes and categories by the year. They were a diminishing breed, the Olivers, Henries, and Phineuses (Phinei?).

As Lydia and I climbed out of the amphitheater, her hand was tight over the navy tote bag that hung on her shoulder, and I plucked hard at the patches of wear in my jeans. With every step,

I got angrier at myself for backing down. Why did it always end up like this? Why was I always the one to cave? Why did I feel guilty that we'd stood up for ourselves, even temporarily?

I tried not to hate the dark-haired boy down the steps, because anger didn't *do* anything, and besides, if I let myself hate him, it wouldn't entirely be for the way he'd acted. It would be for selfish reasons. All my failings were his successes: He could ask for what he wanted without feeling like an inconvenience. He could be totally sure of his own importance, not second-guessing a word out of his own mouth. That kid was handsome and rich and had a voice I remembered, a soaring tenor that was everything it should be. It's too simple to hate the people who have doorways where you have walls.

♫

That night, in my room, I scrolled through the flood of back-to-school audition advertisements. The e-mails had slowed to a trickle and finally stopped over the weekend, and I'd been glad at the time, but now I imagined turning back the clock and trying for any of these, instead of throwing away my chance on the musical. I could have run sound or lights for one of the senior capstone projects. I could have auditioned for *Trazba*, an experimental two-person play inspired by 1950s science-fiction films, in which one of the people is pregnant and the other person plays the fetus, because I guess every other idea for a play was already taken.

The e-mail system refreshed, and the thin stripe of a new e-mail appeared at the top. The subject line read, "Audition Call." My heart leapt, my mind yelled, *FATE!* and my finger stabbed the clickpad.

The message loaded. My excitement died. A cappella *again*.

In a black-and-white photo, eight boys in sport coats and ties sprawled in bored-looking positions on the steps to the Arlington Hall of Music. Stone lions flanked the steps, prowling on the columns that guarded Arlington, carved muscle rippling beneath their alabaster skin. Calligraphy font across the photo read *The Sharpshooters*, and beneath, the audition notice said:

> ONE SPOT HAS OPENED IN THE SHARPSHOOTERS, KENSINGTON-BLAINE'S PREMIER ALL-MALE A CAPPELLA OCTET. WE INVITE TENOR 1S OF ANY YEAR TO SIGN UP FOR AN AUDITION SLOT USING THE FORM BELOW.

Below that, they had an honest-to-God coat of arms, which displayed a pair of crows peeking around a quartered shield. Each crow carried a corner of a banner in its beak, stretching the cloth out to display *VERBIS DEFECTIS MUSICA INCIPIT*. I forced back the urge to laugh.

To be fair, the Sharps had been around since the 1930s, so the crest and the Latin hadn't been these guys' idea. Besides, with the way the school treated them—basically, with the type of reverence usually reserved for religious figures—how could we expect them *not* to have egos the size of your average planet?

Something about the Sharps made people lose their minds. The all-girls' group, the Precautionary Measures, packed Arlington Hall for their concerts, but for some reason it wasn't quite the same. Our whole student body—girls and guys alike—fawned over the Sharps; they were a blank canvas that people could write their dreams onto, a blend between boy-band obsession and artistic admiration. Even Michael had harbored a secret dream of joining the Sharps up until graduation, not that he'd ever had time to audition.

Maybe that was why the Minuets were so unpleasant. An inferiority complex. The thought pleased me a little more than it should have.

I scrolled back up and paused over the photo. The Sharps looked nothing alike, but something about them was identical. The crisp lines of their jackets, maybe, or the loose way they held their heads and hands and bodies. Or maybe just their expressions, which wore the thoughtless confidence that came with practice.

I would've bet all my worldly possessions that the Sharps would win that December competition, and just like that, they'd have a shot at fame. The envy in my mouth tasted hot and bitter. Liquid gold.

Then my eyes fell to the audition notice, to the words *TENOR 1*, and my hands went flat on the keyboard as an idea hit me like a thunderbolt. An idiotic, impossible idea.

"*Your range*," echoed Reese's voice, as I straightened in my seat. "*It's just so deep.*"

It could never work. Of course not.

Could it?

The feeling of failure still itched across my skin, a brand I was desperate to claw away. *How hard will you work to get what you want?* demanded Reese's voice. I remembered that kid from this afternoon sneering at me, and now, eight impassive faces stared out from this audition notice, daring me, questioning if I had what it took: Could I be a Sharpshooter? Could I be hyper-confident, hyper-competent, all my self-consciousness forgotten?

For the sliver of a chance of performing across the sea, maybe I could.

This competition was three months out. Find my way into the Sharpshooters, stay under the radar for ninety measly days, make damn sure we won, and there was the springboard to my future. An international tour would be a shining star on my college apps—something not every other overachieving arts kid would have. It was downright depressing, the lengths it took to feel special when you wrote yourself out on paper. All As? Who cared? That was the standard here. Some shows, some activities? Big deal. How were you changing the world?

Sometimes, when I wasn't too busy, I wondered why we had to change the world so early.

I went for my wardrobe and yanked it open, eyeing myself in the full-length mirror. From my dresser, I grabbed a tissue and rubbed off my purple lipstick, my eyeliner, my blush. Cheap chemical remover stung the air. Barefaced again, back to monochrome tan, I flipped my hair up the back of my skull and over my forehead, the fraying tips hanging above my eyes.

Everyone told me I looked like my dad. Never my mom, who had a delicate nose and chin. I had Dad's prominent features and his stubborn mouth. But I'd inherited Mom's height, plus a spare inch that had come from God knows where. "American food," she'd said, shaking her head, when I'd growth-spurted past her at age fifteen.

I released my hair. As it fell halfway down my waist, I remembered the endless row of wigs in the costume shop. I could even picture the one I wanted—short, shaggy, black. We were supposed to sign them out, and for only three days at a time, but if anyone ever confronted me, I could say I'd forgotten . . . innocent mistake, right?

I worked my dresser's top drawer, gummy with age, out of its slot and rummaged around for the finishing touch—a blunt-tipped pencil, worn down by use. I started filling in my eyebrows, shading the ends out with the tip, making my brows thick and serious.

I gathered my hair up and postured in the mirror, hooking one hand into the pockets of my jeans. Legs swiveled to shoulder-width apart. Tilting my head, I stuck my chin out.

"Hey," I said to myself, and again, deeper. "Hey. What's up?"

I was unrecognizable.

For the first time since Monday, I didn't hate the sound of my voice. I couldn't fix it, but I could use it. I'd solved the unsolvable problem, kept my answer and rewritten the question.

Two knocks came on my door, and I flinched. In the mirror, my shoulders buckled in. I shrank two sizes.

"Hey, lights out," called our prefect, Anabel, from beyond the door. Heart pattering, I flicked the switch, but my desk lamp still shed a remnant of buttery light. As I turned back toward the mirror in the dark, lifted my hair back up, and pulled my guy-stance back on, limb by cautious limb, I felt free and empty and new.

This had the potential to be the most embarrassing stunt in Kensington history, but I had nothing to lose except my dignity, and I'd lost so much of that in June, the prospect hardly fazed me. Besides, theater was all about risk. Risk wasn't scary. Insignificance was terrifying.

The light drew streaks down the thick lines of my arms. I rubbed one elbow, my throat tight. *Michael Jordan*, they'd taunted me every other day in middle school—not so much the girls as the boys. *Incredible Hulk. Hey, Jordan, can you sell me some steroids? Whatever you're on, I want some.* Early growth spurts and a thick frame had gotten me so much shit back then. I'd come out of middle school thinking, that was it, I was done caring what anyone thought.

Of course, if I didn't care, I wouldn't still be trying to prove myself, would I?

I wouldn't still want to win.

I SPENT FRIDAY AFTERNOON ON THE PALMER STAGE practicing my audition piece, serenading the empty theater. With my chin drawn back toward my neck, I muted the brightness of my upper notes, adjusting my delivery to hit the sweet spot between scratchy and strong. I sang out the stress of the week until my throat felt raw.

On Saturday evening, I fixed on my wig and warmed up in my dorm, nervous froth bubbling in my stomach. Then I headed for West Campus.

The second I set foot outside Burgess, I became hyperaware of my posture, the way I usually kept my elbows tucked in and my strides short. That wasn't masculine. Was it? I loosened up and tried to walk like a dude, at which point I discovered I had no clue how dudes are supposed to walk. It took me the entire journey to figure out a gait that didn't look like a velociraptor pretending to be a *West Side Story* character.

The first time I passed someone, a girl who glanced up for a second from her phone, I nearly turned and sprinted toward Burgess. She said nothing. Once she passed, I unleashed a huge breath that I'd been holding for some reason, as if suffocation would make me look manlier. This happened four more times.

I jogged down a grassy incline into the music quad, toward Arlington Hall, an elegant sculpture of weathered brick and poured beige pillars. I pushed through the backstage entrance at the side of the building, stopped outside the stage door, and waited.

At 6:15, one of the Sharpshooters emerged. He was half a head shorter than me and slender. With his neatly organized ginger-blond hair and a pastel button-up, he wouldn't have looked out of place in the children's section of a J. Crew catalog.

"Are you Julian?" he said, and I choked back a nervous giggle. A deep bass voice had spilled out of the kid's tiny body. It was like a Chihuahua opening its mouth and emitting a Rottweiler bark, or possibly the Darth Vader theme song.

I cleared my throat. "That's me," I said, pitching my voice down. I'd gotten used to pitching up in theater classes, both for projection's sake and to sound more feminine. I could get used to the opposite.

J. Crew Junior eyed me a second longer than he needed to. My fight-or-flight instinct burst into life, beating its wings frantically against the inside of my skull. I saw the conversation play out in quick, horrible flashes. He was going to say, "Um . . . you're a girl," and I would laugh nervously and bleat, "Yep! Psychology project! Ha!" at which point I would sprint out of Arlington Hall and never again let myself see the light of day, because in what *possible universe* could I *ever* have thought this was a viable plan?

But no. He just glanced over my clothes with obvious distaste.

"What?" I said, looking down. This was my most masculine outfit: worn-out tan corduroys and a blue flannel. Had they expected me to rent a tux?

The kid shrugged, smoothing a lock of his hair back into place. "Nothing," he said, meaningfully. "Come in." He stood aside and held the door open.

Lightheaded with relief, I folded into the backstage darkness. J. Crew Junior swaggered ahead of me, out onstage, and down the steps, tan boat shoes squeaking. For somebody who had never set foot on a boat, I had seen about three thousand too many boat shoes.

I emerged onstage and white light struck me. Scars glared from the black slick of the stage: blemishes left by screws and sets, splinters torn up by spike tape, shreds of gray missed in repainting.

Arlington Hall could have eaten three of the Palmer Theater and still had space for dessert. The house was a yawning chasm stretching endlessly ahead, and the wings to the right and left felt a few days' journey away. I felt very small and very naked, especially without makeup, which always reassured me onstage. It wasn't so much the feeling of wearing it as the preperformance ritual of sponging on foundation, dusting on blush, the tracing and blending of lipstick, eyeliner, eyeshadow. I couldn't remember the last time I'd even left my dorm without it.

I peered into the first row as J. Crew Junior joined six other silhouettes. Suddenly, horribly, it occurred to me that all seven Sharpshooters could be like the kid from Wednesday. How would I survive three months of *that*? Was the competition worth the very real possibility of me spontaneously combusting?

Another silhouette sat off to the side, his face illuminated by an iPhone screen. I recognized the beaky nose and permanently downturned mouth, which belonged to Dr. Graves, one of the music teachers.

I planted my feet, tilted my head, and ignored the way the underside of the wig made my pinned-up hair itch. A picture came to me: the wig flopping off like a dead pigeon, mid-song, onto the stage. Hysterical laughter built up in my throat.

Paper rustled somewhere. My audition sheet, probably, with the batch of lies I'd typed into their form, from fake name to the matching fake e-mail account I'd made. "Julian Zhang?" said one of the silhouettes—not the bass kid, and not Dr. Graves, who was still frowning down at his phone. This guy had a bright, amused tenor.

I nodded. Julian Zhang was a cousin in Seattle.

The silhouette attached to the voice leaned forward, allowing the stage light to tinge his features. I recognized the guy instantly, the long, rumpled hair looped back into a bun, the serious eyebrows. This kid had sung Justine Gray's "Slower Faster" in the Sharps' last spring concert, a raw, crooning performance that had reduced about 60 percent of the audience to pools of sexual frustration.

"Welcome to auditions," he said. "I'm Isaac Nakahara. I'm the president."

"Of the United States?" said my mouth, without my permission. In the hideous silence that followed this total nonjoke, I wondered how much it would cost to hire someone to stand next to me with duct tape, ready to prevent these sorts of situations.

I started to apologize, but Isaac replied cheerfully, "Yep. Leader of the Free World." He waved at the doors. "If Secret Service tackles you outside, that's why. Because I, the president of the United States, am never safe from—"

"*Isaac*," said an unimpressed voice beside him.

Isaac aimed a quick grin at whoever had said his name. "So, how's it going, Julian?"

I deepened my voice and tried to look nonchalant. "Not bad. How about you guys?"

A couple of laughs came from the silhouettes. Some groaning and shifting. "It's been a long-ass day," Isaac said.

"*Mister* Nakahara," said Dr. Graves to his phone, his permanent scowl deepening.

Isaac shot a careless glance over at him. "Sorry. A long gosh-darn day, by golly."

The other Sharps snickered. Dr. Graves tore his eyes from his screen to give Isaac a withering stare, which Isaac responded to with a thumbs-up. Eventually, Graves shook his head and returned to his phone, and Isaac returned to me. "But yeah, we've been here since nine a.m."

"God."

"You're the last one. Not to make you nervous." He cracked a smile. "You nervous? I was like 90 percent nerves when I auditioned. I mean, I was a freshman, but I guess it never gets better, the auditioning thing."

Somehow, his showy, joking patter was only making my nerves worse. I wished he would fold back into the dark, just let me sing and then get violently ill somewhere, probably. "I've had worse," I lied.

"Good attitude." Isaac leaned out of sight and addressed the others, a bit calmer. "He's a Theater junior. Looks like we've got trumpet and choir in middle school, plus musical theater classes."

A hazy sense of unreality sank over me. This boy, this actual human male, was talking about me like I was an actual human male. They were all buying this: the deeper voice, the wig, the too-small sports bra I'd used to strap back my already-flat chest under my baggy clothes. I hadn't realized exactly how little I'd expected this to work until this second.

It was finally sinking in: This disguise looked convincing enough to turn me invisible. I was just some *guy*. Anonymous. Nobody. The world saw exactly what it wanted to see.

A different, deeper voice jerked me to attention. "Do you beatbox at all?" it said crisply.

"Uh," I said. "No, I—"

"Any arranging experience?"

"Sorry. No."

"Any background in music theory?" the voice demanded. It had slowly increased in volume, and the acoustics in Arlington were so crisp that it echoed from all around me. It was as if God were a baritone and had nothing better to do than lament my lack of musical experience.

I shook my head, praying the School of Music wasn't filled with beatboxing and arranging experts. It seemed unlikely. Singers were a minority; the music kids were mostly instrumentalists. Pianists, flautists, guitarists. There were weirder music focuses, too. From the ones I'd met, I felt like every other Music kid had some focus with a name like Siberian Conducting Methods for Countertenor Rat-Choir.

"All right," said Isaac's voice. "Go ahead and—"

"Hang on," interrupted Baritone God. "Do you need a starting note?"

"No, thanks," I said. "I'm good."

"Are you pitch perfect?" he asked, sounding tense.

"I . . . don't think so? What exactly—"

"Sing a middle C." Baritone God leaned into sight. He was gaunt, with a shaved head and a pierced ear. Over his crisp button-up lay a tie in Kensington carnelian red, patterned with tiny black crows—our mascot. He looked as grave as if he were attending my funeral.

I picked a note and sang it. Baritone God drew a shiny disk from his pocket and blew into one of the apertures along the side. It whistled out a note a full third above the one I'd sung.

"Oh, well," he said, looking disappointed. He flicked a hand and sank back out of sight.

"You done, Trav?" said Isaac, his voice smiling.

"Yeah, yeah," muttered Trav.

"All right." Isaac looked back up at me. "What are you going to sing?"

"I'm going to do 'The Man for You' by Season Sev—"

I cut myself off. Silence fell, absurd silence. I'd sung this song for two straight hours yesterday, and it somehow hadn't occurred to me before this second—"The Man for You"?

". . . Season Seven," I finished, strangled.

"Cool," Isaac said. "Whenever you're ready."

I breathed out the jitters. One breath, two, and then I was singing, and the tension in my body sank through my feet, forgotten.

"You came through like a hurricane," I started, slow, steady. *"You said you'd stay until the end of the rain. You never asked me where I come from, never asked me where I've been. I never asked you about home, or why you never let me in."*

I shifted my focus to the back wall, my head clean of

everything but the basics: posture, breath support, loosening my tongue. *"But you're leaving town tomorrow, girl, now I'm feeling new,"* I sang, shifting the last note around in a short run. One of the Sharps moved in his seat as I upped the volume. *"I guess I never knew before, I never knew I needed you."*

I took a quick breath into the chorus, straightened my back, and belted: *"And now I stop. Wait. Breathe a little, talk too late. You're all I got, babe, and now I never want to hesitate. I'll let you in now, I'm gonna show you how, so baby, kiss me 'til our time runs out."*

In the audience, Dr. Graves looked up from his phone.

My heart gave a panicked leap. I heightened the scratchy quality in my voice, disguising my high notes. *"All I want to say is I'm the man for you, no doubt."* The notes cascaded down, down, and I ended near the bottom of my range.

The echo faded. Silence from the Sharps. Dr. Graves's face, still tilted up toward me, was lit ominously from beneath by the white blur of his screen. Somewhere, a pen clicked.

Then Isaac said, "Thanks for swinging by. You'll get an e-mail after dinner."

I hurried offstage in a cold sweat.

♫

At dinner, something jumpy and paranoid settled under the surface of my skin. Every time someone passed, I felt sure they were craning over my shoulder to stare at my face. But the nearest kids continued building a tepee out of their French fries, and not a single person gave me a second look, even ones I'd seen in class yesterday. Theater kids probably thought I was a film kid, and film kids probably thought I was a theater kid.

Kensington had two dining halls. Here on East Campus, the Film and Theater schools used McKnight Hall. On West Campus, the other three disciplines ate in Marden Cathedral, a hulking Gothic building that had been an active church until the fifties. Then they'd built the tiny, feather-gray chapel at the corner of town and converted the elegant cathedral into what had to be the fanciest cafeteria in the Western Hemisphere.

McKnight wasn't hard on the eyes either. It felt like an experimental film set. Spindly wooden frameworks covered the floor-to-ceiling windows, mapping outlines of trees that sprawled across the glass. The walls leaned deep inward to prop up the raftered ceiling, a weird architectural choice made weirder by the paint job: dark floors and carnelian walls, to show some Kensington spirit, and also presumably to remind us vividly of blood while we chewed our questionable meatloaf.

Someone crossed close behind me. I got a whiff of lavender and stiffened—I would've recognized Lydia's perfume anywhere. I angled my head directly down at my food, counted to ten, and snuck a glance upward. Her platinum hair bobbed into the distance.

Sitting out in the open was too risky. If I ever had to do this again, I would sit at the single-person round tables that lined the back wall, the lands of exile, designed for kids who wanted to read or study in peace while they ate. As far as the rest of McKnight was concerned, people in the back were invisible. I wouldn't have been surprised if one of them had died and nobody noticed.

I inhaled my dinner. The last bites always tasted better than the first. I slowed down enough by the end to savor the crisped texture around the edges of roasted chicken and the clean-tasting juice that snapped from fresh vegetables. Nothing here was ever canned, nothing saturated with salt or preservatives. Except the meatloaf, which consisted entirely of salt and preservatives. A real heart attack of a loaf.

My hands jittered as I scraped my plate clean. I pictured the Sharps in a seven-person circle on the black expanse of the Arlington stage, separating the callbacks from the rejects, Dr. Graves looming over them like a bird of prey.

I didn't dare to hope I could beat all the actual boys who'd auditioned, but that didn't stop my imagination from dancing all the way to the end of the road—the possibilities of that tour. I estimated that the average Kensington kid had been to 5.4 European countries, the way everyone talked about the continent like it was a second home, but I'd never left the US. I could only picture Paris as they showed it in movies, flooded with golden baubles of light, with streets that meandered downward like veins of lava glowing down a volcano's slope, a quiet restaurant on every corner. I pictured what I'd seen of Berlin from photos in textbooks—its square and practical apartment buildings, pastel or neutral, with parallel lines of molding that underscored rows of flowering window boxes. I pictured what I'd heard of London—bad teeth? worse weather?—and knew I was missing everything. Everything: a particular cold scent in the air, I was sure, or a turbulent mix of sounds that flooded busy roads, or the kinetic dart of a bicyclist throwing caution to the winds while a black cab blared its outrage. I wanted all of it. The world in its honking yelling breathing glowing entirety.

♫

Dorm check-in on Saturdays wasn't until 11:30, but after dinner I couldn't get back to Burgess fast enough. I power walked down August Drive, a black stripe of road that twined through the green of campus. The September dusk smelled thick and humid. Coils of clouds promised rain.

My mind drifted into forbidden territory as I walked. Last year, any given Saturday night, Michael and I would have been heading for the tiny coffeehouse in town, the Carrie Café. Carrie was a boisterous woman who had told me not-so-privately she wanted an invitation to our wedding. I'd smiled at so many versions of him across her rickety café tables: junior-fall Michael with braces clamped over his teeth; senior-fall Michael with scruff at the jawline for his part in *The Crucible*; senior-spring Michael, clean-shaven again, hair in a smooth fade at the sides of his head. Older in a way I couldn't describe. Each one mine.

I passed a militia of brick administrative buildings, quaint colonials with white trim. The high-rise dorm for the film kids stood ahead, a concrete interruption that some donor had erected in honor of himself in the eighties. Past the high-rise, August Drive curved toward West Campus.

I split off through the grass toward the theater quad and hurried to the Burgess girls' entrance, keeping my face ducked. Nobody paid attention, not the guys by the quad statue kicking around a Hacky Sack, not the girls up on the Palmer steps blasting "In the Heights" through a Bluetooth speaker.

I paused in the threshold. Those clusters of people looked so unworried, so unified, in their miniature worlds sealed away from mine.

I felt alone, but I had no one to blame but myself. It was the worst mistake to build your world on somebody else's back. Only took one motion for everything to fall to pieces.

I gripped the pieces for a second: Michael's voice, cocky and declarative, and the way the left half of his mouth smiled harder than the right. As the drizzle finally misted down from the sky, I imagined he would have had something to say about it. Probably the Dublin accent. *Jaysus, man, this weather's shite, y'know?* Or the detective. *It rained every night that week, cleared the cigar smoke right up. Sure, the dame had been on my mind, what she and I had done. There was nothin' else to do but sit there and think, wait for 'em to catch me.*

♫

My laptop clicked like an insect as it started. It had a new series of worrying noises to give me every day. I appreciated its effort to keep things interesting.

The wig came easily from my hairline, the cap damp with sweat. My fingers fumbled bobby pin after bobby pin from my hair, and locks of black cascaded around my face, rippled with a curl. I stripped off my flannel. The open space breathed cool air onto my sticky shoulders, around the lines of my sports bra, and a corset of heat dissipated from around my torso.

The computer bloomed into light. I threw a flurry of clicks and typing its way and bit down hard on my cheek.

One new message in Julian Zhang's otherwise-empty inbox. *Audition Results*, read the subject line. I tapped it.

Dear Julian,

Thanks for coming to auditions today.
We'd like to invite you to a callback tomorrow evening in the practice rooms underneath Prince Music Library. Room 003, 7:30 sharp.

Best,
The Sharpshooters

The tightly wound clockwork in my chest spun loose. Bells and whistles and noise clamored in my chest, but all around me was silence.

The world saw exactly what it wanted to see. Finally, it wanted to see me.

4

THE PRINCE MUSIC LIBRARY WAS KENSINGTON'S OLDEST building, perched at the southwestern tip of campus. Tall and elegant, with slender colonettes running up its dark walls, the library looked like a watchtower. A coppery sign stood outside, burnished by 160 years of terrible upstate New York weather, explaining the building's historical significance: A slightly important soldier had stayed here for a night, one time.

I made sure my wig was secure, my hair curled into locks and pinned beneath, and pushed through the ancient doors. As they boomed shut behind me, I stopped.

Most of Kensington's Gothic-style buildings were beautiful on the outside, but their interiors had walls the color of oatmeal and carpets the undecided green-gray of ditchwater. The interior design smacked of dentist waiting rooms. Not Prince Library. Here, copper-bracketed sconces on the walls peeked out from book cases that loomed like beasts. Overhead, miniature spotlights aimed their beams at artful positions to avoid shining on the books, drawing pools of light on a weathered oaken floor.

I wound through the imposing bookcases toward the center of the building: a sunken lounge space outlined by red sofas.

Above, the ceiling was conspicuously missing. Instead, the hollow expanse of the music library stretched up overhead. Upper levels with wooden railings gazed down on where I stood. Iron staircases glinted on the corner of every floor.

This, I thought, was the Kensington they'd had in 1850, when nobody like me could have set foot inside. This was the unchanging part of this place that belonged to the older world, the part that I could only ever spy on.

Shaking off the feeling of having time traveled, I headed for the basement door.

♫

I was early. I waited. I'd half-expected to find ancient catacombs down here, lined with flickering torches and maybe some disturbingly humanoid skulls, but the basement wasn't as old-fashioned as the rest of the music library. The underground halls had the shabby appearance of something built on a whim in the seventies and totally ignored ever since, with chintzy still-life paintings dangling here and there.

After a few minutes, a tall kid shouldered his way out of practice room 003—my competition. He was handsome in a baseball-player sort of way, with a round face and floppy chestnut hair. He nodded to me before disappearing upstairs.

Shit. Did the Sharps care how good-looking the auditioners were? That was part of their whole shtick, right? Being stupidly attractive? Maybe I could pass as a guy, but I somehow doubted I could pass as a hot guy.

J. Crew Junior wasn't hot, I reassured myself. But that was because he hadn't looked old enough to be hot yet. Even he was *pretty*, like one of those weirdly old-looking Renaissance babies from art history slides.

I should've found a suit. A suit could turn a 6-out-of-10-looking dude into a solid 8.

My watch's second hand ticked across home base: seven thirty. I knocked, and deep within practice room 003, a muffled voice called something that the soundproofing blurred into nothing. I cracked the door and slipped in.

The room was bigger than I'd expected. Filing cabinets were lined up along one wall, and a grand piano sat against the other, sleek and black, lid down. Isaac Nakahara sat on the lid, legs crossed. Baritone God—Trav—was perched at the piano bench with the ramrod posture of a soldier. He was even more solemn up close. His face looked as smooth and unlined as marble, like he'd never smiled in his life.

Dr. Graves was nowhere to be seen, but the other Sharps littered the room. They weren't all hot, thank God. Mainly, they were just intimidating, eyeing me with such obvious evaluation that I got the urge to somersault under the piano.

The seven of them made up a decently representative sample of Kensington kids: majority white, but not by much, overall well-dressed, and covered in symbols of the Kensington "middle class," which was a pretty ill-defined term around here. They wore crisp neon running shoes, Mizuno or Asics or Nike, barely broken in, a new pair bought every season or so. On wrists gleamed watches that bore zero resemblance to the scrap of Walmart plastic on my arm. These were a different species, muscular chunks of silver with miniature dials set into their generous faces, which made sense, because if your watch is as expensive as multiple watches, why not get a few extra dials in there? And tossed over shoulders were Kensington hoodies from the bookshop, soft and thick.

I only envied the school gear. Everything emblazoned with the Kensington logo was marked up obscenely for no other reason than that it was part of this place, and if you wore it, then you were part of this place, and eighty dollars—for most kids here—wasn't too steep a price to belong a little more.

"Julian!" greeted Isaac from the piano, with so much familiarity in his voice, you'd think we'd known each other for years. "Great to see you."

"Y-you too."

"You have a good weekend?"

"It, um, yes, good," I blurted, and resisted the strong urge to whack my forehead repeatedly on the door. *God, get it together.*

Isaac grinned, showing pointy canines. "Well, welcome to callbacks. First, let me tell you a bit about us." He flourished a hand at the guys. "We are the Sharpshooters. Originally, the group was called the Wing Singers, and they performed at the cathedral services, but that was ages ago. We've been here since Kensington added the music school in 1937. I mean, not us specifically, *we* haven't been here since the thirties." He reconsidered. "Except Trav, who has absolutely been here for eighty years."

Trav closed his eyes. "Isaac . . ."

Isaac shot him a grin and barreled on. "In terms of workload, we practice every night from eight to nine. We've got two gigs for the school in fall, another three in spring. And this year, we have that competition in December against the other groups, and if we win, we'll get to tour in Europe with Aural Fixation."

From the corner, J. Crew Junior let out a snicker. "Oral," he said.

Isaac looked like he was trying not to laugh. "Yes, Erik, thank you for your contribution." He unfolded his legs, letting a mile of dark wash denim hang over the edge of the Steinway. Scanning his outfit, I felt a sudden flash of insecurity about how I looked in my cheap, formless disguise. I hated how sensitive I'd become to minuscule markers like the Polo player on Isaac's gray V-neck. It wasn't that I wanted to care about brand names, but they were *loud*. When I met one of those kids wallpapered in brands, it felt like they wanted me, specifically, to know they were wearing a thousand dollars' worth of cashmere or cotton or silver or leather. It was the least I could do to acknowledge it.

Trav lifted the lid from the piano keys. It creaked very slowly. When he spoke, it was with sinister softness: "We will win that competition. Or else."

Isaac nodded. "There's that lighthearted attitude we love so much."

I suppressed a laugh. Isaac looked at me in time to catch the tail end of my grin. "I think that's it," he said, looking satisfied. "Questions?"

I shook my head.

"Then it's all you, Trav."

"Mm." Trav's nose wrinkled. "Off the piano."

Isaac rolled his eyes but jumped off the lid. He leaned deep into Trav's personal space, pulling one of those boy-stretches that showed the flexing sides of his underarms.

Trav sighed, shoved Isaac away by the shoulder, and looked back to me. "Let's get started," he said, in the tone that most movie villains would use to say, "Prepare to die."

The other Sharps leaned against the wall as Trav guided me through a range test, marking my results in a leather-bound journal. He played a series of notes on the piano and ordered me to sing them back, adding a new note to the end with each repetition. Finally, he played a set of chords and asked me to sing the top, middle, or bass note.

His facial expression didn't flicker, offering no clue as to how well I was doing. Finally, he scribbled something in his journal and flipped it shut.

"Circle up," he ordered, standing. "One last thing. A blend exercise, to see how you sound with the group."

The Sharps came forward from the wall. I hesitated before joining the circle. It was one thing to fool them from a stage, another to do it a foot in front of their faces. I stood between Trav and a boy wearing a turban, keeping my face tilted downward.

"Erik, lights," said Trav. The tiny bass hit the light switch and darkness clamped down. The sudden invisibility felt freeing. I waited for a pitch, for a direction, anything.

Then a hand grabbed me.

"Hey." I twisted away from the contact, staring blindly around. Another hand landed on my shoulder. One grabbed my arm. "*Dude*," I said, stumbling back. "What—"

"Shut the fuck up," said Trav's voice, calm and steely. It shocked me so much I went still. Someone's hand found my face, and a piece of cloth stretched over my eyes in the dark, back behind my head.

What the hell?

I prayed the wig would hold. The clips were strong, but not that strong.

The tugging sensation stopped. The blindfold stayed in place, and the wig hadn't budged, thank God.

"What ar—" I started, but a hand hit my back, shoving me forward. My hands shot out instinctively, feeling for the empty space in front of me.

The hand pushed me again. I stumbled into a walk. Soon, threads of dim light framed the top and bottom of my vision, creeping in around the blindfold's edges. I focused on the feeling of my sneakers padding on the tiles of the practice room hall, then up the stairs, then over the moaning floorboards of the main library. The scent of yellowing pages and dust descended.

The shock had faded into a frenzy of disbelief. *Initiation*.

I wondered for a split second if they were going to make me wrestle a bear, but on second thought, bear-wrestling was way cooler than most hazing I'd heard about. Usually, it sounded pointless and humiliating, like chugging hot sauce, or swallowing live goldfish, or sitting on blocks of ice naked until certain body parts went numb. If they even *tried* the goldfish thing, that was the end. I had limits.

We clanked up the iron steps that led from library floor to library floor. I bumped my shins repeatedly. I could already picture the watercolor of bruises that would be my legs tomorrow. After three staircases, a door clicked, the air cooled, and the floor scraped under eight pairs of feet, summoning up an image of worn stone. We walked up more stairs, steeper this time.

A hinge ahead whined. The hand at my back guided me forward and stopped me still.

I waited for a minute. Footsteps creaked and shifted in the darkness—and another sound, the distinctive strike and hiss of a match. Then a hollow *shhh* noise I couldn't identify.

A slight pressure worried at the back of my head, and the blindfold fell from my eyes. I blinked rapidly, praying my eyebrows hadn't smudged. Thank God I'd used enough setting spray to freeze a ferret in place.

The room was circular, like the top of a fairytale tower. The shadow of an upright piano stood opposite the door. Sheets of heavy cloth covered patches of wall where the windows must have been, creating thick darkness. The beat-up pinewood floor, scarred and uneven with age, reflected the only source of light: the line of long candles in the Sharps' fists. Thin, dripping candles, propping up curls of flame that danced at the tips of their chins.

About eighty smartass comments jumped to the tip of my tongue.

There must be some mistake, I wanted to say. *I auditioned for a singing group, not the Freemasons.*

Wait, shit, I wanted to say. *I forgot to bring all the goats I raised specifically for sacrificial purposes.*

All right, I wanted to say with a sigh. *Which one of you do I have to exorcise?*

None of it came out. Their faces lit from beneath by the firelight, the Sharps looked weirdly menacing—even J. Crew Junior, who, true to form, was wearing salmon-colored shorts.

Directly in front of me, Trav—the only one without a candle—held an open book. I squinted through the flickering light. A list of names, handwriting leaning every which way, was splattered down the aging pages. One cursive scribble read "Demetrius Dwiggins," and I blinked at it several times, expecting the name to disappear, sure that it was some terrifically ridiculous stress hallucination. Near the end of the list were Trav's name, neat and printed, and Isaac's, extravagantly looped.

"Um," I said. "Should I sign this?"

Trav stared ahead as if he hadn't heard a word. I took half a step and heard a gentle trickling, clicking sound. I looked down. My feet were surrounded by a spread of tiny cardboard fragments: an unassembled jigsaw puzzle.

I scanned the Sharps and their candles again. Each candle was a different length. I understood at once: finish putting this together before all six burned out, or . . . or what? Was some poor goldfish awaiting its fate in another room?

No time. I stepped out of the spread of pieces, crouched, and got to work.

The pieces were a chaos of bulbs and corners, layers of compacted cardboard loosened by years of hurried fingers. The first candle had already gone dark by the time I pieced together the border, an intimidatingly large rectangle.

I sorted the mess of black and white pieces by color and started forming patches. The activity was weirdly hypnotic, a mindless cycle of testing curves against each other, searching for a perfect fit. Time slipped away. Forming Rorschach blots against the floorboards, I nearly forgot where I was.

Then the distant Palmer bell chimed eight o'clock, and I glanced up to find that half the candles had already died. When I went back to the puzzle, the half-light started doing its work. Black and white both started to look like dark gray. The edges of pieces blurred. In the twitching shadows, their shapes became uncertain.

Then I linked two patches together and saw, suddenly, what this was. The fragment formed a sloppy but distinctive letter *T*. The puzzle was some sort of message.

A fourth candle burned down to a wax-coated fist, and the wick sputtered out.

My knees ached against the floorboards. My eyes were strained and watering. I squinted and rubbed them, focusing in.

Soon the first word was finished: *THE*. I bricked together an R near the bottom left and a *K* in the right corner. I shuttled an island of completed puzzle around, rotating it, trying to force the lines to match up. Then it joined to form *THE CROW'S*.

The light seemed to lurch. I looked up. The fifth candle had gone out. One left.

As the glowing tip of the fifth candlewick faded from red to nothing, Trav hummed a note, and the Sharps began to sing.

"*Oh, Danny boy, the pipes, the pipes are calling . . .*"

The solemn arrangement of the Irish folk song was so full, so startling, that I couldn't think. With the words curling into my ears, splintering my focus, I looked down at the mess of cardboard under my fingers and started to panic.

THE CROW'S . . . the crow's what? With this music distracting me, finishing the puzzle was all but shot—could I figure it out with a guess?

No. I'd made it this far. I didn't need to guess—I needed to work harder.

I gritted my teeth and hunched to the side, throwing my shadow away from the remainder of the puzzle. Problem pieces that hadn't seemed to fit anywhere started slotting into place, even as they turned into fragments of nothing beneath my clumsy fingers. Fighting the Sharps' serenade, I formed *B*, then *E*. I already knew what the phrase was by the time I pressed the last puzzle piece into position. *THE CROW'S BEAK.*

Our mascot was somewhere in this room, and it was carrying something for me. I shot to my feet, peering into the music-filled dark, when something tickled the back of my neck. I reached to scratch or slap it and my hand froze. A thick lock of hair had uncoiled from its bobby pins, slipped out of the wig, and fallen down my back.

The darkness offered cover. I twirled the lock of hair around two fingers and prodded it back into place under the wig. If the Sharps noticed, they didn't show it. As they sang, they gazed uncannily ahead, their eyes out of focus, as if they'd left their bodies.

I tried to swallow and nearly choked. My mouth was drier than the yellowing pages of the initiation book. The final candle was barely a stub now, lighting up Isaac's sharp chin. I turned—and found the crow.

Behind me was the door, painted red. On it hung a massive black flag with the Sharps coat of arms embroidered in gold. It looked disproportionately impressive in the flicker of the firelight, and the two crows stretching out their Latin motto looked almost alive. I reached for the birds. A patch of soft cloth was sewn below one of their beaks, and from the deep pocket, I extracted a silver fountain pen, its barrel cool and heavy.

I turned back to the seven boys, strode up to the initiation book, and scribbled *Julian Zhang* at the bottom of the list just as they finished a verse.

For a second there was silence.

"Aaand *cut*," said Isaac, swiping the book from Trav. He snapped it shut.

The Sharps broke into enthusiastic exclamations. One of them stripped away the heavy cloths from the walls, revealing four round windows that framed porthole views of the darkening campus in thin iron. A wooden chest sat beneath one window, a cable peeking out from the lid, two black sound monitors keeping guard beside it. One of the Sharps broke the puzzle back into a box and slid it behind the chest.

Isaac blew out the last candle, which turned to an undramatic finger of wax in the evening light. A few of the guys closed around me to clap my back, and a nervous laugh dislodged from where it had stuck in my throat. I held my neck rigid, urging my hair not to come loose, overwhelmed by the whirl of chatter.

"—did it *by yourself*," crowed a huge boy with dark flyaway hair. "Man, Nihal and Jon barely finished with two people—"

"Fucking nailed it," said a tall blond kid at his side, and gave me a vicious high-five that definitely sloughed off a layer of skin or two.

"Marcus, lights," called Isaac, and a boy with shaggy brown hair scampered over to plug in a power strip near the door. Lighting flickered into life: white-gold strip lights that encircled the stone wall, dim orange globes that dangled near each window, a rope of Christmas lights wrapped around one of the rafters. The place warmed a few degrees in the gold wash of light, and the boys became real all of a sudden, solidifying, their eyes bright and their hair shining. Isaac sprang onto the piano bench, rose to his tiptoes, and slid the book of signatures onto a crossbeam.

"So I'm in?" I said, breathless. My eyes prickled with the flood of light. I blinked hard several times.

"You are in," said Trav, perching on the bench beside Isaac's feet. "Initiation used to require the rookies to climb out a window onto the roof, too. Fifty-foot fall, if you slip. That's been phased out."

"What, did someone die?"

"It's just the hazing policy," Isaac said. He hopped down from the piano bench. "No one likes fun anymore."

I looked around. "Is this a reading room?" There wasn't a library book in sight, but an aging leather sofa stretched out beside the piano and matching armchairs flanked the door.

"This is the Crow's Nest," Isaac said proudly, flopping into an armchair. "It used to be a bell tower, but they took the bell out in the seventies, and it's been Sharps territory since then."

"Crow's Nest," I repeated. "Like a ship lookout?"

"Yep," Isaac said. "Except instead of a ship, we're looking out for the most haunted building on campus, and by the way I've definitely seen ghosts here before."

"Shut up, you have not," said the tall blond kid from the sofa.

"Scared?" said the dark-haired guy with the flyaway hair, and they engaged in a flurry of elbowing.

Realizing that the Sharps had all found seats, I went for the open armchair. With a creak of ancient springs, I sank a mile into the scraped leather cushioning.

My hair tickled with heat. I brushed a finger around the line of the wig. Still safe.

"So," Isaac said. "Now that you've proven yourself, initiate, let's do some introductions." He made a sweeping gesture around the room that involved his whole body. Somehow everything he did seemed to involve his whole body, every motion of the hands, every sentence he spoke. The way he moved reminded me of very giant dogs who think they're very small dogs and are accordingly careless with themselves.

He lifted a hand. "Again, I'm Isaac, your president. And the one who always looks like he just sniffed paint is your fearless musical director, Traveler Atwood."

Trav's nostrils flared. He said nothing.

"You met Erik yesterday." Isaac pointed at J. Crew Junior. "He's on bass and VP."

"VP?" I said.

"Vocal percussion," Erik said proudly, tilting his nose up. The light glinted on his freckled cheeks. Where everyone else was sitting, Erik was on his feet, stance comically wide, elbow postured against the wall. It really didn't make him look any larger. I wanted to offer him some of my height.

"Beatboxing," Isaac explained, interpreting my silence as confusion. "Drum noises. Weird explosion sounds. Whatever we need." He nodded to the boy with shaggy brown hair, who had curled up to sit in the windowsill. "Other freshman, go."

The boy waved. He was stocky, and his shoulders were slumped so low it looked uncomfortable, the sort of posture that suggested he wanted to disappear. "Hi. I'm Other Freshman, apparently." He gave a nervous laugh and cut himself off with a cough. "I'm Marcus Humphreys, and . . . yeah." Marcus's searching, desperate eyes landed on the sofa. "J-Jon Cox?"

"Hey. Jon Cox," introduced the guy sprawled over one arm of the sofa. His golden hair fell over one side of his high forehead, brushing one wingtip of his tortoiseshell glasses. Jon Cox looked more like a mental image of the Sharps than a real person—tall and handsome, with prominent cheekbones. The undone collar of his Polo showed a flushed patch of skin at the divot between his collarbones.

"And I'm Theodore Pugh," said the guy sitting next to him, whose bulk took up a good third of the sofa. His deep, resonant voice smacked of movie trailers, and his eyes were a startling light blue.

Jon Cox gave Theodore a laughing look. "Bro, don't even try. You're never going to get rid of it."

"Get rid of what?" I asked.

"His nickname," Jon Cox said. "Call him Mama. Everyone calls him Mama."

Mama aimed a scowl at Jon Cox. "Why are you so gung-ho about this?"

"'Cause you keep wet wipes in your backpack," said Jon Cox patiently, "and it's important that people know this about you."

Mama folded his arms. "I like clean surfaces!"

The boy at the sofa's other end, the boy with the turban, cleared his throat. He had patchy facial hair growing in on his chin and jawline, but puberty didn't seem to have mustered up the energy to give him a mustache. "I'm Nihal Singh Sehrawat," he introduced, in the driest deadpan I'd ever heard. "Your fellow Tenor 1. Welcome to the falsetto club."

I nodded, trying not to look at his turban. I'd seen this kid around campus once or twice—it was hard to forget the number of people staring at his head. I didn't want to be the next in a long line of turban-gawkers.

"Before you ask," he said, still in that flat tone, "I'm a Sikh, not Muslim; and I'm Indian, but I'm actually from New Jersey. So. Do with that information what you will."

"Cool," I said. "Good to meet you." I straightened in my armchair, trying to keep their names from slipping away. "I'm Julian. I'm a junior from San Francisco."

"Juniors, represent," Mama said. "Why didn't you audition our freshman year?"

I shrugged, faking unconcern. "Trying to focus on theater stuff."

Mama scoffed and scrubbed a hand through his dark hair. "Theater."

"Um, sorry, what?" I said, defensive.

Nihal Singh Sehrawat intervened. "Theodore is convinced that everything that isn't music is an inferior discipline, which is why I was mercilessly hazed all of last year."

Mama gave a luxuriant roll of his blue eyes. "I didn't *haze* you, you asshat," he said. "I just said that it's a national embarrassment that you don't know what parallel fifths are."

"See what I have to deal with?" Nihal said to me. "Asshat. I will never recover."

I decided not to admit that I also didn't know what parallel fifths were. "You're not School of Music?" I asked, relieved.

"No," Nihal said. "Visual Arts."

"Nihal actually doesn't even sing," Isaac said, his eyes sparkling with enjoyment. "We just hired him to Photoshop our posters so they look like Beatles album covers." Sprawled in his seat, his legs spread obscenely and his hands tracing circles over the chair's leather arms, Isaac looked like an emperor surveying his kingdom.

Nihal raised one eyebrow. "If you want to look like a Beatle, Isaac, you may have to get your first haircut since you exited the womb."

"Yeah, over my dead body," Isaac said, one hand flying defensively to his man bun.

Trav cleared his throat. Everyone fell silent.

"To business." Trav turned his eyes on me. They glinted brighter and harder than the stud in his ear. "For rehearsal tomorrow, arrive at least five minutes to eight. Lateness is not acceptable." Trav fished a thick spiral-bound journal from his backpack. "Don't schedule anything over the eight to nine o'clock hour. Ever. And yes, we do rehearse Friday and Saturday night. If you need an exemption for any reason, talk to me well in advance—two to three weeks." He tapped the journal. "I keep everyone's schedules here, but Sharps should always be your priority."

"Got it," I said, wondering about the air of obsession that hung around this guy like a strong cologne. Was he getting paid for this?

"Other things," Trav said, stowing the journal. "Firstly, our faculty sponsor is Dr. Graves, but don't bother asking him anything. To put it generously, he's *very* hands-off. Secondly, we take a three-day retreat at the beginning of Thanksgiving Break. Talk to your parents; factor it into your flight plans."

I nodded. It wouldn't be an issue. With the obscene cost of flights around Thanksgiving, I stayed at Kensington for break every year, so my parents never had to know if I left campus.

"Thirdly," he continued, pointing at a scrap of paper nailed above the piano, "don't discuss our competition set with anyone. You're bound to secrecy. And fourthly . . ." Trav tugged a black pouch from his pocket and tossed it to me. I caught it, pulled the drawstrings loose, and tugged out a silver key.

"That's a key to this room," Trav said. "Prince automatically locks at midnight, but one of the practice rooms has a broken window lock. Easy to sneak in. So, this place is always open for you, 24/7, 365." His voice grew stiff and uncomfortable. "The Nest is like a second home for most of us. That's how it is."

"Aw, Trav," Isaac said, with a lopsided grin. "I'm getting all warm and fuzzy."

"Fifthly," Trav added loudly, "ignore everything Isaac ever says. President isn't a real job."

Laughs bounced off the high ceiling like the sound of pealing bells. With my sound lost in the mix, I let my voice rise high.

♫

The moon was a bright disk outside my dorm, and I sat across from my mirror with a pair of scissors. The empty swirl of a new wig sat on the desk. I'd swapped out the first for a copy of my hair as it looked now, waist-long and simple, straight locks stitched tightly into the cap.

I'd been sitting here for minutes, waiting for the urge to hit. I couldn't trust my hair to stay put, so the solution was obvious: cut my long hair short, swap out a short wig for long, and use the wig to look like a girl instead. But cutting my hair felt so irreversible, a symbolic sign of total commitment. There'd be no rewinding, no panicking, no second thoughts. I'd be halfway through college before this regrew.

I narrowed my eyes at myself in the mirror. I was already committed. I was initiated. I'd conquered auditions, solved the puzzle, weathered Traveler Atwood's icy stare for a truly inhumane amount of time. It wasn't going to be for nothing.

My hair swung around my shoulders and face, crumpled by the grip of the pins. I let myself touch it for a minute. Then I lifted the scissors, took a steady breath, and cut. The metal brushed my jaw, a little sting.

Tinny shearing sounds tinted the air. I accelerated, snipping ends at angles, scything it all away. Years' worth of hair fell into the trash can between my knees, forearm lengths of it. I was weightless. My mother loved the thickness of my hair—"you'll never go bald"—but in the San Francisco summers it always glistened, oily, a heavy beacon for the sun.

Cut by cut, my new reality settled around my head. Every kiss of the scissors was a goodbye to what I used to be. The only thing left was December.

ANDANTE

5

THE FIRST MORNING AFTER MY INITIATION, I PUT ON so much makeup that my face felt like a wax mask. Between 7:15 a.m., when I woke up, and 3:00 p.m., when classes ended, my girl self was in charge, and she had to be deep undercover. Afternoons worried me—after lunch, theater kids left the quad for our core classes: math, science, history, and English. The core academics building rose thin and conspicuous in the center of Kensington, closer to West Campus, and everything music-related, than I would've liked.

Since the West Campus kids had morning core classes, there wasn't technically any overlap, but it still felt unsafe. If the Sharps found me out, I was done, even on the off-chance that the guys themselves were okay with having a girl as one of their tenors. I had a feeling that somewhere along the line, any petition to change Kensington's most historic all-male society to coed would be stamped out mercilessly in its tracks. The administration had miles of bureaucratic red tape running around our student organizations. You wanted to change your club's name? Switch your meeting space? Find funding? Get ready for a whole world of forms. A list of gatekeepers had to sign off on them, from faculty sponsors and deans to the Grand Duke of Luxembourg, probably. Then the forms vanished into a black hole of Student Life paperwork where they took weeks or months to process. No wonder nothing ever changed around here.

Still, none of that was scarier than the public shaming that would follow if I was discovered. I imagined a senior year where nobody would look at me, afraid of being associated with the girl who'd infiltrated an a cappella group, like the least impressive spy of all time.

It didn't matter. I wasn't planning on getting caught.

For the first time since June, I felt grateful for my ex-relationship. I'd spent so much time with Michael that I'd never made any legitimate friends in the School of Theater. Kensington friendships took upkeep. I'd never done the work. I knew the others in my grade, of course, and I still waved in the halls to Lydia and my other ex-roommate, Katie Woods, a stylish girl from Providence even taller than me. But we never went out of our way to see each other. I was scenery; I was set dressing; I was never center stage to anybody but Michael.

This summer, the idea of returning to Kensington without him had terrified me. Walking into Burgess Hall on move-in day had felt like walking into quicksand: the sensation of slow drowning, with nothing to grasp onto.

Now, being alone was useful. The usefulness wasn't a cure-all, but it lessened the sting.

After seventh period, I locked myself into my dorm. I rubbed off that morning's red lipstick and peeled off my false lashes, slipping my long wig into its drawer. Minutes later, Julian stared out of the mirror at me, arranging his boy bangs into place, attaching fake sideburns in front of his boy ears with a Q-tip and spirit gum, courtesy of the costume shop.

Lastly, I slid on a pair of thick-rimmed glasses I'd found in the shop's recycling bin. One of the hinges had been bent out of shape, but with a miniature screwdriver from the scene shop, I'd put them in working order. They were the perfect finishing touch. I officially looked like some grungy hipster.

The problem was the clothes. I'd signed out a few outfits from the costume shop for this week, but there was no chance of hanging on to those—the department rarely used wigs, but they would miss costume pieces soon enough. The current plan: raid the annual Dollar Sale this Saturday. During the week leading up to the sale, Kensington kids abandoned their unwanted bits and pieces in donation bins. On Saturday, everything was equal-opportunity dirt cheap, a dollar apiece. Snakeskin belts, leather brogues, and dorm accessories became a secondhand patchwork blanket strewn across the Marden Cathedral lawn.

With the twenty-three dollars left in my wallet, I needed boy clothes that could disguise my silhouette as thoroughly as possible. I also needed dresses and heels—Jordan had to be more feminine than I'd ever been, to make her 100 percent unrecognizable as Julian. I had makeup galore, raided from bargain bins and gifted from friends since I could remember, but I'd outgrown all but one of my dresses, and my single pair of heels had broken last fall.

Just as I finished my transformation, a knock came on my door. I froze with the pencil hovering over my eyebrow.

"Room check," called Anabel, the Burgess prefect. The sound of a pen tapping on a clipboard rang through the door. I could picture the expression on Anabel's face to the millimeter: dignified and determined, with one eyebrow arched high. With her golden barrel curls always perfectly in order, and her seemingly endless, neatly pressed array of semiformal blazers, Anabel Jennings looked exactly like the word "prefect" sounded.

"Shit," I breathed, looking around. I had to hide. I had to escape. No way I'd fit between the wardrobe shelves, and under the bed or the desk was too obvious.

I dashed for the window and grabbed the iron latch. The first-floor windows weren't supposed to open—it would make it too easy to sneak out—but I twisted anyway, gritting my teeth, praying they'd somehow forgotten to fix this one.

A horrible crunch came from the latch. Then the chunk of iron was dangling in my hand.

I stared at it for a split second, horrified, bewildered. How? This was iron! What was I, a wizard?

"Room check, second call," Anabel said, and I hissed a stream of curses, smacking the window open. It swung wide with an appalling squeal from its ancient hinges. I snatched my backpack from the bed, shouldered it, and hauled ass out the window as she said, "Coming in."

My sneakers sank into the dirt beside the rosebushes. Amid the distant scraping of Anabel's master key, I swung the window shut and ducked under the sill. She wouldn't see the broken handle, right? She was only checking for fire hazards, making sure we hadn't draped dynamite over our lamps or anything. No reason to look at the window.

Doubled over, I fled down the side of Burgess like someone trying to outrun a hail of bullets, iron latch still clutched in my fist, and as I skirted the corner, I wondered why I hadn't just told Anabel not to come in because I was naked and needed a second to become not naked.

Day one was going excellently.

♫

That night, I got to rehearsal half an hour early, imagining that Trav would skin me alive if I wasn't sufficiently on time. I expected to be the only one, but when I reached the top of the jagged stone steps, I found three of the guys sitting around the Crow's Nest.

Nihal, who sat cross-legged on the floor, glanced up and offered a solemn nod in greeting. A square of butcher paper was splayed in front of him, pinned open by a pair of textbooks. With black-smeared hands, he sketched the outline of something huge and oblong, the charcoal nub hushing across the rough paper. Freshman Marcus sat in the same windowsill he'd claimed last night, typing in furious spurts on his laptop. An angry constellation of acne had lit up on the center of his chin, and he kept rubbing it, looking upset. Meanwhile, Isaac sat on the piano bench with a guitar in his lap, strumming a chord progression. With his long hair bound loosely, messy strands all over the place, and his omnipresent T-shirt-and-dark-jeans combination, he looked kind of like an extra from *Grease*.

"Julian," Isaac sang in a ridiculous nasal voice, as I shut the door. *"Yeah, Julian the hooligan, oh. There's no foolin' Julian, oh-oh. Or droolin' on Julian—"*

"By all means," Nihal drawled, "keep going until I'm completely deaf." He tilted his head to scrutinize his sketch from another angle.

Isaac grinned, slapping his palm over the guitar strings. They gave an atonal complaint. "My bad. Didn't mean to interrupt your self-portrait."

I walked around the butcher paper, squinting at it from Nihal's perspective. The drawing was missing his facial hair. It also had no ears. Or a neck. "That's a self-portrait?" I asked.

Nihal sighed, giving me a long-suffering look. "It's an avocado."

"Ah."

He leaned over the butcher paper again. "I would advise taking Trav's advice and ignoring everything Isaac says."

I glanced at Isaac, who seemed happy with himself, like a cat that had just shoved something breakable off a counter.

"Oh my God," Marcus whispered from the window.

We looked over. "What?" Isaac said.

"Grimsley," Marcus said, turning his laptop to face us. A graph took up the left half of the screen. "Look at his poll numbers," he said, his voice growing frantic. "Is this really happening? I can't believe this."

Isaac shot a knowing glance at Nihal. "Kid's the second coming of Ted."

Nihal hummed a tuneful little chuckle—"hm-hm-hmm!"—before going back to his charcoal avocado.

Isaac saw my questioning expression and said, "Ted graduated last year. He commuted like forty-five minutes to Lake Placid to canvass for local midterm elections, if that gives you any idea."

"Hey." A frown darkened Marcus's round face, making him look ridiculously young. Borderline fetal. How did the freshmen age backward this much every year? "Th-the locals and mid-terms," he protested, "are just as important as presidential elections." He turned his laptop back to himself, rubbing his acne patch again. The computer screen streaked blue into his ash-brown hair. "Maybe more important," he said, "if you look at the math. Like, your vote gets more weight by proportions and stuff. Since less people vote."

"Fewer people," Nihal corrected, not looking up from his drawing.

"Yeah. That." Marcus's voice slid into a mumble. "God, who would actually vote for Grimsley . . ."

"Definitely not you," Isaac said, "'cause you're, you know, fourteen."

"Well, *yeah*, and also 'cause I have a *conscience*."

Grinning, I set my backpack next to the door. The hanging flag caught my eye, and I leaned close, inspecting the crows' beady eyes, remembering how they'd flashed in the candlelight. Since we had no sports teams, you couldn't find our mascot printed on cutesy pennants, but you'd find the birds lurking around campus if you knew where to look. Crow statues clung to the ends of the stone banisters outside the Ewing and Wingate dorms, and the chapel's stained glass windows had deep blue birds worked into the designs. The most obvious, though, were the pair of iron crows perched at the apex of Arthur's Arch, our main gates, named for Arthur Blaine of Kensington-Blaine fame. The birds' wings were spread, and they gazed down at everyone who entered campus.

I touched the banner the embroidered crows held, tracing the cursive golden swirls of the Latin motto. *Verbis defectis musica incipit.*

"Music," said Nihal behind me, "springs from failing words."

A chord sang out from Isaac's guitar, mellow and lovely, and then he ruined it by breaking into that fake nasal warble again. "*Music springs from failing words, yeah, yeah. Latin springs from total nerds, yeah, yeah.* Um. *Ostriches are giant birds? Yeah?*" He picked out a quick scale on the guitar, maneuvered it from his lap, and leaned it against the wall, moving with the painstaking care of someone setting down a newborn. Then he unfolded from the piano bench and loped toward the door. "Back in a bit."

He hummed down the stairwell, leaving silence behind him. A breeze floated in through one of the open windows and stirred the warm air. I loosed a slow breath.

"Welcome to Isaac," Nihal said, outlining the avocado's center stone.

"Is he always that . . . ?"

"He says whatever comes into his head, 100 percent of the time. And nobody has the heart to tell him to shut up. It'd be like kicking a kitten."

I laughed. If singing and drawing didn't end up working out, Nihal had a future in narrating nature documentaries. He spoke like he was reading from a script, every line laden with careful disinterest.

Marcus let out an uncertain laugh too, a split second too late for it to sound natural. Glancing over at the boy curled on the curve of the window ledge, I wondered what it must be like, being a freshman in the Sharps. He and Erik had gotten to Kensington only a couple weeks ago—they probably didn't know anything but the reputation, the obsession, the fan following.

Then again, what did I really know about the Sharps besides that? They didn't seem as full of themselves as I'd assumed they were. They were something else, an unknown variable, a family I wasn't a part of yet. I felt like the weird estranged aunt crashing the reunion. The estranged, cross-dressing aunt.

I relaxed into the sofa. Nihal straightened up, serious brown eyes fixing on me. "So, Julian," he said, "how long have you been singing?"

I was instantly suspicious. Was he trying to wring information out of me? Had he noticed something off?

But no. He was just curious, and I was just paranoid, and it had been a while since I'd had a personal conversation longer than thirty seconds.

Nihal told me he lived outside Newark. He was a sophomore, which surprised me, since he seemed older than any of the Sharps except maybe Trav, although maybe that was the beard at work. And to my disappointment, he had no interest in narrating nature documentaries, even though fame and fortune were obviously waiting for him there.

"Thank you, though," he deadpanned. "I've always wanted to sound overeducated and uninteresting."

"Ha. Goals."

"In all seriousness," he said, "my sister's applying for med school, and is looking at nine straight years of school, and I've started to wonder if there's a point at which your brain hits a plateau and can't absorb any more information."

I tugged *Antigone* out of my backpack. "I bet."

"She went to Kensington, too," Nihal said, carving shadows into the avocado pit. "Imagine my parents' relief when she said she was more interested in pre-med than jazz theory."

"God, that's the dream," I mumbled. "Getting interested in something that's actually going to make money." I always wondered whether other Asian kids had as tough a time as I did, convincing their parents to let them come to an arts school. "Are your parents doctors?" I asked.

"Yeah, my mom's an anesthesiologist and my dad's an orthopedic surgeon."

"I hope my job title never has that many syllables."

He raised an eyebrow. "You're setting the bar pretty low with 'actor.'"

"Same with 'painter,'" I retorted.

"Please." Nihal gave me a wounded look. "*Visual artiste.*"

It caught me off-guard. I laughed, desperately tried to keep the sound deep, and it came out as a strangled sort of *hurr-harr, horf!* noise. The sort of laugh a cartoon dog would have.

"Um," he said. "Are you okay?"

"Yep absolutely. Yes. Just something. Caught in my throat." I snapped open my copy of *Antigone*, face burning, and chewed on the end of my pen.

"Well, there's a water fountain downstairs, if you need." Nihal sank back into his drawing. Contented silence took over. In the evening light, a thin barrier collapsed from around me, connecting me to the Crow's Nest, its centuries-old walls, its scuffed-up armchairs, its summer air. The black flag on the door rippled in the breeze.

Loud, casual voices surged in the stairwell, reawakening my first-rehearsal jitters. Jon Cox and Mama piled in, Adidas logos splashed across their chests, shiny running shoes double-knotted. I blinked rapidly, my eyes playing tricks. The pair of them were complete opposites, with Jon Cox's golden tan and Mama's milky complexion, with Jon Cox's top-heavy muscle and Mama's evenly distributed fat, with Jon Cox's swish of blond hair and Mama's frustrated tangle of dark brown—but their best-friendship was so immediately recognizable, they still somehow looked like twins. They moved in that same bouncing, space-occupying way.

Erik strutted in after them. He had a hand folded in front of his mouth, and with the beat that clattered out from his cupped hand, it sounded like he'd managed to hide a full drumkit between his fingers and his lips. Over Erik's meticulously parted hair, Jon Cox and Mama continued a heated argument. From the cheerful tone of their bickering, they were enjoying it.

"—like, I'm sorry, but Haydn is bullshit," Jon Cox said. "All his concertos sound like that boring startup music that plays whenever you open Sibelius."

"*What?*" Mama looked like he'd been slapped. "That's the worst thing you've ever said to me. I'm disowning you."

"But you'll give me mommy issues," Jon Cox said.

"Dude, suck a dick."

Jon Cox adjusted his tortoiseshell glasses, grinning. "You've got to be the only person in the world who cares this much about Haydn."

"*Thousands of scholars*—you know what, I'm not talking to you. We're in a fight." Mama shook his head, but his eyes were bright with good humor. He headed for the window closest to me and swung it open, waving in more cooling evening air.

Through the open door, Isaac strolled in, and Trav followed, carrying a black folder. Everyone went quiet. Erik stopped beat-boxing. In the sudden hush, I heard the air stirring outside the library, curling around our tower.

"Gentlemen," Trav said. "Let's get started."

IN ALL MY TIME IN THEATER, CABARETS, AND PERFORMANCES, I'd never seen a group with this rapt focus, especially not a group of boys. Even Marcus, who was on the solo line and had barely anything to learn, shifted in place and waited patiently.

After we'd warmed up, Trav handed me a thick, stapled piece of sheet music. "Love You Forever," it said at the top, and the subtitle added, "by the Lonely Wingmen." It was one of those Top 40 radio songs you'd try to escape by switching the station, only to find the same song wailing through every possible wavelength. Just the sight of the title made its infuriatingly catchy hook blare in my head ("*I can't do that / I can't do that / I can't do that, oh no, no, no*"; repeat until you want to pour boiling oil in your ears). Trav had written my name in crisp blue pen beside the system's top line. His handwriting looked like a bundled Windows font.

It was all very official until I read the words beneath the notes. *Jin jah,* it said. *Dah din deh dat. Jin jah, love. Jah wah, if you promise you'll, din deh dat.*

I tried not to look amused. It would be like laughing at Trav's religion.

As we dug into the piece, time fell away. The darkening world outside the windows vanished. Half the time, it seemed like the others weren't even breathing, they were trained so hard on Trav's solemn comments.

And those comments. With a few years of trumpet and choir under my belt, I could sight-read decently. I knew my mezzo-fortes and my crescendos. But what was a "diminished two in second inversion," and why were Mama and Jon Cox nodding along like it was totally standard? What the hell was a "deceptive cadence"? An obscure supervillain?

I kept my mouth shut, trying to absorb as much as possible. Reassuringly, some of the others weren't great sight-readers, Jon Cox especially. But the guy could sing back a line perfectly the instant Trav played it, even though line by line, the arrangement didn't sound like much of anything.

After five minutes' teaching, Trav ordered us to put the parts together. He counted us in, a collective intake of breath rustled around the circle, and the richness of the sound hit me so hard, I nearly stopped singing. We were *loud*. Erik and Mama's voices, deep and vibrant, thrummed like a bass guitar. The soft excitement of the higher parts punctured the baritone lines, creating a texture that popped and danced. This was what I'd heard onstage last spring, the sound that made people in the seats around me shift, tense, and jog their knees in rhythm.

We finished the eight measures he'd taught. Trav, with patient displeasure, gave us an itemized list of everything we'd done wrong, absolutely none of which I'd noticed.

"Again," he said, finally. "And don't make me repeat anything."

So it went. Measure by measure, part by part, line by line, and every so often, we rewound to assemble the phrases. Someone always fumbled something or other, losing a note or the thread of a harmony in the mix, and Trav's face reflected the problem instantly, a downward twitch of his mouth or a concerned-looking eyebrow.

Half an hour in, Isaac said something to Mama while Trav was teaching a part. It wasn't loud enough to hear, not even loud enough to distract, but Trav went quiet and still, like a predator going rigid before a killing pounce. Mama's face slackened with dread.

Trav turned toward Isaac, who looked back unconcerned.

"Your part, Isaac," Trav said crisply, tapping a note on the piano.

Isaac cleared his throat and sight-sang the line as if it were nothing. Even the weird chromatic part, which Trav seemed to have written in just to make life difficult.

The two guys held eye contact for a long moment. Trav's lips thinned.

He went back to teaching. The tension cleared. Beside me, Nihal let out a slow breath, his expression telling me this wasn't rare.

It seemed like hardly five minutes before the bell across campus in Palmer tower was hammering nine o'clock, the deep strikes droning through the windowpanes. We passed our music back to Trav, who shuffled it into his binder.

I slipped my backpack on, but the others seemed happy to stay, even with our nine-thirty curfew creeping up. Erik settled at the piano and improvised some soothing jazz, looking unconcerned in the most intentional possible way. If he wanted approval from the older guys, he needed a new tactic—Mama and Jon Cox were already sinking back to the sofa, watching a video on Jon Cox's phone. And Trav . . . the instant his messenger bag landed on his shoulder, he was out the door without a word to anyone.

What was the guy's deal?

Mama jabbed his finger insistently at the screen. "Okay," he said, "*hard evidence* of Haydn being the best. This is the second movement of the Surprise Symphony. Just wait for it."

"What am I waiting for?" Jon Cox said.

"The *surprise*," Mama said, soulfully. "He puts this random fortissimo chord at the end of a pianissimo theme, out of nowhere. Haydn has the best sense of humor of *anyone* from the Classical period."

"I don't know, man." Jon Cox stretched his legs out. "Mozart literally wrote a song called 'Lick Me in the Ass.'"

"Well, that's just immature," Mama sniffed, and then his phone blared an orchestra hit so loudly that, over his shoulder, Marcus nearly fell out of the windowsill.

"Hey, Julian," Isaac said, bopping me on the shoulder. "Could I get your number?"

I jerked back to myself, remembering my disguise. I'd managed to forget I was wearing it. My *number*? Why did he want my number?

I straightened up, puffing my chest out. "Uh," I said gruffly. "Sure?"

He gestured with his phone. "Cool. I'm gonna add you to the group text."

“*Oh*. Sorry, right.” I deflated, mentally pinching myself, and rattled off the number.

“Sweet.” Isaac typed something and hit send, and my phone buzzed in my pocket. “Brace yourself for constant updates,” he said. “This thing is a nightmare.”

I tugged out my phone. *ALL HAIL JULIAN*, said the message Isaac had sent to the group.

“Julian,” said a voice behind me. Nihal was holding the door. “Are you going east?” he asked. “Want to come with?”

I was taken aback. “Y-yeah, sure.” I looked back at Isaac. “Later.”

“See ya.” Isaac took a running jump onto the sofa beside Jon Cox and Mama, who protested loudly. Leaving the Nest filled with rowdy exclamations, all warmth, light, and noise, Nihal and I disappeared into the coolness of the stairwell.

The heavy door shut behind us, nestling us in silence. Nihal adjusted the portfolio slung across his back as we descended the stone steps. “Enjoy your first rehearsal?”

“It was . . . intense.”

“Fair,” he said. “Trav’s a lot at first. Give him the benefit of the doubt.”

“I can do that,” I said, glancing at Nihal. In the dim light of the stairwell, his expression was unreadable. “Why’s he so . . . ?”

Nihal shook his head. “Family stuff. Probably best not to ask.”

I loosed a sigh. That mantra was depressingly familiar. When Michael had lost the lead role in a show after breaking his arm, he’d been the same way: Don’t ask, don’t talk, don’t even try. When his chronic pain acted up, my dad did it too: Don’t ask, don’t talk, don’t even try. But they weren’t showy about their avoidance. They didn't go quiet or dramatic. They carried on like normal, making enough noise that you couldn't pick out the silence underneath.

♫

That night, I jerked awake to a text tone. My room swam in darkness as I slumped over, grabbed my phone, and stared at the time: 3:25 a.m.

It was a text from Trav to the group message. *Thinking about rearranging the opening bars of Love You Forever. Don't get married to the cutouts after the jin jahs.*

"What . . . why," I whispered. "Go to sleep."

Even as the words slipped from my mouth, a text from Isaac ballooned up in gray: *SLEEP NOW, JIN JAHS LATER*

More complaints followed.

From Jon Cox: *thanks, gr9 to know, ive been weighing the pros/cons of that stylistic choice for 4 hours, thats why I'm up at ~3:30 in the goddamn morning~*

From Mama: *Wait no!! The texture of the cutouts is the best part!!!*

From Isaac: *SILENCE, mama, do NOT encourage him*

From Jon Cox: *how dare u speak to yr mother that way*

From Nihal: *Gentlemen. I have a test in five hours. Kindly shut up.*

They took his advice. The text went quiet. I shook my head and rolled back over, but for some reason, a smile pressed at my cheeks. A feeling was budding warm in my chest, and after a second of searching, I pinned it down: the feeling of being among family.

It had been over a year since I'd felt this with my actual family, this specific blend of humor, understanding, and comfort. A year and two months, to be specific.

I remembered that day's details—the call, the white-knuckled trip to the ER, the news about drought that had flashed soundlessly on the televisions in the waiting room—in the way I remembered those overplayed songs on the radio: the memories were suspended, dormant, in my brain cavity, waiting to surface without me needing to try. Weird, how one day your life could be swallowed up in minor inconveniences, the bad weather and late arrivals of the mundane world, and the next, nothing existed but a turning point. For some people, that would be a death, or a fire, or an overdose. My family was sent lurching out of control by something that, at first, seemed like a minuscule upset to the balance: my father getting a cough.

Here's what can happen at the crossroads of being poor, disabled, and sick, a road that's about as pleasant to travel as I-80 during rush hour. Let's say, as a totally hypothetical example, you're a paraplegic dad in San Francisco who works a checkout job, enabling your daughter's flights out to a fancy boarding school in New England. One particular month, let's say July, you get a nasty cough, but you need the hours, so you work through it. The cough evolves into a chilling fever. You soldier on, determined to support your family. But when that cough starts turning up blood and rattling sounds, and a fist of pressure builds in your chest, and one day you can no longer breathe without choking, you land in the emergency room with a tube draining a thick packet of fluid out of your left lung and an $18,000 medical bill accumulated before you're conscious again.

You don't have the money. Not even close. To date, your family has mustered up $3,500 of savings. Actually, you find yourself wishing you'd saved *less*, because past a $3,000 threshold, your disability benefits evaporate and, along with them, your health insurance.

Your wife thinks that this must be a mistake—that policy can't work like this—but it does. Now, without insurance, you somehow need to come up with the difference, $14,500 that the three of you have no way to pay. Your family starts to fight. First, about money; next, about everything, because it becomes impossible to put energy into things that are not money. The stability you built up over the years has evaporated because of one germ that got ambitious.

If, hypothetically, this were to happen, then the hypothetical daughter in the situation would feel, on any given day, angry, helpless, and guilty, in a steady turntable rotation. Angry, because in an apartment where a stalemate is now the best possible option, she eats and breathes tension. Helpless, because she can't magically erase that hospital bill. Most of all, guilty, because she wants to leave. She wants to run as far as she can, away from her parents to her oasis in New York, and she knows they can tell.

I knew they could tell. Here I was, thousands of miles away, still running.

After a year and two months, with a third of the bill paid off somehow and twice as much to go, we were still clawing our way back to some sort of normal. Maybe the missing element was Mom finding a part-time job that gave her more hours, or maybe the solution was me going back to California and staying there. I didn't know. All I knew was that home had a lonely feeling stapled to its side. We were just another problem I couldn't solve.

I looked back at my phone and let myself savor the feeling it gave, that spark of warmth and reassurance. Tomorrow, I would wall myself off from all this. For tonight, for a minute, I could let it linger.

7

REESE UNDERLINED THE WORDS ON THE BLACKBOARD: *anagnorisis* and *peripeteia*. She wrote so vigorously that her hair, bound in a dark knot at the base of her skull, bobbed with the impact of chalk to board. She finished the final *A* and clapped her palms. They puffed dust. "Recognition," she said, "and reversal. Cornerstones of Greek tragedy. A character's sudden epiphany, imposed by newfound knowledge—and the choice they make as a result. Who can give me the final recognition and reversal in *Antigone*?"

Most of us raised our hands. Reese aimed her stare around the table, lingering on the kids who avoided her eyes. Eventually, she picked Ash Crawford, whose hand was crooked above his head. Reese's method for starting a discussion wasn't harassing the kids who hadn't done the reading. She expected competence and didn't fawn over excellence; she wasn't going to chase us down to get us to do the work. If you slacked, you just *knew*, somewhere in your marrow, that she knew; she figured it out just by looking at you, and a dark patch of guilt grew like mold as the class churned forward and left you behind.

My phone buzzed in my pocket. I squeezed it, shutting it up.

As Ash Crawford barreled into an explanation of why Creon might be the protagonist of *Antigone*, Reese perched at the oval table and scanned the fifteen of us. The roundtable discussion format was part of the air of collaboration that Kensington wanted to foster, that we weren't "anonymous faces at desks, but equal-footed members of an ongoing discussion!" Or so all the admissions pamphlets exclaimed.

My dad, who'd gone to a disorganized disaster of a public high school in 1980s Los Angeles, referred to Kensington's methods as "hippie garbage." This baffled me. For somebody who ranted enthusiastically and often about the countless problems with his own schooling, Dad was weirdly fast to condemn any method that differed from it in any way. But at least he'd made it out with a diploma. His high school class, he'd told me, had boasted a 45 percent dropout rate. Social pressures aside, Dad's spinal cord injury had happened his sophomore year. Adjusting to a wheelchair had never made anyone's life easier.

My phone buzzed again. Reese's eyes fixed on me and narrowed. The woman had the directional hearing of an owl. I could've sworn she grew a foot taller in that instant.

The second the bell rang, I tried for the twentieth time that week—and failed—to disable the vibrate function. I was going to have to start burying my phone deep in my backpack. Every waking second, new messages barraged the Sharps group text. During Greek Monologue, I'd missed this collection of gems:

Isaac (11:48 a.m.): Okay guys, who wants to sing a background part on my EP?
Jon Cox (11:48 a.m.): ooooh I am Isaac, I am so fancy, I

am making an album, ladies look at me and my guitar

Isaac (11:48 a.m.): I swear to god, Jon

Jon Cox (11:48 a.m.): Can I borrow your guitar, does it work on girls?

Isaac (11:49 a.m.): Yeah. Like a magic wand basically.

Jon Cox (11:49 a.m.): really?

Isaac (11:49 a.m.): Of course not, you sentient walnut

Nihal (11:49 a.m.): Isaac, have you settled on a title? Because if this is the same EP with that "Smaller Cities" song, I like that as a title.

Jon Cox (11:49 a.m.): ok HEAR ME OUT how about u title it 'eelectric eel'

Isaac (11:49 a.m.): . . . I'm just saying what we're all thinking: that seems really Freudian

Nihal (11:50 a.m.): Literally nobody was thinking that.

Mama (11:50 a.m.): I assume none of your background parts are written for basses?

Isaac (11:50 a.m.): Uh, no, you're right.

Mama (11:50 a.m.): Okay so frankly the anti-bass discrimination in our society has gotten out of control. And as usual, your part of the problem.

Nihal (11:50 a.m.): *you're

And on, and on.

The freshmen and I didn't say much. Marcus only popped in to volunteer his services, always punctuated with an exclamation mark: "*I have an XLR cable you could borrow, Isaac!*" or "*I can print the arrangements, Trav!*" His eagerness to help was a tiny bit excruciating, but it made sense. What else did he have to contribute yet? The same went for Erik and me, too new to joke around with the others.

Anyway, I didn't intend to reach the point of joking around. No more easy conversations with Nihal; no more feeling like this could be some sort of family. I was glad that the Sharps were decent guys, and that they were funny, and surprisingly down-to-earth, and that making music with them got more exciting every time, and that I looked forward to eight o'clock all day. All that was fine. But it was not the point. I didn't need friends—I needed the competition, and so I would stay under the radar. Arm's-length acquaintanceship only.

I'd started studying random boys in a way that could be described as either subtle or incredibly creepy. Research! They moved in different ways, obviously, because they were not all part of some male hive mind controlled by a remote queen, but there were similarities. They led their stride with shoulders and chests, their spines straight, less of the curve you sometimes saw with girls, especially dancers. Hip movements were minimal. Also, sometimes, they sneakily adjusted their crotch areas.

The crotch area was a simple enough fix. I rolled up a sock and stuck it into my pants. The first day that I did this, the sock dislodged itself during rehearsal, slipping lower and lower down my pant leg until my fake penis had reached my knee. I excused myself to the bathroom. Trav was less than happy, but he didn't notice the knee penis, so I counted it as a victory. The next day, I folded the sock into my underwear in an elaborate loop the loop. This was more effective.

The more I tried to lead my gait with my shoulders and chest, though, the more my chest felt like a stumbling block. Luckily, I was on the small side of a B-cup, but my boobs weren't invisible. A sports bra only got me so far.

At the end of the week, I consulted Google. *How to flatten chest*, I typed into my laptop, sitting on my bed, and clicked on the result that looked the least like porn.

I scrolled down to a section that warned about the health risks of strapping your chest back with ACE bandages. There was a list of shirts called "compression shirts" that you could buy, but I kept reading, hoping for something free. One bullet point suggested using the control top of nylon pantyhose. I had a pair that I didn't mind disemboweling. I fished them out of a drawer and settled back on my bed to follow the directions.

I'd already snipped off the legs of the nylons when I looked back at the computer screen, suddenly curious. What was this site?

I scrolled up.

Here, said the introductory paragraph, *are some tips for passing that worked for me before I started hormones.*

I stopped. I reread the sentence. Hormones.

I set my scissors down and peered at the sidebar. It read, *Charlie. 24. He/him. My unofficial collection of emotional and physical resources for trans people. FTM resources, which I have the most of, are here. Click for MTF, genderqueer, genderfluid, agender, non-binary, and general resources.*

For a moment I was taken aback. Then I felt a sudden, distinct twinge of guilt. My hand found its way to my mouth, and I started chewing my nails.

I didn't know how big Kensington's trans population was. I'd met two trans kids here who were out: One was Will Teagle, a genderqueer kid in my grade; he was co-president of the Sexuality and Gender Equity club. The other was Jo Cavaliere, a trans girl in the film school who'd asked me to act in her senior capstone film last year. She'd come out halfway through filming, and then started her transition, which was followed by a week or so packed with people's mortified apologies every time they referred to her with male pronouns. Some days she waved it off. Others, she seemed too tired.

It stunned me how awkward a bunch of well-meaning people could be. There was something exceptionally clumsy about a bunch of cis kids trying to act nonchalant about her transition, rotating between aggressive supportiveness, curiosity, and intense silence around the topic for fear of saying the wrong thing. Trying to normalize—but not to ignore. Trying to be chill—but not distant. Things had grown steadily less weird as we came to the collective realization that this was not, shockingly, even sort of about us.

I reread the website's sidebar and tried to tease apart the bud of unease in my stomach. I hadn't given it serious thought, how my act contrasted with the way some trans kids lived their lives. I was just playing a role, and trans people weren't, so it hadn't felt relevant, hadn't felt like it was in the same ballpark. But it had weird echoes, didn't it? I was on a website that trans people used for their day-to-day. I felt like I was poaching, fishing earnest resources out of this site and turning them into ruses to trick the Sharps.

I lay back on my bed, staring at the ceiling. Cross-dressing and drag had their own history. I wasn't doing anything unprecedented. Still, I felt that I'd edged into a place that was not mine.

Worse, I pictured some nightmare scenario in which the Sharps found out about me cross-dressing, got furious at me for lying, and somehow carried that anger over into a situation with someone trans who was just living their life.

If they would act that way, though, that had to be something deep-seated, some land mine of darker thoughts waiting for a foot to hit it. Kensington, probably because it was an arts school, was such an overwhelmingly liberal place when it came to social issues—I couldn't imagine what it would be like to have that sort of opinion around campus. Or anywhere, really. It was a strange thing to have an opinion on somebody else's existence.

I thought of Nihal's contemplative air and Isaac's carelessness. I thought of Erik's peacocking, showing off every talent he had, and Marcus's desperation to please, and I tried to make sense of the possibility that any of these normal, decent-seeming people could secretly hate an entire subset of the Kensington population. It didn't compute to me. And it struck me, all of a sudden, how incredibly lucky I was not to have to worry about those opinions when I walked out into the world every morning.

From what I'd seen, none of the guys seemed that way, but I hadn't seen much yet. I didn't want to believe it, but I couldn't know. I imagined the sort of stone that's smooth and gray on the outside, which splits open to reveal a jagged red mineral interior. I wished I could tell who was gentle all the way down, and who turned to sharp edges the deeper you got.

♫

That evening, as usual, Nihal and Marcus were working in the Nest when I arrived. Tonight, gentle guitar music echoed through Marcus's laptop speakers. He was always playing something that threatened to send me to sleep, classical piano or the occasional Gregorian chant, probably to calm him down. Marcus was so anxious, so excitable, ready to be startled into laughter or nerves by virtually anything. Talking to the kid stressed me out.

A serene counterpart to Marcus's furiously bouncing leg, Nihal sat by the piano in meditative stillness, tracing line art on a series of cartoon panels.

I hovered over his shoulder, peeking at the cartoon. Bold line art gave the characters exaggerated features, heavy-lidded eyes and dramatic mouths. He'd done the background in dappled watercolors.

"That's really beautiful," I said.

"Hmm?" He looked up at me.

Shit—I hadn't fixed my voice. I straightened up, shoving my hands in my pockets. "Uh," I grunted, "looking good, bro."

". . . thanks," Nihal said, sounding a little weirded out. I backed off and considered the merits of melting into the floor.

As I set down my things, a clicking noise rang through the window where Marcus sat. He flinched away, lost his balance, and toppled onto the sofa, his laptop folding shut beside him.

"Wh—that guy threw something at me," he yelped, scrambling up on his knees.

Nihal's hand stilled against the paper. He set down his pen, stood, and strode to the window. Grim recognition flashed across his face. He tugged at one side of his turban, distaste settling across his expression.

I approached the circle of dusky sky. Marcus twitched away on the sofa so I could see.

A boy was at the bottom of the library building, standing on the long strip of pavement that stretched toward Arlington. He wore a brown leather backpack and was unreasonably tall. His dark hair gleamed in the sunset. It was the kid from the amphitheater.

I sank down, hiding most of my face from view. He wound up like a pitcher, lashed out a hand, and another pebble clattered off the side of the building.

"Hey," Nihal called sharply. "Cut it out."

"Make me," the boy called back, flashing an infuriating grin. "Those your rooks?"

"None of your business."

"What's a rook?" Marcus asked.

"It stands for rookies," Nihal said. "Also a crow pun."

Marcus gave his usual halting guffaw. I peered down at the boy. "He's a Minuet, right?"

"Yeah, their music director. Connor Caskey," Nihal muttered, a deep scowl settling on his face. "He's the only other Visual Arts person in an a cappella group, so he's the closest thing I have to an arch-nemesis, basically. He lives a floor up from me and spends all his time being the absolute worst."

"Caskey?" Marcus repeated. "Like Dr. Caskey?"

"Yep," Nihal said, and glanced at me. "His dad's the Dean of Music."

"He teaches my Baroque and Bach class!" Marcus exclaimed. "He's kind of a tool."

"Yes," Nihal said. "It runs in the family."

Connor Caskey's voice rang up. "I saw your desperate e-mail the other day, Singh. What happened? Someone finally crack under the weight of Trav being a total nutcase?"

For a long moment, I watched Nihal trying to decide whether to take the high road, his mouth thinning in frustration. Finally, he muttered something indistinguishable and stuck his head back out the window. "For *your* information," he called, "someone transferred to Andover."

Caskey let out a slow whistle. "Wow! The lengths people will go to escape you guys."

". . . *rrrghshnff*" was the noise that ground out of Nihal's mouth.

Caskey grinned toothily up at us, running a hand through his hair. Behind him, someone opened the Arlington side door, calling something that the breeze snatched away. Connor said something in reply, backed up from the Prince building, and gave us a salute that turned into a middle finger. "Later, Muppets," he called, and jogged toward Arlington.

We leaned back from the window. "Muppets?" Marcus said blankly. "Why?"

Nihal shuffled his comic into a black portfolio case and tucked his ink pen into a pouch. "We do not deign to absorb insults from lesser groups. Got it?"

"Yeah," I said. "What's his problem?"

Nihal shrugged. "He acts like it's all a joke, but I think he might still be bitter about the Sharps not letting him in. Which is actually sort of sad, since it's been three years." He rolled his eyes. "Or he may just enjoy the whole rivalry thing, because, again, he is the worst."

The worst? Maybe. Still, it was a little exhilarating, having an actual sworn enemy. *Rivals*—the word was exciting, a dare. A hurdle to jump. More than that, the term made everything so cut and dry. It wasn't often the world offered you on a silver platter an enemy whom you could dislike instantly and irrationally, no guilt involved. Connor's cocky grin fixed itself into my mind's eye, and it made me want to grin right back.

♬

On Saturday, I arrived at the Dollar Sale the moment they opened the roped-off enclosure, trying to avoid the inevitable crowd. I'd added a ratty baseball cap to my glasses, casting a deep shadow over my face.

I darted through collections of swiveling chairs and clumsily constructed side tables. In one row, beside a forest of wobbly lamps, a fleet of fans turned in the breeze, abandoned. Those were probably donated by kids who'd been lucky enough to get air-conditioned housing this year. The AC life was a life the theater students would never know. Not even Pepper House, the dorm for theater seniors, had AC. It had been a constant sore point for Michael, who heated up like a radiator in his sleep, always ending up with his sheets banished to the foot of his bed, a mess of soft, crimped cotton.

Stop thinking, sang a voice in my head. *Stop it, stop it, stop*.

I doubled my speed.

A sprawling map of clothes lay farther down the lawn, spread across picnic blankets in the deep shadow of Marden Cathedral. Near the stone path that led to the cathedral doors, I scooped up a six-pack of men's T-shirts, all varying shades on the grayscale, zipped inside a plastic case. I tucked it into the huge red bag they handed out to shoppers and next added multi-packs of undershirts and boys' socks. Buying guys' clothes was like buying bulk cereal.

Instinctively, I checked the tags, keeping the names I recognized. The more I dressed like the Sharps, the more I was one of them. Invisible. And, honestly, it would be nice to blend in for once. I snatched up twenty-three dollars' worth of Vineyard Vines, Barbour, and Joe's Jeans so quickly, the crowd was just starting to seep in when I brought my red bag to the counting table.

Approaching the table, I halted in my tracks. The school got the prefects to work this event, and the prefect manning the table . . . just my luck. It was Anabel, beautiful in a summery sundress, the fine point of her nose lifted in the air.

I swallowed, looking around. With people arriving in earnest like this, theater and music kids alike, it was too risky to wait for the workers to change shifts. I could get through one thirty-second interaction with Anabel, right? The hat, the glasses, the hair . . . I looked nothing like myself. Besides that pair of Hall Standards meetings right after move-in, we'd barely seen each other this year. All I had to do was keep my head down and act normal.

I strode up to the table, sliding the bag across to Anabel. "Yo," I grunted, staring at the table. The white plastic had the stubbly texture of plaster.

“Hi there,” she chirped, spilling the bag out. With crisply manicured nails, she picked through the bag’s contents item by item. I felt spoiled, with all the pricey denim and classy button-ups she was sorting through. A silky tie and—I was officially a sellout—a pair of boat shoes. I’d also stumbled on a pair of khakis perfect for performance and black dress shoes a size and a half too big. It wasn’t like I’d be running a marathon in the things. They just had to fit *enough*.

Anabel’s hands slowed as she moved to the next clump of items: three dresses and a pair of sparkling heels. I shifted in place.

“My, uh, my girlfriend couldn’t come,” I blurted.

“Oh.” Anabel let out a silvery laugh. “I was going to say, performing in *Hedwig* or something?”

“Yeah, no, she’s got me doing her dirty work.” I pulled on the lopsided smile I’d been practicing in the mirror, more of a smirk than a real smile. “Ha ha, typical B . . . Bertha.”

Mentally, I gave myself a hard smack. *What the hell?* Who was actually named Bertha, besides that seventy-two-year-old administrative assistant at my middle school?

“That’s considerate,” Anabel said. “Nice to know chivalry isn’t dead.”

I coughed. “No, yeah. Chivalry is just, uh, super alive.”

Then, like a moron, I looked directly at her. Mild confusion flickered across her expression, and she tilted her head, one curled blonde strand bouncing forward across her eye. “Wait, sorry, have we met?”

“Nope. No. I don’t think so.”

“You look really familiar.”

I shrugged, angling my face firmly down at the table. *Ohshitohgodohshit*, I thought. "Probably just the Kensington effect," I mumbled. "I think I would, um, remember you."

She laughed again. "That's sweet. Again with the chivalry."

There was a teasing edge to her voice that made my cheeks heat up. Was that—was she *flirting* with me? Why was I getting flustered? She couldn't be pursuing me—I'd told her I was dating Bertha. I would never cheat on Bertha. We had a beautiful relationship.

Unsure what to do, I very loudly said, "*Ha ha ha*," and then wanted to die.

Anabel shuffled the clothes back into the red canvas. "All right," she said, sounding amused. "That's twenty-three dollars."

I handed her the crumpled bills, and she sorted them into the beige metal box that served as a register, humming a song from the musical. Anabel had gotten one of the three leads this year, her first lead part. She was going to be good—she'd always impressed me in smaller parts. It was always tough to begrudge other kids their victories. Most people at Kensington were nice enough, even with the bloodthirsty levels of competition. It would've been so much easier if they were divas and assholes and I could hate them comfortably from the sidelines.

"Aaand here you go," she said, handing me my bag.

"Thanks." I grabbed it, turned, and froze in place. Jon Cox and Mama stood behind me in line, a lamp arching its neck between the two of them. A smile spread across Jon Cox's face, his tortoiseshell glasses glinting in the painful sun.

"What's good, man?" he crowed, dragging the lamp forward.

"Hey," I said, trying not to sound too flustered. "Um. Nice lamp. I'm gonna—" I took a few halting steps back, trying not to look like I was engineering an escape. They approached the table. The two halves of my life faced each other down.

Mama folded his arms, leaning back to talk to me. "I don't see *why* we're getting another lamp," he huffed. "We have one in our room already."

"You're roommates?" I said, wondering if they ever left each other's side for more than five minutes at a go. Mama nodded, his dark curls flapping in the wind.

We looked over at Jon Cox, who was leaning deep over the table, giving Anabel his confident grin. "Hey. How's it going? You're Anabel, right?"

A supremely bored look spread across Mama's round face. "Oh, God, not this again," he muttered.

I looked toward the road, and freedom. "Sorry, bro, I really have to go, but I'll see you at reh—"

"He always does this," Mama said tiredly. "Don't abandon me. I spend 90 percent of my life third-wheeling."

I bit the inside of my cheek and stayed put, giving the table a cautious glance.

"Sucks that you have to work this thing," Jon Cox was saying, giving his glasses a nudge up his nose with a knuckle. "How long are your shifts?"

"Not too bad," Anabel said. "An hour each." Her attention flickered over his face, from his blue eyes to his even smile.

Watching Jon Cox's performance was kind of fascinating. With his balanced, patrician features and the way his golden hair caught the sun, he was hard to look away from. He also had *it*, whatever *it* was—the charm some guys have that radiates out like a gravitational field. Michael had had *it,* too.

"Jon," Mama said loudly, "you're holding up the line."

Anabel came back to herself. "Right," she said, glancing down at the box and back up at him. "That'll be a dollar."

"Yeah." Jon Cox pulled his wallet from his pastel-yellow shorts and paid. "Thanks. I'll see you around."

As he backed away from the table, I drew the guys toward the exit. The line flooded up, hiding Anabel from sight, and the tension unknotted from my shoulders.

"What the fuck," Jon Cox said, battering Mama around the torso with the lamp. "She was like an eight."

Mama swatted the lamp away. It swung toward a tiny freshman girl with a messenger bag who dodged it with a squeak. "My bad," Mama called after her and turned back to Jon. "I'm doing you a favor. Remember Laura?"

They pulled identical grimaces.

"So, yeah," Mama said. "Leave theater girls alone."

"Not everybody is gonna be *Laura*."

"All I'm saying is," Mama rumbled, "maybe something would go *well* if you spent less time picking up random girls, and more time, I don't know, making friends with girls, so you can find someone who actually makes sense with your terrible personality."

Jon Cox grinned. He didn't even seem to hear the insult. "The Internet disagrees," he said. "Pickups work. They make you look like an alpha. Women love alphas. It's a real thing."

I couldn't contain myself. "Oh my God it completely is *not* a thing," I mumbled.

Jon Cox elbowed me. "Back me up here." I rubbed my bicep, scowling at him. We reached the entrance of the enclosure and slowed, waiting for the crowd to clear.

"Well," Mama said, "not to sound like a sixty-year-old, but—"

"You always sound like a sixty-year-old."

"—*but* maybe you shouldn't believe everything you read on the Internet."

Jon Cox flicked the lamp over his shoulder. "I officially like this lamp more than I like you."

"I'm just trying to help," Mama said. "It's sort of sad watching you bounce around from girl to girl like a hormone pinball, just so you can pretend you're not pining afte—"

"I'm not *pining*," Jon Cox said as we passed the teachers who manned the entrance. "I don't *pine*."

Mama looked skeptical but stayed quiet. As we reached August Drive, Jon Cox nudged me. "Julian, what're you up to? We're gonna go for a drive. I texted the group—we're picking up Isaac in a second."

"A drive?" I said. "You have your license?"

"Yeah."

"Aren't you a sophomore?"

Red tinged his cheeks. "Yeah, but I, um."

"He's old for his grade," Mama cut in, sounding strangely protective. "So, you coming?"

I hunted for excuses. This didn't fit the whole become-a-hermit-and-hide-forever plan. "I don't know, guys. I've got this essay to write, and—"

"Aw, come on," Jon Cox said, his composure re-forming. "Look at this." He waved at the volumes of blue sky overhead. "It's not gonna last forever."

Don't tempt me. I never got the chance to go off-campus. It didn't take long for Kensington to start feeling like a room whose walls were steadily moving inward.

Also, I felt a little gratified that these two wanted to hang out with me. At some point, it had become hard to tell if a boy genuinely thought I was cool and wanted to be friends with me, or if he wanted something different and wouldn't admit it for fear of rejection. This made for the worst kind of twilight zone. You didn't want to *assume* a guy was into you, but you had to have a plan lined up just in case, because what if he sprang feelings on you out of nowhere in a guerrilla attack and you were unprepared to deflect them in a tactful way? Also, it made a shitty foundation for a friendship, the constant worry that someone would stop caring about you overnight if you didn't want to date them. It was all very stressful.

But in disguise, this was not an issue. When I wasn't a girl, I could be sure that guys liked me for *me*, not for some hypothetical person they thought I could be to them.

It took a moment, but I shook off the gratification and the campus claustrophobia. I had to focus.

"I'm sorry," I said. "I have so much work."

Jon Cox scoffed. "Don't be sorry, just do it later." He slung an arm around my shoulders, and I tried not to tense. "Everyone has work, it's fucking Kensington."

"Think of it as a study break," Mama added.

"Yeah," Jon Cox said. He and Mama split off from me, heading up toward the parking lot. "We're going to drive by the theater quad in like ten minutes," Jon called, "and if you're not there, we're gonna come in and find you."

"But—" I called back, but they'd already turned their backs and started jogging away, perfectly in sync as always.

I watched them go, helpless.

♫

I snuck in through my bedroom window. I'd glued the latch back into place—when I'd studied the broken handle, I'd spotted traces of old glue. I wasn't a wizard. It was already broken when I broke it. Half reassuring, half disappointing.

I flicked my hair into place in the mirror and fastened my baseball cap back on. It wasn't surprising that Jon Cox had a car. With Kensington's limited parking, permits were pricey as hell—you could usually tell on sight which people could afford them.

The issue of wealth at Kensington was built into the walls, and not just in the sense that all the portraits on the literal walls were of old rich guys. This was true, but it wasn't really a concrete problem. The problem was the money this place asked us to drop on textbooks and supplies, even those of us on financial aid. A lot of other boarding schools were adopting full-ride scholarship options that paid for books, travel, laptops—the whole deal. Kensington hadn't caught up yet. Every semester, I calculated my textbook costs, usually three or four hundred dollars, and prayed it was offset by the money my parents weren't spending to feed me.

I put away my new clothes and headed down to August Drive. As I waited at the curb, my nerves slipped toward anticipation. I could stay at arm's length and still let off some steam. Didn't I deserve it? I'd made it through a whole week of my charade with no slipups. I'd just looked my own prefect right in the eye and fooled her. I, Jordan Sun, was pulling off the most outlandish acting performance in Kensington history, which was saying something, since a couple years ago, the School of Theater had put up an adaptation of *Macbeth* set on a space shuttle in 2405. (Half the roles had been turned into malevolent AIs.)

I wasn't just pulling it off, either. I was enjoying it, maybe too much. I liked the invisibility of being a boy, inhabiting a bigger and broader space. I was feeling less apologetic about it by the day.

Lately, I'd been eyeing the male roles in The Greek Monologue and Character and Humanity with envy, too. The parts girls workshopped in classes were usually filled with flirting, swooning, seducing, or heartbreak, only one of which I'd ever been any good at. I found myself wishing I could switch into being Julian. He could dig into some of those guys' roles, powerful or stubborn men, stoic or genius men, authoritative men—parts I would've loved to play for wish fulfillment, if nothing else.

I'd started asking myself: What had I ever gotten out of being a girl, anyway? What did I even *like* about it? Femininity had always felt inaccessible to me—my best attempt at it had always been putting on makeup and pretending to be more patient and graceful than I actually was, mostly for my mom's sake. Sometime in middle school, feeling awkward had become my default. Because I wasn't patient. I wasn't graceful. I was prematurely tall, I wasn't skinny, I wasn't pretty, and I didn't care about any of it as much as I was supposed to. Square peg, meet round hole.

Maybe, I'd thought for a while, the sense of not fitting was part of the package. But I didn't know if other girls felt this way. I'd never talked about it with anyone, even Jenna, Maria, or Shanice; and so many girls at school had seemed completely at home with girlhood that for me to admit the weakness—it would have felt like giving up control.

The only thing stranger than being a girl was turning into a woman. "Such a talented young woman," an aunt visiting San Francisco had said about me last summer, and at "young woman," I'd felt a pang of confusion. Had I alchemically morphed from a girl into a woman without noticing? When had that happened? Sometimes you heard that getting your period meant you were becoming a woman. But I'd first gotten my period when I was ten, the only one of my friends to walk up to fifth grade with tampons stuffed in my backpack, and nobody had called me "young woman" then. I'd been a kid—a surly, reclusive kid, a little too used to fending for myself.

Maybe the idea of turning from a girl into a woman freaked me out because I still didn't understand what it meant to become one. What was the woman origin story? What were we, and how did we get there? It was funny, because for boys, it seemed simple, in a way. The world had told me what becoming a man looked like: conquering one thing or another, one way or another. Becoming a woman, as far as they'd told us, looked like blood.

When Jon Cox pulled up a minute later, I stared rudely. He drove a steel-gray convertible, sleek and low to the ground, keypads on its silver door handles. The aerodynamic curves that formed the car's wide hood emphasized the checkered BMW logo embedded above the grill.

"Climb in," Jon Cox called from the driver's seat, one hand lazily resting on the dark curve of the wheel. Isaac lounged in the back, his guitar in his lap. Mama sat in the passenger seat, fiddling with the bumping radio.

“Climb?” I repeated. No way was I putting my dirty shoes on a car that had probably cost what my parents paid for five years’ rent.

“Yeah, I mean, within reason,” Jon Cox said.

After a second, Mama snapped his fingers at me. “*Maaake haaaste,*” he sang, a rumbling operatic sound.

I braced my hands on the door and vaulted in. My elbow buckled a second too soon, and I barreled into the neck of Isaac’s guitar. He snatched it away, instantly inspecting it, fingers skimming every inch of the wood. It was a beautiful instrument, sleek and rosy.

“Sorry,” I mumbled, settling in the soft black leather of the backseat.

“All good. She’s intact.” Isaac peered at me through narrowed eyes. “But watch it. Damage my baby, and I *will* ship you back to California in my guitar case.” His face lit up. “Did you guys know there was this girl who tried to ship herself to the Beatles in a box? Apparently she forgot to put air holes in the crate, which was, like, amateur mistake. If *I* was going to—”

Mama turned up the music, drowning him out. Isaac gave him the finger, Jon Cox laughed, and we revved down the street and through campus.

I kept one hand on my head, holding my baseball cap on. The film houses passed by, identical dollhouses, square black windows shielding musty-looking curtains. We rounded a corner and slid between the two biggest dorms on campus, Wingate and Ewing, which faced each other down as if in a Western standoff. Finally, we passed through Arthur’s Arch, leaving campus behind, framed by that imposing iron *A*.

Instead of continuing through town toward its array of shops and restaurants, we headed down a side street and out into the open countryside. Jon Cox accelerated until the wind started to billow around us, heavy waves of air. The woodland that encircled Kensington was assuming the tinge of autumn yellow, worn out by a long summer. Every so often, a peeling clapboard house cropped up on the side of the winding road, or a clearing dipped into the woodlands, fields rippling with tall grass and wildflowers.

The breeze tasted like loam and the coming fall, and it made the golden tassel of Jon Cox's hair ripple. "Hey," he told Mama, "can you Insta this?"

Mama sighed. "Like I said. Slave to the Internet." He picked up Jon's phone, entered his password, opened Instagram, and snapped a stupidly photogenic picture. "You should pay me for doing your branding," he grumbled.

Isaac glanced at me. "Jon Cox has, like, eighty thousand Instagram followers," he explained.

"Ugh," I said, involuntarily. He laughed.

"What can I say?" Jon Cox said, sounding satisfied. "Insta girls love me."

"It's probably 90 percent bots," Isaac shot back. "The spam algorithms love you."

"Follow me," Jon Cox called back to me, ignoring Isaac. "Join the crowds."

"I don't do social media," I said, which was true. If I'd had it, I would have deleted it to stay under the radar, anyway.

We were far off-campus by now, and the music faded out. After a second, a plucking guitar riff rang through the speakers.

"Love Me Forever."

"Yes," Jon Cox yelled, turning it up, summoning the bass to thud against my back.

"Here we go," Mama groaned, sinking in the passenger seat. I glanced into the side mirror. He'd sunk so low, all I could see were his thick eyebrows hiding beneath the chaos of hair over his wide forehead.

Jon Cox and Isaac were already singing along at the top of their lungs. Isaac was strumming along on his guitar, too, the strings vibrating inaudibly under the crisp envelope of the sound system. "Last night you said you love me," he and Jon wailed. "You said you can't stop, can't stop thinking of me—"

In front of me, Mama started to sing an octave down. His voice cut through the song like a bassoon. "Baby, I hope it doesn't tear you apart . . ."

Jon Cox cracked up. The persistent bray of his laughter was infectious. I couldn't stop myself from grinning, and as my smile spread wide, a warning chimed in me. *Arm's length. Keep your cover. Don't get in too deep.*

As the chorus approached, Jon Cox turned up the volume even more, drowning my thoughts. That huge, splashy hook blared out, and before I knew it, I was singing too, yell-singing at the top of my lungs. *"And you asked, 'When you gonna tell the truth?' and I said, 'Never' . . ."* The sound of our voices dissipated instantly, whisked away in the rush of the wind barreling through Jon Cox's car. Lost out in the world. *"'Cause you're looking for somebody who can love you forever, and I can't do that—I can't do that—I can't do that, oh no, no, no."*

The sun glowered down at us. The wind rose. We rushed by a house where a pair of middle-aged women sat on the lawn in plastic chairs, reading yellowing novels, dressed in florals. They glanced up as we passed, and their deep-set eyes tracked us until we were gone. The woods around us broke into rough waves of grass as we headed for a steep hill, and when the car crested and plunged down the incline, my stomach lifted. My heart lifted. Everything lifted, and I looked around at the guys in the car, laughing now, laughing about those dumb lyrics, all love and yearning, and I thought, *This is wonderful, this is wonderful, this is never going to last.*

Nothing lasts. I knew that, and I spent half my life repeating it to myself. Only Michael had ever managed to make me forget. He lived in the moment so much, he threw away everything other than the world in his immediate orbit. Sometimes I could've sworn he had no past and couldn't give a damn about the future, that he was some temporary blessing that flickered in and out of existence exactly as he wanted. You had to grab Michael by the shoulders and bully him to wring out any information about his life back home: Seattle and his three little brothers. His parents' calm suburban life did not interest him, and neither did Kensington kids' usual obsessions with what was coming next, colleges or conservatories or auditions. All Michael wanted was the wildness of the present, and he wanted it all at once. It was exhilarating, right up until the point that it became selfish.

I sat in the back of that glimmering car with its purring engine and I let myself think about him without anger, without longing, without anything. Michael wasn't perfect, which I'd known, but maybe he wasn't even perfect *for me*, which hadn't occurred to me. It seemed a little clearer to me now. It wasn't enlightenment to live like you had no history and no consequences. The world wasn't just made out of instants—it was made out of plans, too, and the ability to learn from your mistakes. I wished he'd learned.

The song reached its bridge, falling back in order to build into the final chorus.

Isaac wedged his guitar securely between seats. He grabbed the shoulders of Jon Cox's seat and maneuvered himself to his feet, craning his long body over the driver's headrest. The wind clawed at his hair, clearing the straggling locks back from his forehead. My throat tightened—if we hit anything, or even braked too fast, Isaac was getting pitched straight over the windshield—but Jon Cox and Mama didn't say a word. It wasn't until Isaac leaned forward to fiddle with the bass levels on the sound system that Mama smacked his hand away, shouting over the music, "Sit down, moron, you're going to hurt yourself."

"I've been thinking," Isaac yelled, sitting back down, "and the lyrics to this song kind of suck. I told Trav we shouldn't do it. People are gonna think we're dicks." He put his legs up over the side of the car, crossing them at the ankles.

Jon Cox turned the music down. "Nah, bro," he called back, glancing in the rearview. "Everyone knows the Minuets are the asshole group."

I suppressed a laugh. It was true. Everyone knew the reputations: The Minuets were assholes. The Sharps were pretentious. The all-girls' group—the Precautionary Measures—were super-gay. The jazz group—the Carnelian, named for one of our school colors—

were a bunch of drinkers. And the two coed groups, Hear Hear and Under A Rest, were quagmires of in-group incest.

It had been only a week, but I couldn't imagine what in-group dating would feel like. You'd never get a break from the person you were seeing.

Had the Sharps ever had a problem with that? They must have. The School of Music was less gay, proportionally, than the other schools, but that wasn't saying much.

"Hey, do you have a phone charger?" Mama said.

"Yeah," Jon Cox said, nodding at the glove compartment. "In there."

Mama reached for the glove compartment's handle. It snapped open, and there was a loud, distinct *pop*.

Out exploded a twinkling burst of glitter. It danced and twisted in the air like flour in a hurricane.

For a second, I just stared, unsure what the hell was happening.

Isaac flinched and drew his legs back into the car. Mama spluttered helplessly, his pale face screwed up and smothered in sparkles. He scrubbed at his forehead, spitting glitter over the side.

"What the *shit*?" Jon Cox said, as it settled. "Is that *glitter*?" A million flecks reflected the sun from the seats, from the backrests, from the dashboard—every last leathered crevice. Tiny, blinding points of light. As Mama hit the power button, killing the music, the hollow rush of the wind whipped up to fill the silence.

"Did you lend your car to someone?" I asked.

"Of course not. I don't let anyone borrow this thing."

"Hang on." Mama leaned forward, staring into the glove compartment. "I—there's a note in here," he said, sounding disbelieving. He yanked it out. "It says, 'Might want to put your roof up. Signed—' and there's a dotted half note." Mama lowered the note, his expression injured. "Oh, come *on*."

"The Minuets," Isaac said.

"How do you know?" I asked.

"Minuets are in 3/4 time," Mama said. "Dotted half note. It's a joke."

"Great joke," Jon Cox said. He slammed the heel of his palm against the steering wheel. Once, twice. "*Fuck*. I'm gonna be vacuuming glitter out of this thing for the next eight years."

"And not all minuets are even *in* 3/4," Mama said, as if that were the worst part of the whole thing. "Some of them are in 3/8. Or even 6/8, for some of the Italian—"

"Man, shut up," Jon Cox said. Mama emitted a sigh and went quiet.

"It's okay, Cox," Isaac said, a grim smile stretching across his face. "We're gonna sort this out."

♫

When I got to the Nest that night, Isaac was sprawled on the floor in front of a hefty mason jar, snipping the heads off matches. They danced in the glass as they toppled in, *plink, plink, plink*. Nihal sat nearby with a sketchbook open in his lap. Jon Cox and Mama were in their usual spots on the sofa, both on their laptops.

"Hey," I said, dropping my backpack into my chair. "Isaac, what's that?"

He didn't look up. "Science project."

"Sure," I said. "Is this about the glitter?"

"Maybe." Isaac snipped another couple of match heads into the jar.

"Isaac has an evil plan," Jon Cox said, looking up from his laptop. "He won't explain."

"My theory," Isaac said, "is that they did it 'cause of the competition. They want to put us on edge, you know? Distract us. Which is, obviously, never going to happen, 'cause you could probably shoot Trav in the knee and he'd still show up at rehearsal ready to go."

"You think they could win?" I said.

Nihal let out a merry chuckle but didn't answer.

"I don't know." Isaac set his scissors on the ground. "I guess it depends. Aural Fixation has nine people, all male, so they might want their opener to contrast with that more than we do. Our best shot is to be so freakishly good that they have no choice but to hand it to us." He flicked the empty matchbook into the trash can. From his backpack, he tugged out an unlabeled white bottle the size of a shampoo bottle. The cap popped open, and clear liquid *glug-glug-glugged* its way into the jar.

Isaac screwed the cap onto the jar and swirled it a few times. The match heads swam around, tiny red fish caught in a whirlpool.

"So," I said slowly, "just to make sure: That's not an explosive, right?"

He hopped to his feet, and Isaac took up his guitar by its rosewood neck, flopping down hard on the sofa. Jon Cox and Mama grumbled with no real malice.

"No exploding," Isaac said, tugging a pick out of his wallet. "But in a couple days, those off-key degenerates are going to be sorry. And we're still going to win the competition, and get famous, and that'll be that."

I sat down hard. "I can't believe those guys sell out stadiums. Do people really care about a cappella that much?" I shook my head. "*I* don't care about a cappella that much."

Jon Cox, typing something into his MacBook, mumbled, "Nobody does except Trav. But it's a thing now."

"It's probably those movies."

"Right." Jon Cox grimaced. "Girl power."

The derision in his voice stuck into me like a pin. I shot him a look. He probably didn't mean anything by it—he'd been in a shitty mood since the glitter incident. I got the sense that the Minuets' sabotage had gouged a deep wound into his pride.

"They're not bad," I said. "The movies, I mean."

"Not to nitpick," Mama sniffed, shutting his laptop, "but their group only sounds *good* after they augment the bass. That's essentially a coed sound."

Isaac chuckled. "Aaand there's the verdict from the pretentious peanut gallery."

I thought for a second. My words kept falling apart before they reached the front of my mouth. "But—I mean—" I took a deep breath. "The Precautionary Measures are really good, though."

Isaac nodded, spinning the lid of the mason jar around his thumb. "No, definitely, they're great musicians. But believe me, they're not winning this thing." He shrugged. "Girls' groups have a reputation."

"What reputation?"

Isaac went back to his matches, picking around the words carefully. "Some people would say, um, that they don't really . . .

it's a vibe thing. If we're looking at musicality, the Precautionary Measures are obviously better than the Minuets. But the Minuets *sell* it. There's comedy, you know?"

Drop it, warned a little voice. *Let it go*. But I couldn't. "Why can't girls' groups have comedy?" I blurted out. Jon Cox, Mama, and Isaac looked at me with confusion, obviously baffled about why I was fighting them on this. Nihal had stopped sketching.

"Guys' a cappella is just funny," Jon Cox said blankly. "A bunch of music nerds jamming out pretending to be instruments."

"To be fair," Nihal said, his voice a quiet reassurance, "that is the same thing that girls' groups do."

Mama waved his hand. "I think we're all kind of missing the point. Again, let's look at the *music*." He pointed at me and Nihal. "You two sing up to what, an F5?"

I glanced at Nihal. "I can kind of get a high E out," I said reluctantly.

"G-ish on the better days," Nihal said.

"Well, yeah, then," Mama said.

"Well, yeah, what?" I said.

Mama shrugged. "Even girls' groups hardly ever write parts that sit on a high F."

With a snip of the scissors, Isaac finished guillotining the last of the matches. "The Measures obviously have ranges above that," he added. "I think a couple of them have the F an octave up, which is wild."

"Well, yes," Mama said patiently. "But nobody's ever going to arrange anything up there for more than about two seconds. Having bass gets you a hundred times more mileage than being able to sing notes from, like, *Die Zauberflöte*."

Jon Cox grinned. "Here's a fun game. Try to make Mama go a full conversation without name-dropping Baroque music."

"Oh my God," Mama said. "*Die Zauberflöte* is Classical Era; I'm embarrassed to know you."

"Really digging yourself deeper here, Theodore," Nihal said.

Jon Cox raised his hands. "Yeah, sorry my parents aren't music professors."

They kept bantering. I stayed quiet. Discomfort had settled like a bed of needles beneath my skin. My teeth were clamped tight together to keep the words in. I almost wanted to go to the Precautionary Measures right now and vent to them, but I sat there, wondering. Were the Sharps right? They knew more about music than I did—was my reaction a knee-jerk denial that girls' groups were necessarily worse than guys'? It was true that all the songs we covered were bass-heavy, from recent thudding pop songs all the way back to the jazz standards from the thirties, whose double bass plucked along beneath flaring horn sections. Obviously, girls' groups had a different sound quality.

How could it be objectively worse, though? Plenty of songs in the coed and all-guys' concerts were missing something, too, not innovative enough to hook an audience in either. That seemed like the real battle—making each song engaging moment to moment. Not something as indefinable as "vibe."

It just didn't feel right. Music aside, didn't they hear what they sounded like, with all the vague talk about comedy? It smacked of the same old argument that "girls aren't funny," as if all girls had one specific sense of humor and the Powers that Be had decided along the line that it missed the mark.

I didn't want to fight the guys on it. All I wanted was for them to think a little bigger. For the first time, sitting among them, I felt inadequate, struggling to reach some tier they'd put themselves on. This was supposed to be the place where I was finally good enough.

I felt eyes on me. I glanced over at Nihal, who gave me a resigned-looking shrug and went back to his sketchbook.

♫

Before rehearsal, the guys asked me to pull "After All" from the archives—a classic Sharps song, originally by sad indie boy Hendrix Bird. Since I didn't know where the archives were, Nihal led the way. We wound down into the practice room where I'd done my callback, opened a filing cabinet, and started rummaging.

Nihal's careful hands drew out two bursting manila folders. He shouldered the filing cabinet shut and placed the folders gently on the piano lid. "Here we go. The esteemed Sharpshooter Archives. You check this one." He angled a folder my way.

"Not alphabetical?"

Nihal's lips quivered, making his beard twitch. He didn't bother answering.

I opened one of the folders and flipped through the clutter of arrangements. "God, there's so much."

"Mmhmm." Nihal licked his thumb and started paging through the arrangements with a caution that verged on tenderness. "There's twelve years' worth of music in here. Everything after they stopped teaching by ear and before they started arranging digitally."

As my fingers flipped aging pages, rivers of handwritten notes splashed across yellowing staff paper, a glimpse of memory folded against my vision. Last year, Mr. Rollins had asked me and Michael to alphabetize his cabinet of audition sides, its drawers crammed with photocopied excerpts from *A Streetcar Named Desire* and *The Aliens* and *Much Ado About Nothing*. I remembered sitting on the floor cross-legged in this sort of quiet. Easy and natural.

Nihal asked, "Do you have friends in the Precautionary Measures?"

"Why?"

"You seemed a bit—" He made a strained face. "—earlier."

I kept my tone casual. "It's nothing. I just didn't think the guys were the type to throw shade."

Nihal hummed his usual little chuckle. "They probably didn't even realize they were," he said. "Isaac, Jon Cox, and Theodore are delightful people who tend to get so far up their own asses they lose sight of daylight."

I laughed, but my smile faded fast. I was doing exactly what I'd said I wouldn't do. Random afternoon car rides with the Sharps, long conversations, feeling betrayed by opinions that distanced me from them—this was too much.

But I didn't want to pull back. It was hard to miss isolation.

"Hey," I said quietly. "Do you have a lot of friends in the Visual Arts school?"

Nihal's hands faltered. "Why?"

"No reason."

Nihal glanced at me. He had the kindest eyes, hazelnut brown, tapered at the edges as if in a permanent smile.

"No, really, it's nothing," I said. "The Sharps are so—" I broke off, shrugging. "Everyone's so tight."

"Yeah, and?"

"And what if I'm not like you guys?" The words fell out before I could stop them. I backtracked. "I mean, what if I don't . . . fit?"

Nihal looked at me curiously for a second and said, "Julian, last year we only had two rooks: me and Jon Cox." He raised his eyebrows. "Jon Cox, the most archetypical Kensington kid in the history of Kensington kids. And then me."

He went back to paging through the music, still unhurried, serene. "I worried about what it'd be like in the Sharps. If I'd get staring, or weird questions, or the feeling that . . ." He switched folders. "But it wasn't like that."

"Why?" I said.

"I suppose it's the work, right? It has to be." He shrugged. "You can be weird. You can be a frickin' furry, for all the guys care. We're just trying to make something."

I looked back down at the folders. Weird, sure. But would they be as forgiving of a girl? Someone who broke their circle of brotherhood, or all-male back-patting, or whatever it was at heart?

"Thanks, man," I mumbled, nearing the middle of the folder.

"Sure."

"Also, why do you call Mama Theodore?" I asked.

"Because he asked me to."

"Oh."

"Found it," he said, plucking a stapled piece of music from his folder.

The archives went back in the cabinet, and Nihal shut off the lights when we left.

"—BUT IT WAS JUST ONE KISS. SHE WON'T MAKE IT A big thing. Right?"

"I don't know, Jenna," I said, lying back on my bed, wrapped in a towel. "I feel like if you kissed her, it's your job to make it 'not a big thing.'"

"Yeah, well. She kissed me back." I heard cars rush by in the background. Jenna was the only one of my friends from home who actually called, instead of texting or Snapping, and she only ever called when she was walking home from school. People were slightly less likely to say shit to you on the street if you were on the phone, and Jenna had it rough with catcallers. You could see the girl's curves from three blocks away no matter how shapeless her outfit was.

"Still," I said. "You kissed her first, right?"

"I guess . . ."

Something unsaid lurked in the pause. I grinned. "You *liiike* her, don't you?"

Jenna let out a jumbled stream of embarrassed-sounding consonants. "Forget it! Whatever. I'll figure it out." A car horn beeped in the background, a male voice yelled something indistinguishable, and Jenna's yell came through, muffled: "Grow up!"

I smiled. "Okay, well, keep me in the loop."

"Are you sick?" she asked.

"What?"

"Your voice sounds kind of weird."

I cleared my throat, lifting my voice. "Oh, yeah, I'm kind of getting over a cold." I had to be more careful—I kept slipping, speaking in Julian's voice during classes by mistake.

"Aw, okay, get some rest," Jenna said. "Talk later?"

"Later."

"Love you!" she sang, and hung up.

I rolled off my bed, adjusting my towel. These days, I'd been showering infrequently enough to disgust even myself. A bit of a journey separated my room and the bathrooms, and where I was going, my wig could not follow. That chamber of pure humidity would have made it soggy and sad for the rest of its lifespan. Burgess's floor plan didn't exactly help, with its seemingly random map of twists and turns. You never knew who was waiting around the corner, waiting to discover you wigless.

Shower caddy swinging from my right hand, I cracked my door and peered out.

All clear. I dashed forward, flip-flops clapping between the teal carpet and my heels. I stopped at the corner, peered around it to make sure the next stretch was clear, and accelerated back into a run. The decorations on doors flapped in my wake.

I slowed at the water fountain, tight grip on my caddy. One last turn.

As I peered around the final corner, Katie Woods shouldered

through the bathroom door, looking down at her phone. I whipped out of sight. She was heading right for me. There was no time to make it down the hall—I only had seconds.

My eyes lit on the door labeled *TRASH* to my left. I barged in. My momentum brought me crashing into the unforgiving edge of the wooden trash container, which held a heaping tower of knotted white bags. I lost my balance, my arm flew up, and my caddy sailed into the infinite depths of trash mountain.

The door clicked shut behind me. As I breathed in, the foulest of stenches washed through my nostrils, so strong I tasted it. I gagged. *What the fuck?* What were people putting in their trash-cans, sacks of rotting produce? Literal feces?

Trying not to breathe, I extracted my caddy, which had landed between two bags, one seeping a horrible liquid. My shampoo had escaped, sliding all the way to the back, near the wall. I reached up with both hands, one for levering bags out of the way and the other for shampoo retrieval, which meant dropping my towel, and that was how I found myself naked in the trash closet digging through the garbage like a sad hairless raccoon.

My fingers collided with smooth plastic. I tossed the shampoo bottle into my caddy and snatched up my towel. I fled my garbage realm and dashed into the shower without a look back.

♫

Disguised, vigorously cleansed, and out of Burgess, I headed for the dining hall. I was breathless, having left the quad as fast as possible, as usual.

My phone buzzed. I unlocked it to find a text from my mom:

Hi sweety . Good news and bad news . Bad news first, I was late to a shift so , Pattons said that was my 3rd strike . But good news, we r approved for calfresh ! Ebt card came today . Hope everything is good w u .

I stopped dead on the sidewalk, my breathlessness switching registers. Bewilderment washed cold down my back.

She'd said it so casually, as if this were the last in a long line of messages about losing jobs and reapplying for benefits. Like this wasn't completely out of the blue.

It was so typical of my parents, not telling me anything until it was so late in the day that my opinion felt totally irrelevant. What should I say? Did it even matter?

I forced myself to start walking again, past the hulking film dorm, up toward the picturesque colonial houses.

Why didn't you tell me you were applying? I texted back.

We'd been on CalFresh before, for ten months, back when it was still just called "food stamps." I'd been seven and hadn't understood. Back then, the EBT card—that special debit card, the Electronic Benefit Transfer—had seemed like an exciting gift from a mysterious helper. I didn't get that it meant something bad had already happened, that the layoffs had reached us and we were scrambling to catch up.

Dad found a new job, though—his current job—after the better part of a year. Sure, the hours were shitty, mostly night shifts, but it was something. Then a part-time position had fallen into Mom's lap like a gift from God, and we clawed our way over the poverty line. Paid off our debts, started getting bills in on time. For half a decade, we were normal-poor, instead of missing dinners. Regular-tired, instead of exhausted. And then the hospital bill from hell.

Good news, I reread, feeling sick. *Good news?* Without Mom's job, were they going to have enough to make rent, or pay the bills for the phone in my hand, let alone make payments to the hospital? How long would they have to stay on SNAP?

Growing up poor meant getting intimate with acronyms. SNAP, the Supplemental Nutrition Assistance Program. FNS, the Food and Nutrition Service. CalWORKs. LIHEAP. On and on. Dad's disability had its own list: SDI, State Disability Insurance. SSDI, Social Security, which had denied my father's application because he wasn't *quite* disabled enough. SSI, Supplemental Security Insurance, the benefits that had disappeared because my parents had saved a little too much. Honestly, the only thing more sobering than being poor was *dealing* with it. Everything needed paperwork, interviews, renewals—and strict, merciless verification. Are you sure you're poor; are you sure you're disabled? How much do you really need this? How much do you still have left to lose?

My phone buzzed. Mom's next text said, *Didn't say anything bc did not want to make u worry !*

Okay well, I typed, *I'm worried now... so are you going to find another job? Are you and Dad talking about this?*

My finger paused over the Send button. After a moment, I reread her text. *did not want to make u worry !*

I closed my eyes and exhaled a long, slow breath.

Then I selected my reply and deleted it.

Are you okay? I asked instead.

Fine, Mom said after a minute. That was all. Fine. Sure.

The muscles in my stomach were tense. I looked up from my phone. The dining hall had come into sight, perched on an incline. On the lawn spilling down from its doors, clusters of people lounged in the late afternoon, a stippled landscape of brightly colored backpacks and summer clothes. They all looked free, and free sounds tinged the air, careless laughter and energetic exclamations. In the same breath I felt entirely outside the world and as if I were drowning in it. I listened to flutters of crows' wings from the trees and the distant whir of car tires over asphalt.

When I felt inside my body again, I started to walk, and I thought determinedly about the homework I'd partitioned into hours for tonight. I thought about keeping my head down along the back wall of McKnight. I didn't let myself think about the way Mom and Dad might simmer over the dinner table tonight without a word to each other, because there was no use torturing myself over something I couldn't change. I was going to learn this one way or another: If you can't fix it, leave it behind.

♫

That night, I lay in bed, turning over again and again. My legs weighed too heavy on each other; my hands felt too empty; my eyes wouldn't stay shut. Snatches of tonight's arrangement cycled in my head. *"Your touch is heaven falling, heaven, din din dah dat, fall, whoa way ah."* As if it weren't bad enough hearing these songs on repeat. When the nonsense-syllable version got stuck in your head instead, you couldn't even sing it out loud, at the risk of seeming seriously deranged. *Your eyes so starry, jah wah! Bow! Your eye-eye-ah-bah bow.*

After what felt like hours of trying to sleep, my phone buzzed on my desk. I sat up at once and checked it. It was past midnight, and Isaac had texted to the group, *Meet at the side gate in 20 min or be condemned to everlasting suffering!*

Replies from the others rolled in. *If you insist*, from Nihal. *Roger that*, from Trav. A hands-to-God emoji from Jon Cox.

More texts rolled in, but I didn't stop to read them. My feet hit the floor of my dorm, sheets thrown aside. Live energy hummed in my veins.

I didn't think about the two-day suspension kids got for sneaking out. The only thing on my mind was how isolated I'd felt since my mother's messages, how restless. My heart was on the other side of the country and I had no control. It took every ounce of energy not to slip into dismal hypotheticals—but maybe the best way to get distance from yourself was to never be alone.

♫

The side gate peeked out of the woods behind Marden Cathedral, guarding an old maintenance road. When I got there, Nihal and Trav manned the pillars, hands in their pockets. Trav looked cold and thin, a beanie pulled down over his forehead, his dark skin turned slate gray by the scant moonlight. Nihal wore pajamas. Button-up red flannel, top and bottom, his kirpan slung around his waist as usual. The ceremonial knife never left his side.

"Hey," I said breathlessly, breaking from my jog.

"Where is everyone?"

Nihal pointed past the gate. "Theodore, Isaac, and Jon went on ahead."

Two silhouettes appeared by the hulking outline of Marden Cathedral. Erik's slight frame moved with its usual cocky swagger. Marcus hurried afterward and muttered to Erik as they approached, a low, nattering stream of words. Erik had his arms folded and met my eyes with exasperation. I kept getting that vibe from Erik during rehearsals: that because Marcus talked too much, and wore cargo shorts, and, okay, was kind of a suck-up, Erik thought he belonged at the "humiliating" end of the uncoolness spectrum. Maybe Erik would grow out of it. Being earnest wasn't the disease people made it out to be.

"Let's go," Trav said. He grabbed the bars of the side gate, planted his sneakers on the wrought-iron crow motifs peeking out, and grappled his way to the other side. His forearms flexed past the rolled-up cuffs of his sweatshirt.

I grabbed the bars, the first to follow. Up and over. The burst of activity lit up my muscles, made my vision clear. I'd barely hit the ground before Trav was striding down the side road into the woods.

I waited for Nihal before following. "What is this?" I asked.

"Don't worry. No hazing." Nihal gave me a serene smile, and looking at it, I felt a wave of gratitude that he was here, that he was reliable and kind and himself.

The maintenance road was more pothole than actual road, the asphalt cracked and crumbling as if there'd been an earthquake. The moon bobbed along overhead, a waxing gibbous following us through the trees. Eventually, the path turned to gravel, and we emerged from the trees into the scattered weeds beside a country highway. Across the road, a field was chock-full of moonlight. White wildflowers drooped in clusters throughout the grass, glittering diamonds laced into green embroidery.

Isaac, Jon Cox, and Mama sat in the middle of the field, waving. We jogged across the street, picked through the field, and settled in a circle. Surrounded by long grass stalks and knotted flower stems, Jon Cox had abandoned his usual uniform of pastels and crisp khaki, slouching in an oversize hoodie. Isaac's hair was down, thick and wild and dark, and he lay on his side, stripping the leaves off weeds. Mama was setting out a line of glasses in the grass, his big arms pale and bare in the moonlight. The dewy ground dampened my jeans. The breeze cut through my jacket. I shivered.

"Gentlemen!" Isaac said, sitting up. He looked, as always, as if he hadn't expected to see us but we were the best surprise all day. "It's time to celebrate a victory over our mortal enemies."

Trav's expression darkened. "What did you do?"

Isaac held up his hands in a *wait-there's-more* gesture. "As we all know, I'm sure, ammonia plus matches equals ammonium sulfide, which smells so bad, it makes Jon Cox smell amazing in comparison."

"Wait, what?" Jon Cox said, sniffing his own armpit.

"Tonight," Isaac continued, "sixteen terrible people are going to find their mattresses saturated with this smell. Will their noses ever recover? Who knows?" He lifted a bottle of whiskey with an aged honey-brown label. The liquor glowed tawny in the starlight. "Courtesy of Jon Cox, a toast to vengeance."

He started pouring, and I eyed the bottle, uneasy. I'd been drunk all of once—Shanice's fifteenth birthday party, the summer between freshman and sophomore year—and it hadn't gone well. Jenna had kept flirting with me, and alcohol, I learned, made me uncontrollably happy about everyone and everything. So when she kissed me, it lasted a minute or two before the alarm bells in my head blared, reminding me that, oh, right, I had a boyfriend. And I was straight. At least, I'd thought so.

Michael and I fought about it for hours the next day. It had been one of our dumbest fights. He freaked out at me, stunned that I'd never told him I might be into girls. *That's because I don't know if I am into girls!* I'd yelled back.

How can you not know? he'd demanded.

I hadn't had an answer then. I didn't have one now. I just didn't *know*. I'd never been sure if I was attracted to girls, or whether it was a too-strong awareness of how attractive I thought girls might be to other people. Three or four times, I'd had what I chalked up as weirdly intense friend-crushes: I'd meet a girl, get flustered, get fascinated, and for months, I'd want only to be around her.

Where was the line, though? Did I want to be around her, did I want to be her, or did I want to be *with* her?

"If you're bi, that's so much more competition, babe," Michael had said at the end of the fight, sounding exhausted. I'd spent the following weeks convincing him that he didn't have competition. That nobody would ever compete.

I took a glass and stuck it out. Isaac let the neck of the whiskey bottle clink to the glass and tilted. Amber liquid rushed out. "That's good," I said quickly.

"Lightweight?" Isaac said, a hint of a challenge in his voice. I didn't rise to the bait. He grinned and moved on.

"Cheers, gentlemen," Isaac said, after pouring Marcus's drink. He lifted his glass, and seven hands followed suit. Nihal and Trav, who hadn't taken glasses, mimed the toast.

"To us," Isaac said, "for being handsome and brilliant."

Nihal's merry chuckle punctured the declaration. "I think maybe 50 percent of us meet maybe 50 percent of those requirements."

Laughs rippled around the circle. We drank. The whiskey was as bitter as rust and burned all the way down my throat. My face screwed up. By the time I untwisted it, the conversations had broken open again, low voices filling up the night, and gratitude flooded me for this field on this night with these boys, who knew so little about me and somehow seemed to know everything that mattered.

To my left, Trav spoke quietly to Isaac. "There's going to be hell if anyone finds—"

"Nobody's ever watching the side gate," Isaac said, low and careless. "And if someone does show up, whatever. We'll run."

"I was going to say, if anyone finds out it was *you* who poured that on their beds."

"Oh, well, they'll obviously know it was me." Isaac smiled. "But that'll be it. The Minuets aren't going to say anything, or I'll tell the school they broke into Jon Cox's car, and that's no good for anyone, right?"

Trav wasn't satisfied. "Right, well, no more of this. We should focus."

"We are focused. We're ahead of where we thought we would be." Isaac's voice softened, and in the space of a second he became someone I hadn't seen before, who used words like they mattered, who knew how to wield them to push away or edge a little closer. "Hey, look at me, Trav." He raised his eyebrows. "You're on top of all this. I promise."

Trav took off his beanie and scrubbed his hand over his shaved head. “Yeah,” he muttered, almost too quiet to hear. “I know. You’re right.”

Isaac clapped him on the back and met my eyes. I glanced away, embarrassed. I shouldn’t have listened in.

The night wore on. I sipped my tiny amount of whiskey down to nothing, but the others poured more and more for themselves. I had drunk just enough to turn the world to gold. I looked over at Trav around one thirty, while the others looped a song into existence, making up parts as they went. They folded in snatches of popular songs every so often. *Da-dah, hmm, yeah. What do you love? What do you love? What do you love?* Trav’s eyes were shut. He looked peaceful.

I closed my eyes and felt it, too. That potent thing distilled out of familiar voices, hidden in the lovingly painted strokes of rural New York, nestled in the lazy weeks before the cold cut down. Peace. We’d locked the world out, frozen time, trapped a little idyll in the isthmus of the hourglass. As for Michael, and my life in theater, and the big bold question mark of my family’s future—the competition, even, sitting ahead like a bull’s-eye at the center of a target—gone, gone, gone.

9

ISAAC WAS WRONG, IT TURNED OUT.

Not about everything. We didn't get caught in the field, thank God. And the Minuets didn't go to the administration about the mattress stink bombs.

But it wasn't over.

The day after the Great Ammonium Sulfide Retaliation, Nihal and I jogged up the steps to find a giant fluorescent penis spray-painted on the red door to the Crow's Nest. Nihal "borrowed" some red paint from the Visual Arts painting studio, and I helped him fix the graffiti. "My finest work," Nihal said in a mournful drone, painting over one edge of the penis. "*Penis on Red Door*, mixed-media, 2016. Lost forever to revisionist history."

I chuckled. I'd finally mastered that—a laugh fixed low enough in my register that it didn't sound like a giggle. "You," I said, "are so pretentious."

"I will do what I must for My Art," he droned. I cracked up.

The day after the penis attack, Isaac, Erik, and Jon Cox caught about six-dozen crickets and let them loose under the Minuets' dorm room doors.

At the start of Thursday's rehearsal, Trav asked everyone to sit down. I felt, all of a sudden, that incoming sense of doom of getting back a Chemistry test.

"So," Trav said, perching on the piano bench. "The Minuets' music director came up to me today and told me about eight different ways to go to hell."

"What, Caskey doesn't like his new friends?" Isaac said innocently. "His loud, six-legged friends?"

Mama and Jon Cox slapped hands.

"No," Trav said, giving them a sharp look. "That's not a high five. I don't care what they do next. We're not retaliating anymore."

"But—" Isaac started, but Trav cut in.

"Not a discussion." Trav looked around the room. Everyone avoided his eyes. Marcus shifted uncomfortably in his windowsill.

"It's October 2nd," Trav said quietly. "I know you think the competition is way off in the future, but nine weeks isn't an eternity. These four arrangements are not easy. Besides, the Spirit Rally's the 16th, so leading up to that, we'll have to waste three rehearsals on learning the school songs. And we'll lose a big chunk of time at the end of the month, since we have to prepare for Daylight Dance. Then there's Thanksgiving, which—"

"Hey. *Hey*," Isaac said, lifting his hands. "Trav, breathe, all right? We're not pressed for time. We're already almost half-done, and putting the Minuets in their place isn't distracting anyone from learning the music."

"Also, they deserve it," I muttered, thinking of the giant penis. The persistence of dick graffiti made no sense to me, especially coming from straight guys. If they were thinking about sex all the time, shouldn't they have been scrawling vaginas all over the place?

"I, um." Marcus's hand jerked into the air. Everyone looked at him, and his hand faltered. "I kind of think Trav's right. Like, a couple of the new Minuets are in my Theory class, and it's really awkward. I-I told them I didn't do the cricket thing, but they didn't believe me, so—"

"What, Xander and Gonzales?" Erik said, lip curling. "Those guys are morons. Why do you give a shit what they think?"

Marcus quavered, his voice shrinking. "Because I—it just doesn't seem like it has a point."

"Exactly," Trav said. "It's pointless. My having to fend off Connor Caskey is pointless, and this discussion is pointless, and we don't need any more like it."

"What?" Isaac said. "This so-called discussion was your idea."

And with that, the whole room was talking all of a sudden, talking over each other, bubbling up and up until Trav snapped.

He shot to his feet. "Quiet," he breathed. His hands were out in front of him and shaking. The half-dozen rings on his fingers glinted, polished pewter. "Quiet. *Now*."

For a moment, I thought Trav was having some sort of attack. After a second, though, he lowered his hands, which came to fists. His piercing eyes scanned each of us in turn and stopped, fixing on Isaac. "We're done here. That's final. Unless you've thought up any other ways to waste my time."

The air went cold and still.

My time, he'd said. Rehearsal time—all his, and never contested. The question had never floated so clearly to the surface.

Who did we belong to? Trav, with his strangled intensity, the gorgeous music he wrote, the balletic precision that he brought to rehearsals? Or Isaac, with his easy charisma, welcoming and omnipresent, the force that held us together?

Isaac's eyes were set alight. His lips were an arrow shaft leading to a sharp crease in his cheek. He looked ready to snarl. All fire to Trav's ice.

Jon Cox and Mama traded a look. Nihal closed his eyes, lashes dark against his cheek.

Isaac shoved a loose lock of hair behind his ear and leaned back in his armchair. Relief, then discomfort, prickled over my skin.

"Circle up," Trav said, snatching his folder from the piano bench.

That night, nobody stayed after rehearsal.

♫

"All right," Mr. Rollins said, as the clapping dispersed. "Take a seat."

It was first period on a Friday. I was wrung out—I'd barely slept. My scene partner, Douglas, took the seat we'd been using in our scene, and I dropped to the Palmer stage, smoothing the long locks of my wig over my shoulders.

"Well, what'd you all think?" Rollins turned to address the rest of our Character and Humanity class, fifteen kids dotted among the front rows of blue-covered seats. "Don't be shy," Rollins said, folding his arms. The command boomed out, rippling like thunder into the corners of the Palmer house. Rollins had graying cheeks, scruffy silver hair, and the sort of gravelly, dramatic voice that usually got assigned to mythological creatures in movies, which, incidentally, he'd made his living on for twenty-odd years. Then Hollywood had found a new, more famous guy to voice their dragons, and Rollins had enjoyed a respectable stage career before retiring into teaching. "Speak up," he urged. "Shy won't help anyone."

Finally, Lydia raised her hand. The silver charm bracelet on her forearm slid toward her elbow. Rollins pointed to her.

"So," Lydia said, "I enjoyed the scene. But . . ." She looked to me. My heart clanged like a bell; my nerves reverberated. Nobody's critiques were more accurate than Lydia's. "Jordan, you're supposed to be playing a refined lady, and I'm not quite seeing . . . that."

Heads wagged up and down in the audience. Rollins snapped his fingers and pointed at her. "Good, Lydia. I'm glad you hit on that." He faced me. "Jordan, to be honest, this wouldn't be a part you'd land on, because part of the plot of *The Duke* revolves around Lady Calista being short enough to disguise herself as a twelve-year-old boy." He raised his eyebrows at Douglas and me. "Which you both know, of course, because you read the entire play before performing this scene. Right?"

"Of course," Douglas said. I nodded.

"Okay, good. So—" Rollins's hands made grand gestures through the air, wringing the booming words out. "We're back in the Restoration. Remember: This is the first time that actual *women* were allowed to play women's roles onstage. This sort of seduction scene was the height of titillation back then, okay? Yeah, titillation, thank you, guys," he aimed over his shoulder at the couple of people who were failing to stifle their laughter.

"So, Jordan. *Imagine* it. Imagine being that restricted! That's going to show in everything, okay? When every second of your life is shaped by being a woman, at a time where women are so defined by this idea of extreme femininity, you need to play this seduction sequence as if this guy is the first guy, *ever*, that you've seen behaving like this, showing interest like this." He had worked himself into a frenzy. "It's scandalous! You know? That's why the unflappable Lady Calista's so appalled by it. So delighted by it."

I glanced at Douglas, my cheeks burning. He met my eyes, looking equally humiliated. I had this private theory that hell was an eternity of sixty-year-old teachers explaining seduction scenes.

Mr. Rollins took a breath and placed his palms flat on the stage. "Long story short, there's some stuff happening with your body that doesn't match that. Remember your Hagen, right? *Who am I: How do I perceive myself?* Part of character is how you take up a space. Part of humanity is how you think of your own human body. And Jordan, you're a confident girl, that's great. But at one point, I look at you and you're sitting with your legs stretched out like you're some guy on the subway. You're laughing like someone modern laughs, not like a demure member of the aristocracy who was raised not to draw attention to herself. And you've got this arm thing going on, your arms are so involved when you talk. If you're in the clothing typical of the period, right, you're not going to be able to *do* that. You've got to make it all match, okay?"

"Got it," I said.

"Great. Let's try some of this when we run it again later. Anyone got something for Douglas?"

As Rollins turned back to the class, I frowned, looking down at myself. I hadn't realized it at all, about the way I was sitting or moving.

At the end of last year, people's comments had been the exact opposite. "You need to push it more." "You look scared to reach out of your space." "It's like there's this box around you." The longer I thought about it, the more I realized that it had started to feel restrictive not to carry myself with the sloppy confidence I'd adopted for Julian. His persona had worked its way into the crevices of my normal life.

A hint of confusion awoke. What did it say that I'd gotten so addicted to my male disguise? If girlhood felt frustrating, and boyhood felt freeing, did that say more about girlhood, boyhood, or me?

I'd never questioned being a girl until now. I sat on that stage, detached, suddenly weighing every part of myself, wondering.

But the longer I thought about the possibility that I might not be a girl, the more I became sure that I was one. I knew it innately. The struggle to fit into some narrow window of femininity didn't exclude me from the club.

At the same time, even just pretending to be a guy was changing me. It was letting me access parts of me I'd pushed back, and parts I didn't know I'd had, and I *wanted* that version of me. I liked her better. She was new, she was interesting, she felt in charge.

My old self was losing traction, and as she fell further behind, I realized I didn't particularly miss her.

♫

Nihal texted me late that afternoon. *Hey, what time are you going to Bonfire?*

I stretched out my legs on the Nest couch, glancing around the room. Marcus sat in his window, brown hair lit up gold by the receding sunlight, reading a peeling copy of *Leviathan*. Mama hunched over the piano, examining sheets of staff paper spread out on the music rack, his huge hands occasionally darting over the keyboard with a surprisingly light touch. Erik was slouched, texting, in my usual armchair. It had been a subdued afternoon.

"Hey, guys, what time are we going to Bonfire?" I asked.

"Um, I don't know, whenever's good!" Marcus said, sounding awed, like he always did when someone included him in something.

"I dunno," Mama said, pulling at the strings of his hoodie. His eyes were fixed on a page so densely packed with chords, it looked like somebody had spilled an inkwell over the systems. "I'm still waiting for Jon to get back to me."

Erik laughed. "What are you, married?"

Mama didn't turn around. "Simmer down, rook," he said absentmindedly. His pen tapped F-sharp on the piano over and over.

"Hey, whatever." Erik arched one eyebrow, still texting. "I don't judge."

Mama glanced to me. "I'm thinking early. Maybe right at seven?"

"Cool," I said. "I'll tell Nihal."

I went back to my phone. *Probably 7,* I typed. *You?* I hit send, lying back on the couch. With September out the door, the Nest no longer felt like the inside of an oven, so I'd been spending more and more time here. Which meant less and less time out of disguise. These days, my voice fell naturally into its lower register, more than the occasional slip—whenever I was on the phone with Jenna, or even Mom and Dad, it felt like a performance.

Meh, Nihal texted. *I was going to wait until after practice.*

You'll miss all the food tho, I said, before remembering Nihal didn't eat meat. *Wait. Ok. Never mind.*

He texted back a cow emoji. *Please, spare me!! I like wandering through fields!! Being alive!!*

Aaand thanks for the guilt trip.

You are just so welcome, Nihal said. *See you at 7.*

I grinned, tucking my phone between the couch cushions. October Bonfire was the best fall tradition at Kensington, with the long tables of sizzling hamburgers and the flickering rumble of fire in the parking lot. The huge pyre they set up burned long and low, embers sparking and cracking up into the dusk.

"Seriously, though," Erik said after a second of quiet. "Are you guys . . . you know? You and Jon Cox?"

It took a second for me to realize what he was asking. Marcus suddenly seemed too interested in Hobbes, his Adam's apple bobbing in his beefy neck.

Mama went still for a second before turning to face Erik. "I mean, why do you care?"

"Maybe 'cause we spend all our time together?" Erik said, as if it were obvious. "Why do you not want to answer?"

Mama looked unaffected by the baiting. He tilted his head, letting the silence stretch until I felt this impulse to clap, or stomp, or yell, to snap the tension. Finally, Mama said, "I don't want to answer because you've never bothered to ask me a question about my life before. And this is a weird, presumptuous one to start off with."

Erik went red. He shifted in his chair and looked back at his phone. "Okay, forget it. I don't care."

I restrained a sigh. *I don't care*—people always used that as a get-out-of-jail-free card for arguments, as if by pretending the whole thing meant nothing, they could hide their obvious losing hand.

Mama ran a hand through his flyaway hair, which settled over his heavy eyebrows. For a second, I thought he was going to back-track, cave, and answer the question. But he shook his head and looked back at his staff paper. "Handel's my favorite composer," he said gently, "and I have two little sisters, and I'm from Kansas City. Just some stuff to start you off with."

Erik didn't look up from his phone, but it was obvious that he wasn't concentrating on the screen at all.

♬

We got to the bonfire as the sun dipped red toward the horizon. Buffet tables stretched down the parking lot, which had been cleared of cars, leaving a plain of asphalt to catch the sunset in its jagged fissures. The fiery crown of the bonfire roared up ahead. Teachers unsettlingly dressed in jeans and casualwear were hauling hay bales into rings around the fire, a safe distance back from the blaze. Once we'd heaped our plates high with food, the seven of us tugged a few bales together to sit.

Trav hadn't shown. He'd been silent on the group text since last night. Isaac, on the other hand, was here, making quips with the sort of snappy preparation that made me sure he was more bothered by the fight than he would ever admit. The amount of food he shoveled into his face stunned me. He didn't even have time to hog the spotlight, he was so busy putting hot dogs and rolls away.

A few teachers manned the bonfire, standing close to ensure that nobody threw anything in. It had become an unofficial student tradition, trying to distract the teachers long enough to sneak something into the fire. In my freshman year, Michael had done it to impress me, darting up while Mr. Yu's back was turned. He'd sent his empty plate arcing up into the inferno like a grease-stained Frisbee, turned back to me with that triumphant smile, and pressed a kiss on my eyebrow.

That memory didn't hurt anymore, which was strange. It just twinged. Pressure on a paper cut.

Nihal and I shared a bale. Erik perched to our right, and for once, his blustering attitude had vanished. He didn't talk, didn't sneer when Marcus talked, and didn't jump in with opinions on every tiny topic. Most noticeably, he didn't look at Mama once.

When a hand fell on his shoulder, Erik jumped, spilling water all over his khakis. "Shit," he said, wadding his napkin against his leg. He looked up at the girl the hand belonged to and scowled. "Thanks a ton."

"No problem," the girl told Erik with a grin. "And wash out your mouth, child."

I looked up at her, too. *Victoria Taylor*, I realized. Her sudden proximity was a shock. Victoria, the music director of the Precautionary Measures, was a Kensington celebrity, as well as a real-world celebrity: one of those rare ex–child stars who had actually kept her life together. She'd been the lead of a sanitized cable sitcom for three or four years—and she'd looked totally different onscreen, preteen pigtails and bubblegum-pink smile. Now, sharp black eyeliner drew her hooded eyes up into wings, and rippling golden-brown hair fell to her waist. Her left ear had about a half-dozen piercings.

The other guys had stopped talking to each other. Victoria glanced around the circle. "Hey, Sharps," she said, all casual. The family friend at the reunion. "How's it going?"

"Pretty well," Mama said. "You know Erik?"

One of her eyebrows rose. "Yeah. He's my brother, so, like, we've met a couple times."

Jon Cox made a noise that made me worry, for a moment, that he was choking to death. "*He's your—?*" Then he fell silent, staring at his plate, embarrassment written all over his face. It made him look like a different person. Victoria studied him for a second, looking baffled.

"He, um," Jon Cox mumbled. "He didn't mention."

"Yeah, I hope he's been good," she said. "Mom was so worried about him making friends, since he has all the social skills of a dying moose."

Marcus sprayed a bit of Sprite from the corner of his mouth, and I traded a delighted glance with Nihal. Even Isaac stopped eating to laugh.

Erik's cheeks went bright red. "*Victoria*," he said through gritted teeth. His voice cracked dramatically, flipping from bass to soprano and back within the space of four syllables.

Victoria shrugged, a wicked gleam in her eyes. She had an impossibly commanding presence, for someone who couldn't have been more than five feet tall. She'd worn flats at the Measures' last concert, and with all the other girls in heels, she'd been about a head too short to blend in.

"Erik's been a real problem," Isaac said, tapping his chin in mock thought. "The Measures are probably gonna have to take him on as some sort of fake alto."

Nihal chimed in. "He set off fireworks during rehearsal the other night."

"Yeah," I said, "and he eats string cheese without peeling it into strings. So messed up."

Victoria laughed. "A new low." She looked me over with curious eyes, glancing from my hair down to my clothes. I picked hay out of the bale, suddenly self-conscious.

"Eh, he's been fine," Mama said, breaking the stream of criticism. "Nothing we can't fix."

Erik, whose ears were bright red by this point, looked Mama's way. After a second too long, one corner of Mama's mouth lifted, and he went back to his food.

Nobody seemed to notice the tacit forgiveness bouncing across the circle, but I knew that was it. The weird fight was done and forgotten, and thank God. We didn't need any more clashes.

"Well, good, since you're stuck with him," Victoria said, flashing a smile. She had brilliantly white teeth. "You know what? We should all go into town for a group dinner sometime. Sharps and Measures. Best of pals."

"Absolutely," Isaac said. "I'll get you in touch with our schedule-master."

"Ah, Traveler," Victoria sighed. "Where is he, anyway?"

Isaac shrugged. "Probably making a blood sacrifice at his shrine to the Yale Whiffenpoofs."

The others laughed, and I spluttered along, more at the name than anything. The *Whiffenpoofs*? I could only guess that was an a cappella group, although it sounded more like a breed of dog that rich blonde ladies kept in their handbags.

Someone called Victoria's name a few hay bales over, and she said, "Gotta run. Later, guys." She flashed chipped red nails in a wave and jogged off.

Everyone watched her go, and then turned back to the center of the circle. An immediate air of conspiracy sank over us. Jon Cox hissed to Erik, "Victoria Taylor is your *sister*?"

Erik didn't look pleased about it. "Yeah, duh."

Isaac spoke through a mouthful of burger. "Jon'sh been in love wiff your shishter f'r like a year."

Jon Cox shoved him. "I'm not *in l*—it's not like a—it—"

"I have to put up with the pining 24/7," Mama groused.

"*I don't pine!*"

"As you can see," Nihal said, "he can't even really look at her without his brain turning into a sea cucumber."

"Nature documentary," I muttered to Nihal, and he elbowed me.

Jon Cox buried his face in his hands. His glasses slipped up, getting tangled in his swishy hair.

I couldn't help a grin. Jon Cox losing his shit was kind of cute. I'd wondered why he didn't have a girlfriend, if his pickup attempts were as frequent as Mama said. Hot guys didn't stay single long at Kensington, since the girls here were on the whole so much better-looking than the boys, it was almost embarrassing.

By senior year, attractive single boys turned into famously

single boys. The way people talked about, for instance, our seniors, you'd think it was a personal insult that they had no apparent interest in dating. I couldn't blame them for not wanting to get wrapped up in Kensington's ridiculous dating culture, though. This place bred long, intense relationships with lots of poetic love declarations and romantic serenades. Valentine's Day at Kensington could induce nausea in even the sappiest people.

Obviously, Trav was already in a relationship with his arranging software. As for Isaac, whoever he eventually landed with, I'd be warning them to keep some sort of industrial-grade muzzle on hand.

The sun had set. With Mama and Isaac still teasing Jon Cox mercilessly, we rotated our hay bales to face the bonfire, which roared up into the purpling sky. I scanned the faces in the bonfire crowd. They flashed yellow-orange in the changing light. A few Theater sophomores sat half a dozen hay bales to the left. To our right, the Minuets hooted with laughter, cluttering up the air.

All of a sudden, the other Sharps fell quiet one by one, their eyes fixing behind me. I glanced up.

Trav stood by our hay bale, looking out of place in neatly pressed slacks.

We were all too still. I could feel the line of attention drawn from Trav to Isaac like a spiderweb, but Isaac was busy examining his tightly laced black sneakers. The noise of people milling around persisted, cupping our silence inside, as clear as spring water.

Trav cleared his throat. "I didn't want to waste our rehearsal time, but I wanted to talk about yesterday."

Isaac glanced up, looking wary.

Trav smoothed down his linen jacket. "I shouldn't have lost my temper. It—"

"Hey, Atwood," jeered one of the Minuets. We looked over. The guy jabbed a finger toward the bonfire. "Check it out."

I squinted in the direction of his finger to the corner of the bonfire nearest us, where somebody stood dangerously close to the pyre, cast into a tall silhouette by the light. His dark hair caught the firelight.

"Connor," Nihal murmured, his voice filled with suspicion.

Nearby, the shortest, stockiest, and beardiest of the Minuets stood in front of a teacher guarding the bonfire. The Minuet wore a huge, kiss-ass smile, talking up a storm.

Foreboding settled over me like a cold blanket. As we watched, Connor Caskey unzipped his backpack and pulled out something I couldn't make out in the brightness of the bonfire. He darted close to the fire, stashed it among the flames, and darted back again before any of the teachers noticed.

The group of Minuets were all wide smiles.

By the fire, Connor reached into his bag again, shuffling out another object.

"Is that . . ." Nihal murmured as it caught the light. This time, I recognized it. A manila folder bursting with stapled papers.

No.

My stomach clenched. I shot to my feet. "The archives," I choked out. "That's our music!"

Isaac was already moving. He vaulted a bale of hay and bolted toward the fire, but too late. The second folder landed in the fire and roared into life.

My heartbeat felt hollow, a small mallet knocking against a large, deep drum. I watched with detachment as Nihal darted after Isaac and seized his wrist, pulling him back from the fire. A few people nearby stared, but mostly, in the mix of voices and motion, the whole thing went unnoticed. Just a few guys acting out.

The decoy Minuet left the teacher, who turned to see Caskey a safe distance from the bonfire, strolling backward. For one second, Caskey flashed us an arrogant grin. There it was again: *I win*. Isaac's face gleamed in the light as he snarled something at Caskey, and with the rest of the Sharps' faces a mix of disbelief and fury, unfamiliar rage built in my chest, too, white-hot and righteous.

Fists curling, I looked around. Trav had vanished.

I caught sight of him disguised by the fluttering light. Past the tables, behind the crowds, his black backpack bobbed into the darkness, away from the lot and down the road.

WHEN I OPENED THE DOOR TO THE NEST, I FOUND TRAV sitting on the sofa, his shoulders high and rigid, hands clasped hard in his lap. One thumb rubbed a pink scar on the back of his hand over and over, tight tiny circles. His backpack lay on the ground, half-open, a corner of the black scheduling journal jutting out.

"Hey," I said.

No answer.

"Look, Trav," I said, "if I can help rewrite anything, just say the word."

Trav seemed dazed. He looked at me like he'd never seen me before, sizing me up, slicing me apart and fitting me back together in ways I didn't recognize. "That's for me to deal with," he said quietly.

"You can't do it all yourself. That's got to be years' worth of work."

"It has to be done correctly. So I'm going to do it." The words seemed to give him resolve. He stood, picked up his backpack, and headed for the piano.

I didn't argue. It wasn't smart.

During practice, nobody said a word to Trav. Everyone could sense it—he was brittle. Right on the brink. At nine o'clock, he vanished like a whisper.

The rest of us settled around the room. "So. Plan," Jon Cox said. "What do we do?"

"We ruin them, obviously," Isaac said.

Everyone looked toward the piano bench where he sat. For once, he wasn't joking.

"Not to rain on that particular parade," Nihal said, "but personally, I think we should focus on getting back what they burned. We can transcribe a lot of these arrangements from recordings. I'm not a great arranger, but we can figure it out. Work in shifts."

Isaac pulled his hair loose and started working his fingers through the tangles. Methodical. Steady. "Yeah, don't get me wrong. That's a good idea. Let's do that." He pointed out the window at the hulking shadow of Arlington. "And let's also stamp those assholes into the dirt."

"Isaac," Nihal said, sounding uneasy.

"No, don't. I mean, come the fuck on. That was like responding to a spitball with a shotgun. I want them *sorry*."

Nihal straightened in his seat. "If we do anything, Trav's going to lose it. Remember yesterday? 'This is not a discussion'? Nothing's changed." Nihal sighed. "You really want to make this situation worse for him?"

Everyone else started laying out opinions. The Nest filled with voices trying to batter each other down.

"Marcus," Isaac called. His clear tenor broke through the noise. "What?"

Marcus had his hand raised. It stayed high as everyone looked to him.

"What if we voted?" Marcus said with more confidence than I'd ever heard from the kid. Democracy at work. "There's seven of us, so it won't be a tie."

A spark of amusement darted across Isaac's face. "Great. Sure." He stuck his hand in the air. "All in favor of getting the Minuets back?"

Erik raised his hand. I hesitated, remembering Trav's expression last night, the one that left no room for debate. *Unless you've thought up any other ways to waste my time.*

I met Isaac's eyes. They urged me to take the risk. I thought of the quietness of his voice in the field when we'd snuck out, the way he'd talked Trav down, and I realized the hardness in his expression came from loyalty. This wasn't on Trav's time. It was meant to make the Minuets pay for wasting it.

I raised my hand. Jon Cox and Mama traded a look. I saw a whole conversation in the second of eye contact. When they looked away, neither of their hands budged.

"All opposed," Nihal said. Three other hands joined him.

Isaac's lips thinned.

"All right," Nihal said, standing. He didn't look at Isaac. "It's settled." The perpetual amusement in his voice had faded. He sounded tired. "We've got a performance in two weeks. We should keep our eyes forward."

The others filed out, but Isaac and I didn't move. He was staring at the floorboards, one foot tapping in slow, deliberate rhythm, as the door closed behind Marcus.

After a minute, Isaac looked over at me and said, "You going home?"

I shrugged. "Are you waiting for me to leave?"

He shrugged back, a tight roll of his narrow shoulders.

"You all right?" I said.

He ruminated. I waited for words. It was Isaac; words were coming.

After a second, he said, "Yeah. I mean, I'm fine. Just, this is bullshit, right?"

"Right."

"And, I mean, I *did* want them to stop. After a point, I figured they'd—but now Trav has more to deal with on top of everything."

"Is he okay? Is something going on?"

Isaac closed his eyes. I could sense the explanation building up, a rising tide held back by a weakening wall. Finally, he caved. "Yeah, it's college stuff, family stuff. His parents went through this shitty, messy divorce last year, and they're both kind of scary. Not even regular Kensington-parent scary, seriously unreasonable." He tied his hair back up, twisting it into a bun. "It's not applications, so much. He's going to get in everywhere, obviously. He's a genius. But his mom's this famous movie critic, his dad's an oncologist, and his mom's all like, 'Pursue music, only the arts matter!' and his dad's literally said, 'If you don't do pre-med, your mother's going to be shouldering your college bills alone.' It's really fucking with his anxiety, trying to pick a track."

"God," I said.

"Yeah." Isaac grimaced. "Obviously, it's not really my business, but I think leading up to them separating, he got this totally unrealistic concept of what he needs to do to be a person, you know? His whole thing with feeling like he has to do *everything*—

that's got to be some sort of holdover. Like, if he isn't totally adjusted and responsible and on top of his shit all the time, he's the reason his parents didn't end up happy."

"He knows that's not true, right?"

Isaac shook his head. "I don't know. They've never done anything to reassure him. I kind of hate them, dude. They haven't come to a single concert, even though they live in the city. It's not that bad of a drive. I do it every break. Six hours out. And you know how much he cares about this stuff."

"They sound awful."

"Yeah. I don't know. He frustrates the absolute shit out of me half the time, but the guy's one of my best friends, and most of the time I feel like I can't do anything to help."

Isaac pushed the sleeves of his sweater to his elbows, accordions of charcoal wrinkles. His sneaker tapped the floor faster and faster, and the longer I sat in my armchair, the more pressure piled onto my shoulders. The storm crackled in my chest, rolling thunder, ladder lightning. Images flashed. Connor's smirk as he backed away from the fire; the way he'd looked at me with pitying disdain when we'd first met. Trav rubbing the scar on the back of his hand so hard, the healed gash faded from brown to pale. All those handwritten arrangements, hundreds and hundreds of painstakingly written pages, some of them dated years before I was born, incinerated in a matter of seconds.

"Look," I said quietly, "I'm still down to get them back."

Isaac went still. After a moment, he glanced up at me, his eyes dark. There was that hesitant look, the weight and the measure.

"Yeah?" Isaac said.

"Yeah."

He cracked a smile. "All right, then."

♫

The week flew by. Nihal learned that his sister had been accepted early-decision to Yale Med School, and he bragged about it so often, I started to suspect he felt sort of insecure by comparison. Marcus badgered each of us individually to volunteer for the Democratic Senate candidate, irritating Trav to the point that he vowed not to vote at all. And one evening, on a dare, Isaac climbed halfway out a window of the Crow's Nest, aiming for the roof ("I'm going to get old-style initiated!"). Before he could get there, Marcus's protests escalated so much that a librarian stormed up and ordered us to stop being so disruptive, and also what are you *doing* dangling out of a fifty-foot-high window, Mr. Nakahara, are you *trying* to break your neck.

Meanwhile, I turned in a long essay for The Greek Monologue, finished mapping a project for Lighting Design, and delivered a biweekly critique for Character and Humanity. All fine.

The world outside Kensington wasn't as manageable. The only interview Mom had gotten for a job came and went without a word, and I knew what that meant. Sometimes, when I ate, my mind ended up back in California, imagining my mom or dad at some cash register, swiping our EBT card quickly so the people behind them in line wouldn't give them judgmental looks.

I prayed for Mom to find another job. I convinced myself it wasn't useless, although prayer hadn't done an awful lot for us in the last couple years.

If anything could distract me, it was the looming promise of the Sharps' first performance. For the back half of the week, we spent rehearsals learning the school songs for the Spirit Rally. We all hated them, these boring four-part arrangements that Trav taught us by ear. The main one went:

O Kensington, we sing to thee; our voice doth fill thy halls!

When far away are we, the winter clamors at thy walls!

O Kensington, we sing to thee, 'twixt stands of oak and maple;

When far are we, we'll still serve thee, as long as we are able!

Really just vomit-worthy stuff.

A secret sense of purpose powered me through. Isaac and I had stayed late the night of the bonfire talking over possibilities. We'd decided to wait. Wait for Trav to settle, wait for the group to feel unified again—wait for the Minuets' guard to be down. And then we'd steal the Golden Bear.

The Golden Bear was the Minuets' pride and joy, featuring in all their concert posters, CD covers, and e-mailed advertisements. A glass statue of a bear on its hind legs, covered in actual gold leaf, it had been passed down since the Minuets' founding year, 1985. The Bear had lived in their common space ever since.

The problem: Nobody knew where the Minuets' common space was. According to Isaac, they rehearsed in one of the Arlington recital halls, but that wasn't *their* space. They had to have something like the Nest, a home base, but they'd kept the location on lockdown.

Isaac and I were going to figure it out. And then they were going to pay.

♫

"There you are," Trav hissed as I rounded the corner. "Where *were* you?"

"Sorry, I left my clothes at home," I lied. "Had to run back." I messed with my tie, trying not to breathe in. In a list of Kensington stenches, this gym out-stenched them all. The trash closet smelled foul, sure, but this place was like rubbing your nose into the armpit of somebody who'd just done back-to-back marathons in eighty-degree heat.

I looked down at my tie. Last night, Trav had pulled out eight carnelian-red skinny ties from the chest in the Crow's Nest. The eight of us made perfect duplicates: sport jackets single-buttoned, khakis pressed, rigid dress shoes squeaking, red ties neat at our throats. Except for my tie, which had somehow turned itself backward again. Or sideways? God, why were these things so impossible?

"Jesus," said Erik, eyeing my neck.

"What, freshman?"

"Do you not know how to tie a tie, or what?"

I scowled. "I—have not needed to know, no."

He looked at me with the scathing condescension of a twelve-year-old watching his grandmother try to operate Twitter. "Like, ever?"

"Oh my God."

"Here," Isaac said, stepping in. Exasperated, I let my hands drop. Isaac met my eyes. I gave him a warning look, and his eyes danced, but he didn't say whatever smartass comment he was clearly dying to make.

Isaac straightened the knot and stepped back. "There."

"Are we done with the sartorial conference?" Trav said through gritted teeth.

"The what conference?" Marcus said.

"Oh, never mind. Just—come on, Julian." Trav grabbed my elbow and yanked me into my place in line, at the bottom of the concrete steps. The announcer—it sounded like Mr. Hall, the theater school's voice coach—was already in the middle of his opening speech. He'd be calling us up into the gym any second.

I let out a slow breath, my heart still pounding. My seventh-period teacher had ushered our class over from Blythe Tower to the gym. On the way, I'd given the group the slip and sprinted ahead to the girls' locker room, where I'd stashed my change of clothes this morning. I'd worked fast, but it had still cut too close for my liking.

The idea of being in front of the whole school had my palms sweating up a rainstorm. At least the student body wouldn't be too close. The Sharps performed on the court, behind one of the basketball hoops. Everyone else stood up in the bleachers, all shifting limbs and folded arms, a bunch of awkward art kids trying to summon school spirit.

". . . for their sixty-eighth annual performance of the school songs, please welcome the Sharpshooters!" rang Mr. Hall's voice. We filed up the steps toward the sound of thunderous applause.

The gym echoed, bouncing one and a half thousand yells down at us. As we emerged from the stairwell into a wash of sickly light, I kept my eyes fixed on the back of Marcus's neck. Three shiny zits, scrubbed into agitation, encroached on his hairline.

We passed Dr. Graves, who clapped each of us on the shoulder, and formed a semicircle around the microphone behind the basketball court's baseline. The floor squeaked under eight pairs of shiny shoes.

Trav waited for the applause to end. He looked more at ease here, in front of this massive crowd, than he had since that night in the field.

He blew the pitch, counted us in, and we sang.

"O Kensington, we sing to thee, our voice doth fill thy halls . . ."

Trav's steady hands cut the air as he conducted, metronome-precise. Downbeat. Swipe left, swipe right, like he was ushering away an insect. Upbeat . . .

As we started the second verse, my attention strayed across the gym. Floods of faces stared our way. The five disciplines stood in sections, partitioned off from each other by rows of teachers. The School of Music stood closest to us, familiar faces studded in the ranks: Victoria Taylor peered out of the second row, barely taller than the kids a row down. But Connor Caskey, beside Victoria, wasn't gracing us with his attention, because—

My voice faltered. Anabel was out of place, standing in the music section, her golden hair glinting in the sharp light. She and Connor were talking, and in one brisk second, he leaned down to kiss her forehead.

I looked back to Trav. He'd heard my part slip. I picked it back up and held his critical eyes for the rest of the song, but my mind tumbled through the possibilities, already conjuring up the sparks of a plan.

When we finished the final piece, applause washed us back down the steps, and Dr. Graves followed. There was a note of superiority to the unchanging displeasure on his face, as if he were proud that he had never experienced happiness. As we collected our things and prepared to head back up, Graves gave us more claps on our shoulders. It seemed like he meant these to be supportive. The man did not have supportive hands. It felt like getting whacked on the deltoid with a granite club.

He gave Isaac's hand a businesslike shake, then Trav's. "Gentlemen," he said. "Sounding pretty good."

Trav's mouth formed a thin smile, but his nostrils flared. His brain had probably translated the phrase "pretty good" into "categorically inadequate."

Graves turned on me, his detached expression unchanging as he glanced me over. I froze. "Now, I know the other new members from class," Graves said, "but you are a theater student, no?"

"Yeah." I stuck out a hand. He shook it, granite hand like a clamp. "Julian," I said.

"Congratulations on your first performance," he said, every syllable rigid. Maybe he actually meant it. It was impossible to tell. "You know," he continued, "it isn't too late to transfer between disciplines. A year and a half is just enough time to complete the basic elective requirements, and Sharpshooters are always welcome in the music school."

"I'll think about it," I said. I looked determinedly above his gray eyes, which were set deep into his tan face, piercing me. It took him about eight hours too long to look away.

"Traveler," Graves said, doing an about-face, "let's meet soon to talk about December. Dr. Caskey seems convinced that his son's group will emerge on top, and that cannot be allowed to happen. I enjoy nothing more than embarrassing that man."

Trav nodded, and Graves marched back up the steps.

I let out a slow breath, feeling uneasy. "Jeez," I muttered to Nihal.

"He tried to convert me, too," Nihal said. "He even talked to one of the Visual Arts teachers about it. Apparently he told her I was, quote, wasting my talent, unquote, which is insulting on about six different levels."

I loosened my red tie, feeling choked. If Dr. Graves asked any theater teachers about Julian Zhang, the act would collapse. This whole thing relied so much on people's disinterest in each other's private lives—that if I stayed under the radar and out of everyone's business, nobody would go out of their way to do much digging on me. If they did, they wouldn't have to dig far before hitting gold.

♬

Anabel lived in a single on the floor above mine. I knocked on her door and pressed my lips together, feeling the prickle and give of the purplish lipstick.

Anabel answered. "Jordan, hey," she said. "What's up?"

"Hey. Not much. I've just got a quick question."

"Sure. You want to come in?" She held her door open. I glanced in and did a double take. I'd expected gleaming surfaces, designer bedding, some sort of meticulously organized wall calendar. Nope. Her room was a bomb site. Clothes were strewn everywhere, half a dozen pairs of heels decorating the mess.

"Nah, it's okay," I said quickly. "I was just wondering if—oh, wait!" I played up an *I'm-an-idiot* expression. "I just realized I never told you congrats on the musical. It's going up soon, right?"

She smiled. "Thanks! Yeah, we're getting pretty close, so . . ." She broke off, seeming to realize who she was talking to. A crease appeared between her neat eyebrows. ". . . so yeah," she finished awkwardly and bit her lip.

I let the silence stretch.

"Look," she said, "it sucks that they didn't find a part for you. Like, everyone is totally on your side. I feel like they should be required to get you into the ensemble if you're a junior."

Excellent. "Yeah, well." I grimaced. "I mean, altos, you know?"

Anabel let out an apologetic-sounding laugh. "Theater is so unfair sometimes. The voice part thing is so arbitrary."

"It's okay." I shrugged. "I was actually thinking of auditioning next year for one of the a cappella groups or something. It's senior year, why not?"

Anabel lit up. "That's a great idea," she said. "It looks so fun. Honestly, sometimes I wish I'd gone for the School of Music instead."

"I feel you. And it doesn't hurt that the guys' groups are . . . you know." I raised my eyebrows. "Appealing, or whatever."

Her cheeks went red. "Seriously."

I waited, wondering if I needed to prod further. In my experience, talking about guys was the absolute simplest level of conversation for Kensington girls. It required no thought and no effort. The concept of dating in this place and getting any privacy about it was totally foreign; so most people chatted about it reflexively, like they'd talk about the weather or an upcoming quiz.

Anabel tucked a curl behind her ear, bouncing on her toes a bit. "I'm actually sort of talking to one of the guys in the Minuets."

Bingo. I feigned excitement. "Really? They're amazing," I said, nearly choking on the blasphemy. "And apparently they have a secret hideout somewhere, which is so cool."

Anabel snorted, then covered her mouth. "Sorry. I mean, yeah, they do. But it's—" She waved a hand. "Whatever."

"Wait, you've seen it?"

"Yeah, but you know boys. They love thinking they're so dramatic and mysterious and stuff, when it's honestly not even . . . like, don't encourage them."

I laughed but felt a twinge. I'd thought the same thing about the Sharps before getting to know them—that they needed taking down a notch. It had seemed comical how seriously the groups took themselves, a product of narcissism or low self-awareness, but I understood now, as I remembered the hold of the red tie around my neck and the way it had looked on the eight of us side by side. It was impossible not to love the feeling of owning something and belonging to it in return.

"So, what," I said, "they're squatting in some vacant single somewhere and pretending it's a secret home base?"

"I mean, not quite, but it's not what it's cracked up to be. And I have no idea what they're going to do when it's winter." She rolled her eyes. "Anyway, Connor would kill me if I told anyone I've been inside, let alone where it is. I . . . yeah." She gave her head a shake, making her curls bounce. "So, what did you want to ask? Also, how have you been? I feel like I haven't seen you at all this year."

No, come on, I wanted to say. *Just tell me!*

I couldn't push. It'd be suspicious. This had to seem casual—a two-minute chat, something she'd forget within the hour. So far, she probably thought she'd steered the whole thing.

Besides, I had the sneaking feeling she'd already told me what I needed to know.

"I've been good," I said lightly. "This year's been pretty hectic—I've basically been living in the library." I pulled out my copy of *Lysistrata*, which I'd brought along. "Anyway, I'm in Reese's Greek Monologue class, and I saw you do this one last year, so I wanted to ask what you thought about this section . . ."

I tugged apart her words. *I've been inside. I have no idea what they're going to do when it's winter.*

Whatever building they were using didn't have heat. With the brutal Kensington winters, that narrowed the possibilities down to practically nothing.

11

THAT WEEKEND, ISAAC AND I TOOK A SHARPIE TO A map of campus, locating the buildings that might not have heating—the ones that were never used. That meant one of two options: the defunct single-screen cinema near the film dorm, or the old greenhouse behind McKnight. We agreed to stake them out. Isaac, the cinema; me, the greenhouse.

Every night, after check-in, I crept out through my window and snuck up-campus to lurk in the woods by the greenhouse, whose doors were boarded up. As I waited, I studied by flashlight against the bole of a tree that was slightly less smothered in ants than the others. I didn't retreat to Burgess until 1:00 a.m. It got to the point where I couldn't remember the last good night's sleep I'd had, but I wasn't about to let these guys slip by. They were going to pay.

The end of October crept up, and with it, the Daylight Dance. The Kensington administration knew how terrible an idea it would be to unleash a bunch of arts kids on Halloween. (Imagine the costumes.) Instead, they'd placed a semiformal dance a week into November, on Daylight Savings. The Sharpshooters and the Precautionary Measures performed at the Daylight Dance every year, two songs each; for a week and a half, we broke from our competition set to learn the pieces, but the time we lost wasn't an issue. We'd already memorized half the competition set, and if Trav still wasn't satisfied, knocking out the performance at the Spirit Rally had at least mollified him.

He never seemed to leave Prince Library anymore. Any time of day, we could find him in the lounge area, headphones on and a MIDI keyboard plugged into his laptop, transcribing. The ghost of his fight with Isaac still drifted over rehearsals every so often, but what the Minuets had done had glued us back together, left us twice as determined to triumph in December.

Then, one Saturday afternoon, Isaac texted me: *Hey, swing by my room. Got news. I'm in Wingate 420, insert obligatory weed joke here.*

I booked it to Wingate and took the elevator to the fourth floor. The sour light of the hallway made my hands look green. I passed a bulletin board plastered with hall rules—check-in schedule, lights out, living agreements—and knocked on Isaac's door.

The sound of feet bounded toward the door. It flew open. "Hey." He waved me in.

The Wingate corner rooms had four windows, showering them in natural light. This room might have benefited from a little less visibility. Sci-fi paperbacks, well-worn fantasy hardbacks, and thick textbooks had been chucked at random onto the shelves. Pads of staff paper featured prominently on both desks, balled-up wads of paper littering their edges. Jackets and jeans dangled off bed frames; shorts and socks lay in trails on the mottled carpet.

"Wow," I managed.

Isaac grimaced. "We're gonna clean this weekend."

"No sweat. I've seen worse." I eyed the walls, which were plastered with posters. Isaac's walls wore a spread of angry-looking rock bands, a rainbow of electric guitars clutched in their front men's hands. His roommate's side advertised an array of blood-splattered movie titles, as well as a vaguely pornographic-looking video game. The animated lady's spandex-clad boobs didn't follow any laws of gravity I'd ever encountered.

"Where's your roommate?" I asked.

"He lives in the Arlington practice rooms. Like, there's definitely a pillow down there."

"Who is he?"

"His name's Harry. He's a cellist from Arkansas." Isaac saw where my eyes were fixed and glanced at the video game poster. "Um, he just genuinely likes the game."

"Sure he does."

Isaac leaned over his bed. A silvery microphone in a foot-tall stand sat cushioned by his comforter, set up beside his laptop. The equipment looked spotless, heavy, professional. "Wanna shut that?" He waved at the door.

"Right." I shouldered it shut, feeling awkward. We weren't allowed to be in boys' rooms unless the door was wide open and it was before 6:00 p.m. "So," I said. "What's up?"

Isaac moved his recording setup to his desk with a heavy *thunk* of the mic stand. "I saw Oscar and Furman and Caskey skulking around the cinema last night. We got 'em."

"Oh, thank God. No more lurking in the woods until one in the morning."

"Yeah, stakeouts are surprisingly boring, is my takeaway from this."

"Seriously." I navigated through the ocean of discarded clothes to his desk. "Nice job, by the way."

"Thanks. I'm a legend." He gazed into the middle distance. "I am destined for a future in espionage."

I couldn't help a laugh. "'Cause subtlety is your middle name."

"I'm the subtlest person I've ever met. I'm basically James Bond."

"Right. James Bond is really well-trained in—" I glanced at the worksheets on his desk. "Identifying imitative polyphony."

He gave me a catlike grin. "Imitative polyphony is how you beat the Russians."

I failed to suppress a smile. He brightened, rubbing his hands together. "So, *anyway*, when do you want to do this thing? We could wait until after Daylight Dance, if—"

"A whole week? Nah, forget that."

"Sweet. I didn't want to wait either." He turned to his desk and flipped a couple of pages. "I've got a test Thursday, so I'd rather not sneak out Wednesday. How about Thursday night? That work for you?"

"Sure. We could meet around midnight? One?"

"One sounds good. I'll—" A knock interrupted him. I wound through the maze of discarded clothes and pulled the door open.

Nihal stood in the threshold. His turban was dark blue today, matching his stiff felt coat. His brown eyes met mine with unshakable calm.

I slipped a smile on. He hadn't heard anything, had he? If Nihal found out we were going ahead with retaliation, even after the vote, he would . . .

I wasn't sure, actually. What, would he get mad? The most negative thing I'd seen from him was stress irritation, and even then, hardly any, compared to the rest of us. I wondered what Nihal looked like angry.

"Julian," he said, looking between me and Isaac. "How are things?"

"Going fine," I said, standing back. "Come on in."

As I shut the door, I shot Isaac an urgent glance. He cleared his throat. "We were just, uh. Talking about the retreat. Julian wanted to know what it's like."

Nihal smiled, leaning his backpack against Isaac's desk. He took a seat. "It's the best."

"We're staying at Jon Cox's mountain house," Isaac said.

Of course Jon Cox had a mountain house.

"His mom was there last year," Isaac said, "but I think his grandparents are flying in to Boston for all of Thanksgiving Break this year, so we're on our own."

"We've been specifically instructed to leave the place in one piece," Nihal said.

"*You've* been instructed," Isaac said. He gave me a knowing look. "Jon Cox's mom loves Nihal."

Nihal shrugged. "I'm good with moms."

Piece by piece, Isaac disassembled his recording equipment, unscrewing the cage-like shock mount from the mic stand. As his quick hands worked, my heartbeat slowed. Maybe he wouldn't have gotten outright angry, but Nihal would've said *something* if he'd heard us.

He slid open one of Isaac's desk drawers, peering in with mild interest. "Isaac, do you have time to double-check some of the Fall '99 stuff I transcribed?" he said, pulling some sort of hair-product aerosol out of the drawer. "The 'Baby One More Time' arrangement is strangely complex—I might have gotten the bridge wrong."

"Yeah, sure," Isaac said. "Also, I can start on Spring 2000, if you haven't yet."

The guys glanced at me, as if waiting for me to offer my help. I would have, if arranging weren't a foreign language to me. Instead, I checked my watch and grimaced, as if it had told me something important. "Oh, I gotta run. See you at rehearsal?"

"Later," Isaac said, lifting a hand. I ducked out of his room and hurried for the stairwell.

♫

Thursday night arrived, clear and bright. At 12:45 a.m., I zipped up my dad's old winter coat and slipped out my dorm room window.

My body went tight with cold. California had nothing like this sort of chill, although the air still hadn't started to bite properly. Winter was sinking slowly into the earth, layering the crisp scent of frost over campus night by night.

I slunk down the wall of Burgess and paused. Three windows down, Reese's light was still on.

I snuck a peek over the windowsill and through the glass. The housemother's quarters were a more legitimate-looking living space than any dorm in Burgess. We had diseased-looking carpets and furniture that looked like it'd been swiped from a rejected IKEA concept catalog. This room had hardwood floors and a kitchenette, and Reese sat at a sleek glass desk, poring over a thick stack of essays. Her thin hair was down, half-curled from being in the grip of her bun all day; her reading glasses were on and her eyes unlined. She looked entirely relaxed.

For a second I watched, weirdly entranced by the quiet, personal sight. Then she stretched and looked toward the window, and I flung myself flat to the flowerbed, my cheek pressing hard into the mulch. I shimmied forward with my forearms and hips, cursing my own curiosity, and once I'd escaped sight of her window, I fled toward August Drive.

The starlight showered around me, stark and revealing. Brightness you'd never see in a night sky in San Francisco. I always found myself staring up on nights like this—cloudless, infinite sky nights. I brushed mulch off my jacket and hustled forward, curls of white warm breath winding between my lips.

I froze at the southeast curve of August Drive. A mechanical whir echoed down the road—one of the ATVs that electricians and maintenance used to navigate campus. I dashed for the nearest cluster of bushes and crouched behind them, waiting for the sound to pass.

A minute later, the ATV's back lights disappeared down the street, a distant pair of red eyes. I crept out and up the road. Movement caught my attention—Isaac crossing the street. A long silhouette stretched out from his feet, cast by the streetlamp. His narrow shoulders were wrapped in a black fleece, his hood up.

I jogged up. "Hey," he whispered, eyes bright with mischief. "Ready to break and enter?"

"Definitely." We darted behind the row of film buildings, heading for the rim of the woods.

The old cinema was a single-screen theater from the 1940s that had been on the renovation list for a decade and a half. I doubted it'd ever happen. The newest film house had a screening hall in the basement, complete with a projection and sound system, so there wasn't much reason to fix this old place up. Still, there was something to the aesthetic of it. The cinema stood, tall and rickety, on the edge of the woods, looking like something out of a horror movie with its boarded-up windows and padlocked doors.

"All right," Isaac whispered, stopping at the tree line. "That window's the way inside. Let's get in, get the Bear, and get out."

"How do we get the boards off?"

"Uh. Not sure." We advanced. A thick white band of stone ran above the double doors, where the shadow of scrubbed-away letters read THE CARNELIAN PICTURE HOUSE. Isaac crept to the corner of the building and brushed a hand over the thick board that lay across the window. His finger caught on its underside. One of the board's edges rested on a nail, unfixed to the frame. He rotated the board up until the window was free.

Isaac pushed on the peeling white frame. The window whined upward.

I nodded to the dark gap inside. "Wanna go first?"

"Go ahead."

I braced my foot against a pipe that ran down the building's edge, planted my palms on the rough stone windowsill, and hoisted myself up and through.

My shoes hit filthy tile that might've been beautiful mosaic once. I blinked a few times, letting my eyes adjust to the darkness. Years and grime had made this foyer the picture of decay.

The damp air smelled earthy, something like mold. Near the ceiling, the wallpaper had swollen and wept with water damage, long streaming stains that flanked the smeary windows.

Isaac landed lightly next to me. He pushed the window back into place and flicked his hood back, revealing excitement that made his dark eyes gleam. We prowled toward the crimson double-doors in the center of the hall.

I heard something and stopped, throwing my arm out to catch Isaac. He stilled. I leaned toward the door.

Low voices echoed in the theater.

"They're here," I breathed.

Alarm flashed across Isaac's expression. He glanced around the foyer.

The voices grew louder. I heard the clutter of footsteps. "They're moving," I hissed. "I think they're leaving."

"Come on." Isaac dashed for the opposite end of the foyer, where a dark archway led to a pair of bathroom doors, *Ladies* and *Gentlemen*. I grabbed the *Ladies* knob. It wouldn't turn. Isaac tried the other, which rattled and stuck as he twisted it. "Shit," he hissed.

I spotted a tiny closet in the corner and lunged for it. The door squeaked open, revealing a space barely larger than a crevice. Isaac folded himself in. I squeezed in afterward just as the theater doors opened. Isaac reached past me to grab the knob, pulling the closet shut with a *click*. Unyielding dark folded over us.

The sound of voices in the foyer seeped, muffled, through the door. Isaac let go of the knob, which made a tiny sound. The air stirred. Something bumped into the side of my face—his chin, maybe? His nose? I flinched.

"Sorry," he whispered. The word landed light and warm on my forehead. I became acutely aware that I was crammed against his chest, knuckles against his heartbeat. I tried to move back, but my shoulder blade met the door with an audible creak, and I froze.

As we stood there for what felt like several weeks, embarrassed heat lit up all over my body, patching over my cheeks, flushing my chest. I took a slow breath to steady myself. It was a terrible idea. I could smell the hint of cologne that clung to the softness of his fleece: half bitter, half sweet, like resin or rum. It made me think of dark, rich colors, maroon and cobalt and amber. Of course Isaac had to smell good, with his well-cut clothes and his long hair and his whole guitar-boy rock-star shtick. Just one more piece of the costume.

The Minuets' voices were still milling around. *Get out*, I wanted to scream. I needed space. I hadn't been this close to anyone since June, and it reminded me too much of that afternoon. I'd tried repeatedly to forget it. But I remembered everything, down to the weather—those weird beige clouds had cast amniotic light over the whole city. In the darkness, I saw with pristine clarity the image of myself standing in my kitchen, leaning close to kiss Michael, and I heard him saying, "*Wait*." I felt the grip of his big hands as he took my shoulders, moving me back a step. "*We should talk*." I felt all of it, all over again.

He'd road-tripped down from Seattle to have the talk. Because even then, he'd needed to make it all a presentation. Drama queen Michael. Center stage Michael. Couldn't he have taken it down a notch that one time? Let me feel like my feelings belonged to me and weren't just some event in his life story?

I swallowed. I felt weak, and stupid, and like months of progress were slowly rewinding. I let a silent breath pour in over my tongue.

The sounds of voices outside faded, and the squeaking of sneakers stopped. I heard the distant whine of the window frame, a clunk as the plank fell back into place, and I grappled around for the doorknob. The door popped open. I practically tripped over my feet in my haste to get away.

"Hey," Isaac said.

I glanced back at him as he shut the closet door.

He looked wary. "You all right, man?"

"Fine," I said. My voice cracked—I'd forced it too deep. I turned away. "Claustrophobic, it's fine. Let's go."

Calm, I thought, as we slipped through the crimson double doors. *Calm*. I felt around for a light switch, found one, and flicked it, making small bulbs bloom into light far overhead.

We'd emerged at the top of an aisle that led down to a long white screen. The wall behind the screen was painted a bold, dark red, like the dining hall walls in McKnight. Cobwebs clouded every corner like Spanish moss. Legions of thin wooden seats stretched to the left and right, some of them folded up, some hanging down like dangling tongues.

At the front, a dozen-odd crates had been gathered into a circle. Isaac and I padded down the aisle toward them. Once, this carpet had probably been carnelian red, too. It was dusky pink now, all grayed out.

"This place is actually pretty cool," Isaac said with a touch of reluctance, looking up at the ceiling. Painted panels stretched overhead, showing faded pastel clouds and apple-cheeked angels, blocked off by wooden beams. One light bulb for each panel.

"Yeah," I murmured. My heart had calmed. The air in here hung eerie and still. We stopped at the circle of crates. "Where do you think they keep the Bear?" I said.

A noise rang up the aisle. Isaac and I ducked, dropping like there'd been a gunshot. We crawled behind the front row of seats on opposite sides of the aisle.

"Hello?" came a voice. *Shit*. One of the Minuets had come back for something. We should have waited. I shouldn't have panicked in that closet.

I pointed toward the emergency exit door and mouthed, *Run?*

Isaac gave his head a hard shake. *Locked*, he mouthed.

"I know you're in here," said the voice. "The lights are on."

My thoughts of escape faltered. That voice . . .

"Wait, what the hell?" Isaac said, standing up. I stood too.

Trav stood at the top of the aisle, the red doors framing his square shoulders. His hands were balled up at his sides.

"Trav," I choked out. "I. How did you find us?"

"I followed Isaac from Wingate."

"But how—" I closed my eyes. "Nihal." He'd heard after all. And instead of confronting us, he'd done *this*.

I bit back disappointment. I would have thought he could be honest enough to . . .

Honest? The sheer hypocrisy of the thought stopped me. When had I ever been honest with him? How could I expect him to owe me that?

Trav nodded to the door. "Come on."

"Yup, nope, not happening," Isaac said, moving back to the circle of crates. "We're already here. We're going to find this thing."

"Find what?" Trav said.

"The Golden Bear," I said.

"The *Bear*? You're stealing the Bear?" Trav sounded unimpressed. "What are you planning to do with it, exactly? Hold it for ransom until the Minuets apologize? Threaten to smash it unless they throw the competition?"

"Hey, that's not a bad idea, actually." Isaac started flipping the crates over with his toe, carelessly disrupting the Minuets' space. Under one sat a six-pack of wheat beer. Under another, a pair of black binders. He picked one up and started flipping through.

"Huh," he said. "Rehearsal notes. Do you do this, Trav?"

"Let's go," Trav said. "It's 1:00 a.m. I'm tired."

Isaac stopped turning pages and frowned at the binder. "Wait," he said. "What *is* this?"

"What's what?" I said, leaning over to look at the binder. I caught only a flash of narrow handwriting before Isaac snapped the binder shut.

"You wrote those shitheads a peace letter?" Isaac said, staring at Trav with open disbelief. "After they landed you with hundreds of hours of unnecessary transcription?"

"Yes," Trav said. "I did. Because someone has to be mature in this situation, and it clearly isn't going to be you."

I felt the venom in Trav's voice. Isaac stiffened. Something kindled in his expression: pure belligerence.

"Now come on." Trav turned and opened one of the double doors. "We're going. You're not taking their ridiculous statue."

"Yeah? Or else what?" Isaac's voice was as rough and unyielding as cement.

Trav closed his eyes. "What exactly do you want me to say, Isaac?" He spoke crisply, each word a needle going in. "Fine. Let's see. I could tell the others at rehearsal tomorrow that I caught you. Would that be humiliating enough? Or I could report this to the emergency line and get you two suspended. Does that work for you?" His volume rose steadily. "I don't want to have to dangle something over your head, Isaac; I want to know that you respect me enough to back off something when I ask you! So can you stop turning me into the villain here and be a little cooperative? Please! Just once!"

His words echoed around the movie house for a long second. Finally, he shook his head and left. The door banged shut behind him.

Isaac stood stock still, potential energy coiled up in every inch of his body. After a long second, he dropped the binder and kicked the crate back into place over it. "Fucking *Christ*."

He stormed up the aisle.

For a second I stood alone, looking around the empty theater. I stood tall and unbending, a hollowness in my chest, unsure what I was feeling, unsure what I was even thinking. Everything seemed to swim. Was this what boyhood was supposed to feel like? A power struggle, a punch to the stomach? It was foreign and inaccessible. It was something I could feel in my blood. It was only just beginning to grow clear.

I'd set down the burdens of being a girl, unstrapped them one by one and left them on the roadside, but my shoulders didn't feel any lighter. They were carrying different, unfamiliar weights now. As I stood there in that derelict husk of a theater, I felt like I'd gotten lost in between my lives, and the road ahead looked long and strange and poorly lit.

DURING FRIDAY'S REHEARSAL, I COULDN'T MEET ISAAC'S eyes, or Trav's. Staring down at my sheet music, I got the overwhelming sense of their mirror-image disappointment in me, Isaac's for not backing him up, and Trav's for my betrayal. I was the bad seed, now, the disobedient kid, and it stunned me how much I cared. I kept remembering the ringing silence after Trav had pleaded for us to just work with him, and the heady scent of Isaac's cologne in the dark.

Nihal hadn't texted me all day. Good. I had nothing to talk about with him.

If the other guys noticed something was off, they covered it up valiantly. Marcus, at the very least, was even more excitable than usual. "Guys," he exclaimed after rehearsal, "I can't wait to perform for people. It's going to be great. Right?"

"Yeah, Daylight's always a good time," Mama said.

"It'll be weird not watching it this year," I murmured, perching on one arm of the sofa. The Measures and the Sharps performed at the start of the night, a ploy to get people to show up on time. Daylight Dance, like every other Kensington dance, was awkward by nature. Too many teachers standing around the periphery of

Marden Cathedral's cleared dining hall. Too many kids from class getting weird on the dance floor.

My plan: perform, then make a break for it. This wasn't like the Spirit Rally, where everyone up on the bleachers had seen barely anything of me except a blur of black hair and hipster glasses. The makeshift stage they set up for the DJ at the Daylight Dance was close and personal, and I had a short solo part in our second song, "After All."

Still. The idea of leaving early left a sour taste in my mouth. I loved that dance.

Jon Cox made a grumbling sound, and Marcus wilted a bit. "You don't think it's going to be good?"

Mama rolled his eyes. "He's just bitter he didn't have the balls to ask Victoria to go with him."

"I have a date," Erik declared from the piano bench, changing the subject with all the subtlety of a rhinoceros crashing into an even larger rhinoceros.

"Who're you taking, rook?" Mama said, sounding half amused and half proud.

"This girl in Carnelian. Her name's Camilla; she plays string bass."

Jon Cox gave his sleaziest grin. "Good with her hands, huh?"

I rolled my eyes.

"Jon," Mama chided. "Please, have some *decorum*. Erik's, like, four years old."

Erik's cheeks went red. "Shut up. She's cool." He busied himself with his phone.

"Hey, Julian. Can we talk?" Nihal said from the door to the Nest.

He looked cautious. It irritated me more than it should have. *No*, I wanted to snap, but I managed to muster up an "Okay."

I followed him into the dimness of the stairwell. We headed to the bottom of the steps and halted by the door that led back into the library.

Nihal sat on the windowsill. "So," he said.

"Yeah," I grunted, sticking my hands in my pockets. I scanned his face but couldn't hold his eyes—he was examining me in that careful, knowing way of his, a look that exposed as much as it questioned.

He chose his words carefully. "You know, this is probably exactly what the Minuets wanted."

"What did they want?"

"To get us fighting. Nothing sounds worse than a group that hates singing with each other."

I closed my eyes and let out a slow breath through my nose. He needed to stop being reasonable. The only thing worse than arguing with someone who was clearly wrong was arguing with someone who was clearly right.

Nihal stayed quiet for a minute. Something like guilt niggled at me, and I kicked it away. Why was *I* feeling guilty? Nihal had been the one to go running to Trav without even talking to us. Weren't guys supposed to be confrontational, or something?

Examining his downturned face, though, I began to see the other side of the coin. He'd probably felt like he had to rat us out. We'd put the Minuets issue back on the burner two nights before a performance.

Maybe Nihal deserved an apology. Just a bit.

I opened my mouth, searching for words, but trying not to look apologetic. It felt too close to my actual self—like if I apologized, the lines and contours of my real face would glow right through.

Nihal spoke first.

"Sorry for telling Trav," he said.

I blinked a few times, taken aback. "If you're sorry, why'd you do it?" I asked. Something bolder than I ever would have said out of disguise.

"I'm sorry to you specifically. Because I know Isaac's hard to say no to."

Guilt set in. *It was my idea*, I wanted to say. *I suggested going behind your backs. Not Isaac.*

Nihal shrugged, rubbing his scraggly beard. "I don't regret it, but I'm still sorry. Anyway, I thought I should at least try to clear the air, since . . ." He shifted on the windowsill. "I don't know. It's been good getting to know you this year, and I guess I didn't want hard feelings. But if you don't . . ." Uncertainty dragged his voice into silence.

Something softened in me and melted. The resentment faded as I studied him, Nihal with his unassuming gentleness, with his quiet but firm desire to do the best thing for as many people as possible.

"No, of course," I said, my voice thick. "No hard feelings, man."

♫

"'Cause after all, you know I love you,
And after all, you know I want you,
Baby, after all, you know I need you,
After all this time."

The last "time" hit an A-flat above middle C, the very top of my belt. I only held it for a second before riffing downward—disguising my voice up there was way more of a task.

At the high note, the crowd broke into scattered cheers. Isaac took the solo part back over, and I faded back to my background part. *Dum dah det, dum dah det, din din.*

I kept my focus on Trav. Some of the crowd was already dancing, but most people just stood there, hardly ten feet away, smiling up at us or yapping with their friends. The knot of people thinned out about twenty feet from the stage's edge, turning into a scattered sea of disinterested kids in formal wear, eyeing the wintry decorations. Marden Cathedral looked gorgeous tonight, its soaring interior decked in glass snowflakes on thin white threads, pine boughs arranged over stone arches. My freshman year, I'd thought November 5th was ridiculously early to ring in the winter. Then, the day after the dance, the New York sky had dumped several inches of heavy snow onto the ground, and I got the point.

Trav lifted his hand. We crescendoed out on the final note and made a crisp cutoff. Cheering broke out, ringing off the vaulted ceiling. As we filed off the stage, the DJ, some guy in black with a neckbeard, jogged up to take our place.

Nihal and I descended the steps into the crowd side by side.

"Do you think you'll stay?" he asked, shrugging his blazer off. As he rolled up the sleeves of his blue button-up, I longed to do the same—this place was already heating up beyond belief—but my white shirt's fabric wasn't as opaque as I would've liked. I was wearing my makeshift nylon binder and an undershirt, but it still felt safer to keep the jacket on.

I shook my head. "This dance is like a four-hour headache," I lied. Daylight was better than prom and the Valentine's dance combined, and everyone knew it.

Nihal chortled, but his smile curdled as Connor Caskey approached us, tall and broad-shouldered, dark hair swept back.

"Sharps," he said.

"Caskey," Nihal said stiffly. I inclined my head in an unwilling nod.

"You guys sounded great." He flashed that irritating smile. "For half an a cappella group."

I gritted my teeth. "You know," I said, "you've got some nerve, saying shit to us after you ruined our music."

Connor's smile faltered. A long, awkward second passed. Then he blurted, "I mean, we didn't expect you guys to just give up."

I traded a glance with Nihal, who looked blank.

"You what?" I said.

Connor fidgeted, clumsy hands adjusting his tie. "I mean, this is kind of the whole point of a rivalry."

". . . *No*," Nihal said, utter disbelief dripping from the single syllable. "No, the point of rivalry is *not* to ruin each other's lives. It's an incentive to make everyone better."

Connor arched an eyebrow, and humor snuck back into his voice. "Jesus. Your version sounds boring, Singh."

"I used to wonder why all the Minuets call me Singh," Nihal shot back, "and then I realized, it's probably because you Neanderthals can't pronounce Sehrawat."

"To be fair," I muttered, "I've misspelled your last name like eighty times."

Nihal gave me a withering look. "It is a mystery that I keep you people around."

A hand landed on my shoulder. I turned to find Victoria Taylor and one of the other Precautionary Measures, both in black dresses. "Julian, hey!" Victoria said, and went right for the hug. I froze for a second before awkwardly patting her back, praying I didn't smell too feminine. Hell if I could afford cologne; and I did not have the time, resources, or desire to buy one of those dude body washes that looked like ultrasound gel and came in a dispenser shaped like a torture device.

Victoria's head fit under my chin. Her wavy hair smelled like peppermint. I glanced around for Jon Cox, but he'd disappeared into the throng.

Victoria pulled back. She looked stunning, put together in the way rich girls could afford, with pearls dangling from her earlobes and draped in a line over her delicate collarbones, set in rose gold. A loose sack dress disguised her curves. I couldn't look away. In some other lifetime, if she hadn't left her sitcom for reality, she might have worn this on a red carpet with paparazzi crowding in to ask who she was dating or how she stayed wire-thin. She'd abandoned that lifestyle just before diets and dating became the questions that defined her. A lucky near-miss.

I was looking too hard at her. I looked down instead at the silvery heels that brought her up four inches or so, making her regular-short instead of hobbit-style tiny. Her weight shifted easily from one spindly heel to the other. "You were great," she said. "You and the other new guy, what's his name?"

"Marcus?"

"Yeah. Your solos sounded awesome." She smiled. "Erik told me you're a junior. You should've tried out before this year."

I looked over at Nihal for backup, but he and Connor Caskey were in the middle of a duel of wits for the ages. "Right, well," I said. "You know how busy . . . stuff . . . things are."

Both Victoria and the other Measure looked like they were trying not to laugh. Mentally, I kicked myself. With my best friends excepted, I was awful at talking to girls, especially if they were prettier than me. It felt as if they had some sort of answer key to girlhood—how to walk and how to laugh and how to flirt—and they could tell that I was bullshitting my way through the whole female experience.

Logically, this couldn't be true, but it still seemed like it sometimes. I would've thought it would be easier to be a guy, talking to girls. Apparently not. I felt defensive under their scrutiny.

Music boomed into life over the nearby speakers. *Shit.*

"You okay?" Victoria said.

"What? Yeah. Why?"

"You just—" She mock flinched.

"Nah, it's nothing." Nothing except that, now that the music was playing, the beat was slipping under my skin. I wanted nothing more than to stay and dance. And Victoria—she was all smile and interest and attention, and I couldn't stop looking at the way her hair fell, collected, shifted, brushed over the curves of her collarbones. Why?

I should've escaped the second I got offstage.

"Here," Victoria said, stepping closer. From the folds of her dress, where a pocket was apparently hiding, she pulled out a flask, keeping it low and hidden from any wandering eyes. "Want some?"

I absolutely did. My nerves were leaping, and the heat was getting unbearable. A bead of sweat itched its way down my spine with torturous slowness. The beat made me want to lose it, break into a dance in front of the speaker.

Victoria raised an eyebrow. She had exclamatory eyebrows, dashes of dark paint, a few shades darker than her hair.

I took the flask, unscrewed the cap, and hunched down to take a swig.

The rim was wider than I'd thought, and a rush of straight bourbon whited everything out for a second, a battering ram of bitterness. I swallowed hard and my ears went hot, the top of my nose burning. Victoria took her flask back, screwed the cap on, and tucked it away. "Feel free to have more, please," she said. "I'm set for the night, and I have to get rid of that."

"She can't hold her liquor," the other Measure said to me, knowingly.

"Hush, freshman," Victoria said.

I gave her my guy-chuckle, the bourbon's sting still chewing over my tongue. The room already looked brighter, the laser lights wilder. Threads of neon blue and green spun through the dark, drawing bright spots on the distant walls. Outside, night had fully settled over Kensington.

I spotted Jon Cox and Mama in my periphery and flagged them down. They forged past shining dresses and pressed button-ups.

"Hey, um, hi," Jon Cox said over the music, leaning in to hug Victoria. It lasted longer than it needed to. As they pulled back, the DJ transitioned into another song, and to my right, Mama broke it down. I watched for a second, trying to hold back my dancing impulse—but watching him only made it worse, because shit, but Mama was a pretty good dancer. The vocal line soared. The beat pulsed. I felt it in my hips, my shoulders, my ribs.

When the others started dancing, too, I caved. *One song,* I told myself. *One song, then I'll go.*

We formed a circle, the five of us, and I looked down at myself, trying to blend. Guys at school dances always did that awkward knee-bobbing move, nodding their heads, obviously hoping to grind on someone. I tried to strike a balance between that and my need to swivel my hips until my waist ached.

The lights dimmed, turning the crowd into a thousand frantic silhouettes. After the song ended, I tried to leave, but Jon Cox slung an arm around my shoulders. The song after that? "Love You Forever," so obviously, I couldn't leave then, either.

Soon, I resigned myself to the fact that I wasn't going anywhere. I didn't want to, and besides, did it really matter? Nobody was looking at faces in here. You could hardly see facial features in the blinking strobe, in the whirling flood of purple and green.

Our circle gravitated toward the deafening speakers, getting closer and closer to each other with every song. Soon, we weren't so much a circle as a clot, a tangle of arms and legs and moving hips. To my right, I could tell Jon Cox was trying to get up on Victoria, but either he couldn't work up the guts to ask her, or he assumed it was too loud to try verbal communication.

A couple of teachers kept having to break up kids who were grinding too obscenely. Worst job ever.

Victoria's flask rotated between us. By the time it reached me, what I'd had earlier had sunk in. My head felt light and frothy and open, like someone had skimmed off the top of my skull, and I thought, *What's the harm?* I took another secret swig. And a second. And a third.

Time disappeared. All around us, the crowd screamed the lyrics to "Lightning," to "Club Love True Love," to "Haley's Eyes." Sometime during "Haley's Eyes," the crowd shifted, and suddenly Victoria was pushed into me, her back against my chest. I expected her to pull away, but a beat later, she was moving against me. The bright mint smell of her hair intoxicated me more than the alcohol. My hands found her hips instinctively, the slick satiny fabric of her dress folding under my fingers, and we locked together. She pressed back into me, and the feeling of her curves made my stomach twist. My mind had gone blank.

Then she looked up over her shoulder at me. Bright, daring eyes, and thick black eyeliner. Smirking coral lips. She moved—twisted—and leaned up.

Her mouth pressed to mine. Something ignited in my stomach. I melted down into her.

The sensation lit up patterns of memory, sparks that set each other off in a chain reaction. I remembered how I'd used to kiss a year ago, when kissing had been a commodity: eager and greedy and reaching, all action, all fire. Right now, I was sinking down inside myself, where everything felt like the ocean, the slow but unavoidable sway of want. I wanted to wait, and savor, and watch. It was all different, but the same fundamental fascination.

So it hadn't been a fluke with Jenna that summer. The way I'd felt something stirring.

Hang on, I thought vaguely. *Isn't this girl way out of my league?* Another thought: *I shouldn't do this.*

But I couldn't remember why not. Victoria tasted citrusy and whiskey bitter, she kissed with total authority, her hands were hard knots on the back of my blazer. My eyes fluttered shut and I floated upward. I imagined, for a second, silence or stillness, the two of us at a quiet movie or a windy hillside or a mountain view that went on for miles. Walking with my arm around her waist, or her hand in mine. I imagined her powerful soprano voice kept to an absentminded hum as we worked side by side, tucked away in a corner of the library, maybe. And through it all, she felt, against me, like a line of electricity. My hands didn't know where best to be. All of her was the perfect place, every inch the most intriguing inch.

Then she touched the front of my blazer, the heel of her hand brushed against my breast, and my mind snapped back into place. My eyes shot open. I stumbled out of her arms.

What the hell was I doing? She thought I was a boy. Maybe she wasn't even into girls. And to my right, Jon Cox was dancing with zero rhythm, no heart in it at all, determinedly avoiding my eyes. Mama gave me a look: *What the hell?*

Julian was an asshole. I was an asshole.

This was a mistake. I needed to get out. I had to stay alone.

"I—I'm sorry," I said. Victoria's smile faltered. I turned from her. "I gotta—I have to go."

I forced my way through the crowd, the wash of bodies and heat and humidity, and my tongue felt like a strip of tanned leather sitting at the bottom of my mouth, and I was blinking and sweating with every hit of the bass. As the song surged into the chorus, confusion swam over me, dulling the panic. Everyone was jostling everyone else, causing stumbling chain reactions, and only half the crowd even looked like they were having a good time, and *what did I just do, what did I do, what did I do?*

You're drunk, said a voice in my head. That explained it. Definitely drunk. Was I into girls, or just drunk? Or was I both drunk and into girls? Why hadn't I stayed sober, so I could make a controlled experiment out of this?

Near the door, someone's hand landed on my back, and I turned. I tilted my head up. Isaac. Relief flooded me, cold. The face of someone who didn't hate me yet.

"Hey, are you leaving?" he said.

"Isaac," I said. Was I talking too loud? The music wasn't so deafening back here. "Hey, Isaac."

He tilted his head. "Are you drunk?"

"Ha. What? Me? No. Yes."

Isaac sighed.

"I think I'm going to head out, too," he said, scanning the room. "Not sure how much more of this I can do."

"You don't dance?"

He laughed. He was always laughing. There was something off about it this time. "No," he said. "When I dance, I look like—you know those flailing inflatable tube guys that are always, like, thrashing on the side of the highway to advertise car sales? That's how it looks."

I laughed and wandered past him toward the door, by column after column. Marden Cathedral was so beautiful. Even this mess of people couldn't hide it. Biblical scenes were hewn into the pearly gray rock, shepherds herding, women weeping, the Messiah lifting His hands. Grooves ran up from the carved vignettes to flowery scrollwork at the top of the columns, where they bled into the arched ceiling.

"Julian," Isaac said, nudging me.

I gave my head a shake, realizing I'd stopped to look up. I'd been staring at the ceiling for a while. I wondered how long. "What?"

"We should go." He glanced along the wall. So did I. Teachers, a line of them, one for every dark, stained glass window. The nearest one was eyeing me.

"Yeah, got it." I focused on keeping myself steady as we headed for the doors. They stood wide, letting freezing drafts into the cathedral's sweaty interior.

We passed Principal Busse, the Supreme Overlord of Kensington-Blaine Academy, who stood at the door checking people's invitations. She was a short, round woman wearing bright red earmuffs. She didn't spare us more than a passing glance. Her face was a blur. Everyone's faces were blurring. Red mouths and black eyes.

Outside, in the dry cold, the sweat and heat under my blazer evaporated in what felt like seconds. For an instant, it invigorated me, the shock of the temperature, and I wanted to sprint, or climb something, or dig deep into the world. But soon the back of my neck stung with the chill, and then I couldn't feel my nose, and my eyes were globes of ice in their sockets. August Drive had grown to twice its usual length.

They'd said it on the news the other day—a storm was coming. Winter Storm Saul. Or was it Paul? Some Biblical boy name. Whoever it was, he was going to drench us in snow.

"Look," Isaac said, "we'll talk about this when you're not drunk, but what happened Thursday with Trav shouldn't have happened. I'm going to figure this shit out." The words circled my head, not quite sinking in. An array of vaguely important sentences I wasn't quite hearing. "I don't know," he went on. "You and Nihal seemed stressed out today, and that's not a good rehearsal vibe, and I feel kind of bad since it's your first semester and the president is supposed to, like, set an examp—"

I walked into his shoulder.

He stopped and steadied me. After a second I levered my head upward because I had been staring at my feet. There were his eyes. Not laughing now.

"How much did you have?" Isaac said.

"It's cold," I said. It was important that he knew this. How cold it was. Isaac had on a coat—the same hooded black fleece he'd worn the other night. Why hadn't I brought my coat? This blazer didn't keep the warmth in at all.

"Pretty cold, yeah," he said. Then, after a second, "Where'd you even *get* a drink?"

"Victoria," I said, and the back of my hand came to my mouth.

"Girls. Terrible influence." Isaac sighed. "Okay, you live in Burgess, right?"

Bad. The plan was bad. He wanted to make sure I got back to my dorm. If he saw where I lived . . .

I hunted for a diversion. We stood across from the administrative buildings, that curving line of brick cubes. Identical gables stood out over their doors. To our right, a shallow hill led down to the music buildings. What to do?

"No, don't," I said. "You don't have to w—don't worry. About it, man, don't worry."

"I'm not gonna risk you passing out outside somewhere. It's fine. I'll walk you back."

We kept walking down August Drive. I had to stop him. "It's cold, though," I reminded him. "I'm really cold . . ."

I shivered. And then my leg was somewhere left of where I'd wanted it to be. I staggered, and Isaac caught my upper arm. I regained my footing. We stood by a stop sign. The single intersection on campus. Four corners of white sidewalks glowed like paint in the moonlight. The narrow stream of August Drive crossed over the wide black river of Main Street. "Can I get some water?" I said. "Use a bathroom?"

"Water. Good plan," he said, looking around. "Here, come on."

We turned right on Main, heading downhill toward the dappled stone of Wingate. Isaac took a wallet out of his khakis and scanned us in. The warmth of the Wingate lounge enveloped us. Hardwood floors beneath my feet and uncomfortable-looking leather sofas passing by my legs. On the wall hung portraits of old people in wigs, rimmed in thick golden frames.

I spotted a water fountain in the corner and made for it. Isaac's footsteps followed. As I hunched over the fountain, quaffing mouthful after mouthful, I got the urge to call Jenna. Tell her what had happened at the dance with Victoria.

Jenna had known since forever. Since she was six. How could I still not know? I had to be a fake. She wouldn't believe me. Would she? Did I believe me?

Thoughts wandered around my head unrestricted. It was better being drunk and alone than drunk and crowded in. Everything felt important. Isaac stood a few feet away.

"I made out with Victoria," I told the water fountain.

"Uh. What?" said Isaac's voice. The water fountain had nothing to say.

"I mean, she made out with me. We made out with each other. She started it. I don't know. What?"

"Classy," Isaac said, sounding amused.

"I feel bad. Jon Cox was *right there*, and I felt bad."

"That's shitty luck. Same thing happened to Ted last year with this girl Cameron. I think I told you about him? Ted? He's . . ."

Isaac's steady voice soothed me. I listened to the cadences and rhythms of it for a minute, unable to wring any meaning out of the sounds. Eventually, I straightened up from the water fountain. Swayed. "You ever miss New York City?" I asked, cutting him off from some tangent or other.

He leaned against the wall. "I guess, yeah."

"What do you miss?"

He looked bemused. "I don't know. The size of it. My parents."

"I miss my parents too. Are they—what generation are you?"

"Honestly, I couldn't tell you. Way back. Like, both sets of my grandparents lived in New York City." Isaac paused. "Are you even gonna remember any of this?"

He had a point. I could hardly remember what he'd said about Thursday. Something important.

I looked around the lounge. "Is there a bathroom?"

"Yeah, but this is a girls' floor," he said.

I laughed.

"What?"

"Nothing," I said, with a snap of lucidity. I had to fix my voice. When had it slipped up? When I'd laughed? Before? I tamped it down, deepening my words. "Let's go."

He headed to the silver elevator doors and thumbed the button. "Why do you ask?" he said. "About that stuff?"

"Because I don't know. I mean, I don't know that sort of thing about you guys. Except Nihal. He's so cool, you know? He's so good at everything."

"Yeah, he is," Isaac said.

"I'm being annoying. I'm sorry."

"It's fine," he said. I felt unsatisfied. The best answer you could hope for after an apology was *you don't have to be sorry*. Still, it was funny. These days it was so much less instinctive, the feeling of being sorry, the unstable drive to say I was.

The elevator doors slid open. We entered. Isaac's finger hovered over the second floor for a second. Then he pressed the fourth floor button, saying, "Let me grab you a coat, while you're here." The doors shut.

"Thanks." I leaned against the wall, facing Isaac. Two thick locks of hair hung down from his forehead, framing his face. He had a long, thin nose. Everything was quiet. The car jolted upward and my spine compressed. I thought of the elevator in Ewing Hall across the street, identical, my back to the wall and Michael's hand tangled in my long hair and his lips against my neck and the shudder of the elevator downward that had made me feel, for a second, weightless.

"You remind me of someone sometimes," I said. The words were slippery and came out dreamy.

He'd already said, "Who?" when I realized I shouldn't have said anything. He didn't look like Michael. He didn't act like Michael. He was just tall, and a boy, and good-looking enough for me to notice it. And he smelled like cobalt and rum.

I looked at Isaac and remembered my panic in the dark against him, and I wondered if it hadn't been because of my memories of closeness after all. Maybe I had felt the need to run from him like I'd run from Victoria. Terrified of being within reach. Terrified of the exhilaration or my own inevitable inadequacy. What did it mean that I'd wanted her? Was it making me want him, want everything, suddenly, all at once?

Last time I'd felt the heat of attraction, I'd been Michael's girl. Now I was my own again. I was my own. It took being your own to want somebody else. Now I could, and it was drowning me, and Victoria was mint and Isaac was a smile and every person I knew was such a work of art. Beauty was beauty and want was want and a beating heart was a beating heart. I was drunk and my synapses were firing in sluggish delirium and everything was absolutely stupid and utterly profound.

What came out of my mouth was, "You smell good."

"What?" he said.

"Um."

He looked hard at me for a second. Then the light of slow realization dawned on his face, which I realized, somewhere, was a very bad thing.

His mouth opened a fraction.

I began to feel ill. The door slid open. I exited the elevator. Something had gone wrong. I had to get away from it. The hall blurred. My eyelids were falling. Then Isaac's dorm room door shut behind me. We'd gotten in somehow. Walked down a whole hallway, and I'd already forgotten every step. Getting a coat. Right.

I saw a bed. That bed was mine. I headed for it, shrugging my blazer to the floor. Isaac said something, but I had already become horizontal, breathing in that bittersweet smell that hung on his navy pillowcase. It was soft against my cheek. My eyes were closed, and I was gone.

SCHERZO

I JERKED AWAKE AT 5:00 A.M. ON SUNDAY MORNING, blinking stickiness out of my eyes. Why was it so dark? Why was glossy paper plastered all over my walls?

Because they're not my walls. It flooded back—the drinks. The performance. The kiss, the gravity that had kept me clinging to Victoria, the way she'd tasted, the roughness of her lips beneath the gloss. What I'd said to Isaac.

I jerked up in bed, whispering a stream of detailed and elaborate curses that would've made your typical Kensington mother clutch her pearls. Isaac lay on a mattress pad on the ground, breathing deeply in his sleep. His roommate snored in the other bed, invisible under the covers. As Isaac's covers fell from me, I realized I wasn't wearing my blazer. *Why?* What possible reason? Had I lost all sense of self-preservation?

As I looked in the window, the reflection offered a glimpse of my left eyebrow, a glaringly obvious brown-black smear pointing toward my cheekbone. The moment in the elevator came back to me, then. The way Isaac had frowned, scanning my face, and gone completely blank.

Horror paralyzed me. My hands went still on Isaac's dark

sheets. I couldn't do anything but let the alarm bells in my head ring on, on, and on.

Isaac had figured it out, because regular eyebrows did not migrate down people's faces, and Isaac wasn't an idiot. He'd tell the others, and they'd shun me and tell the rest of the school, and I would be humiliated beyond belief.

That had been the biggest flaw in my plan, hadn't it? Of course I had no backup plan for failure, because at the start, I hadn't cared about failing. I'd had nothing to lose. Nothing at all.

Now I had something, fields at night and songs in the dark and wind in the afternoons and the eight of us together and home. The idea of losing it felt catastrophic.

I slid out of bed. Isaac shifted in his sleep, but I moved faster, grabbing my blazer from the end of the bed and dashing for the door, head splitting. *Go. Go. Go—*

By the time I burst out of Wingate into the freezing early morning, I was in a full spiral of panic.

♫

Evening approached. I felt pinned and helpless.

None of the guys had texted me all day. The group text had been unnaturally quiet, too—and Isaac hadn't said a word.

They must have started another group text, just the seven of them, to talk about it. Maybe they were meeting in person to figure out what to do. Even with the Sharps' eighty-year history, I somehow doubted they'd had this particular issue come up.

It was a weird day if figuring out you were bisexual made up the *least* of your mental turmoil. I considered calling Jenna, but I felt too sick with nerves to talk about it. Instead, I buried myself in memorizing lines for The Greek Monologue all afternoon. I had to deliver a monologue from *Antigone* on Tuesday. "Last of all shall I pass thither, and far most miserably of all, before the term of my life is spent!" The anguish of it all didn't help.

Sitting in my room as eight o'clock approached, I figured there was nothing for it. I slid my wig off and brushed my bangs into place. Black jeans belted, gray shirt buttoned, winter jacket on, I stepped into the skin of a perfectly average boy, and with it came the sting of self-assurance, still a little fresh every single day. I braced myself and slipped out the window one last time.

♬

At the top of the stone steps to the Nest, I hesitated. I ran a hand over the red-painted door and took a deep breath, breathing in the dust and oldness of the stairwell. The faint tang of fresh paint still hung in the air from when Nihal and I had put a new coat on the door.

I blinked hard, looking up at the ceiling. *Breathe. It'll be over soon.*

My watch read 7:59 p.m., closer than I'd ever cut it with rehearsal. No more delaying.

I walked in. Isaac, who stood by the piano with Nihal, looked over to me and stopped talking. Nihal wouldn't meet my eyes. The rest of the conversations went quiet, too.

My face and neck flooded with heat. The last, tiniest hope I'd been harboring—that somehow Isaac hadn't noticed, or if he'd noticed, hadn't said anything—died.

The door shut behind me. The black Sharps flag fluttered a bit, brushing me as if in comfort.

"Julian," Trav said slowly. "Hi."

I swallowed. "Yeah."

"Listen," he said. "Sit down."

I sat down. The armchair squeaked beneath me. I slipped my hands under my thighs and gripped the leather cushion hard. Seven pairs of eyes fixed unwaveringly on me.

"So, um," Isaac said. "We . . . this . . ."

"Spit it out," I murmured.

Mama leaned forward, resting his elbows on his knees. His eyes were warm. "Look, it's fine," he said. "Okay? It doesn't have to be weird."

I stared at him for a full ten seconds before I could muster up a sound.

"Wh-what?" I said. My heart hammered. They didn't *care*?

"Yeah," Isaac said. "Um, look, I'm sorry. I shouldn't have said anything, but I didn't know if . . . anyway, I'm sorry."

I opened my mouth, then shut it again.

Jon Cox shrugged. "I mean, if we had a problem with gay guys, this would be the actual worst place in America to go to high school, you know?"

Oh my God.

After a strangled second, I released a shout of laughter that was way too much for the joke. Laughs rippled around the room in the wake of the sound. The others looked relieved, but those looks were barely a shadow of what I felt.

They thought I was a *gay boy*. Isaac must not have noticed anything when I took off my blazer. Of course, it had been dark.

The makeup smear must have happened in my sleep, and I'd left this morning before he'd seen it. Even the dance—Jon and Mama had seen me run away from Victoria like her kiss had burned me.

"We should start rehearsal," Trav said, "but we wanted you to know that you don't have to expect anything different here. I hate to make a presentation out of it, but since maybe you had reasons for not saying anything, and since finding out en masse like this is a little . . . um, unorthodox, I thought it might be best to make sure you . . . are all right." He looked around for backup. Marcus was nodding so hard I thought he might give himself a minor concussion. Even Erik gave me a single thumbs-up, although red tinged his cheeks, like the idea of *gay* Julian was scandalous.

"I . . . thanks, guys," I said helplessly. Part of me wanted to break into hysterical laughter. But mostly, as I looked around the Nest, at the scored floorboards and the out-of-key upright, I wanted to melt into a puddle of relief. This was still mine. The circles of night sky through the windows and the guys around me, with their dumbass jokes and their silences and their complexes. The sight of the Sharps flag on the back of the door made something shaky and warm start glowing in my chest. *Verbis defectis musica incipit*. Words were failing me.

I still belonged.

♫

At the end of rehearsal, Nihal and I set off together, as usual. Rehearsal hadn't been different, just like Trav had promised. Of course, Trav was the only one talking, and the guy was as unchanging as a faulty chameleon, so that wasn't saying much.

Nihal wrapped a thick woolen scarf around his neck as we set up the shallow hill toward August Drive. For a few minutes, we were quiet. As we crested the hill, he said, "Julian, I'm sorry everyone found out at once like that. As usual, Isaac couldn't keep his mouth shut."

I shrugged, but my throat went tight, the same twinge I'd felt when I'd come across the trans resource website. I'd slipped beneath another mantle that wasn't mine—as if I could understand what being a gay guy was like. All I understood about sexuality was its uncertainty, discovering your way through yourself day by day, stepping tentatively, hitting on some term that seemed to fit and hoping it stuck.

We hit the sidewalk and headed toward East Campus. Thick white clouds had settled over Kensington earlier this afternoon, and they had turned cannonball dark in the night. Our school's towers and buildings reached toward the belly of the sky, outlined in orangey streetlight.

"It was good to see the guys like that, though," Nihal said. "I mean, because . . . you know. You never know who comes from what sort of mindset. So it's comforting."

I glanced at him, not sure where he was going with this. I nodded.

"Comforting," he continued, and from the strain in his voice—strain I'd never heard before—I realized what he was going to say before he said it. "Because I am, too, actually. Gay, I mean."

I looked at Nihal, then, with his prominent nose pointing down at the pavement and his hazel eyes more guarded than I'd ever seen them. He said it like a shield. He said it like he'd never in his life said it out loud.

"Hey," I said, stopping in my tracks. And for a second I considered telling him absolutely everything. Spilling the truth out in a rush, coming clean.

It caught in my throat. *No, be smart. Be smart about this.* I'd just gotten my freedom from the truth—it had happened like a miracle. Plunging myself back into that uncertainty, cold and thick and neck-deep . . . I couldn't do that.

Nihal might tell. He'd told before.

Instead, I reached for his shoulder and let my hand rest there a second. He was a couple inches shorter than me, I realized. I'd always thought of Nihal as tall. Tree-tall, tree-solid, tree-serene. Right now, he was just a scared-looking boy a year and a half younger than me.

"None of the guys know?" I said quietly, lowering my hand.

"No." We started walking again, approaching the crossroads where our paths usually split. "But being here is good," he said. "There's so many people who are, it feels normal. I started getting a grip on it at the end of last spring, and I was going to get back after summer and tell the Sharps, but now I can't."

"Why not?"

We slowed, then stopped at the crossroads. "It's . . ." Nihal sighed, searching for words.

"Is it because—?" I glanced at his turban. Maybe I couldn't say this without being insensitive.

Nihal must have caught the look, because he said, "No, not really." He half-smiled. "It's actually funny. There's nothing about gayness in the Guru Granth Sahib. That's our, you know. Holy book. Scripturally, it's just not mentioned."

"That's . . . good?"

"Yeah, you'd think. But the Guru Granth Sahib maps out the course for our lives, and since the only thing that *is* mentioned is straight marriages, that's all that's technically allowed. So gurdwaras won't allow for gay marriage ceremonies."

I studied his expression, which was uncharacteristically closed.

"That's frustrating," I said carefully.

"Yeah." He grimaced. "Very. Some people think that since it isn't mentioned, being queer lines up fine with Sikhism. I guess that's what I think. I mean, I have to believe that, otherwise what am I doing, you know?" He sighed, looking up at the spools of nighttime cloud. "Honestly, it doesn't make sense otherwise. I mean, being a Sikh is—it's love, acceptance, equality, oneness. For *every* person. It should be simple." A hint of bitterness touched his voice. "But I still can't make the pieces fit right in my head."

"Have you—maybe it would help to talk to your parents about it?" I suggested.

He puffed out a sigh. "I haven't told them. I don't really have plans to. I have this lesbian cousin who lives in Ludhiana, and when she started being open about it, about half my extended family stopped talking to her, or even about her, because in India a lot of people still think it's this purely sexual thing. I mean, not that people here are so much better about understanding that that's not true." He rubbed his forehead. "But it is tougher over there for a lot of reasons. Maybe it'd be different for me, but I don't want to take the risk."

A bundled-up figure headed up the sidewalk on the other side of the road. I lowered my voice. "You could talk to the Sharps about it. I mean, look how they acted tonight. It'd be fine."

"I can't."

"Why?"

"Because—" He glanced at the figure until it turned the corner and bobbed away. "I'm kind of involved with someone. His family doesn't know, either, so he doesn't want the whole school knowing."

"Oh." After a second, I said, "But that's great. That you're seeing someone."

A shadow of a smile touched his mouth and faded. "Dating is kind of a murky thing too. My mom says I shouldn't see anyone until I'm ready to get married, because that's the point, that's what I should be thinking toward. But I . . . this isn't really *dating*. We kissed one time, but I told him I couldn't do the physical stuff, so since then we've just spent a lot of time together. Just talking."

"What's he like?"

Nihal's lips quivered in suppressed laughter.

"What?"

"Nothing. Just. You know him."

I frowned. "Is he a Sharp?"

"No. Definitely not."

"What do you mean, definitely n—wait." I mouthed uselessly for a moment before getting ahold of myself. "Is it a Minuet? Is—is it *Caskey*?"

Nihal winced. "Okay, so, hear me out."

"Oh my God. It is."

He lifted his hands. "Let's all just breathe."

"Isn't he dating Anabel?"

"No, they were only talking for a couple of weeks."

"Okay, but—I—you're so much of a better person than him!"

"He's not actually like he pretends he is." Nihal struggled for a second. "I mean, Connor's very smart, and he's an exceptional painter, and he has a great voice. We actually have everything in common, when he's not being inflammatory, and that's only because he wants his dad to think he's, I don't know, *manly*."

"What? His dad's a high school music teacher. Not exactly hypermasculine."

"See, that's what I said." He grimaced. "But it's *Kensington*, so it's apparently different in a way that has not yet become clear to me. Anyway, his family has this mansion outside Boston, and they've all been Kensington alumni since the late nineteenth century. So they aren't go-hunting-and-be-a-lumberjack masculine, they're, like, sip-old-fashioneds-and-adjust-your-six-hundred-dollar-tie-while-disdaining-the-bourgeoisie masculine."

I tried to undo my face of disgust.

"Yeah," he said. "Same. Trust me, though. Connor isn't his dad."

"But he *is* the guy who burned our archives."

"Yes. We had words about that. Don't worry; I can hold my own." He raised one eyebrow at me. "Although I'm very flattered by your concern."

I sighed, my knee-jerk revulsion finally simmering down. "No, I just—I thought you hated him."

"Well, obviously. Connor's infuriating, all the time." Light humor colored his voice again. "The worst."

My phone buzzed with low battery. I checked it and startled. Nine thirty had crept up while we'd been standing here. If I was going to make it back through my window by the time Anabel knocked on my door, I had to run.

"We should go," I said. "Check-in."

"Right."

I paused, meeting his eyes. "But I won't tell anyone, trust me."

"I do," Nihal said. "That's why I told you."

The words hit a little too hard. As he left down the street toward Wingate, guilt fastened over my body, a mass of pinching claws. It was the most basic trust, expecting someone to be himself.

AS WINTER STORM SAUL LOOMED IN THE DISTANCE, the season snuck up on us. The cold unsheathed its claws, releasing the sort of chill that had you hiding your frozen lips between your teeth for safekeeping. The year's first snow came that Monday, showering down from wet skies, plastering Kensington in layers of thick white. By the next day, it had been tramped, sledded, and salted down to mud and slush. From winter wonderland to miserable hellscape in under twenty-four hours.

The midterm election happened that day. Marcus blamed the outcome on the weather, as well as voter apathy, and the poor alignment of the stars, and also there being no God. He couldn't stop talking about how Anderson Grimsley was going to be the worst senator in US history. He threatened to move overseas a few times. "Ah, of course," Nihal said. "Our largest emigrant population always has been politically disgruntled fourteen-year-olds." Marcus turned fire-hydrant red and emitted a sound of protest that sounded like a balloon deflating.

The week after my fake coming-out was filled with questions and adjustments. I meant to ask Erik to say something to Victoria, to follow what had happened at the dance, but I couldn't settle on the right words. An apology for fleeing, sure, but then what? "I only think of you as a friend"? "I think we should see other people"? "It's not you, it's the fact that I'm secretly a girl who sacrificed a foot and a half of perfectly good hair to the dark gods of a cappella"?

Erik himself could no longer stand within a few feet of me without blushing. I wanted to tell him he wasn't my type, but something told me he would've gotten weirdly offended.

And Isaac—I wouldn't have thought he was the type to act differently around gay guys, but he'd changed too. Vaguely, I remembered something he'd said after the dance—some promise to fix things between him and Trav, to patch everything over. The exact opposite had happened. Isaac stopped coming to the Nest early and stopped staying late. His guitar disappeared from its usual corner. During rehearsals, unless Trav was teaching him his part, he messed around with his phone, an air of avoidance hanging over him. I expected Trav to shatter that phone with his bare hands, but surprisingly, he didn't seem to think it was an egregious interruption, since it was silent.

I wanted to ask Isaac if he planned to figure out their issues before we had to live in a house with each other in the middle of the mountains, but we were barely talking anymore. He looked at me with something withdrawn, something that looked horribly like Connor Caskey–brand dismissal. I didn't want to admit how much the cold shoulder hurt. While we'd plotted to steal the Bear, we'd gotten to be actual friends, or so I'd thought from the joking texts fired in each other's direction every other minute.

I let him push away. Instead, I spent more and more time with Nihal, who'd convinced me to start crossing campus to eat dinner with him in Marden Cathedral. I listened to the dinnertime announcements from Dr. Caskey instead of Reese and took the nightly moment of silence in a space where it felt holy. The girl I was last year was a campus away.

The musical went up a week before Thanksgiving Break. I watched it in the back row on Saturday night, feeling only a bit wistful. Anabel's eleven o'clock number got a thundering round of applause that lasted a straight minute.

The next day, Winter Storm Saul rolled in, cracked his cloudy knuckles, and got to work. Temperatures nose-dived toward zero. The slush froze into sheets of three-inch-thick ice, and it snowed again—this time for thirty-six hours nonstop. Fifteen inches total. Kensington cancelled classes on Monday, to the shock and confusion of pretty much everyone. I peeked out of my room and saw a couple people walking around the Burgess halls, directionless, like dogs whose owners had dropped their leashes. We'd never had classes cancelled, not once in the three years I'd been here.

The second they sent the e-mail announcing the class cancellation, Trav texted the group: *We're still having rehearsal.*

I had to laugh.

♬

"I should've gone to Rochester to do door-to-door," Marcus moaned, traipsing up the stairs ahead of me. "There are some counties where people just don't have *rides*—low turn-out areas are *always* the counties where Republicans win—"

"Rides?" I said, exchanging a look with Nihal. I tried not to laugh. "Marcus, have you even taken Driver's Ed?"

"I mean. No." He stopped at the door to the Nest and looked back at us, twitching his head so his too-long bangs flicked out of his eyes. "Guys, come on. I'm a concerned citizen."

I lifted my hands. Nihal choked out, "Well. I will cosign whatever strongly worded letter you want to send."

Marcus went red and shouldered into the Nest. We bustled in after him, stamping snow onto the mat Trav had set in front of the door. Warmth washed over me, courtesy of the space heater plugged in by the couch. Erik was playing some quiet tune on the piano, and bluish shadows of snow were piled on the other side of the windows, and the campus looked dark and hushed and miles away.

"—guess we could bring a sled," Jon Cox was saying to Mama.

"Bring a sled where?" Marcus said, hopping into his windowsill.

"The retreat," Erik said, still doodling around with his chord progression, sparing Marcus a *did-you-really-have-to-ask?* glance over his shoulder.

I couldn't decide if I was terrified or excited by the retreat. We'd be at Jon Cox's place Saturday morning through Monday afternoon, arriving back at Kensington that night. The break in routine made me want to plan everything down to the second, but I couldn't. I had no plan for living with these guys. What did boys *do* at what was essentially a glorified sleepover? Could I find this on Google?

It could work, though. This might actually be simpler—no switching between Jordan and Julian. The only thing I'd have to worry about was showering, but I could just stay up until all the others had gone to sleep. Who needed rest, anyway?

"How're we getting there?" I asked, shrugging my coat onto

the back of my armchair. It rustled, snow showering off the sleeves.

Nihal perched on a sofa arm. "Jon Cox and Isaac drive a car each."

Speaking of which . . . I glanced around. Isaac was really cutting it close tonight. In about thirty seconds, he'd be late.

"Dibs on not driving with him, please," Mama said. "Never again."

Jon Cox grinned over at him. "You're just salty 'cause you don't have your license."

Mama snorted. "I wouldn't call what Isaac does 'driving.' He brakes like he's trying to stamp a cockroach to death. It's the least safe thing since the frickin' *Hindenburg*."

"Ah, Mom, always safety first," Jon Cox said. "Make sure to bring the baby seats for Marcus and Erik."

"Shut up," Marcus and Erik said at the same time.

I grinned, slumping into my armchair. "Why don't y'all just get Trav to drive?"

"He doesn't drive," Mama said. "He—"

The door creaked open. Trav hurried in, shrugging off his black peacoat. He lifted his folder. "Last arrangement's done."

A ragged cheer rose. Trav headed to the piano, we hopped to our feet, and the stack of music made its way to me. I grabbed a packet, passed the others, and smoothed my thumb over the title. This song, all bare piano and wistful theme, had been unavoidable a couple years ago. The song of my freshman fall. I'd been listening to it after my first mainstage audition, the first time Michael had walked up to me. "Halloween," by Girl on a Ledge.

"We'll start with the pre-chorus. Turn—" Trav cut himself off, glancing around. "Where's Isaac?"

We all traded looks. "I don't know," Mama said. "Did you see him downstairs?"

Trav twitched his head, a quick shake. He pulled his phone from his jeans pocket. "He hasn't texted." Disapproval made his voice rigid. "Someone call him. Now."

Jon Cox tugged out his phone, tapped the screen a few times, and held it to his ear. He waited, staring up at the ceiling. The lights wrapped around the rafters reflected in the lenses of his glasses. After a second, he lowered his phone. "Didn't pick up."

Trav's nostrils flared. He looked back down at his music. "Page four," he said. "Tenors in unison . . ."

I wondered what Isaac could be doing. Hopefully he hadn't slipped on the ice and broken something. It was dangerous out there, especially coming downhill to Prince.

I shouldn't have worried. He strolled in twenty minutes late. His expression was completely blank, as if there were nothing weird about showing up a third of the way into rehearsal, when nobody had been as much as twenty seconds late the whole year.

We all watched him grab the extra copy from the piano and join the circle.

"Anything you want to say?" Trav said, dead quiet.

Isaac shrugged, stiff and detached. He barely resembled the Isaac from callbacks, so comfortable, who'd looked at everyone as if he felt lucky to have them around. That kid was absent. Some shallow avatar of him had stepped into his clothes.

Trav seemed at a loss. After a long moment, he said, "We already did the first four pages."

"Got it," Isaac said, looking down at the music.

A needle of irritation prodded me. Of course he could just sight-read it, but why did that give him a free pass on showing up on time? Trav probably would have flayed the rest of us alive. Glancing around the circle, I saw hints of the same feeling on the guys' faces. I wasn't the only one a bit confused, and a bit more annoyed.

♫

Isaac came late the next night, too. He rolled in at 8:15, and this time, Trav didn't stay quiet about it. "Talk to me after," Trav said, his voice like gravel.

"Can't," Isaac said. "I've got a counterpoint project to finish."

"I don't care."

"You don't care about my grades? That's funny. I do." Isaac shrugged off his backpack and set it down by the piano. "So I'm going to go home after rehearsal, although you're welcome to try to stop me."

I stared at my shoes, baffled. *One of my best friends*, Isaac had said about Trav. Who acted like this to a friend?

Unwillingly, I found myself wondering if this was my fault. Had my coming on to him freaked him out this much? Was Isaac secretly a Westboro Baptist–type or something? After all, he barely even looked at me anymore, and when he did aim a furtive glance my way, he looked completely walled off.

The tension didn't ease during rehearsal. Whenever someone failed to get a part perfect the first time, Isaac shifted in place like he could barely contain his exasperation. As nine o'clock crept up, Marcus fluffed some line on his second try—not an easy line, either; a fast harmony with a surprise natural—and Isaac sighed audibly. Marcus shot a hurt glance his way but, of course, didn't speak up.

My vision sharpened with anger. I couldn't hold it back. "Hey, Isaac," I said, "if you think you can help, how about you go ahead and sing Marcus's part with him?"

"Julian," Trav warned.

"I'm serious." I kept my eyes on Isaac. "I mean, apparently it's obvious to you when we don't get everything 100 percent right the first time. So, how about you help out, genius?"

Isaac's eyes burned into mine. For a second the walls fell away, and I saw a flash of bitterness, of disappointment. I stared mulishly back, my heart pounding.

Finally, he yanked back the sleeve of his coat and twisted his watch to check it, fingers tight on its brown leather band. He hadn't even taken his scarf off, ready to go at the soonest possible opportunity. "We're done," he said.

As the clock tower began to strike, he grabbed his backpack and disappeared.

♫

The next night, he was on time. I felt a pang of embarrassment when he walked in. I shouldn't have snapped last night. It wasn't my job—I'd probably just made Marcus anxious.

Isaac settled by the window near my armchair. Silence hung between us like a thick, opaque veil. I drew it back with a clearing of my throat. "Hey, listen."

"Don't worry about it," he mumbled, not meeting my eyes.

". . . yeah, sure, but—"

Trav walked in, and I sighed, standing. When Trav's searching eyes found Isaac, his expression cleared.

Maybe this was just another blip on the radar. Isaac would explain in a few weeks what was going on. College apps stress, maybe. And then he would get into every school, and we'd think it was hilarious in hindsight.

Maybe.

"We're in the home stretch," Trav said. "First thing: Rooks, I need you to go to a meeting Friday afternoon with Dr. Caskey. He's working through the competition's program order, and we need to be last. Got it? Second-to-last at an absolute stretch. Nothing else is acceptable. I don't care if you have to extort somebody to make this happen. His e-mail said 3:45 in Arlington, so be there at 3:30, in case the chronology of your arrival makes a difference."

We grumbled our agreement.

"Next." Trav handed the arrangements to his right. "If we finish this tonight, we'll have tomorrow and Friday night to focus on memorization before even getting to the retreat. That's ideal, so let's focus up. Got it?"

Heads bobbed.

"All right. Page sixteen."

We learned quickly. As the minutes passed, the thick discomfort in the air lessened, turning less oppressive, until I could almost tell myself it felt normal again. We'd finished the arrangement before eight thirty.

We had a set. Jon Cox let out a whoop, and Mama clicked his heels, nearly crashing into Erik as he landed.

"From the top." Trav joined the circle, closing it. He tugged his pitch pipe from his jeans pocket, lifted it to his lips, and blew a pitch. The arrangement gathered momentum and took off.

About twenty seconds in, Trav suddenly stopped singing the solo. He gestured for us to keep going, but a grimace worked its way onto his face. I heard it too. The background was cluttered instead of smooth, just off-key enough to hit the ear like an accident. Trav leaned forward into the circle to listen, his arched eyebrows practically meeting above his nose. "Whoever's suspending the second, don't," he called halfway through the verse. I had no idea how he heard it, but somebody's note shifted back into place.

As the song went on, the tonality sank even further. With dissatisfaction fastening into place on Trav's expression, we were getting nervous, depressing the sound, tending flat.

"Pitch," he warned. Backs straightened, and the sound lurched about a quarter-tone sharp, buckling into place part by part. By the second chorus, we'd grappled our way on top of the piece. But as we cycled through the chords leading into the bridge, Trav called out, "There's no flat seven in these chords!" and then, "Stop, stop."

He looked around the circle. "Who's doing that? This isn't fucking *jazz*, guys." He glanced at Marcus, and his voice softened a bit. "Is—do you need to go over that part again?"

Marcus looked hurt. "I thought I got it right."

To my surprise, Erik said begrudgingly, "He did get it right, I'm pretty sure."

“But the Tenor 2 line . . .” Trav rounded on Isaac. “Is that you doing that? Are you just adding random sevenths?”

Isaac gave him a blank, confused look.

“Okay. Never mind,” Trav said. “One more time from the top.” He took a deep, exasperated breath.

Then he froze. Dread seeped into the room as if the coldness outside were slipping through the windows. Trav leaned past Marcus, closer to Isaac, and took a second, sharper breath through his nose.

Isaac moved back, but Trav was dropping his pitch pipe into his pocket. “Why do you smell like weed?” he said, his voice low and dangerous. “Are you *high* right now?”

I—and all the other guys—turned a disbelieving stare on Isaac. Jon Cox and Mama smoked in the woods pretty often, but never anytime close to rehearsal, out of sheer self-preservation if nothing else. Since when did Isaac even smoke?

A long moment drew taut, a quivering string. Isaac glanced around the circle, as if for backup, then back to Trav. “Yeah.”

“Answer something for me.” Trav’s voice was taut with control. “When are you going to start taking this seriously?”

“Calm down,” Isaac said.

“No. Not until you get rid of this new attitude, treating rehearsal like it doesn’t matter.” Trav’s voice rose. “Look at you. You’re late, you’re distracted, you show up like *this*—”

Isaac snapped. “Maybe that’s because this *doesn’t fucking matter*!”

A flinch impacted the circle, and something awful happened. We were punctured and began to deflate. I felt ridiculous, sheet music drooping in my hand. All this—it *was* kind of silly, wasn't it? Singing nonsense words until they sort of fit together, trying to massage pop music into a format that lent itself to humor more than anything else? And Trav's absolute seriousness made it ludicrous, if you thought about it too hard. I glanced around the circle and knew everybody else was feeling it, too. A sudden blast of unwelcome perspective.

"What?" Trav said. "What's that supposed to mean?" The fury had evaporated from his voice. He sounded hollow.

"What do you think it means? Look at this." With a toneless laugh, Isaac threw his sheet music on top of the piano and turned on the rest of us. He searched blank face after blank face. "What do you think we're doing here? Curing cancer? Jesus, what do you think this *is?* Eight guys standing around making noise." He rounded on Trav, and for the first time, it was obvious the height Isaac had on him. "I'm done with you, acting like this is life and death."

I wanted to step in, but this had been coming since that night in the theater, since that first rehearsal when Isaac hadn't been paying enough attention for Trav's taste. It had been coming since before I'd even auditioned.

"Forget it. I can't do this." Isaac went for the door. The bang when he slammed it made tingles run down my arms.

"Jesus," Jon Cox muttered.

"I—I can go after him," Marcus said, "if—"

Nihal shook his head. Marcus fell quiet.

The air was still. One by one, we looked to Trav. There was nothing behind his eyes. Usually, you could see calculations, or judgments, or appraisal. Or that rare dash of happiness. Now, nothing.

"We're done for the night," he said, his voice raspy.

Every movement slow and methodical, he collected the music, closed his binder, and left, as silent as a shadow.

15

IT BECAME CLEAR ABOUT HALFWAY THROUGH THURSday's rehearsal that Isaac wasn't going to show.

We managed to do a full run of the set before the hour ended, but the difference in our sound shocked me. With Isaac's hypersensitive ear, Trav always put him on the strangest notes, those tight harmonies that made some chords sound like they were glowing. Without those parts—and without Isaac's soaring solo lines, which always made my heart clench, no matter how many times I'd heard him sing them—everything sounded empty. Wrong.

Trav had a hand on the doorknob at the end of rehearsal when Mama stopped him. "Trav. Look, would you like me to call him?"

Trav froze, not facing us. "No."

Jon Cox sighed. "Man, if you're waiting for Isaac to crawl back and apologize, we're still gonna be standing here by the time competition rolls around."

"No," Trav repeated, turning now. His eyes were cold chips of black glass. "We're not waiting for anything."

The rest of us traded uneasy glances.

"I get it," Nihal said gently, "but two of our arrangements have eight-part splits. We need eight voices."

"I'll consolidate lines," Trav said. "Rearrange, reteach. We can take Erik off VP for 'Clockmaker' and 'Open Wide.'"

I closed my eyes, collapsing into my armchair. "Trav, we just finished the set. Nobody wants to relearn it."

"Also," Mama said, eyeing the rumpled collar that peeked out from Trav's sweater, "you look exhausted. You've put in how many hours? I mean, the Minuets have five arrangers, and—"

Trav pulled his hat on, zipped his Patagonia, and took the doorknob in a stranglehold. "Do you think I care what the Minuets do?" he said. "This is what I do. I'll handle it. And if Isaac's not interested in contributing, he can stay out of it, as far as I'm concerned."

Before we could say anything else, the door was closing at my elbow, the flag rippling in Trav's wake. I made a hopeless gesture.

Jon Cox and Mama sat down on the sofa in unison. The freshmen just stood there, staring after Trav.

"So," Marcus said, finally. "Does this . . . has this happened before?"

"I mean." Jon Cox glanced at Mama. "No, but I saw it coming for sure."

Mama sighed. "They had issues last year, but last year's seniors always put them in line."

I tried to imagine anyone putting Trav in line. It didn't work.

"Same with the year before that," Mama said. "Trav's a transfer, so he joined the same year I did, which made it sort of weird. Maybe it would've been better if they'd been freshmen together."

I caught the two freshmen trading a glance. Erik looked startled, like he hadn't considered the fact that he'd be in the group with Marcus for four long years.

"Okay, um," Marcus said. "I've got this composition homework to do, so . . ."

"Me too," Erik said. He cleared his throat. "You, um, you want to work together?"

Surprise and doubt warred on Marcus's expression. Eventually, he said, "S-sure, that'd be, yeah. Let's."

"Right."

They headed out, both their heads ducked. Nihal hopped up on one of the arms of my armchair. We sat opposite Jon Cox and Mama, silence suspended between the four of us.

Nihal nudged me. "What ended up happening the night of the prank?"

"What prank?" Mama asked.

"Um." I cleared my throat. "Me and Isaac had this plan to get the Minuets back after Bonfire. We were gonna steal the Golden Bear—"

Jon Cox spluttered. "You what?"

"—but Trav found out, so nothing happened." I glanced at Nihal. "I've been thinking, though. What if this whole thing is because of, you know, what happened after the other weekend? I mean, Isaac seemed fine before he found out I'm . . ."

Mama shook his head. "No, don't worry. It's not that."

"How do you know? It—"

Jon Cox waved his hand. "Because he's been rooming with that cello kid for three years. Harry whatever. And cello kid is pretty much the gayest person this side of the Mississippi."

"*Oh.*" I fell quiet. The theory evaporated, landing me back on square one with a thud, and with an unexpected rush of relief.

At my elbow, Nihal let out a breath, and I knew he'd been wondering the same thing.

Another lapse. Brows stayed furrowed. Lips buttoned shut.

"What if he doesn't want to do the retreat?" Jon Cox said. "Who's going to drive?"

Nihal nudged me. "Do you have your license, Julian?"

"Yeah, but I can't drive more than one person. And I'm not allowed to have anyone younger than twenty in the car until March." I frowned. "Actually . . . Jon, how are *you* allowed to drive more than one person?"

A guilty look crept over Jon Cox's face. He threaded his fingers through his golden hair.

Mama jumped in, just like at the Dollar Sale. "It's, uh, different in Massachusetts. The—"

Jon Cox sighed. "Leave it, Mama." He glanced at me, his blue eyes guarded. "I turned eighteen in August."

"What? How are you a sophomore?"

"I got held back. Twice."

I opened my mouth to reply, but nothing came to mind. Sure, some Kensington kids couldn't have cared less about core classes, but they'd still tested into this place. The whole point of this school was excellence.

After a second, I wiped the surprise from my face. *Stop. God.* I hated getting snobby about grades. None of my friends back home got good grades, and I didn't judge them for it; it was dumb to hold Kensington kids to a different standard.

"Jon's dyslexic," Mama explained. "It was worse in elementary school."

"*Oh.*" I looked back at Jon Cox, who was shrinking back into the sofa. Tiny things fell into place—the way Trav always taught Jon's parts last, and with uncharacteristic patience. Jon Cox's deeply smothered insecurity. The way he was always reading the same book for weeks at a go. "I mean," I said, "but you can't help that."

Jon Cox let out a mumbling laugh. "Not according to some people."

"Fuck them," Mama said.

Jon Cox didn't look satisfied. His expression grew doubtful, as if his own thoughts were hounding him. I wanted to say something reassuring, but nothing came to mind.

"Right," I said, clearing my throat. "Okay, so. We'll just . . . hope Isaac comes around?"

"That's pretty much my plan," Mama said, standing.

The four of us collected our things, huddled down in our jackets, and shuffled out together into the icy clutches of campus.

It wasn't until Nihal and I were alone and halfway up the hill, coated in snow to our knees, that I spoke. "I know nobody wants to say it, but if Isaac doesn't show for the retreat, the driving thing is going to be an issue."

"Yeah," Nihal said. "He's also *loud.* Next to everyone else in the competition, seven people will sound anemic. We're already so small."

"You want to track him down?" I said. "Tomorrow after classes, maybe?"

“We can’t. I have transcribing to do, and you have to go to that meeting with Graves.”

We broke onto the cleared sidewalk. “How about tonight?” I said. “I could sneak out after check-in. Ten o’clock?”

Nihal checked his watch. “I can do that. I’ll meet you at his room.”

♬

I knocked on Isaac’s door, using only one knuckle to dampen the noise. The Wingate prefect couldn’t see me on this hall—he’d chase me out.

After a second, the door creaked open to reveal Isaac’s roommate, a light frown on his face. It was the first time I’d seen Harry: a pale, scrawny kid wearing white Converse and neon yellow jeans, which made him look just a little bit jaundiced. “Isaac’s not here,” he said.

I loosed a sigh. Of all the nights Isaac had picked to sneak out to work . . . good thing Harry was actually home for once, then.

Nihal glanced at me. “We can wait in my room for a bit.”

“Yeah, word.” I looked back to Harry. “Did Isaac say if he was getting back before lights-out?”

Harry frowned. “No, guys, like, he’s not *here*. He left Kensington this afternoon.”

After a beat of uncomprehending silence, I said, “He what?”

“Yeah.” Harry adjusted his glasses, the thick black rims framing owlish blue eyes. “They let him out before afternoon classes.”

“Why?” Nihal said, sounding as blindsided as I felt. “Where did he go?”

"Back to the city," Harry said. "He didn't tell you? His dad was in a wreck, and there's been, like, three different surgery complications. He still hasn't been discharged."

"*What?*" Nihal spluttered. My mouth was wide open. I couldn't help it.

"I thought he would've told you. At rehearsal, or whatever."

We were quiet for a minute.

"No," I managed. "Nothing. He didn't tell us anything."

16

FRIDAY AFTERNOON WAS COLD AND DARK, 3:30 P.M. disguised as 3:30 a.m. Erik, Marcus, and I met in front of Arlington Hall to sort out the competition order. I passed between the twin statues of lions that flanked the stairs, following Erik, who looked like a turtle, shelled in an olive coat that was absurdly big for him. His parents must have expected a growth spurt soon, but judging by Victoria's height, they might be waiting a long time.

The freshmen dipped easily into conversation, but secrecy had its hand across my mouth. Nihal and I had agreed not to tell the others—it wasn't our information to dole out. If Isaac didn't want the Sharps knowing, that was his business.

Still, I couldn't help thinking about the way he'd been acting. Guilt tinted my recent memory blue. I'd read his attitude as hostile or sullen. *This* had been the last possibility on my mind. It felt wrong, all the others still trapped in that blue space, unknowing.

We clanked through the front doors and traipsed through the foyer, where murky-looking oil canvases hung on the wall that curved down to the box office. A door to the auditorium was propped; we filed in. A trio of people glowed at the edge of the stage, shirts and skin whitened by the lights.

The three of us traded a look and broke into a jog. We were fifteen minutes early to the time Dr. Caskey had given Trav—why were people already here?

But as we neared the stage, I recognized Connor, and it all cleared right up. Dr. Caskey must have given his son an earlier time than the rest of us. Just nepotism. Nothing complicated.

I clomped up the reverberant steps at the side of the stage, Erik and Marcus trotting up afterward. We flocked toward the table at the edge of the stage, where a pair of Minuets—Connor and his lanky ginger henchman—were talking to Dr. Caskey. Dr. Caskey had a well-groomed thatch of salt-and-pepper hair topping a face that looked uncannily like Connor's, right down to the self-satisfied look that seemed built into the architecture of his expression. The two Caskeys loomed over the redheaded Minuet like twin skyscrapers.

"Gentlemen," Dr. Caskey said, scanning us. "Welcome. Let's get your time slot squared away." He had a confident, genial tone of voice that didn't match the hardness of his blue eyes.

"Connor, Oscar," he said, waving a dismissive hand. As we approached, they cleared away from the table to reveal a poster with six slots. The last—of course—was taken: *NEW YORK MINUETS.*

Marcus fidgeted, looking between Erik and me. "What do we do?" he murmured.

"Trav said second-to-last," I muttered back.

Erik picked up the pen and reached for number five, but Dr. Caskey said, "Wait."

Erik looked up at Dr. Caskey, who had a foot and a half of height on him.

Dr. Caskey showed his teeth. A manufactured-looking smile. "The program needs genre separation, so we need some distance between the men's groups. Fourth or earlier, please."

Erik let out a slow breath. "Cool." He and Marcus looked at each other, then, in unison, they faced me.

"Why are you looking at me?"

"Because you're a junior?" Erik said.

I shook my head. "Okay. Maybe first? What if we did first? It's better than getting lost in the middle, probably."

"Totally, yeah," Marcus said. "That makes sense. Do that."

I picked up the pen and scribbled *SHARPSHOOTERS* into the first slot.

"Thanks for stopping by," Dr. Caskey said. "Have a good break, fellas."

We headed for the backstage door, passing between the stripes of deep blue curtain that hung stage left. "That was bullshit," Erik muttered, looking mutinous. "Trav's going to be so mad."

"Yeah," Marcus agreed. "Yeah. But he can't really do anything, I guess. Dr. Caskey is the *dean*."

"This better not throw our chances," Erik grumbled.

I opened my mouth to reassure him, but something interrupted: a sensation of sudden warmth blooming between my legs.

I froze. My period wasn't supposed to come for another week. These sweatpants, light gray, weren't going to hide stains, and I couldn't remember if I had a tampon in my bag. I'd never *wished* for period cramps, but good Lord, a little heads-up would have been nice.

"You good, man?" Erik said.

"Yeah, I'm fine," I grunted. "You guys go ahead. I'm going to use the bathroom."

"See you later!" Marcus chirped, and they headed for the stage door. I moved for the greenroom, trying not to waddle too much. What was the best way to walk when you were trying not to bleed everywhere? Unclear. Someone should've done studies on this.

The Arlington greenroom planners had taken the name too literally, with rich emerald-green carpeting and walls painted a light mint. The L-shaped room had sofas along every available wall, the boys' restroom to my right. I darted around the bend, hunting for the girls'.

There it was, tucked into the corner of the *L*. *Please*, I prayed, pushing inside. In Palmer, the bathrooms under the stage were always stocked with pads and tampons, lined up along the mirror like a feminine hygiene buffet. I didn't know why they were there, but I'd raided those supplies more times than I could count.

I flicked on the lights. This bathroom wasn't equipped. It had been a slender hope anyway.

I swung into a stall and sat for a while, contemplating the terrible timing. Now I had to deal with my period on the retreat. How was I going to get rid of a shitload of bloodstained objects without the Sharps noticing?

Only one option, really: Bring a bunch of plastic bags and hide it all in my suitcase. Smuggle my used tampons back to school after the retreat like contraband.

Sighing, I double-checked the front pocket of my backpack. Empty. Time to make one of those makeshift pads out of toilet paper, position it awkwardly in my underwear, and pray it held up until I got home, then.

Makeshift pad made and applied, I flushed, washed my hands, and left the bathroom. My phone buzzed as I crossed the green-room threshold. I paused to check the group text.

Trav (3:36 p.m.): *You didn't even try to request he change the order? You didn't ask him why the Minuets knew to get there so early? He might have backed down if he thought you were going to bring this to other teachers.*

Trav (3:36 p.m.): *I asked you to do one thing. You might have taken a bit of initiative.*

Shit. Usually, this would be the point at which Isaac would dive in to calm him down. None of the rest of us knew how to handle this. The others were probably resenting Isaac right now for disappearing.

I found myself wanting to be angry at him, too—as if by not telling us, he deserved the resentment. Of course not, though. He didn't owe us the down-low on his dad's medical procedures.

I tapped Isaac's contact on my phone screen and opened a new text. Seeing our text history was a weird flood of memory—the rapport we'd had before the Golden Bear disaster, before the dance.

I typed a message. The words didn't come smoothly.

Hey, Isaac. Your roommate told Nihal and me last night what the deal is. We haven't told the guys. You don't have to reply to this or anything, but if you want to talk about it, I'm here. Hope your dad's feeling okay and he gets better soon.

I reread it a few times. Would this help at all? Was it too emotional? Too girly?

I gave my head a hard shake, disgusted. How selfish *was* I, worrying about whether my phrasing in a text was too feminine, when on the other end, Isaac was sitting in some hospital by his post-op father? I knew what it felt like to sit in that seat: lonely.

Besides, Marcus was plenty compassionate. Nihal was plenty kind. Kindness had no gender, had no race or age or category. It didn't matter if this made me sound like myself—I'd built a thick enough wall for it to withstand a few blows, and Isaac could use some sympathy. I couldn't offer much, but I could be genuine for once in my damned life.

I tapped Send, put my phone down, and walked out of the greenroom.

On the way to the backstage door, a low, serious voice stopped me. I caught a glimpse between the dangling curtains at the side of the stage—everyone had come and gone, except one tall figure facing another down. Connor was nearly as tall as his father, but Dr. Caskey wielded those few extra inches of height like a weapon. After a second's debate, I ducked out of sight and listened.

"—still remember what it was like to be here," said Dr. Caskey's clear, tuneful voice. "I know what it's like, the real Kensington. Fooling around with girls in the cathedral. Getting drunk on Dom Pérignon in the woods. Going out after dark without the housemaster noticing . . . and you know, when I was in the group, we had real rituals, real *tradition*, none of that watered-down Kumbaya trash they have people doing now. I had a brush with death on the night of my initiation. Still got a scar or two." He said it as if it were his proudest achievement, and I wondered what the Minuets' old initiation might have been. What could they get away with out in the woods? Branding, maybe, like I'd heard about college frats? One of those get-blindfolded-and-lost-in-the-wilderness scenarios?

Dr. Caskey loosed a long, deep sigh. "So, I understand."

"Yes, sir."

A pause. "But you need to understand something," he went on, his voice getting soft and dangerous. "You know what I'm thinking when Mr. Yu tells me I might want to talk to you, because, well, do I know your performance this semester hasn't quite been up to your usual standard? I'm thinking I shouldn't have to babysit you and your grades for you to perform. And I'm thinking, maybe I need to get worried about December, because maybe you're not getting into Princeton without that tour."

Connor was quiet.

"The rituals, and breaking the rules," Dr. Caskey said, "it only means anything if you're a winner. I mean—" He laughed. "It's the difference between those guys on Wall Street doing cocaine and a coke addict, get it? The difference is control. If you're going to mess around, pick fights, fine. Don't tell me about it, but it's fine. Kind of character-building, at the end of the day. But the first thing you're going to do is be the best, or the rest is wasted time. Hear me?"

"Yes, sir."

Dr. Caskey's voice lost its last shred of humor. "You're not going to embarrass me again?" he said, colder than sea ice. "Because if you don't get results here, and I get wind from *anyone* else that you've been fucking around this semester, I am not going to be happy."

"You don't need to worry." Connor spoke with utter neutrality. Without seeing his face, I knew the disconnected expression that would be locked into place over his steely eyes and thin mouth. I understood suddenly where and why he'd adopted it: here, a foot in front of his father, for survival's sake.

"Good." The sound of a hand on a shoulder. "Eyes on the prize. Now put that table up and let's go."

I slipped noiselessly out the backstage door, feeling like nothing of what I'd just heard could be real.

♬

"Okay, we're good," Erik said, putting down his phone. "Victoria says she can get a ride to the airport with, I don't know, Ariana something. So we have a car."

I issued a sigh of relief. It caught in my throat as Jon Cox turned toward me. "All right, buddy," he said. "Are you up to drive?"

Four hours there, and four hours back. For eight hours, I'd have to make sure the speedometer never even nudged the speed limit. I couldn't risk getting pulled over. It wasn't just driving someone under twenty that would get me busted—the cop would get curious why I didn't match the girl on my license.

But with Isaac gone, what was the other option?

I looked around for a sympathetic face, but the guys all looked expectant. I hedged. "Just, we don't drive in this weather in California, so . . ."

"The roads are going to be salted," Jon Cox said quickly.

"Well," Mama said, "not the whole way. Up in the mountains, it gets pretty snowy. You really think—"

Jon Cox hushed him and looked back at me. I understood the pleading look in his eye—we needed to get out of this place. Too many angry words hung around the Nest, cluttering our corners, perching on our rafters, peering down at us. They needed time to drift away.

But as far as my parents knew, my semester was a total non-event. All I needed was one missed speed limit sign, one cop having a bad day, or one patch of black ice, and everything was done. Nobody in my life would trust me again.

A voice came from behind Jon Cox. "I'll do it," Trav said.

I turned with all the other guys. "What?"

"I thought you couldn't drive," Mama said.

Trav pursed his lips. "I *can*. I just . . . don't." He crossed his arms. "But it's better than Julian getting arrested. I-I can do it."

More than anything, he sounded like he was talking himself into it. Unease flashed across my thoughts. Isaac had mentioned Trav's anxiety. How bad was it around driving? Should I jump in? Tell him not to worry about it, not to push himself if he didn't feel comfortable?

But Jon Cox was already saying, "Thanks, man. So we're set."

"We're set," Trav said, sounding more confident.

Under my skin, excitement and guilt grated against each other, shooting sparks.

17

IT WAS EARLY AFTERNOON, THE WHITE SUN SLIPPING down from its peak, when Trav said, "Music off. We're here."

I punched the power button and leaned forward, peering out the windshield. The view made a welcome break from the phone in my lap. I kept checking it, wondering if Isaac would reply to my message. I didn't really expect an answer, but I hoped, a little, if only for the human contact. I'd spent the car ride in crushing silence, with Erik in the backseat watching the entire Bourne trilogy on his phone, while to my left, Trav operated the wheel with the acute focus of a brain surgeon mid-procedure.

My mind kept circling back to Connor Caskey's conversation with his father. Dr. Caskey had fit so many terrible sentences into such a short period of time that it was like he'd been trying to horrify me specifically. For weeks, Nihal's frustration had mounted as their secret grew heavier, but I hadn't understood before yesterday how much of a disaster it would be for Connor if word got out.

The seatbelt locked tight against my chest as Trav braked too quickly. In the back, Erik made an irritated noise. We crunched onto the spread of snow before Jon Cox's mountain house, a three-story confection of honey-colored beams. It stood in the Adirondacks at the bottom of a sweeping slope, stands of powdered pines peeking over its snow-dusted roof. Panels of windows high on the front face of the house gazed down on a frozen river, which pooled in the crease of the valley. Crisp, untouched snow stood all around in thick drifts and layers.

Trav had barely put Victoria's Lexus into park before Jon Cox came vaulting across the hood with a whoop. His jean-clad ass wiped off the thin crust of snow that had accumulated over the four-hour drive. Trav went rigid in the driver's seat. Jon Cox squeaked off, making the car bounce, and landed with a *crunch* on the iced-over gravel.

"Watch it," Erik said, scrambling out of the backseat. "If there's one scratch on this thing when we get back, Victoria's gonna murder me."

I slid out and shut the passenger door behind me. "Rest in peace."

"What took you so long?" Jon Cox asked, loping after me as I headed to the trunk. "We've been here for, like, fifteen minutes."

I glanced over my shoulder. Trav still sat in the driver's seat, extracting the keys with the slowness of your average sloth. "Trav drives with one hand on the horn, if that tells you anything."

"Jesus," Jon Cox said.

"I know." I hoisted my fraying suitcase out of the trunk. "But whatever," I said, yanking Jon Cox's hat down over his eyes with my other hand. "We got here alive, didn't we?"

"Being alive is important," Mama boomed, walking up with a huge duffel slung diagonally across his back. "C'mon, let's get inside. It's freezing."

Once Trav had locked the car, backing away from it as if it might explode, we all trudged up the side steps, two flights of damp, rickety wood, to a sliding-glass door.

"Honey, I'm *hoo-ooome*," Jon Cox sang, as he flung the glass door wide. Hearing Jon Cox sing always came with a bit of a shock—he had an operatic baritone, solemn and controlled, like a fifty-year-old's.

The seven of us trailed into a gleaming kitchen. I tried not to stare and failed spectacularly. A sheen of dust softened marble countertops. Slim windows hugged the pine-beam ceiling. A beaten copper ventilator rose above four shining burners, facing a row of polished cabinets, and the refrigerator looked big enough for about half a dozen people to fit inside, if they got creative.

"Dibs on the master bed," Mama called, kicking off his shoes. He slid in his socks over the hardwood toward the darkened great room. We trailed after him, and when he hit the lights, my mouth drooped open. Cherry columns propped up a ceiling twenty feet high. Tasseled rugs lay beneath long sofas and chairs whose dark leather was faded under translucent dustcovers. Beneath the dappled stone chimney, the wide fireplace's iron grate was swept clean.

As the other guys went for the steps to the second floor, I looked down at my beat-up suitcase and felt minuscule. On some level, I felt like I should've been seething with envy, but this place was so far removed from everything I'd ever lived that I couldn't even feel jealous. All I had was a numbing awe: that real families had houses like this, that one of the Sharps had spent his whole childhood in rooms where even the color of the treated floorboards screamed money.

Nihal stopped next to me. "He's an investment banker," he said quietly. "Jon Cox's dad."

"Got it. Forget theater. Investment banking is my new plan."

Nihal chuckled. "If you want to never see your kids, go for it." He followed the others upstairs.

I mulled over the words, chewing on the inside of my cheek. The subtext wasn't subtle: the huge house Jon's family didn't even live in, his beautiful car, everything—it couldn't substitute for an absent father. I felt like I'd heard this story a thousand times.

Still, I would've taken this option any day. Back in San Francisco, I hadn't exactly been drowning in family time either. Dad worked night shifts as a gas-station cashier, leaving for work before I got home from school and not getting back until I was already asleep. I had years of memories of myself—nine, ten, eleven years old—walking around the back of our apartment building, digging the spare key out of a gravel-filled flowerpot, and letting myself in after school. Mom came home from her part-time job around six, in time to cook up beans or powdery mashed potatoes.

The older I got, the less I saw of her, too. She took more hours. I took care of myself. Rich kids with millionaire dads weren't the only ones raising themselves.

I never felt like a poor-little-poor-girl, though, some tragic character out of a story—it was mundane. Everything in my life was sketched in the same bland shade of disrepair. Clothes, apartment, furniture: fray and decay. Bulk tins and stained utensils. So normal to me.

Looking around this mansion of a mountain home, I wondered—did Jon Cox think this was normal, too?

"Hey," said a voice. I startled. Jon had come up from behind me.

"Hi," I said. After a second, I waved around. "This place is . . ."

Jon Cox shook his head. "Yeah, don't . . . I don't know. It is what it is."

He looked embarrassed. I wanted to cringe, or say, *Don't be embarrassed that your life is a fantasy*. But I stayed quiet, my thoughts chasing each other's tails. After all, if he'd looked smug or satisfied, I would've thought, *arrogant*. Maybe there was no right answer to being born filthy rich, like there was no right answer to being born dirt poor. Maybe everyone was just looking for reasons to think everyone else was ungrateful.

It was so stupid, too, because what were *we* supposed to do about the Very Wealthy Elephant in the Room, me or Jon Cox? We still had people telling us when to turn out our lights. We still had to ask permission to use the bathroom. Yeah, this boy drove around all ostentatious in his flashy car, with his Ray-Ban sunglasses and his Brooks Brothers jackets, looking like a grade-A assclown. But he'd also bought us that fancy whiskey that night in the field. He was always buying people food, giving rides, self-consciously generous with his time and money. Now we were all here together, living under his roof. Did all that equal out to my vacuum-silence when it came to my family's situation?

I wanted to talk about it all, but I didn't know what to say, or whether it would do any good, anyway. Did anyone else even want to talk about it? Why was it such a slippery subject, wriggling its way out of everyone's grasp?

Maybe I'd figure it out in ten years, or maybe when I was my parents' age, when I knew what it felt like to lose jobs, skip meals for my kid, scrape the barrel so hard the splinters tore up my fingertips. Maybe then I'd know how to talk about money without feeling like, somehow, the whole thing was imaginary—something human beings had pulled out of thin air without an instruction manual for how to do it all right.

In the uncomfortable silence, Jon Cox took off his glasses, which had fogged up around the edges, and wiped them on his knit sweater. "Do you want to check out the attic?" he said. "It's, um, it has a view . . ."

"Lead on," I said, taking the handle of my suitcase.

♬

The attic had its pros and cons. Pro: the king-size bed and the huge circular window that overlooked the frozen river. Con: over the bed, on the bare wooden walls, hung a giant deer head that looked so freshly dead I expected it to blink. Strong pro: I had the room to myself, so setting an alarm in the middle of the night to shower wouldn't be conspicuous. Strong con: The bathroom was down the stairs and two hallways, past the rooms where four of the guys would be sleeping. More sneaking than I'd hoped for.

I'll make it work, I told myself, leaving my suitcase by the bed. I jogged downstairs. In the great room, Trav and Mama were lifting a coffee table, clearing the center of the room. From the kitchen, the scent of sizzling hot dogs flavored the air, flooding my mouth with saliva.

Trav set down his end of the table. "Lunch," he called, "then choreo."

"I can't dance," Marcus said beside me. "At all."

"Everyone can dance," I said.

Half an hour later, Marcus was doing his very best to prove me wrong. Mama demonstrated for about the fifth time how to turn over the left shoulder. Marcus spun the wrong way for the fifth time, looking green.

"Here," I said, stepping in. "Right foot over left, okay?"

"I'm the worst," Marcus mumbled.

"No, you're not. You just gotta learn it. Then it's done."

"How do you know how to do pivots and stuff?"

"Theater. I've taken a dance class every year since I've been here." I didn't want to tell him that this hardly qualified as actual choreography. Mama had referred to it as "choralography," which sounded about right. A lot of walking on-rhythm into different formations, dramatic lifting of arms, and quick shoulder movements. Nothing that would interrupt our breath support.

I settled for saying, "You can get this. It'll look so simple by the end, you won't even remember how you had trouble with it."

Marcus planted his right foot over his left and spun so enthusiastically, he wheeled off-balance into Nihal, who let out an undignified splutter.

Mama sighed, coming to a halt beside me with his hands in his pockets. For a moment, we watched the others practicing the steps. "I wanted to stick in some hip-hop," Mama muttered, "but Trav vetoed it."

"Put it in anyway," I muttered back. "Make him do it."

We exchanged grins, watching Trav. He moved like a robot that hadn't been greased for a couple decades.

We worked straight through the afternoon. This was tough for Marcus, but tougher for me. While he could gripe about his lack of coordination, I couldn't say a word about my issue: a vicious set of period cramps that—over the hours—escalated slowly from "mild abdominal discomfort" to "my entire uterus is getting extracted with a spoon and sacrificed over a violet flame to the unholy uterine gods who are placated by naught but pain." I escaped a few times to knock back Advil like a seven-year-old popping Skittles.

By the time we finished choreographing the first two songs, the sunset was glowering, and sweat made my T-shirt cling to the small of my back. We collapsed before the fireplace, slices of gooey instant pizza making our fingers drip with grease, and ate until the spread of windows that flanked the chimney held a grayish dusk.

Jon Cox went about building a fire in the hearth, striking a long, thick match that hissed as it flared. When the fire was popping merrily up the chimney, Mama slid a video game into a thin black console and a dim logo glowed into life on the screen above the mantel. I settled back into the sofa as Trav navigated through a hellish horror game, complete with oozing monsters lurching out of the dark.

Trav's reflexes with that arsenal of weapons were frighteningly fast. I averted my eyes from the screen as he took a meat cleaver to a monster's arm with a messy-sounding squelch. A fitting soundtrack to the carnage I'd endured all afternoon.

Nestled in the sofa, I rubbed my stomach ruefully. If life had taught me one invaluable lesson, it was that being aware of the walls of your internal organs is universally a bad thing. Right now, if you'd given me a Sharpie, I could have traced a perfect outline of my uterus onto my abdomen. Like using translucent parchment paper to trace an image beneath, if that image was of a war-torn battlefield or a sun exploding or three hundred simultaneous shark attacks.

Nihal had his sketchpad in his lap next to me. I glanced over and got a jolt—my own face was staring back from a line of facial sketches. The seven of us who were here. Isaac's face was conspicuously missing.

"I texted him," I muttered.

Nihal's pen slowed against the page. "Yeah? He say anything?"

"Nope."

Nihal shook his head and outlined one of Erik's arched eyebrows.

My phone lit up, blaring my ringtone. *Isaac*, I thought. That was some timing.

I grabbed my phone and stood, but when I glanced down, my grip went rigid. The number on the screen didn't have a contact associated with it—just a string of digits. Of course I recognized that number, though, even if it'd been half a year since I'd deleted it.

The last time Michael and I had talked, he'd been considering a gap year. I resented my curiosity. Had he ended up at NYU after all, or was he auditioning for Broadway shows instead? Had he gotten that union card and started racking up Equity points? Why was he calling—was he okay, was he safe?

The urge to pick up was so strong that I wondered for a moment if I was still in love with him. These days, Michael-related thoughts had faded from omnipresent to sporadic—more in the lower single digits per day than in the upper doubles, less of browsing the Internet and wanting to send him everything that made me laugh or think.

These days, the only ways he lingered were the ways he'd changed me. I knuckled my forehead in late-night exhaustion like he always had, sitting by the Burgess fireside. I highlighted my scripts in two colors, the darker shade reserved for beat shifts; he'd told me I should try it sometime. Really, it helped him memorize, helped him pick what to care about the most. Love was a sea of red ink, and once you folded under the waves, there was no solvent that could scrub it out of your skin. You could only wait to discover what you were when you wandered out of the shallows: something rose, or crimson, or carnelian.

I hit the Decline button and sat back down on the sofa, exhaustion sinking into me like heat. Even my cramps had suddenly subsided, as if they'd decided that I had enough to deal with at the moment. I couldn't believe I still *wanted* to talk to him. You'd think I would have gotten sick of hurting.

"Who was that?" Nihal said.

"Ex," I said before I could stop myself.

"Ah." He raised one eyebrow. "Recent?"

"June."

"Not a good ex, I'm assuming."

From my other side, Jon Cox grunted, "Good exes are a conspiracy theory."

Mama nodded. "Laura," he said, with significance.

I glanced around, not liking the looks the others had, as if this was going to turn into an actual discussion. How weird would that be, talking about Michael with the Sharps?

"I'm just surprised we get reception out here," I said loudly. Everyone got the hint. Even Trav went back to slaughtering monsters with renewed vigor.

It was strange, though. As I cracked open the book I'd brought to read, I felt almost disappointed that not one of them had pushed it. Shanice and Jenna would have been happy to let it drop, but Maria would have been all over me, badgering me to vent out every tiny bit of feeling, making sure I didn't need tea or chocolate or a ranting session. *Talk it out, talk it out*, she always said, clapping her hands like a coach. *Let's go. Tell me everything.* Businesslike in her empathy.

After a couple minutes, Nihal cleared his throat gently.

I glanced over at his sketchpad. A caricature stared back: a guy-face with greasy-looking bangs, a lopsided nose, and a sleazy leer. Below it, Nihal had written, *Julian's Ex*. Arrows pointing to the picture added helpful taglines like *Obviously an idiot, Has definitely been miserable since June*, and *Julian can do way better.*

I laughed. Delighted, I reached for the sketchpad, but Nihal was already turning the page, a secret smile hinting at his eyes.

18

THE NEXT MORNING, WE DUG INTO CHOREOGRAPHING the other half of our performance set. The first song was "Open Wide." Trav had reinvented it—his arrangement accelerated from a half-tempo slow jam to a firecracker-fast breakdown section. After five hours straight working on the choreography, we were sweaty, discouraged, and still hadn't done a complete run of the song with any success.

"Let's just move on," Mama said, checking his watch. We switched to our ballad, "The Clockmaker," a lilting piece by an overemotional indie band called Hyper Venti Latte.

In comparison to "Open Wide," the choreography for "Clockmaker" was blessedly simple. I kept count of the times we dramatically turned, lifted, or dropped our heads. It came to an even dozen.

We'd finished learning by sunset. My brain felt pumped full of new information, clouds of steps and gestures still hardening into place.

"One last time," Mama called, "from the beginning." We gathered into a clump in the center of the room. Mama's body was big and soft against my back. Erik's knobby shoulder dug into my bicep.

Trav played the starting note on the pitch pipe, counted us in in a whisper, and we started singing.

Nihal stepped forward, tilting his head upward.

"You know what they say:

I can't ever get out of my own way.

And I know this, I know all about myself.

I know myself too well."

In the resonant space of the great room, the humming was as otherworldly as celestial noise. We fanned into a line, facing the fireplace. Nihal's voice carried crisply in the acoustic, and with my part committed so deeply to memory that it was thoughtless, I could finally focus on his words for the first time:

"So I came down Saturday, beside

the statue of a man who died twice,

when his name went quiet, quiet,

and I met her there, and I met her there . . ."

Motion seeped into the background parts. In my peripherals, as we shifted formation, Jon Cox's sturdy body swayed, and Marcus's round shoulders drifted. The sound grew from a soothing chorus of *ooh* to a brassy, ringing *oh*, melding with the solo into something bright and strong.

"And I asked the clockmaker

how much it would break her,

her cogs and bells and wooden ledges,

her painted face and gilded edges,

to turn back the dial

to turn back the dial for a while."

The song built up on itself. The bridge began with a sudden hush, a prickling rest, before circling, gathering momentum. It teetered high on that energy—a violent windstorm of sound—and crashed into the final chorus, which whipped by in a rush.

The last note held, thin and pure. I didn't want to stop singing. I wanted it to cycle on and on, and when we were done, we'd turn back the dial, and I'd still be here, barefoot on the slick floor of this room, or huddled in the warmth of the Nest as Jon Cox brayed his throaty laugh, or in the back of his convertible on an autumn day as Isaac leaned carelessly out the side and Mama turned up the music. But the last wisp of sound floated up to brush against the high ceiling, and then the moment was gone.

"Well," said a voice from behind us. "Guess I didn't even need to be here."

We turned as one to find Isaac leaning against the archway into the kitchen. At his feet lay a long duffel bag and his guitar case. His hands were shoved deep in his pockets, the ends of his dark jeans crusted with snow.

The silence of the end of the piece hung over us. Nobody spoke.

The tip of Isaac's long nose traced undecided shapes in the air as he looked around. His eyes couldn't fix anywhere. They scanned the fireplace. Our bare feet. The steep staircase against the other wall. "My—" he said, and stopped. He swallowed, took a second, and tried again. "My dad's out of the hospital. So I thought I should stop being a dickhead and show up."

"Your dad's *what*?" Mama said.

Nihal and I glanced at the others. Stunned to silence, all of them. The look of comprehension on Trav's face was painful to see.

Isaac's eyes wandered again. Discomfort settled into every inch of his face, every line of his body. He bowed under it, narrow shoulders slumped. "Listen," he said, "I'm going to take my stuff upstairs."

Jon Cox's head bobbed.

Isaac slung his duffel over his shoulder and crossed the room, his head ducked. He retreated with his tail between his legs. It occurred to me that as much as the guy hunted the spotlight, he obviously hadn't figured out how to deal with it.

♫

"Hey! That's my hotel," Marcus protested, leaning over the coffee table to grab at Jon Cox's pastel heaps of money. "C'mon—I—pay up."

Jon Cox clapped his hand over Marcus's eyes and flicked the red plastic hotel off the board. "What hotel?" he said innocently. "I don't see—what are you talking about?"

Marcus pulled away. "I totally called this," he asked, looking mutinous. "It hasn't even been a month since the election, and corruption's already taking over."

"Oh, boy," I muttered.

"Here we go," Jon Cox said, swirling his drink before downing the last of it. "Hey, Marcus, can you give me ten more minutes? I'm not drunk enough for the whole Republicans-are-Satan thing yet."

"Well, they *are*," Marcus grumbled. "*Free trade.*"

"Get thee to an economics class, thou filthy liberal!" Jon Cox declared in a truly despicable attempt at an English accent. "Wouldst thou like to take this outside and *duel for thy honor*?" He brandished a finger at the front door.

“Thine honor,” Nihal said absentmindedly, drawing a card from the board.

Jon Cox rolled his eyes. “Thanks, Nihal.”

“Hey, guys?” Isaac said. He was sitting on the ground in front of the hearth, looking small and folded.

Everyone around the game board paused, and we could hear the uneven licking of the fire again. Trav lifted his pen from his journal, which was open to a spread of staff paper that he’d covered in chord analysis. From the couch, Erik looked up from his phone. He hadn’t set it down all night.

Isaac was picking strands from his bun, pulling thoughts out of place. “I should apologize for the last couple weeks. I don’t know why I took it out on everyone.” He sounded strangled but determined, as if his voice were a solid object that he was trying to cram through the crack of a closed door. “Obviously I think this matters. Not just the music. *This.*” He swung one of his full-body indications around at us, busy arm and bothered torso and sweeping eyes. “Sharps has been my most important thing for a fifth of my life, which, apparently, means I can get shitty and complacent about it, because—I don’t know. I guess that’s what you do with everything you care about. You forget how to care about it right. So.” He grimaced. “I didn’t say sorry. I’m sorry. There.”

“We should apologize, too,” I said. The Sharps’ eyes fell on me. I didn’t back down. “We should’ve noticed there was something wrong.” I hoped he heard what was behind the words. *I’m* sorry. I’m sorry I snapped at you, sorry I saw that flash of disappointment from you and didn’t understand what it meant, sorry I saw you pulling away and assumed it was selfishness.

A sigh issued from the last person I expected. "I agree," Trav said. He twisted the stud in his ear over and over. It refracted the firelight. "This year has been rocky, and to a degree, I think it's my fault."

Isaac eyed Trav curiously. "Why?"

"My parents told me they're coming to watch the competition, and I want them to know what this means." After a moment, Trav shook his head. "Singing is what makes me feel like I'm *here*. But I know for most people, it's the opposite: They're here because they like to sing. That's valid. It doesn't have to be your life's blood. There is actually more to the world than a cappella." His eyes twinkled with firelight. "Or so people keep trying to tell me."

The thickness of the air loosened a bit, and Marcus shifted, and Nihal was holding back a smile. Mama had that serene look he sometimes wore when he forced us to listen to Handel.

"Anyway," Trav said. "I'll accept your apology for showing up late, but nothing else. And even that's—well, I drove here myself. So maybe your dramatics were worth it."

"What, the whole way?" Isaac said.

"Yes."

I expected some sarcastic jab about the number of casualties, but Isaac's mouth pressed into a small and genuine smile. "That's awesome."

"Thank you," Trav said. We were all quiet for a second. I watched Trav carefully. There was less tension in him than usual, from his expression down to his folded hands.

Without a further word, Trav went back to his journal. The others returned to their conversations, but I kept watching. He dotted note heads on the staff with precision and intent, as if he were the captain of a ship charting a course home.

♫

My phone alarm rang at 3:15 a.m. I silenced it, slid out from between the sheets, and lifted the fluffy towel from the end of the bed.

Wrapped up, I crept down the curving staircase to the second floor. The sound of Jon Cox's aggressive snoring rumbled through the door of the master bedroom as I slunk by. The cold floorboards issued protests under my toes, every step a conspicuous squeak. I hurried toward the bathroom, ducked in, and slid the lock into place with a satisfying *shunk*. Safe.

A glass door separated the shower from the rest of the bathroom. I cracked it open, stepped in, and twisted a thin chrome handle. Steaming water cascaded from the broad showerhead to the silvery tile.

Hot water coaxed the tension out of my muscles. I scrubbed shampoo through my hair, letting the water trickle between my roots. Soon I stepped out, glancing at the mirror. I placed the flat of my palm to the glass and swiped a gap into the condensation; then, after a moment, I wiped the whole mirror clear.

I looked different. I always lost weight at school, with the healthy food to eat and the campus to walk, but this was something else. More even than my new posture, head held higher, the squareness of my shoulders, the straightness in my back. Something in my eyes, maybe. I looked brazen.

I wondered if, when I stopped playing Julian, his influence would leave my body piece by piece, like the slow replacement of dead cells. I didn't like the idea. This new face was a treasure I'd stumbled upon. I always wanted to look this sure of myself.

I thought of ignoring Michael's call earlier. In retrospect, I felt strong having done it. At the beginning of the year, I would have given in. Jordan didn't have this much control, this much agency. In the battle between the halves of myself, I felt like she'd finally been eclipsed; only a crescent glow of her still peeked out.

Exhaustion crept over me. I thought of Shanice's fierce loyalty, Jenna's clowning and posturing, Maria's warmth. I could hardly remember what it felt like to have a history. When the girls looked at me, they saw seventeen years of me. The Sharps barely had a few months. And now I was this, something new, so quickly, and what was it? Was I happy this way?

I swept the towel from the rack and wrapped it around myself. I hit the lights, peered out the door, and crept back down the hall. I accelerated as I went, dashing for the steps. Past all the guys' bedrooms.

A door swung open in front of me.

Shit—

I tried to stop, but my wet feet squeaked against the hardwood, and I wheeled off-balance. One hand flailed out, grabbing the doorjamb, swinging me into the person standing in the doorway. My other hand let go of my towel, which, for a second, slipped down to my waist. I snatched it back into place, but too late.

As I righted myself, Isaac stared down at me with total astonishment.

19

"JULIAN?" HE BREATHED. "WHAT—WHAT IS—WHAT?"

I stepped back, the world splintering in my head. *Run*, was my first, stupid, thought. Sprint down the steps and away, and never look back. Second instinct: whack Isaac on the head with the nearest heavy object. That always messed up short-term memory in movies, right? Third thought: *If I have latent powers of invisibility, now would be an awesome time for them to show up.*

He let out a tiny, incredulous sound, but I held one finger to my lips, giving my head a violent shake. This was no time for Isaac-babble. I grabbed his forearm, dragged him around the door, and yanked him up to the attic.

Once the attic door clicked shut, I hit the lights and faced him. His bleary eyes wouldn't focus. "What is happening?" he jabbered. "Are you—is—"

"Shh. Hey. Calm down." I glanced down at myself, at the towel I was still clutching. "Turn around, okay?"

Looking pretty much catatonic, Isaac rotated to face the round window.

I grabbed my T-shirt and sweatpants from the bed, pulled

them on, and hung the towel from a hook on the door. "All right," I said. "So."

Isaac turned back around, looking like he'd figured it out. "So, um, you're trans? Sorry I freaked out, it—"

"No."

His bafflement reappeared. "Then—"

"I'm a girl. I've just been cross-dressing." I scrambled for words. "Everything else I told you is true. I swear. Who I am, where I'm from." I sat on the edge of the bed. "Except, um, my name's Jordan, and I'm not a guy."

He gave his head a hard shake, and then another, as if he were trying to dislodge a stubborn bit of water from his ear. "But *why* did you—why are you doing this?"

"I didn't get cast in the musical, because my voice is. Well. My voice. And I'd heard about the competition, and I wanted—I don't know."

The incredulity faded from Isaac's expression. A light frown creased his high forehead.

Was he angry?

I looked down, picking at the fuzzy specks that had accumulated on my sweatpants. "I mean, it was the competition, but then it turned into . . ." Being part of something. Finally, someone else at Kensington had known me again, like only Michael had.

"It's stupid, I know," I muttered. "Like I couldn't have found some more normal way."

My hope collapsed like a house of cards, fluttering down to nothing. It was over. I'd reached the end of the road I'd been paving all semester, throwing stones desperately at the ground and getting lucky as they stuck.

None of this felt real. I felt like I should want to cry, but nothing came, not a burn to the eyes or a tightening in my throat. Nothing. Some shield of self-preservation had come between me and myself.

A weight depressed the bed beside me. I looked over at Isaac, who inspected my jaw, my nose, my eyebrows. All my features, recontextualized. He looked wary.

"Um," he said, "you want to go for a walk, maybe?"

"It's like twenty-two degrees out."

"It can be a short walk."

"Okay. Yeah."

♬

By the time we crept out of the house, I'd regained some composure. I huddled inside Dad's winter coat, my hands deep in the pockets. Isaac and I sidled through sheets of snow toward the riverbank. At the edge, in the frozen slate of mud and leaves, we stopped still, and the hush settled down in the glade around us.

Time spun out, loosely unspooling. The pair of us had never been quiet for this long. Every time I thought I had something to say, it slipped on my tongue and fell away. I waited for Isaac to unleash the fast-paced monologue—or, if not, to let some angry instinct take over, lash out with something that would hit hard. He said nothing at all.

We didn't look at each other for a long time. When we did, it happened at the same second, and we looked away instantly, like children who'd been caught staring at something rude or dangerous. I examined the flat band of the river, lying lazy and glittering under the moon. On the opposite bank, the snow seized and spun the cold light like a long tray of quartz chips.

Isaac broke the silence, finally. "It's, um," he said. His voice was warm and neutral. "It's kind of unbelievable you pulled this off for three months."

"Yeah."

"How'd you even . . . ?"

I waved vaguely at my face. "I wear a lot of makeup when I'm in girl mode."

His eyes fixed on my hair. "And a wig or something, I'm guessing?"

"It's from the costume shop. I'm going to return it, I swear. Just . . . for now." I twisted my scarf tighter. "And the voice, um, I do a lot of shifting my voice register for my theater classes anyway, since they want me to sound more like a girl."

"You do sound like a girl," Isaac said. "I mean, now you do. Mostly. This voice." Realization filled his words. "After the dance, too, you sounded . . ." He trailed off. The sentence rerouted. "Wait. Didn't you make out with Victoria Taylor?"

"Yeah. I'm bi, as far as I can tell, so."

He chuckled. "As far as you can tell."

"No, I'm serious. I was in this relationship that I'm only now kind of over, and it was impossible for me to figure it out, with that in the way. He took up all my attention, all the time, so . . . yeah, distracting."

"Huh," he said. "It just seems like that would be a thing you couldn't not know."

"Well, yeah, there were signs, but I don't know. I thought they were something else, I guess, or I wasn't focusing on myself hard enough to see what was there. It just got confusing when I did." I curled my hands in my pockets. "I don't like not knowing things."

"I know," he said, with a touch of amusement.

More silence. We went back to observing the river. I imagined I heard it rushing under that thick coat of ice, rolling dark and quick over its bed.

My voice came out in a feeble little mumble. "Do you think the guys are going to be mad?"

He didn't answer right away. *Obviously*, whispered the unspoken response. How could they be anything but livid?

"I mean," Isaac said carefully, "do you want to tell them?"

My heartbeat became a thudding drum in my ears. "You'd cover for me?"

"Sure."

"Why?" I asked.

He was still examining the river. "I mean, it's obvious, right? You didn't give me away, either."

The words made my heart slow.

I let myself look at him for the first time, really look. I never looked at the Sharps more than necessary. Whenever we made eye contact, I felt sure they'd read the truth right out of my eyes somehow. So I avoided it. But it was 3:55 a.m., and I had no more energy for avoidance.

Isaac's thick hair was down for once, hanging in rumpled layers. Moonlight washed his profile. His lips looked chapped and bitten, and acne scars pitted his cheekbones. His thick eyebrows tapered above his narrow eyes, making him look perpetually serious or frustrated.

His calmness was giving me dangerous courage, making me

want to say, *Forget it. Tell the guys, and if they hate me, that's that.* Get everything out in the open. Finally, I'd be able to talk to the Sharps as myself, without filters, without constantly thinking, *What would a boy say? How would a boy act? Is this the way a boy should be?* As if there were a *right* way to be a guy.

I'd never been a one-of-the-guys type of girl. Jenna and Maria and I went way back to the first grade playground, and we'd adopted Shanice in seventh grade, when she'd transferred to our school. We, the Fearsome Foursome of Buchanan Middle School, had never needed boys—they'd been irritants or decorations, hovering around the fringes of our lives. Back then, we'd gotten a lot of the same from guys—panicked teasing in middle school, desperate teasing, the type that screamed *notice me!* or *like me!* or *concede to me!*

Now, when I came back for summers, we hung out with Jenna's wide collection of guy friends—about half of whom had mustered up the bullheadedness to ask her out, even though they knew she was lesbian—and they smirked and pushed each other around and talked shit, talked loud, talked over each other. For the first time, now, I wondered what they'd tamped down beneath that. What were they hiding under the rusty, outdated suits of armor they climbed into before talking to girls? Were they frustrated romantics, like Jon Cox? Know-it-alls, like Mama? Still figuring out how to treat the world, like Erik?

Or maybe they were like the boy in front of me. So impulsive that he got thoughtless, saying anything, doing anything, forgetting himself. For once, there he was in silence, in stillness, all tangled up in knots, this kid standing next to me on the bank.

"Thanks," I murmured, my throat tight.

"No problem."

"Listen. Isaac."

"Yeah?"

"Can I ask about your dad?"

He met my eyes. I couldn't read his. "What about him?" he asked.

I shrugged.

"Like, about the surgery?" he said.

"Yeah."

"Okay, um. He got in this wreck and fractured his femur, so they put a titanium rod in his bone to hold it together. It got infected, so they had to take him out of physical therapy rehab and put him back in the hospital. He's in rehab again now. My mom looks like she hasn't slept in weeks." He paused. "It was kind of weird. He's a comedian, I might've told you that? He writes for late-night shows and SNL and stuff. Does some stand-up. I swear to God I've never seen him go so long without cracking a joke about something. He was so, just . . . I don't know. He looked like eighty years old. Or like someone made a wax copy of him and made it a little too small."

After a second, he said, "Why do you ask?"

"I don't know. I just thought, if you haven't talked about it with anyone, you might want to."

"I guess." Isaac looked down. He was stretching the edge of his thick sweater over his thumb. "I mean, thanks. But I don't know. There's some stuff that it kind of doesn't feel right to talk about. You know?"

"Like how?"

"I mean, if it makes you get all weird. I don't feel like me, talking about some stuff. Like, who's this boring sad boy who's probably going to go home and listen to depressing indie rock until he stops feeling shitty? Who wants to talk if it's just going to get you upset? What good's that going to do?"

I folded my hands under my arms, warding off the piercing cold. I knew exactly what he meant. I'd thought about bringing up my dad's hospital stay, to commiserate or relate, but that episode was wound so tightly into the way my family had lived for the past year—hell, the way we'd lived for most of my life—that it felt too huge even to touch. I didn't know who I would be if I let myself talk about it.

But I knew how it would go if I did muster up the courage to broach the topic. I would start to talk and for a minute I would hate it. The next minute, I would feel exposed and jumpy and paranoid, but as if I were pushing at a door that needed to be opened. The next minute, I wouldn't be able to stop talking. And then—after a long time—

"You keep going until it feels better again," I said quietly. "Catharsis."

"Right."

"In theater, that's the whole thing with Greek tragedy. You take the audience through the—like, the realest shit, the tearing out the eyes or the worst possible thing, and then on the other side it's like coming out of boiling water and you're clean."

"Life's not a Greek tragedy."

After a long second, I shrugged. "I mean, if *you* didn't sleep with your mom by mistake, that's fine, but don't go around acting all superior to the rest of us."

Isaac gave me an amused look. The corner of his mouth lifted a fraction, and then a broad smile cut his face, a slash of white teeth. "All right, you win," he said. He spread his hands and took a few steps back. "You go ahead and handle the tragedy stuff. I'll just be over here." He edged up on the river and placed one foot on the ice.

My hand flew out. "Wait—"

"I tried it earlier. It's fine." Isaac gave a demonstrative stamp. Not even a groan from the ice—just a heavy thunk, like oak hitting oak. He walked out onto the river.

"Isaac, wait!"

His steps slowed. He halted by an arm of driftwood thrust out from the ice plane, a dark spar like a ship's mast. He glanced over his shoulder. "What?"

"It gets thinner in the center. There are currents under there. You want this trip to have a body count?"

"Come on," he said. "It's got to be a foot of ice out here." He had that look in his eye. The feverish delight of acting out. The adrenaline of it. He didn't move away from the driftwood. "Stop looking at my feet."

"What if it breaks?"

He shrugged. "It won't."

"You don't know that."

"No, I know."

I shook my head. "Why don't you take care of yourself, huh?"

Isaac's head tilted. He looked uncomprehending. A bit of lostness around the angle of his brow.

The wind had picked up again. Loose snow was eddying around his feet. I pictured the ice rupturing, a dark gash of river opening wide.

"Come on," I said. My voice was quiet, but he could hear just fine. We were locked in a snow globe together. "We can go inside," I said. "It's cold."

He took a halting step my way. Then another. The ice creaked as he approached. The wind picked up as he crossed the lip of the river, mounting the bank. He stopped in front of me.

"Okay," he said. "I didn't think it . . . I don't know."

You're a runner, I wanted to say. *I'm a runner too. Rather sprint for the hills than hold on to something you can't figure out.*

I said, "It's all right," and we headed back for Jon's house, the oasis of light shimmering in the blue-dark snow.

♫

We wound up back in the attic. Isaac wanted to see the wig. I hadn't taken it along. Instead, I unlocked my phone and showed him the shot of the Greek Monologue class for our upcoming showcase, where I stood at the end of the row, bright-pink lipstick and long hair. It was 4:15 a.m., and everything had turned vivid with sleepless delirium, everything tenser and funnier and more electric than it should have been. We wound up stretched on the bed, side by side, staring at the ceiling, talking music and home and nothing at all. His guitar was a gift from his mother, so expensive he'd wanted her to return it. My mom's most valuable present had always been her time.

In the slanted attic ceiling, a set of narrow skylights displayed slices of the outside world. Pine branches shivered overhead. A hollow moan of wind passed by, distant, a ghostly lullaby. I had thawed from the trip outside, my muscles tired and empty.

A glittering spray of snow toppled from the branches and scattered across one of the skylights. Time slowed. There was nothing pressing at the edges of the night anymore, not the dawn, not the day. The sun would never come up. The flakes of snow in the yellowing moonlight would keep shifting and dancing for years, graceful in the dark.

"I'm kind of glad you found out," I murmured. It came out vanishingly quiet.

Isaac hesitated. The mattress warped as he edged back. In my peripheral vision he moved into a slender cut of moonlight, his hands folded behind his head. When he spoke, his voice had softened a fraction. "Weight off your chest?"

"Yeah." Something like that. Relief always came after guilt, one way or another. "Have you ever lied for three months?"

"I don't think I could."

I half-smiled. "Must be weird having morals or whatever."

"No, that's not what I meant," he said. "I definitely lie all the time. Dumb little things. People will be like, what'd you do this afternoon? And I'll be like, oh, I was studying, when actually I watched Netflix for a few hours and ate about four metric ass-tons of cheese puffs." He yawned. "But it's never anything somebody's going to hold me accountable for."

"Except the past couple weeks."

"Right. And it was the worst. I can't imagine three months of that. Honestly, I don't think I have the patience."

I was still and quiet, wanting to tell him that the patience couldn't hold a candle to the isolation. How could I explain the ever-present tightness in my chest? The sense that between me and the rest of the school, I'd built an indestructible wall? The sense that I would never belong again, with Kensington, with my friends at home, with the Sharps—maybe even with myself, inside my own head?

"Sometimes I'm trying to go to bed," I said, finally. "And I just think about the people who know me."

After a second, he said, "The actual you, you mean."

"Yeah." I didn't want to sound pathetic. But it felt good to let it out. "You guys are kind of my only friends here, and it's not even real."

"No offense, but how'd you go freshman and sophomore year without making friends?"

I gave a humorless laugh. "Because my ex was my whole life, and then he—" I cut myself off. *Don't get into it.* "He, um. Graduated. And we don't talk."

"Ah."

"Yeah." I closed my eyes. Tiny confetti shapes danced behind my eyelids, cartwheeling down over the darkness. My brain felt wrung out.

"It's kind of funny," Isaac said.

"What is?"

"It . . ." He paused. "I mean, we're so comically, laughably tiny. You know? The universe is expanding forever, and there are nebulas a hundred billion miles away, like, spectacularly shitting out stars, and suns collapsing every twenty seconds, and essentially what I'm trying to say is that we're the tiniest speck of dust on an infinite space plain and our lives are these insignificant little minuscule pinpricks on the timeline."

His spiel petered out into quiet. Outside, the wind was back. That low, gentle whistle.

"And?" I said.

"And what?"

"You said it's funny. What's the punch line?"

"I guess I was going to say, like . . . all this, and human beings act like it's such a big deal if you talk a little deeper than usual and wear baggier clothes. That was going to be the punch line, I don't know, if there was one. I'm not the comedian, ask my dad."

An exhausted chuckle fell out of my mouth.

Isaac's voice had turned scratchy and slow with sleep. "But now I kind of want to say, with all that going on, I guess it's no surprise the world feels totally unmanageable sometimes."

"Yeah," I murmured. I felt like I might melt into the covers and the mattress and the carved bed frame. It all cradled me like gentle hands. I kept thinking of home, for some reason, but in a quieter, sweeter way than usual. No worry. Just my mother humming me to sleep, and my father content in bed. "But it keeps turning," I said.

"Yeah."

"So at least there's that."

"Yeah."

MY LAPTOP EKED OUT A SHRIEK OF COMPLAINT AS I bent the screen back, getting rid of the glare. "Hush," I told it, and double-tapped Skype.

As it loaded, I glanced out my dorm room window. Dusk had fallen. Ropy icicles drooled down behind the glass, and beyond them stretched the tree line, stripes of black wood on white snow. Kensington over breaks looked twice as beautiful as when everyone was here. Burgess fell silent as a cemetery, nobody padding down the hall outside my door or chattering by the water fountain.

The application loaded, revealing an empty contacts list. My parents hadn't gotten online yet. I carried my laptop to my bed, flopped down, and waited.

The retreat already felt like it had happened years ago, although Isaac had driven us back to Kensington only this afternoon. I should have stuck with Trav's car, tight-knuckled steering and all. Mama hadn't been kidding about Isaac's driving: He drove with his knees guiding the wheel, mostly, his right hand occasionally drifting up to adjust the car's trajectory. He sat with a generous lean against the driver's door, peering out the windshield with piercing eyes, as if he were hunting the empty roads for a victim to slam into. I spent most of the ride digging my fingernails into my thighs, doing breathing exercises.

When I wasn't praying for my continued survival, I was meticulously dissecting every second of last night. With Erik in the backseat finishing the Bourne movies, Isaac and I barely spoke. The words we did manage felt hopelessly shallow in the wake of everything we'd let loose a handful of hours before. I couldn't look at him without a reaction fizzling under my surface, a mixture of heat and panic that might have been fear, paranoia, or something significantly worse.

This morning, I'd slipped into sleep halfway through one of his sentences. I woke up on my side to a dawn that was bright and shocking, so close to him that—for a moment—I couldn't breathe. In sleep, we'd fallen toward each other. He looked soft and calm. His serious eyebrows shadowed the slope of his nose. Seeing him so still was like seeing a river stop in its bed, the mess of churning water held perfectly motionless for a minute, the constant rush silenced.

The entire ride back to Kensington, I couldn't stop remembering that image. Staring through the passenger window at the blurring wall of trees along the highway, I saw it. Every time he hummed to a song on the radio or messed compulsively with his hair or drummed his fingers on the wheel, I saw it. It was an indelible film over my eyes.

It was bad news. I set about destroying it at once.

We got back around 8:00 p.m.—intact, miraculously—and the eight of us had dinner at the pizza place in town, at which point Jon Cox attempted to fold a whole pizza slice into a cube to eat in one bite. In penance for being the grossest person alive, he picked up the tab, thank God. I'd agonized the whole time about the best way to ask one of the guys if they could spot me.

Afterward, the other Sharps packed up for the rest of break and got back on the road—one car to Watertown, for the airport, and the other back to New York City, for Isaac, Marcus, and Trav. They'd be driving all night.

Meanwhile, I returned to my dorm, pinned my break residency permit on my door, and shut myself in.

My parents had badgered me all afternoon to Skype them. I donned my wig, rolled on some lipstick, and lined my eyes. If I ever Skyped my parents without makeup, they asked if I was getting enough sleep. *Are you sick? You look tired.* Maybe they'd just forgotten what I looked like without it on.

Mom's Skype contact popped up in the list. I clicked it. One big plus of everyone leaving campus: Internet speeds quadrupled overnight. Otherwise, streaming video on this laptop would've been like trying to stream video through two tin cans strung together with dental floss.

My parents, in our kitchen, showed up on the screen in glorious 240-pixel resolution. We had a computer back home. It was from 2005.

Mom was craning over Dad's shoulder. Their blurry smiles settled me. I waved.

"Hi," Mom said. "How is everything going?"

My smile froze into a rictus. Even with the tinny audio, I heard the undercurrent in her voice. Bad news.

"I've just been catching up on reading," I said. Restful. Calm. I'd made it my business being unreadable, but inside, panic bells started to clang. *Idiot*, I told myself. Of course this had meant bad news. Otherwise, why wouldn't they have left the call until Thanksgiving, as usual?

"What's going on? What did you want to talk about?" I said. They looked at each other, then back at me. Whatever this was, it was big enough to have bridged the divide between them. I felt the acute dread of somebody standing in place, watching a cannonball fly toward them.

Dad's voice was uncharacteristically calm. It unnerved me. "Jordan," he said, "the landlord told us today that rent's hiking."

My hands curled up beneath my laptop.

"So we made a decision," Mom said, "and you're not going to like it, but we don't have many options."

A glut of protest built in my chest. Since middle school, they'd talked about moving every time things got tight. If they thought we could dodge the rent escalation by burrowing deeper into Chinatown, then by the time I got to college—assuming I got the scholarship money to afford college—they'd be living in one of those Single-Resident Occupancy rooms, eight-by-ten-foot cubbyholes that whole families sometimes operated from. If we'd been able to afford the relocation costs—if my parents had ever had job prospects somewhere else, if we'd had a car—we would have abandoned San Francisco and its heinous prices, but you couldn't pay for a move with hypotheticals.

If we moved, that was another blow against my already-destabilizing friendships. During the year, the girls slid along like beads down a thread, all together, on a different track than mine. When we met back up, I had to work to dissolve the buffer

Kensington created between us, the distance of perfectionist culture and college-prep focus.

I could imagine it. We would move out of our neighborhood, the one I'd always shared with them, a block down from Jenna, three streets over from Shanice and Maria. Our friendship would turn into something made out of old habits. When that turned irrelevant, we would fall out of touch entirely.

My mother's voice interrupted the spiral: "We're pulling you out of Kensington."

Everything stopped.

As her threat processed, the world began to swing horribly, a trapdoor plummeting on a huge hinge. It dangled. I clung to the edge.

Something had gone wrong in my vision. *Keep control. Keep control—*

"Um," I whispered. "What do you mean?"

"We can't manage those costs anymore." Mom sighed. The camera image focused for a second, and in that instant, her expression was a diagram that explained exhaustion. Stress filled her every wrinkle. More lines had drawn themselves in since last time I'd seen her, encircling her lower eyelids, linking the corners of her nose to her jaw. "And at home," she said, "maybe you can work somewhere."

"But—but isn't it cheaper for me to be here? You don't have to pay for my meals, there's no—"

"Xiao Ming," Dad said, my childhood nickname sounding more like a stiff rebuke. "It doesn't come close to breaking even."

A childish tantrum erupted in my head. I stamped it down, trying to think rationally. I had to be mature. I had to be logical.

Flights, I thought vaguely. Each year was four or five hundred dollars' worth of flights, what with Winter Break, the only holiday when the Campus Residency Office couldn't let me stay on campus. Storage, too—it cost seventy-five dollars to hide my things away in some closet here over the summer so I didn't have to ship them home. And textbooks . . . I had the crumpled receipts somewhere: $335 this semester, $290 last semester, a staggering $415 the semester before that. Not to mention supplies, everything from my stupidly expensive graphing calculator to pens and paper. There had to be other costs, too—costs I was forgetting, or costs I didn't want to admit.

I didn't want them to be right, but if they were, I had to find a fix.

"There's no guarantee I could work at home," I blurted. "Maria looked for a part-time job all last year and she never—"

"*Xiao Ming*." Mom's voice cracked.

I held back, but my mouth threatened to overflow. Words clawed for space, pushing at my tongue. I was finally old enough to apply for the student-worker program, but they wouldn't be hiring until next year, and that was nine months out before I would make a cent. Maybe I could try to find someone to stay with over winter break so flights weren't on the table. The thought of begging for someone's charity made me taste bitterness, but I had to stay here. I was so *close*.

"Please, let me ask the school about it," I said, keeping my voice low. "If I transfer, their withdrawal rate goes up. They want me to stay. They want me to apply to college, they want me to do well—"

Mom snapped. "Then why they never put you in a show, huh?"

I drew back from my laptop.

She sighed. "You went to that place to do something. If they don't let you do it, you should come back home. That's all there is to say." Mom rubbed her forehead and glanced at Dad. "Well?"

Dad lifted his head. The crease between his eyebrows had begun to sag into an immovable frown. "It's not a question," he said. "We're telling you so you can get ready. You're there until Christmas Break. Then you're coming home."

♫

I called Nihal. He didn't pick up. He must have been flying back to Newark. I called the girls one right after the other, but nothing from them, either. I bet they were out together, laughing, talking, normal.

Normal had evaporated. Normal had skidded headlong off a cliff.

Isaac, I thought, and pulled up his contact page, but something kept me from hitting the call button. In retrospect, last night looked like a hallucination, or a dream. I didn't want to ruin it with reality.

I yanked my wig off, bundled up, and tromped out into the snow. No soft, drifting flakes tonight—tiny beads of snow swirled in gray tornadoes, fast and loud. The winter air clamped around me, and wind brutalized my skin, chapping my lips the second I stretched them in a grimace.

A hand of wind slammed the door behind me. Amid the whitish stir, I made for the road and shuffled down toward Arthur's Arch.

I paused between Wingate and Ewing for a moment and peered up at the dorms, glazed and dripping with ice, water stains rimming their peaked windows. Streaks of snow ran along the turreted details at their roofs. My first memories of Kensington had me driving up this street, under those crows pecking at the wrought-iron arch, up to these two dorms. They'd towered over the cab, blocking the sun, cutting swaths out of the deep blue sky, and when we'd emerged from their shadows at the intersection of Main and August, the sky had opened up again, like unfolded origami. I'd never seen a sky like that before, flat and uninterrupted, miles of what instantly became my favorite sort of blue. Our colors were black and carnelian, but when I thought of Kensington, I thought the blue of the glazed-over lake past North Campus. The blue of Lydia's eyes, the first day of freshman year. The blue of that sky.

The sky was an umbrella of black-gray now, thick with bluster. I shunted my way through the wind and down the sidewalk, a mess of slush and corrosive greenish salt, until I reached Arthur's Arch. Red rust glared out at me from the hinges. Slender icicles dangling from the apex of the *A* trembled with the wind. Everything looked ancient and worn out. I wanted to cling to it, gather it all to my chest. Even the cruel winter.

My eyes stung. I hurried down the drive, hat on and my head bowed, keeping my eyes fixed on the closest lights: the Carrie Café. The sweet orange light of the lantern outside bobbed, rising and falling like a candle on a ship's prow. As I approached, the lantern's iron whine mewled into life over the wind.

I shouldered my way in. The door banged hard into its frame, and I wiped my cheeks free of the wet. The café was as quiet as always, the only music a tinkling piano nocturne.

An island occupied the center of the coffeehouse. Rickety tables edged the five walls: The glass front wall looked out on the street, while the other four were white clapboard, covered in framed photographs of a thousand shades, sepia, black-and-white, blue- and gold-framed. Tiny lanterns dangled over every table, making the silvery chairs shine. Every single chair stood empty.

"I'll be damned. Jordan Sun?" called Carrie from the register. "That you?"

I felt a twinge of guilt. I hadn't been here since last spring. Walking through the door without Michael felt like walking in naked.

"Hi, Carrie." I stamped the snow onto the mat in front of the door. It squelched under my feet.

"Really wanted a coffee in the snowstorm, huh? Love the haircut, by the way."

"Thanks," I said, injecting life into my voice. "How's it going?"

"Always fine. Beans. Roasting. You know the drill." Carrie drummed her fingers on the counter. She was a round, dowdy woman with a carrot-orange braid trailing down her back. She always had the same uniform: army boots and a floral dress. Sometimes with an apron, sometimes with thick woolen leggings, sometimes with a quilted winter coat, but the boots and the dress never budged. *Super lesbian,* said some of the Kensington kids knowingly, which was funny, since Carrie was married to the guy who worked every other weekend. Not that they actually cared enough to find out. With so many queer kids at Kensington, people sometimes got weirdly comfortable, like they had a free pass to say anything they wanted about sexuality. I guess it was tempting to stick a rainbow-colored "Ally" pin on your backpack and call it a day, as if that were the endpoint, not the starting line.

"What can I make you?" Carrie asked. "How about a Thanksgiving Special?"

"What's that?"

"Turkey-flavored coffee."

"Um. What?"

"Messing with you." She flashed me her bright, yellowing smile. "Hot cider with cinnamon, cube of chocolate on the side. Sound good?"

It sounded like it would have been heaven, if I had a few bucks to spare. "I actually . . . just came in to get out of the wind."

"Let me make you one anyway." She winked. "On me."

I managed a smile, finally approaching the counter. The scales of cold started to fall away from my cheeks and neck. "Thanks, Carrie."

Carrie rummaged under the counter for a mug, but her shrewd eyes stayed on me. "I haven't seen you here all year. The second Mike graduates, you ditch me, huh?" She set the mug on the lip of a machine and pulled a silver knob. A line of golden syrup glided down into the porcelain. "Tell him I ain't impressed, young lady."

"We, um, we actually broke up. Start of summer."

Carrie went still. She released the knob and set the mug on the counter. "You did not."

"Yep." I couldn't meet her eyes. I didn't want advice. I didn't want sympathy. I'd moved past those phases.

"What happened?" she asked.

"Nothing. We just . . ." I shrugged.

"You don't shrug off a two-year gig. What happened? Between us."

I chewed the words. After a long second, Carrie picked up the mug and went back to the ingredient counter. "Forget I said anything. Of course you don't have to say," she said gruffly. "Didn't mean to push you."

I said it in my head a few times, preparing for the acrid taste the words would leave on my tongue.

"He cheated on me."

Her movements slowed. "Oh, honey."

"For three months, with this girl Alaina. They're both from Seattle. She's this dancer girl who looks like a model, and she got into Yale, and she's on the Kensington website now, and her face is just staring out at me every time I need to use Moodle." The confession poured out of me like hot lead. Staring at the weathered counter, I felt it go cool and dark in the air.

Behind me, the door creaked open, letting in the howl of the wind. It slammed again, but I didn't flinch. I kept staring at the counter, remembering the sheer number of times we'd stood here side by side. Michael, big as a bear, his hand at the small of my back. Small talk over the register.

With the next customer's footsteps padding up behind me, I pulled myself together. Carrie had seen me through the insecure hell of freshman year. I would've shared anything with her. But I didn't want to bare my soul in front of some stranger.

Carrie slid a wooden drawer out beneath the counter, unwrapped a cube of chocolate from rose-colored foil, and set it on a saucer. She nestled the mug in the saucer and slid it toward me. When I reached for it, she put her hand on mine. "Sweetheart," she said, "you are well shot of that. You are too good for that. Hear me?"

I felt a pang, examining the ceiling. "Yeah, well. I've got a life to deal with. So forget him."

"Julian?" said a small, musical voice behind me. "Is everything okay?"

I froze, my lipstick suddenly burning on my mouth. That voice—it couldn't be her. She was supposed to be back in Boston.

I steeled myself, turned around, and Victoria Taylor's eyes went wide. Her freckled face was nestled in a thick scarf, and a black-and-carnelian Kensington hat fit low over her straight eyebrows. They drew together as she stared.

"Oh my God," she breathed.

"Hey, Victoria," I said, with the charisma of a dead anchovy. "Why are you. Um. Not home?"

"This storm was in Boston on Saturday, so a bunch of flights got cancelled," she said, eyes fixed unblinkingly on my face. "My new flight's tomorrow morning. Are you—what is—*how*—"

I picked up my drink. "Let's talk. I'll be over here."

I headed for the nearest table, steeling myself.

♫

"You know, this is almost a relief, from a 100-percent selfish standpoint." Victoria stirred her hot chocolate, examining me with bright, curious eyes. "After the dance, I was like, wow, nobody's ever been that viscerally not into me."

"I mean." I cleared my throat. "Not that I wasn't. Into it. But um. Complications."

"Right." She flashed me her cheeky grin. "Alter egos."

"Yeah. I figured it'd be weird if we, and . . . assuming you're not into girls . . ." I trailed off, not wanting to seem too curious.

Victoria took a sip of her drink. "Mm, this is good." She placed the cup on the scratched wood of the table. "Yeah, no," she said, with a bit of hesitation, "as far as I know, I'm the Measures' token straight girl."

Something quieted in me. A lock flicked shut in my chest. I remembered the way my mind had opened wide when she kissed me—all fantasy and imagination and jumping twenty steps ahead. My heart alive, all of a sudden, remembering how to want someone. Not that any of that mattered, when I had less than three weeks left.

I gave her a tired smile. "Well," I said. "Good to know."

"So, why are you still on campus?" she asked, a little too brightly. "Are—hang on, are you an international student? Am I making that up?"

"Nah, I'm from San Francisco. My parents are . . ." I trailed off. It would be so easy to make something up. A casual fib, thoughtless. *My parents aren't in the city right now*, or *I have this project I needed the library to work on*. On and on.

"I can't afford flights back," I finished. "Or much of anything else, at this point."

Her composure slipped for a second, showing a glimpse of surprise.

"Sorry," I said at once. "I just—sorry."

"Hey. No, it's okay. Why are you apologizing?"

"I don't know." Old habits die hard. I looked down at the table, my throat tight. My heart was beating too hard. I curled my nails into my palms, trying to force out the tension. *Get it together*.

Victoria examined me as if I were a science fair experiment.

My mouth skewed in a grimace. A strangled sound worked its way out of my throat. I couldn't get it together. Not this time. Something had cracked deep inside my body, and if I held it in anymore, its edges would shred my insides open.

"It must be hard not to see your family on Thanksgiving," Victoria said. She sounded uncertain, and it made her younger somehow, hopeful and anxious, a girl I could recognize from her television show. The Family Channel had scripted twelve-year-old Vicky T into a heroine anyone could get behind, all sharp humor when a middle-school bully needed a dose of snark, but warm in her softer moments. I found myself stupidly glad that this version of her hadn't been fiction.

"It's not that," I managed. "They're making me go."

I circled my hands over my cheeks, kneaded my temples with my index fingers. God, I could see it. Meeting after meeting. I'd sit in a thousand stiff leather chairs in a thousand tastefully decorated offices of a thousand well-meaning grown-ups, and they would all try to convince me to stay, and I'd have to smile in a chagrined sort of way, saying, "I've got to do what's best for my family." None of them would know I was fighting back a voice in my head that screamed, *I don't want to go. Don't make me go. I need this.*

Then I'd get on a plane. December 14th, the day after the competition, that useless competition I'd gambled everything on. And I'd never come back.

A hand lit on my shoulder. "Hey," said Victoria. "Hey. Are you okay? What do you mean, they're making—"

"I'm not coming back next semester." I lowered my hands and looked at her. I probably looked like a train wreck. "I have to stay in San Francisco."

Her hand dropped away. "But what about your spring concert and stuff?"

I gave a hollow laugh. "If my parents say it's not happening, it's not happening."

"And they don't know about . . ."

"Any of this. No. Course not."

I cupped my cider mug, letting my hands grow uncomfortably hot. "Victoria?"

"Yeah?"

"You're not going to tell anyone, are you?"

She sat still, looking torn.

"Please," I said, low, intent. "The guys can't find out. It's three more weeks. Singing with them is the one thing since June that's made me feel like—I don't know. Like I'm *going* somewhere. Like this wasn't all for nothing." This whole process. Class after class, audition after audition, fight after fight with my parents just to *stay*.

"It's not for nothing," Victoria said. "What happens if the Sharps win the competition?"

The question didn't even feel like it mattered. The whole thing had been a ridiculous dream. I shook my head, studying my hands at the edge of the table.

"You could still do it," she said quietly. "They pay for the whole thing."

"I mean, yeah. But then I'll have to tell my parents."

"So tell your parents." Her voice gained strength. "You would have had to anyway. What do you have to lose?"

I met Victoria's gaze. She didn't look away, didn't back down. I saw myself in there, all stubborn conviction, hungry ambition, eyes on the prize.

Tell my parents I'd been posing as a guy in every spare hour since September. Gamble on the chance that they'd let me travel with a group of high school and early-twenties guys. Gamble on our winning the competition in the first place.

When was I going to run out of bets to make?

21

ON THANKSGIVING NIGHT, MY PARENTS VIDEO-CALLED me, sitting in the kitchen, sink and cabinets out of focus over their shoulders. Mom had her hair out of its ponytail for once, two streams of tangled black. As the resolution of the video flickered and cleared, I felt my intestines form a deliberate pretzel.

I asked about Thanksgiving. They'd gone over to the Davises' for dinner, as usual—the Davises had six kids, so they never said no to a couple of extra adults to balance things out. Hopefully, they'd managed to keep their tensions out of the Davises' apartment.

Finally, Dad asked, "What did you want to talk about?"

"I need to tell you something." My heart pattered. "So, this year, I got into this singing group."

My parents traded a look. "You what?" Mom said.

"It's a vocal group, and they're really good. There's this competition we've been working for, and it—"

"Why is this the first we're hearing about this?" Dad asked.

I swallowed, improvising. "Since it's not theater, I thought you might not want me to be doing it. But I love it, okay? I really love it. And this competition is a big deal. We've got a chance to tour all over the world with a professional singing group. A famous group."

My parents looked as if I'd switched to speaking Arabic.

"They expense the whole trip," I rushed on. "We wouldn't need to pay anything or do anything. If we win, I—can I go? It's over winter break. Please? It's a big deal. A huge deal. It could be a career-making thing."

They looked at each other, then back at me, in unison. My mom said slowly, "I don't see a problem with that. Who's in the group?"

"That's the thing," I said. "I mean, the tour's going to be a bunch of adults. You know, professionals. But my singing group is, um . . . well, it'd be me and seven boys."

"*Absolutely not*," Dad said. At the same time, Mom spluttered, "What singing group has seven boys and one girl?"

"They sort of . . ." I winced. "I mean, they think I'm a boy, is the thing. I've been kind of pretending. To be a boy. So. Um."

Both of them sat absolutely still for a moment, so still I wondered if the screen had frozen. Then they came back to life. "*What?*" my mom said, aghast.

My dad said, "How on earth have you been pretending to be—"

I tugged off my wig.

My parents' mouths dropped open. I was tempted to screencap the sight and send it out as a Christmas card.

"You cut all your hair," my mom said. She sounded as if she might pass out. "You cut it off."

"Yeah. Yep."

My dad sank a hand into his own hair as if reassuring himself that it was still there. Mom gave her head a violent shake and said in a low, dangerous voice, "So, you're saying you lied to your school?"

"No! Kind of. Not really. It's a club, so there's only one teacher who's involved. The school doesn't . . . really know. It's just the guys."

If my mom heard a word I said, it made no visible impact. She was still studying my hair with unqualified horror.

I bit my lip. "If it makes it better, people cut their hair for parts in shows all the time."

Then Dad let out a noise that sounded suspiciously like a giggle.

Mom looked at him with astonishment. After a second of restraint, Dad cracked. "How dumb do these people have to be not to see she's a girl?" The burst of laughter that came from his mouth was too much for the computer: The audio peaked and cracked, sending across a robotic blare of mirth.

Slowly, my mom looked back at me, and after a second, she started laughing, too. Stunned, I sat there, watching Dad transition from howling to wheezing. He wiped his eyes with his knuckles, caught Mom's eyes again, and they collapsed against each other's shoulders in hysterics.

What the fuck, I thought.

When they finally got themselves together, I said, "So, is that a yes, or?"

"I think," Dad said, looking at Mom, "if it's worth it, you should do the competition."

Mom jumped in. "It really costs nothing?"

"Zero."

"Well," she said, and folded her hands. "If you win, we'll talk more about it. But if you do win, no more of this lying to these boys. No more telling your school you're—" She brandished an indicating finger at the camera. "*You know.*"

"Yes. Okay. Absolutely." If I made it that far, then, I'd have to figure out a way to have my cake and also eat all of the cake. I'd have to explain who I was—but too late for anyone to take it back. I imagined an e-mail from overseas, or possibly a carrier pigeon. Smoke signals?

My plans slowed in their swirling patterns for a moment, stilling as I examined my parents. I wanted to thank them, but I couldn't form a sound. Their laughter had struck a strange, sweet note inside me. I hadn't seen them like that in so long, unified, looking at each other as if they were allies. They looked so much younger, it made me feel ancient.

♫

"Who is it?"

"Julian," I called through Isaac's door.

After a second's muffled noise, the door swung open. Isaac's bun was messier than normal; a thick fistful of dark hair hung under one of his pointy ears. A pair of bulky headphones hung around his slender neck, branded with thick white text reading *Audio-Technica*. Wires snaked around his wrist, black and red.

For a second, we eyed each other. There were fragments of something swimming under his usual careless expression. Had five days changed his mind? Had he thought over everything and decided to tell the others after all—or never talk to me again?

"Hey." He smiled. "Come in."

Relief doused the fires of worry in my head. I wove through his maze of clutter, found a patch of wall to lean against, and summoned the words I'd planned while trying to sleep. Two plain sentences. *Listen, I'm not coming back to Kensington after break. I'm still all in for the competition, but we should talk about replacing me.*

I imagined some boy sitting in my armchair in the Nest, and I felt, for a second, as interchangeable as something sent down an assembly line.

My throat tight, I scanned the room. Isaac's recording setup sat on his desk: the microphone plugged into a preamp with a half-dozen dials, which fed into his computer. In front of the mic, a disk of black nylon was positioned to catch uneven bursts of air, attached to the stand by a goosenecked bracket. "Didn't you just get back?" I said, nodding at the setup.

"Yep." Isaac leapt over his suitcase and folded his laptop shut, hiding the screen full of multicolored recording tracks. "I've got priorities. The muse waits for nobody, Julian. Um, Jordan." Unplugging the mic and unscrewing the stand, he glanced at me over his shoulder. "What name should I use?"

"Doesn't matter. Just don't call me Jordan in front of the guys."

"I'll just call you J," he said, looping the mic cable in a blur of black rubber. "Like a blue jay. Except that you're human and stuff." He gave me a suspicious look. "*Supposedly*."

"You are the weirdest person I know," I said with a grin, and it wasn't even an exaggeration. Under the misleading layers of being well-dressed and good at guitar, he was very possibly the biggest dweeb at Kensington. I remembered my audition, with that heinous nonjoke about the president of the United States, and it seemed impossible that I'd ever been afraid of Isaac thinking *I* was weird.

I forced my smile down. *Three weeks left*, I reminded myself. No reminiscing. Time to start letting go. "How's it going?" I said, keeping the strain from my voice. "The album, I mean."

"Not bad. I did all the instrumentals over break, so now I just have to finish up the vocals." He slid his equipment into a drawer. "I probably should've left my guitar home—I don't really need it now, I guess. Anyway, whatever." He hopped up on his bed and fiddled with the knotted drawstring of his hoodie. He had crooked fingers from holding pencils and picks and handles too tight. "Why'd you come by? What's up?"

I opened my mouth and nothing came out. If I told him, it made this real. It would begin the three-week goodbye.

"Just wanted to . . . you know," I said quietly. "Make sure you didn't drive off the road."

He laughed. "Thanks, asshole." His laugh froze. "I mean, um—"

"Any time." I smiled back.

His shoulders loosened. "Right. So." He cleared his throat. "How was staying here for Thanksgiving? We got more snow, right? That must've been fun. Did you go sledding? You don't look dead of boredom, at least. So that's good."

". . . I survived, yeah," I said past a strangled feeling in my throat.

After a moment, Isaac smiled a confused smile. "Gonna give me any more than that?"

"What?"

His smile skewed uneven. He shrugged. "Well, when we talked—I just. I mean, we talked."

I know. I know. It had been smooth and effortless, the way talking hardly ever is. We'd talked and it had felt like a song.

I couldn't hold his eyes. I studied the posters plastering the walls instead. One displayed a gaunt, stubbly man perched on a stool, draped in spotlights, acoustic guitar tucked into his lap. Another showed a slice of black stage with a guitarist on his knees, the red-and-gold face of his electric gleaming. And there was Freddie Mercury, stripe of mustache above his generous mouth, wailing into a sparkling microphone, sweat pearling on his brow.

My thoughts circled back around, apparently determined to remind me how, five days ago, Isaac and I had murmured into the night until it paled with the promise of dawn. Before that night, I hadn't let myself think of Isaac as anything more than the senior always looking for trouble. Since then, I'd reconsidered. He wasn't looking for trouble. He was trouble.

"Um," he said. "So I guess I thought I'd . . ."

I waited.

"Never mind," he said. "Forget it."

"No, what?"

He swung his legs, his quick voice coming to life. "Did I tell you I burned the turkey on Thanksgiving?" he asked. "I can't cook. It's horrible. I swear I could burn those lazy-person cookies you get in the frozen section. When I was twelve, I basically set our kitchen on fire. My mom still has a grease burn on her forearm."

I let him swing the subject in a wide arc, far away from anything that mattered. But I kept hoping, as we bantered about dining hall food and competition prospects and our upcoming rehearsal schedule, that he'd steer us back.

I didn't want to tell him. I knew I had to.

Then, out of nowhere, he said, "I kind of thought I should call you," and it jarred me back to myself.

"Uh. What?"

"I don't know. After I got back home, I thought, like, she's a girl. You're a girl. That was a weird time at the retreat. Right? So, I should call. Or text. Something." His eyes were brushing me all over, then meeting mine, then darting away embarrassed. He lay back on his bed, examining his ceiling. "You're not mad, right?"

"Wh—mad about what?" I said, bewildered.

"That I didn't get in touch."

"What? No." I pulled his chair out from his desk and sat. "What are you talking about?"

"Fuck. I don't know." He put his pillow over his face and said something into it.

"That's, um, not the best way to make words."

He slid the pillow up until his sharp chin and mouth poked out beneath. "It doesn't make sense anymore. I don't know if you would've wanted to talk, or if it made me an asshole for not talking, or if you were worried about—"

"Isaac. Hey. It's okay." I studied his profile as the pillow slipped from his face. He was still staring at the ceiling.

I wasn't going to tell him to stop overanalyzing. Not until I figured out how to stop doing it myself.

"You're not an asshole," I said, quieter.

He straightened up slowly, a thick lock of hair falling over his forehead. He brushed it back. "Okay. I just . . . I don't get how girls work."

I tried not to laugh, disbelieving. "I work like *me*. Like a person. I'm the same human being, okay? You know me." Sudden resentment needled me. "And also, I'm not suddenly trailing after you and hoping you'll call me, just 'cause I'm a girl."

He made a frantic motion. "What! No, that's not what I—I didn't mean—"

After a moment of his floundering, I leaned against his desk, amazed. No wonder Isaac Nakahara had never had a girlfriend, then, if this was how he talked to girls.

"Then tell me what you mean," I said, and I meant it to sound amused, a little sarcastic, but it didn't come out that way. His room was silent except for the murmur of the heating and a whisper of music down the hall, and in the stillness my words were halting and confused.

He leaned back against the wall. "All right. I wanted to call you, okay?" he said, with an air of finality. Like that explained everything.

I waited a long moment for an elaboration, but for once, Isaac didn't keep talking. He just held my eyes, wearing a serious, unfamiliar expression.

The door opened. I jolted, twisting around.

Jon Cox stalked in, his mouth curled in a snarl.

"They keyed my fucking car," he said, his voice trembling. "Those *shitheads* keyed my car!"

Isaac and I were both on our feet in seconds. "Where are they?" Isaac said.

"Isaac," I warned.

"I saw a couple of them near Arlington," Jon Cox said.

"Guys—"

Isaac grabbed his coat. The stuttering boy had disappeared. The sharp knife of revenge was back. "Let's go."

"Guys!" I snapped.

Two heads turned my way.

"This needs to go to the administration, okay? That's destruction of property. That's not rivalry—with your car, that's a felony."

Jon Cox looked downright offended. "Oh, like we can't sort this out ourselves?" he said.

"Yeah, exactly like that," I shot back. "If they get suspended, or in legal trouble, colleges are going to see it. That's actual consequences. We can't do actual consequences without . . . I don't know."

"Without what?" Jon Cox demanded.

"Without stooping to their level."

"They're not going to see it that way," Jon Cox said. "Connor Caskey is going to go around like, yeah, we won, the Sharps are a bunch of pussies."

A sheen of red lowered over my vision. "Oh, is *that* your priority? Making sure some asshole doesn't think you're effeminate?"

Jon Cox mouthed for a second, looking baffled.

Isaac leapt in. "Okay," he said, giving me a cautionary look. "You know what, maybe it *is* time to just talk to someone. Graves, maybe. Tell you what, let me—"

"No, don't," Jon Cox blurted. He shook his head, pushing a hand through his hair. "He'll tell my parents. I swore I wouldn't get the car hurt." Looking defeated, he backed toward the door. "Forget it. I'll see you guys later."

"Wait," I said, but he was already gone.

♫

The lunch bell rang, and the Greek Monologue class sprang up from our table.

"Tell your friends to come to the showcase next week," Reese called over the hubbub. "Hang up those posters." The posters in question showed us gathered in the Black Box in costume, under harsh lighting, looking suitably tragic and dramatic. We'd been having class in the Black Box, mostly, for a month or so, preparing for the final performance. Reese's critiques were merciless, but the showcase replaced a final exam for this class, so nobody complained.

I was planning on taking down every single poster I found. My face hanging up around campus? Not safe.

"To the bathrooms!" exclaimed Ash Crawford, grabbing a sheaf of posters.

"What?" said Pilar Velasquez, giving him a weird look.

"The best place to hang up posters is the back of stall doors," Ash explained, heading for the door. "People can't escape, you know? If you put . . ."

They made up the back end of the escaping stream of students, and when their laughter was cut off by the closing door, I turned to look at Reese, who stood at the oval table, appraising me. It was only the first day back from break, and I already felt threadbare. This dean's meeting would be the first of this afternoon's emotionally exhausting sessions. Goodbye to Admissions. Goodbye to Financial Aid. Goodbye to theater.

"Let's go to my office," she said.

♫

Long rays of afternoon light fragmented through the old glass in Reese's office window. The rhythmic whip of the fan took over. Her long nails were pressed together, arching a cage up between her palms. I gazed, resigned, at her silver manicure.

"Have you considered work-study?" Reese asked.

"Yeah, I talked to Human Resources. They said they've already finished their hiring for spring, so I'd have to wait until fall. I don't have time to wait, is the thing."

Reese shook her head, toying with a charm on one of her bracelets. "This has come up at every single Board meeting for the past few years," she said. "I can't fathom how the academy claims to meet 100% of demonstrated need, if outside costs like travel and supplies aren't within the student's grasp." Her lips thinned. "We're slow to change, unfortunately."

"Yeah."

Reese folded her arms on her desk and leaned forward. The tightness of her dark bun drew her forehead back, lifting the arches of her brows. Beneath, her softly lined eyes were serious. "Jordan, I've started your parents with the transfer application, but I tried to discourage them from the idea. You're an excellent student. I know the circumstances seem severe, but there are steps you and your family can take to tackle them, if you're committed to graduating from Kensington. We can map this situation out for you; we can take this little by little."

The quiet intensity in her voice took me aback. I didn't know why, but it made me want to disengage, or disappear. I stared at my thighs.

"Let's assume you get a work-study job next year," Reese continued, clicking a pen into action. "That leaves us with two breaks and next semester to account for. Three blocks of time; we can look at them one by one." *1, 2, 3* went the rollerball tip onto blank paper, hollow-sounding on the desktop. "Let's start with next semester first, all right? There may be work opportunities available in town. I can ask on your behalf, if you're not comfortable." A pause. "Jordan?"

I looked up reluctantly. My teeth felt glued together, my voice pushed deep inside a pouch I couldn't open. *It's useless*, said a repeating voice in the back of my mind. *Why bother?* Something would always fall through. It was easy to say this was just a set of Unfortunate Circumstances, but looking back, hadn't we always just been stringing our way from Unfortunate Circumstance to Unfortunate Circumstance? If it wasn't the fallout from a hospital stay, it was getting cycled out of a job. If it wasn't a job, it was the hiking rent. If it wasn't rent, it was some freak expenditure that threatened to unbalance everything: a rattling air conditioner that spat out hot air and rancid water, weeping for replacement; or an abscessed tooth that knotted up my mother's face every time she bit down, which cost some stupid amount of money to extract, because it's a rare part-time job that comes with dental.

If it wasn't any of those circumstances, it was my parents' innate, unshakable conviction that I was more valuable at home where they could manage me.

And if it wasn't my parents, at the end of the day, it was my own failings. My own inability to get cast or find my way into this community as myself. My inability even to hold on to somebody. I didn't belong at Kensington, and trying to belong made it worse every time.

"Jordan," Reese repeated, but I stood up.

"I need to go," I said. "Thank you for talking. But this isn't going to work."

She called after me one more time as I walked out the door.

♫

Usually, Thanksgiving Break made the last couple weeks of school before Winter Break feel unnecessary. This year was different. With two weeks to go, the campus started to buzz with competition talk. Advertisements plastered campus. An Aural Fixation poster the size of my mattress appeared in McKnight above the dish return. A cappella talk started to infiltrate the neurotic pre-exam discussions of study techniques: *Are you going to ask for their beatboxer's signature? He's so cute. Do you think people are going to stake out seats ahead of time? Carnelian has to win. No, the Sharps. No, Hear Hear. Do you think Aural Fixation is going to sing? If they do "When You Call," I think I'm going to pass out . . .*

Soon, the obligatory counterculture discussions about the competition sprang up: *Why is this happening with exams coming up? We need to study. Who cares about a cappella, anyway? It's not even real music. Nobody was this excited when that amazing slam poet toured here. We didn't get posters when that award-winning experimental kazoo artist did a show here . . . he got featured in* TIME *and everything . . . but* nooo, *a cappella is more* important . . .

Trav moved rehearsals to the Arlington stage so we could practice with sound tech. We trained ourselves to avoid the deafening feedback that came from aiming *P*s and *B*s directly at our handheld mics, shots of air that sounded like pressure popping in the amplifiers.

Trav had a pair of kids from the music school sitting backstage left, plugged into a digital soundboard, tweaking dials so that the rocket-launch decibel levels from Isaac and Erik didn't drown out Nihal and Marcus, who sounded like mosquitoes in comparison. These kids didn't seem to have names and didn't talk to anyone but Trav, but they seemed to love telling him things he already knew. They also wore Official Sound Guy Face, which was an intriguing blend of displeased and pompous.

To be fair to the tech guys, it must have been infuriating to watch us mess up in the same ways repeatedly for nights on end. "Hold the mic farther from your face," Trav told Erik one night, for the eightieth time.

Erik looked like he wanted to throw the mic at the wall. "Can't we just use the area mics, like every other group?"

"No," Trav snapped, and took a breath. "No. This is worth it. Otherwise, we'll lose half the arrangement to the choreography, and we'll be hideously quiet in comparison to everyone else, and—just trust me."

He was right, as always. When we were balanced and mixed and polished, the mics were worth every minute we'd spent on them. The curved black spine of the performance hall reflected sound down to the back walls, every consonant as crisp as a cracked knuckle. The Nest had its own resonance, a homey echo back from the rafters, but here, plugged in, amplified, and choreographed, we sounded like another group entirely.

After rehearsals, we packed up our equipment and marched it up the Prince stairs. We had eight wireless mics, heavy black Sennheisers; the eight-channel receiver; the mixer, with its army of sliders and dials and plugs; and a couple of bulky monitors that made my arms ache.

"Why don't the other groups use individual mics?" I asked once, as we climbed up to the Nest, equipment in hand.

"Because they have more people," Nihal replied over his shoulder. "And mics get expensive very fast."

"Careful, rooks," Trav barked as Erik and Marcus accidentally knocked the tech trunk into the wall. They panted apologies. The instant we were back inside the Nest, Trav was under the lid of the chest and inspecting every bit and every piece, ensuring that nothing was scraped or bent. He had a tender, soulful look on his face, as if his father had wrought the sound tech over the course of sixty-one long years and it was all Trav had left of him.

I set down a monitor with a grunt. "How expensive?" I asked.

"$11,000, I think?" Nihal said, glancing to Mama for confirmation.

I choked on my breath. "*What?*"

"Yeah, several years' concert tickets. Dr. Graves helped us figure everything out—he handles the money." Nihal raised his eyebrows, his eyes laughing. "We suspect he's skimmed off the top."

I was still gaping. "What, are those mics made out of platinum?"

"Sapphire, actually."

I couldn't even quip back. I could hardly think about money these days. It was a short slide to an inevitable reminder: *Kiss this place goodbye.*

As the competition clock ticked down from two weeks to ten days to seven, I drifted out from myself like a boat leaving land. I began to count my lasts: the last essay I would turn in to Rollins, the last critique Reese would give on my monologue, the last time I would see Carnelian walking around campus in early December, doing jazz arrangements of carols. During the Greek Monologue showcase: last time I would see Ash perform, then Pilar, then Jamie. Ticking down by the word.

My finals counted down. Core classes had exams first, hour-long blocks of frantic scribbling in blue books; electives took over on Wednesday; and the week ended with a whimper, not a bang, empty class periods filled with distractions. On Friday, I walked out of my last class, English with Mr. O'Neill; we'd read a poem by Eavan Boland he'd said was his favorite, about an Irish couple killed by weather and hunger and history. Emerging into the winter light, I got that feeling that sometimes sets in after waking up from a particularly vivid dream, a disconnection from reality. I almost expected the landscape to disappear around me patch by patch.

Late that afternoon, Isaac and I got a text from Jon Cox: a picture of his and Mama's dorm-room door. I zoomed in on the image.

A whiteboard hung on the door. I'd swung by their room in Ewing a couple times and seen it—usually, inside jokes were scribbled across the board, doodles of comic book characters, thinly veiled sexual references, or the running count of how many times Mama had reminded Jon to take out the trash (thirty-four).

In Jon Cox's text, the whiteboard wore a very different doodle. A drawing of a person filled most of the space, a bulging shape whose head, hands, and feet were exaggeratedly small, toothpaste caps on a bursting tube. The doodle wore a shirt that read in angry capitals, *THEODORE PUGH HUGE.*

They wrote it in permanent marker, Jon Cox texted. *I'm taking it down. Mama's pretty upset about it. He's skipping his last orchestra practice.*

I stared at the horrible drawing. This must have hit hard. Nothing else all year had managed to tear Mama away from Handel, the love of his life.

Furious heat itched up my back. Of every shitty thing so far—the music-burning, the car-keying—this was the shittiest. What had Mama ever done to Connor Caskey?

Yes, fine, Connor's dad was an asshole, but past a point, that stopped mattering. A reason wasn't an excuse. Same genus, different species.

I pulled my coat on and flung my window open, outrage spurring me faster. The snow hampered my rushing steps. It took longer than I would've liked to reach the music academic building, a heather-gray block adjacent to Arlington Hall. Teachers bulky with coats trickled steadily through the lobby, the stairwell, and the second floor. I rushed down the hall, scanning the plaques on the office doors. *Mrs. Chen. Mr. Goossens. Ms. Mburu.* The faculty in the School of Music kind of resembled a United Nations conference.

Finally, I knocked on Dr. Graves's door, praying he hadn't left yet.

"Come in," he called, sounding impatient.

I entered. Wintry sun through an arched window limned the office with white light. A bookcase by the door held titles like *A Brief Introduction to Modal Counterpoint*, and *Religiosity in the Life of Bach*, and *Early Music and the Evolution of Stable Harmonies*. Dr. Graves himself stood behind an oaken desk, hunched over his keyboard, square glasses perched on the prominent bridge of his nose.

He straightened up. "Julian. Hello." His computer sang a tune, shutting down. "I'm on my way out. I'll be at the competition tomorrow; may we talk then?"

"This won't take long."

He checked his watch with a humorless laugh. "Can you make it under five minutes?"

"Sure," I said, drawing myself up. "The Minuets are trying to sabotage us." It sounded so petty out in the air like this.

His expression darkened. "How so?"

"It's been a bunch of stuff. Vandalism, and they burned a bunch of our music, and today they left graffiti on someone's dorm."

"What sort of graffiti?"

I shifted. "Well, it . . . here." As Dr. Graves buttoned up his coat, I pulled out my phone, searching for the photo. Gray leather briefcase gripped in his grayish, leathery hand, he ushered me out the door. Backing up a bit in the hall, I held the screen out to face him.

Graves locked his office, tucked his keys away, and peered at my phone through his glasses. A shadow passed across his expression.

After examining the picture for a second more, he drew back and pinned me with a look I'd never seen on a grown-up's face before. Some withering mixture of disdain and dismissal. "Mr. Zhang, if you can prove who exactly did this, let me know." His gray eyes flashed. "In the meantime, may I give some advice for you and the boys?"

"Yeah?"

"Man up."

And he set off down the hall, leaving me doused in disbelief.

MAN UP. I WOULD HAVE FOUND THE REBUKE FUNNY for the double entendre if it hadn't sliced in like a paper cut and kept stinging. What, I wasn't allowed to stand up for my friend? Mama wasn't allowed to be upset if someone took a sucker punch at his weight? There was something deeply screwed up about that attitude. There is no world where "you're wrong" is an acceptable answer to "this hurts."

Man up. What a cleverly disguised way to say *shut up*. Shut up, or fight back, or you deserved what you got.

Everything was growing clearer. So *this* was why the guys had such an issue backing down—why Mama fought for the last word in every argument, why Erik wanted revenge for every prank, why Isaac said sorry like it was brine on his tongue. I finally understood it. No, I *felt* it. Rage was mounting inside me; not at Graves, somehow, but at Connor fucking Caskey for setting me up for humiliation in front of a teacher. There was nowhere else to put the anger except back where it came from.

I stormed away from the music quad. Soon, I realized my feet were carrying me toward Wingate. Around to the side door. Up four flights of steps, which I powered up mechanically, relishing the burn in my thighs.

When I stopped at room 420 and knocked on Isaac's door, Harry yanked it open.

"What now?" he snapped. Harry was obviously suffering a postfinals hangover. His hair stuck out from his scalp at an impressively vertical angle; Band-Aids wrapped his fingertips. He'd probably resorted to playing his cello with his toes.

"Where's Isaac?" I said. I needed him to talk me down. I needed his endless tangents and distractions.

"Oh my God." Harry shoved his glasses up violently, as if they'd done him an unforgivable wrong. "Some guy literally *just* came by to grab his guitar for his EP thing, so probably Arlington or Prince? I don't friggin' know."

Harry made to shut the door, but I frowned, slamming a palm onto the wood. Isaac had told me he'd finished recording all his guitar parts over break. And . . . *some guy*? Who would Isaac ever trust to touch his guitar?

"What guy?" I said.

"I don't know. Dark hair. Weirdly tall."

My fists clenched. I felt a strange excitement. The sun of anger in me lashed out a flare. "When did he leave?"

"I mean, you knocked about ten seconds after I shut the door, so—"

I spun away, scanning the hall. He couldn't have come up this stairwell. I would've passed him.

I stalked down the hall, hunting. Halfway down, I broke into a sprint. Half-open doors flew by, issuing snatches of soothing study playlists, hints of violin and flute. The sheets of paper pinned to the walls rustled and flailed as I rushed by.

Up ahead, the elevator dinged.

I flung myself around the corner to the elevator bay and through the closing doors, smacking into Connor Caskey.

"*Shit,*" he said. We fell apart, I thumbed my glasses back into place, and he caught himself against the back wall of the elevator. His right hand was fastened about the neck of Isaac's guitar, that smooth rosewood. Strips of cloudy mother-of-pearl in the fretboard glittered behind his fingers. He gripped so hard that white bays pooled around his fingernails.

Caskey straightened up. We stood at an impasse as I fought for breath. The elevator doors drew shut behind us, but the car didn't budge. I glanced at the panel—I'd knocked him away before he'd pressed a floor.

I had him cornered. Finally. "Give me the guitar," I panted, "or else."

"Or else?" Caskey said, and took a tube of acrylic paint out of his jeans. He flicked the cap open, held Isaac's guitar out, and lifted the tube. "How about you move, *or else.*"

The fury that had simmered all afternoon reached boiling point. Something snapped, blanking my mind out like a flood of white paint.

I charged.

As I crashed into him, the guitar slipped from his grip and landed hard against the wall. A discordant complaint rang out from the strings. My hand found the acrylic paint, forced it out of Caskey's fingers, and somehow I had the presence of mind to cap it before flinging it in a generally backward direction.

Then, out of nowhere, Caskey's curled knuckles found my face.

They slammed my jaw with enough force to make glass shatter somewhere deep in my head. My teeth clocked together. Lights burst in the corner of my eye, and my glasses slipped askew, then off my face altogether.

More in shock than pain, I clutched at the pulsing site of impact. All logic, all reason, all thoughts abandoned me. Energy surged from my core into my blood, and suddenly I was wildfire, needing to get the rage out. *Man up*, yelled a voice in my head, and I threw a fist. It found its target, smacking deliciously into Caskey's temple.

He reeled sideways, spat a curse, and bulled forward. I tried to push back, but there was so much of him, six and a half feet of wiry limbs and cream-colored sweater. My spine hit the elevator doors, a dart of pain that scrabbled down my back. I flung out a hand. The flat of my palm found the side of Caskey's neck, and I dug my nails in, driving my knee up toward his crotch. It missed the mark, hitting his thigh.

He staggered, face ugly with rage, and sunk his fist in the soft bowl of my stomach. The wind flew out of me. I hunched over and gasped for breath, a cold rush flooding up to my collarbones.

He grabbed me by the hair, angled my face up, and the second hit landed on my cheekbone. The impact reverberated through my skull, sending a red shadow over my vision. Caskey's grip ripped hairs out of my scalp. Tears pricked my eyes. I lurched forward, righted myself, started to lift my fists—

His third punch careened in like a battering ram and smacked me square in the nose. I crumpled back. Blood trickled over my lips into my open mouth, warm and coppery. The stream felt like it was coming down from my eyes, or my brain, or from the center of my head, and I cupped the dark liquid in one hand as it dribbled off the tip of my chin.

I was bent double, chest heaving.

"Good talk," Caskey's voice said. "Know what? Keep the guitar."

I straightened up. "Fuck you."

He clapped me on the back, but for once, he looked dead serious. "Have fun singing tomorrow." He reached for the *Door Open* button, but I lurched in front of it.

"Come on, Zhang," he said, sounding tired. "Move."

"No," I said, spraying flecks of blood toward him. He recoiled.

I drew slow breaths through my mouth. "I want to know what your problem is."

A mulish look settled on his face. "And I don't want to still be here talking to you."

"You know what people say about you?" I caught my breath and gave him my best sneer, as much as I could with blood seeping over my mouth. I wiped my upper lip with the back of my hand. "You're just bitter you didn't get into the Sharps. Kind of sad, isn't it, holding a grudge over that for four years?"

"Shut up." A purplish flush rose into his white cheeks. "It's not—you don't understand."

"Fine. Then explain."

Caskey's lips scrunched up. It clearly took everything he had to keep quiet.

My eyes fell to the guitar. "What, do you think you're better than Isaac?" I said. "Think you should've gotten it instead of him, when you guys were freshmen? 'Cause I hate to break it to you, but nobody's better than Isaac, man. Not me, not you, n—"

He burst. "It's not Nakahara, for Christ's sake."

"Yeah? Then what is it?"

"I'm a Sharps legacy, okay?"

My mouth drooped open. We stared at each other for a second.

I couldn't help it. I burst into laughter. It made my head pound—I had to stop. Get ahold of myself. "Are you *fucking serious*?"

His face purpled even more. He looked like a ripe plum. "I knew you wouldn't get it," he said, obviously trying for scorn, but it didn't sound right. There was a desperate edge to his voice. "My dad was a Sharps president. My grandfather was in it, class of '65. It's not some stupid thing to laugh at, okay? It's our life. Like you could ever understand tradition. You can't—you don't *get it*!"

The outburst rang around the elevator. Embarrassment flashed across his expression. Then he straightened up, fixed his face into unconcern, and tucked his dark hair into place behind his ear.

As I studied him, the comedy of it curdled slowly, leaving something foreign to me. What *did* I know about tradition? When I looked back on my own history, I had to trace a jagged path full of leaps and shifts, starting with that first transpacific jump: my dad's parents emigrating from Beijing in the eighties, leaving everything they knew behind to give my teenage father California. Then I had my mother, traveling alone from Hong Kong in 1995. What had I inherited from her, really? What had carried over from my parents to me? There was such a massive divide between us, so much difference that they hardly had the cultural currency to relate to what my life was like, born and raised American.

But Connor: Suddenly I imagined his life in Boston, in the mansion Nihal had told me about, raised in the same ancient rooms his family had occupied for a century and a half. I remembered how slight Connor had looked on the Arlington stage as he stood opposite his father and played the part: the arrogant Princeton aspirant who would never fall short, never fall behind, and never fall for a sarcastic boy from New Jersey. I could still hear Dr. Caskey waxing nostalgic, trying desperately, pathetically, to relive everything through his son, to mold him into just what he wanted.

All at once I could see the crippling sameness of those generations. Connor turned transparent for a moment, and under his skin, I saw a patchwork of his father, his grandfather, and his grandfather's father, Massachusetts men with only the smallest variations, pieced together from such a strict and immediate tradition that there was nothing left of *him*.

"You're right," I said. I felt distant from myself and from what we'd just done. "I don't get it."

I stepped aside from the panel of buttons. He looked at me a long time. A bruise was clouding into life on his proud forehead, where I'd gotten revenge. I regretted it, but it felt inevitable for him to wind up blue with bruises and hard with scar tissue. His father had been so proud of getting hurt. Growing up meant inheriting all your parents' injuries.

He punched a button, the door slid open, and he disappeared.

A long time after Caskey's footsteps faded, I leaned over and jabbed the first floor button with a thumb. It left a red smear on the clear plastic that came off with a swipe of my sweater sleeve.

I sagged against the paneled elevator wall. Everything felt swollen: my lips, my stomach, and my brain, which pressed against the confining walls of my skull as if trying to squeeze its way out into the open air. I slid a hand clumsily over my aching lips. Red kept running between my fingers. My vision was narrower than usual, bright and uneven around the edges.

The mirrored elevator doors slid shut and showed me myself. The bruise on my cheek was already darkening, and the lower half of my face was a bloody mess. For a moment it occurred to me that I'd never looked more like a man.

Then I couldn't look at myself anymore. I'd done it. I'd gotten there. I'd trampled out every last vestige of who I used to be. Rest in Peace to my former self. It had taken *this* for me to miss anything of what I'd had before, when I'd been unsure and awkward—but God, at least back then I'd been able to recognize myself in a fucking mirror.

And then tears rushed hot to the inside corners of my eyes, and I began to cry. Some gasping spot of relief uncurled in the center of my chest, cathartic, freed. I held myself against the wall, my shoulder slipped down the paneling, and I crouched right there and sobbed until I couldn't breathe. My mouth stretched wide, and the blurry world jerked and sharpened as the tears unfastened themselves from my eyes, molten down my cheeks. I felt stupid and small, caught up in the pursuit of something I had no business chasing down. Victory, or honor, or selfish vindication. All this bullshit that guys were taught to care about.

It wasn't that I wasn't capable of it, or that it was too much for me to carry. It was that it didn't *matter*, did it? Did it really matter at all?

♫

I drifted over a stamped-down track of snow connecting Wingate's back entrance and the music quad. The thoughts in my head moved like treacle. *Ice*, went one. I scooped up a handful of wet, heavy snow and pressed it to the bridge of my nose. *Nest*, went the next. *Home*. I sniffled a bit, and tight pain shot up from my nose, dispersing over my forehead.

Blood droplets hit the snow, marring the shadows with school-spirit carnelian. I left a trail in my wake. The cold numbed my face and froze my fingers around Isaac's guitar. By the time I reached Prince, the bleeding had slowed, almost stopped. The punches I'd taken to the side and stomach had roared into prominence on the way over, making every step feel like one of Hercules's labors.

My glasses steamed up when I walked in. Stern silence wallpapered Prince Library, punctured by the clicking of keys and scratching of pens. Music kids occupied every chair, filled every sofa. Others huddled in groups on the oaken floor, clustered around outlets with laptop screens illuminating their faces, like survivalists after an apocalypse gathered around their campfires.

I steadied my stride and breathed quietly through my mouth, keeping my face aimed down. Nobody even glanced at me. Final papers were due at 7:00 p.m. In the last academic sprint of the semester, everything else turned transparent.

In the stifling air, sweat beaded on the back of my neck. They'd turned the heat up in every building, overcompensating for the ten-degree weather. I climbed staircase after staircase. In the antechamber that led up to the Nest, I had to stop halfway up the stone steps. I thought I might throw up, my stomach hurt so badly.

At last, I turned the knob and all but collapsed into the Nest. It was blessedly temperate, the only warmth issuing from the space heater beneath a window.

The only other person there sat at the piano, his back to me, scribbling a paragraph on a pad of college-ruled paper. Looking at him, navy sweater stretched over his narrow shoulders, his horrible posture and the way his head was always tilted a fraction to the left, I thought I might cry, and I wasn't sure why.

Isaac clicked his pen and turned around. His eyes fixed on my nose, my mouth. The blood coating the ridges of my upper lip. His mouth drifted open.

"Hey," I managed.

"Holy shit." Isaac snatched the tissue box off the top of the piano and crossed the room in five long strides. "What happened? Are you all right?"

"Careful," I said. "Your guitar." My voice came out thick. It made the top of my nose buzz.

In one impatient motion, he took the guitar from my hand and chucked it onto the sofa. "Who did this?" he said, his eyes darting from my cheekbone to my nose to my mouth.

I glanced back to the door and twisted the lock. It took time. My clumsy fingers wouldn't respond; it was like trying to control someone else's hands. I wiped my mouth with the flat of my palm, feeling like a child.

"I caught Connor trying to ruin your guitar," I said, unzipping my coat. "In Wingate. We—I don't know. Fought." I gestured at my face, and a twinge of discomfort flashed across my torso. I swayed and sat down on my armchair's arm, sliding my glasses off.

"Caskey did this?" Isaac said. A murderous look twisted across his face. "When I see him, I'm going to—"

"*No,*" I said heavily. My eyes closed. "Don't. No more fighting, no more anything. Please." I took a few deep breaths. "He's just confused. He's just trying to figure his shit out. Let's just let each other get better for a second."

When I cracked my eyes back open, Isaac was giving me a strange look, curious and fierce. He turned away the second I saw. "Okay," he said. "Right."

Isaac unlatched the nearest window and scooped up a handful of snow from the sill outside. I maneuvered my way out of my backpack, moving gingerly, and Isaac moved back to my side, stretching out a cloud of damp tissues. I reached up, but he was already pressing them against my chin.

I closed my eyes and tried to ignore my stabbing headache, my throbbing bruises. The tissues passed over my mouth, against the creases of my nose, so gently I felt no pressure, just the cold sapping the heat from my skin. I took breaths past my aching teeth.

"Is it still bleeding?" I asked. A nasal hum edged my voice.

"Doesn't look like it," he said.

The tissues skirted my lower eyelids, pressing away the tear tracks that had crusted up as I walked. When he slid the tissues over my cheekbone, pain burst open on the spot like a bitter flavor. I flinched back.

"Shit. Sorry." His voice was close. I opened my eyes. My face prickled with cold evaporation. A chill blustered through the open window, at odds with the sunset that smoldered like coal in the clear sky.

"What happened to the talking thing?" he said, flicking the tissues into the trash. "Beating each other up is kind of eye-for-an-eye."

"It's the Greek tragedy coming out again," I said feebly. "Retribution, you know? I thought about sacrificing him to Zeus, but it would've been messy."

He didn't smile. "Hilarious," he said. Then two of his fingers were hovering over the swollen curve of my cheekbone. I might have imagined the ghost of their warmth. "But this isn't actually funny, Julian. I mean, Jordan."

My heart took an unsteady swerve. I kept my voice level. "Taste of your own medicine, Mr. Walk-on-Thin-Ice."

"That's not the same. I, unlike some people here, don't get hurt for real."

"Yeah?"

"Yeah," he said, quiet and hoarse. "I kind of make it a habit."

His fingers landed against my cheek, two points of light contact. Second by second, my focus gathered around his touch. *Ignore it*, I told myself. Glancing down, I studied the dots of snow that salted the flagstone floor, the tight knots of Isaac's black sneakers, the white corners worn into his jeans pocket where he tucked his phone, and the cable knit of his sweater. But then my gaze slid up too far, brushed his, and stuck. My composure slipped out of my strangling grip. His eyes were the warm black of velvet.

His touch on my cheek became a conduit for everything I couldn't say: the admissions I couldn't make; the wants I couldn't let myself want; and the fears that came from trusting someone more than he'd deserved. I kept quiet. Isaac would take his hand away, step back, and leave this weird silence where it hung in the air, to extinguish safely. And I would look down at the bloodstains on my dad's old coat, and it would still be December 12th, two days before I left this place for good. Silence was the right answer here.

But he didn't back up. He slid his hand forward, his callused fingers brushing over my ear into my hair. The stiff heel of his hand rested against my jaw.

I pressed the tiniest bit against his touch, a breath slipping between my lips. His expression was written in uncertainty and signed in curiosity.

I slipped forward on the armchair and rose back to my unsteady feet, nearly his height. His hand stayed in place, palm fitting warm against my cheek, and his eyes stayed searching mine, as if I were hiding answers inside instead of a rippling well of confusion. The wind mumbled past the window. The space heater emitted its determined hum. A whisper of breath from him drowned it all out. He was so close.

Isaac swallowed. My gaze darted down to his neck, the bobbing movement of the sharp curve in his throat. My thoughts fragmented as I thought of the voice in him, always going, never tired. The whisper that had brushed my forehead in November in the cinema. The scraping words in Jon Cox's attic as the dawn snuck up. The raw edges of his solos that tore at me every time he sang, and tore at the crowd during concerts, leaving us all dumbstruck afterward. This boy put so much of himself into his voice and spent all his time giving it away.

His thumb brushed the corner of my mouth, and then his other hand found my hip, and I realized I wanted him. With the strength of a thousand gravities, I wanted this. What would he feel like against me? Would he be uncertain, or reckless, or something else entirely, showing some facet I hadn't seen? I wanted his quick, string-callused hands on me.

Where was his impulse now? Where had that gone?

I placed a hand uncertainly on his chest. One of the questions in his eyes resolved. He tilted his head, and we moved together. Then my eyes were shut, and my mouth was landing softly against his. The aching, for a second, melted away.

The moment froze. A moment of feeling, just for a second, what it was like—him and me, lip to lip, tense and hesitant.

He pressed forward. His lips were rough and bitten, scraping mine like salt. The tip of his nose dug into my cheek, and as I drew a breath, the smell and taste of him rushed in, bittersweet and biting.

I reached up and slipped my fingers into his dark hair. It felt how I'd imagined, thick and rough, tangled as if he'd walked out of a hurricane. I hadn't known I'd been imagining it at all.

He pressed too hard and too far, mouth clumsy and immobile, all movements of the head and neck. My nose bumped his, and pain darted up between my eyes. I drew back too fast, remembering myself: my bruises, my swellings, the penciled shading in my eyebrows, and my shapelessness under layers of disguises. I was a collage of cover-ups and bad decisions.

But Isaac didn't seem to have remembered any of that. He was looking at me as if he couldn't breathe from self-doubt. I read it right out of his eyes: *Did I fuck it up? Is this okay? Am I okay?* And I knew, somehow, that if I didn't reassure him, he'd cut and run. I'd lose him, this time, across the river.

I knew Isaac longed to be the mask he wore every day: all instinct, no caution. But I looked at him now and saw a boy made out of contingency plans.

He didn't need one. Not with me.

I leaned up and kissed him again. He pulled me in until we were flush together. Heat snarled up beneath my heart. The quick ache in my chest had turned huge and yearning.

My perpetual doubt clamored up. *Is this right, Jordan?* it nagged. *Is this stupid? Is this plummeting feeling something you want to escape, or something you want to let spin down to your core? And if you give yourself over—if you close your eyes and let gravity have its way—what's it going to feel like when you hit the ground?*

What if it hurts?

What if it hurts, all over again?

When he leaves you too, what if it's as bad as it used to be?

Shut up, I thought. *Shut up and let yourself be happy for a second.*

For once, my brain obliged, going blissfully silent, but it wasn't happiness that bloomed up to fill the silent aftermath. It was closer to shock, the instant of shock that follows an accidental glance into the sun, painful and immense and consuming. Closeness felt like that after being untouched for a while.

The world was quiet. Isaac's hand was rough on the back of my neck, his thumb drawing designs over my skin.

As we kissed, tentative turned to urgent, before fading back to gentle, and finally—when we pulled back—he rested his forehead against mine. I didn't find any guarantees in his eyes. For a moment, I wished I could see certainty there, the cocky arrogance of absolute surety. For a second, I imagined him saying, *This is going to be everything*, the words Michael had whispered at the start of our relationship with burning eyes—with authority.

I knew better, though. Isaac was panic over whether to call and the murmured admission that the world was too big and too furious and too much to make sense. He wasn't about to patch my doubts and make me whole; he wasn't going to be my cornerstone; he wasn't the blanket stretched taut to catch me when I fell. He was this nervous kid, playing with matches and dancing around gasoline, and I was this nervous kid, shying back from the firelight, and we were here nervous together, acting like we had it figured out—as if we hadn't already learned what it looked like to see each other pretending.

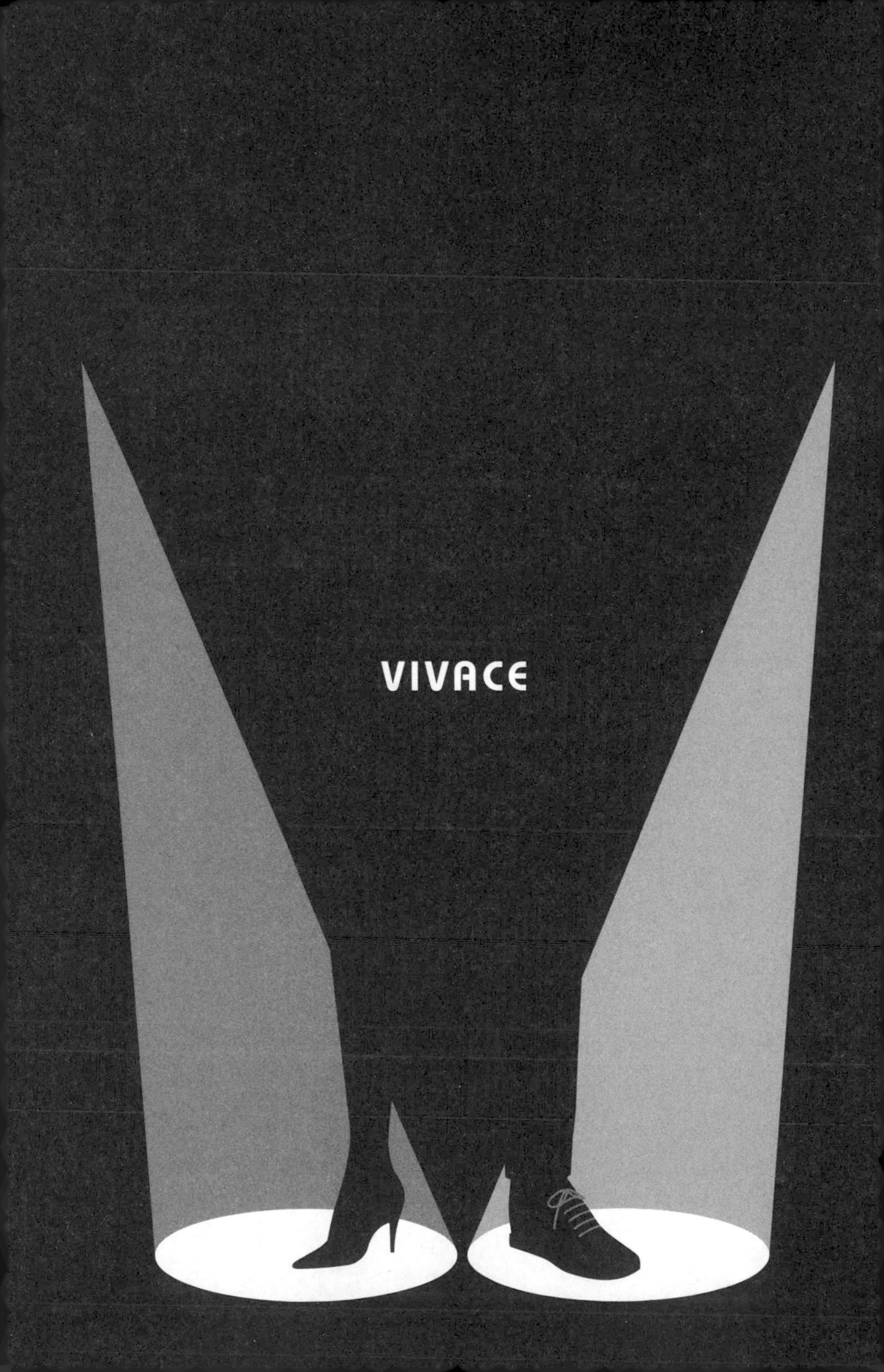
VIVACE

ON THE SOFA, ISAAC WAS PLAYING ME LULLABIES, his fingers switching practiced formations over the fretboard. I watched him for a minute, watched his teeth close on the corner of his lip as vibrations danced beneath his fingers. I thought of every Kensington guitarist sitting under a tree in autumn with his guitar, trying to impress girls. It felt strange to watch in earnest.

The sensation of the end approaching closed in like parallel walls, and when they started crushing me, I loosed a breath, moving in, resting my head on his shoulder. The solidness of him helped the tiniest bit. *Stop thinking forward. Relax. Be present . . .*

It didn't work. The hours ahead were too tight.

The music slowed, softened, and plucked into nothing. "What's up?" he said, slipping his arm over my shoulder. I leaned back into the warm weight of it.

"Listen," I said. He paused, waiting, but my words wouldn't come.

He raised one eyebrow. "Listen to what?"

"I . . . never mind."

After a second, Isaac asked, "Was that going to be the *what-are-we* talk?"

A laugh stuttered out of me. "No. But we can, if you want."

"No, I'm not—let's not," he said. "It's kind of nice not knowing."

"Ignorance is bliss."

"*Whoa, dude, I'm so blissed out,*" he said in a California-surfer-dude voice. "*Ignorance is totally tubular.*"

I fought back a grin that threatened to make my whole face hurt. "California's too good for you, city boy."

"Sure it is." His hand on my shoulder drew me closer.

Voices echoed up the stairs. We jerked apart. I glanced at the clock—an hour had flicked past in fast-forward. I snatched up my miniature sideburns from the sofa arm and tried to stick the gummy strips back to my face, but they had lost all adhesive power.

As the doorknob rattled, Isaac flew to the door and leaned on it, pinning it shut. "Ahe-he-*hem*," he harrumphed through the crack in the door. "Password?"

Protests rose behind the door. "Come on," groaned Erik's voice.

"Wrong," Isaac said.

"Is it Eelectric Eel?" Jon Cox's voice said. "Best album name ever?"

"You know, shockingly, I didn't land on that one," Isaac said. Bracing one hand against the wall to keep the door shut, he gave me an urgent glance back.

I gave up on the sideburns. "Agh," I said, and flung them out the window as Trav's voice said,

"*Now, Isaac.*"

Isaac pulled the door open. "Amazing," he said. "Trav, you're psychic."

Trav gave him dagger eyes, nudging past toward the piano. I leaned my cheek on my hand, trying to look natural, as everyone piled in.

"Okay," Erik said to the other guys, dropping into an armchair. "Fuck Elena, marry Ayana, kill Libby."

Loud exclaiming from Jon Cox and Mama. Apparently a controversial choice.

"Wrong," Marcus mumbled as he hoisted himself into the windowsill. He jerked his head, as if to get his nonexistent bangs out of his eyes. He'd cut his hair short a week ago, but the habit had carried over, leaving him with a new nervous tic to add to his extensive collection of nervous tics.

"Why are you killing Libby?" Jon Cox said. "She's way hotter than Elena."

"Because Libby stands for *Liberty*," Erik said. "Imagine saying that in bed and hearing in your head, *Liberty! Liberty!*"

Jon Cox grinned. "You know nobody actually says each other's names in bed, right?"

"Speak for yourself," Mama said.

Nihal settled on the sofa beside me, looking pained. "I know so much right now that I did not ask to know."

"Hey," Mama said, his eyes falling on me. "Julian. Are you—what happened to your face?"

Everyone's eyes lit on me, and a hush spread. I angled my face downward, avoiding the stares. "Nothing," I said gruffly.

"He walked into a wall," Isaac said. "But, like, repeatedly."

I sighed, glancing around at the guys. "Me and Connor Caskey got in a fight, okay?"

To my left, Nihal grew rigid.

Surprise registered on the guys' faces. "Jesus," Jon Cox said, his eyebrows drawing together. "That's drastic."

Erik jumped in, too eager. "Did you win?"

I shot him an amused look. "Two music geeks beating each other up in an elevator? Nobody's a winner." Chuckling rippled around the Nest.

"You *can* sing, yes?" Trav said.

"Yeah. I'm a little stuffy, but it's already better than an hour ago."

"Good. Put on some stage makeup or something tomorrow." Trav cleared his throat. "And everyone, make sure you're there by five so we have plenty of time to warm up."

Seven heads bobbed.

"That said." Trav folded his hands. "Let's move our—"

He stopped, his eyes falling to the corner where our equipment always sat, the monitors and the chest of mics. It was empty. "Did someone take that down to Arlington already?"

Awful silence spread. And I realized why, all of a sudden, the Minuets had been so intent on distracting us today.

♫

Standing in the Arlington backstage area, I felt like I was reliving the evening of my audition, when Erik had led me onto the stage. The cascades of the spotlights.

Now, darkness smothered everything except for the ghost light that sat center stage. It cast dim slivers of light back here, onto the rack of music lockers, whose metal webbing covered clusters of musical equipment. Tucked into one cage was a deconstructed drum set, the hammered coppery flats of the cymbals glinting. In another, swaths of cloth wrapped up mixers and miniature keyboards.

Trav was rattling through the cages one by one, double-checking that none of our sound tech had ended up inside.

"How about," Jon Cox said, "we ask the other groups if they have any equipment we could borrow?"

"Yeah, of course," Mama said. "They're totally going to turn down a golden opportunity to ruin our performance."

"Pessimist," Jon Cox said. "Let's call some people. Even if we can just get hold of a beatboxing and bass mic, it'll be something." He looked at Erik. "You think the Measures might have any extra solo mics?"

"Maybe," Erik said, not sounding convinced.

"Ulterior motive," Mama mumbled. But he, Jon, and Erik took off, and Marcus scrambled after them. The four of them jogged down the upstage wall, past the rows of taut pulley ropes, into the open greenroom.

Trav had stopped searching the cages. He stood at the side of the stage, staring at a patch of ground like he was trying to set it on fire through sheer force of will. He was twisting the stud in his ear so violently that watching it made a sympathetic pang dart across my earlobes.

Isaac jogged over and took Trav's wrist. He said something too quietly for me or Nihal to hear. We exchanged a look and turned away from the seniors.

After a minute, they approached us. Trav's hands were back in his pockets. He was breathing more steadily.

"So," Isaac said. "Do we have a plan B?"

"We already know where it is," I said quietly. "Where they put our stuff."

We locked eyes. His expression cleared.

"You think so?" he said. "You don't think they'd just put it in their rooms?"

"I don't think they'd risk somebody seeing it."

Trav spoke, sounding hoarse. "You three check the cinema. I'll catch up with you." He pulled his phone from the rustling pocket of his windbreaker. "I'm going to call our sound tech guys. Maybe they know where we can get some last-minute replacement equipment."

"Cool." I glanced from Isaac to Nihal. "Let's go."

♫

When the three of us arrived at the cinema, the dim light seeping under the emergency exit door told us the Minuets were still here. We skirted the building and kept our distance.

"All right," I whispered, as we hunched by a dying pine at the edge of the woods. "How do we get them out?"

"Tear gas," suggested Isaac.

I nodded. "Unleash the wolves."

"Rocks through the windows."

"Set fire to—"

"*Or*," Nihal said, "we could call the safety hotline, like rational people."

The possibility stewed in the freezing air.

"They'll get suspended," I reminded. "All of them."

Isaac shrugged. "Yep, I'm fine with that."

Nihal stayed quiet, picking at the edge of his gray woolen scarf. He was thinking of Connor. I saw it in the distance on his expression.

I nudged Isaac. "You don't want to see their faces when we beat them tomorrow? Fair and square?"

Isaac sighed. "Has anyone ever told you you're as stubborn as a brick?"

"Often."

"Move," Nihal hissed, pulling me behind the tree. After a second, I peered back out at the cinema. A smudge of facial features hovered, murky, behind one of the windowpanes.

I clenched my freezing hands in my pockets, trying to force warmth into my fingertips. "How about the emergency exit?"

"Yeah," Isaac said. "Let's make some noise. Pretend we're unlocking the door."

"How about we stake the place out until they leave?" Nihal said. "They can't sleep there."

I grimaced. "I wasn't built for this weather."

"California," Isaac said, rolling his eyes.

I shouldered him. "Okay, *first* of all—"

"Guys," Nihal said, looking between us with something like suspicion. "A little focus?"

Isaac and I put a few more inches between each other, sheepish. We had to be less obvious.

I couldn't help it, though. I had the buoyant feeling inside my chest of someone who was learning to fly.

I looked at his hand against the tree bark and felt it forceful on my back, careful in my hair, sweeping down my shoulder, scraping across my cheek. I glanced over his features, shadowed in the dark, and thought, *You're mine*. When he caught me looking, the night felt endless again, and we were the only spots of life on a barren plain of snow.

Nihal was still puzzling things out. "How did they get into the Nest in the first place?" he murmured.

"I don't know," I said. "They'd have to have a key, right? Unless someone forgot to lock it."

Isaac shook his head. "I was the last out last night. I locked it."

"They must've stolen a key," I said.

Isaac didn't look convinced. "Who even knows we *have* doubles of the key?"

Nihal's lips thinned. "We should get a move on. Isaac, could you make a diversion? Rattle the door?"

"On it," Isaac said, and loped off through the trees.

I waited until he was out of earshot to look back at Nihal. He was wearing an uncertain-looking frown.

I leaned against the tree. My nose and lips had gone numb. "What's up?" I asked.

"Nothing."

"You sure?"

Nihal closed his eyes hard, his long eyelashes folding up at the top of his cheeks. "No," he murmured. "Just, Connor knows I keep my key in my backpack."

A long second later, he gave me a look that searched for reassurance, his brown eyes deepened by the night.

I shook my head. "Well, text him and ask, then. If he did it."

"I don't want to attack him."

"It's not an attack. It's a—" Movement behind the cinema windows cut me off. As I went quiet, I heard Isaac's voice, distant but sharp, behind the building. He was singing Sam Samuelson's "The Way You Loved Me" at the top of his lungs. Subtle.

The lookout's face vanished from the window. Nihal and I ducked back into the woods, snow crunching beneath our boots. A minute later, a shadowy figure pushed the window up and darted across the lawn. Then the other Minuets poured out. I counted them as they went.

The last one to leave shoved the window down and hooked the board back into place. He broke into a run and tripped not far from us, plowing face-first into the snow with a painful-looking *smack*. I shifted, and a branch snapped beneath my heel.

Nihal tensed. I froze, but the guy had already twisted toward us. It was Connor, a jagged leaf of bruising wrapped over his temple.

He picked himself up and straightened to his towering height, brushing snow off the sleeves of his fleece. Nihal swayed forward, as if to drift out of the woods.

A dozen feet apart, they looked at each other for a long moment. Connor's broad features were weighted with words. For a second, I thought he might approach us—or give us away.

Then he gave his head a shake and backed up, moving after the rest of his group. He broke back into a run and disappeared.

It wasn't until he was long gone that I looked back at Nihal. "Hey," I said quietly. "You good?"

His eyes were still fixed on the spot where Connor had disappeared. A long moment passed, and the tightness around his mouth didn't ease. I could practically smell the disappointment on him, a bitter haze.

Finally, he turned back to me, resignation worn into the creases of his eyes. "Yeah," he said. "Let's go."

♫

The theater was less impressive than I remembered it. In my memory, it was a cavernous space, magnificent but faded, like an ancient opera house in need of restoration. As I stood here at the top of the aisle, though, it looked small and shabby and smelled like winter and dust.

"There's nothing here," Isaac called from the screen at the front. "Just like with the Bear."

I shook my head. "It has to be here."

"Maybe there's a basement," he called. "Like a boiler room sort of situation."

"That," I muttered, "or they're meeting in the bathrooms."

"Up there," Nihal said. He hadn't said a word since we'd come in, drinking the place in with weary scanning eyes. Now he stood halfway down the aisle, pointing up at the back of the theater. The projection window glinted in the center of the wall, a black aperture cut into the paneling.

I exhaled. "Nihal, you're perfect." I scanned the walls for a way up, found nothing, and pushed back into the foyer. A peeling door stood ajar beside the ticket booth. "Out here," I called to the guys, and shouldered into the darkness behind the door.

I held out my phone, revealing the shadowy helix of a spiral staircase. The mold and damp smelled twice as strong in here, pressing the taste of earth into my mouth. The Minuets' snowy shoes had left the steps squeaky. I jogged up. The staircase came out inside the projector room, whose ceiling leaned closely over my head.

The guys came up behind me. "Watch the ceiling," I said to Isaac as he reached the top of the steps.

"Thanks." He craned his head sideways to keep from bumping it. "Jesus. This room is for elves."

Nihal ran a hand along the wall, found a light switch, and flicked it, revealing a long, narrow room. Shelves had come loose from the wooden pegs propping them up; they hung diagonally, handprints disturbing the thick coats of dust they wore. Snatches of drab pale blue glimmered between the concert posters and CD covers the Minuets had plastered over the walls—their own, of course. Except for one Sharps concert poster, which had been mercilessly defaced.

The lone projector hunched in the center of the room, its metal body scabbed with decay, the empty slots for film reels blooming in circles above and below. At the end of a thick cylinder, its lens peered up against the projection window's glass, like a sniper rifle's barrel eyeing a faraway target.

In the corner sat a familiar chest.

"*Shit* yeah." Isaac held out his hands to Nihal and me. We slapped them.

Noise shuffled up from downstairs. "Hello?" said a rich baritone voice. Trav had caught up.

"I'll tell him we found it," Nihal said, winding his way back down the steps. His gray windbreaker rustled away into the dark.

Isaac and I moved to the corner and cracked open the chest, sorting through the materials. Mic carriers had come unzipped and unbuckled. Isaac grimaced. "Trav's going to have to check that everything's still in here," he said, glancing over my shoulder at the staircase.

"Yeah, I'll grab him." I dodged the projector, spiraled down the steps, and stopped.

Nihal's voice was echoing past the door, low and urgent. "—said you were done with this stuff, you promised you'd stop!"

"Nihal, I said I'm sorry," said the other voice. It wasn't Trav.

Lurking in the darkness, I craned my neck to see through the cracked door: Connor Caskey stood in the foyer, dark-cheeked and glassy-eyed from the wind, knit hat pulled low over his arched eyebrows. Everything was bluish in the night.

Had he brought the other Minuets back? Decided to give us away?

No. He was alone, breathless tension on his face, as if he were about to jump out of an airplane.

"Okay, but *are* you sorry?" Nihal said. "Because you've said that before, but actual guilt makes people act differently, and as far as I can see, you haven't gone out of your way to do anything you said you'd do."

"Like what?"

"Like acting like a decent human being! What you drew on Mama's door wasn't funny. It's not funny. Connor, you beat up my best friend!"

I leaned back from the door. It should have felt wonderful to hear that—*best friend*. But guilt soured the glow, seeping around the edges.

"Come on." Connor's voice was low and embarrassed. "Don't be like that. It was just—"

"Answer the question. Did you take the key or not?"

"I . . . look, I didn't want to hurt you or anything. I didn't think you would . . ."

"Didn't think I would what?" Nihal said. "Care? You didn't think I would care that you swung by my room for the first time just to *steal* something from me? Or was it that you didn't think I'd hold you accountable?"

Silence.

The manic edge to Nihal's voice dulled. "Because I suppose, you know, I haven't really done that. I've given you a dozen second chances." He sighed. "I don't understand. I've done everything you asked. I've kept myself in the closet, even though I've wanted to be out for months now, and all I want is—I just want to know you *give a shit*, don't you get it? That's all I've wanted, this whole time."

Silence.

Nihal let out one of his little laughs. It sounded like an injury. "I mean, what," he said, "are you so ashamed of me, you can't even admit you care in secret?"

The hurt in his voice gutted me. Numb, I turned to head back up the stairs. This wasn't for me. I shouldn't have listened to any of it.

"No, come on," Connor murmured. "Of course that's not it. Hey."

"Don't *touch* me," Nihal said. And then they were out of earshot.

When I got back to the projection room, Isaac was holding the Golden Bear.

24

THE BEAR'S BLUNT NOSE GLEAMED, ITS RIDGES OF fur coarse with daubs of gold. Here and there, patches of frosted glass shone through the leaf. The statue was smaller than I'd expected, maybe eight inches tall, and almost delicate, with its outstretched paws less fearsome than pleading. It looked like it knew it was in the wrong hands.

As I approached, Isaac turned the Bear over and over. "What do you think?" he said.

My brain said to put it back. Everything I'd just heard made me want to smash the thing against the wall.

"I don't know," I said.

Isaac set the Bear on the projector. Its heavy resin base thudded onto the metal. "Is Trav coming up?" Isaac asked. "We should show him."

"That wasn't Trav," I said, trying not to sound so hollow.

"Then who?"

"It's one of the Minuets. Nihal's talking to him."

"Shit." Isaac made for the corner. "Let's get our stuff before he tips them off."

"He won't," I said quickly. "He and Nihal are friends."

"Huh." He stopped. "I didn't know the Minuets had 'friends.' Isn't that against their cult rules?"

"Yeah, well." I approached the projector, tracing the contorted line of the Golden Bear's back. "People probably say the same thing about us."

"And they're right," he said. "I don't really care about anyone else." Isaac stopped on the other side of the projector, folding his arms on top of it. We looked at each other for a second. His attention flickered down to my lips, and my body was too warm, all of a sudden. I remembered how kissing him felt, a searing memory.

I leaned on the projector too. Our arms lined up against each other, and he slipped his hand over mine. "How's your face doing?" he asked.

"Not bad."

"Good." His thumb passed across my knuckles.

Feet clattered up the stairs. We jerked back as Trav appeared in the threshold, scanning the room.

His eyes lit on the chest, and he sighed. "Thank God. Let's get this to Arlington."

As he made for the chest, he passed the Golden Bear, and his steps faltered. He stopped by the projector, his eyes fixing on the statue.

"I found it under the—" Isaac started.

Trav's eyes narrowed. Then, in one sharp motion, he smacked the Bear into the air.

It caught the light as it spun for a split second, resin base over distended golden jaws. Then it crashed to the floor, shattering into a thousand glass splinters. And the most wonderful look spread across Trav's face, a look I'd never seen before—a broad, dizzying, don't-give-a-damn sort of smile.

"My mistake," he said. He crossed to the corner, hoisted the chest, and carried it toward the steps. "Let's go."

For once, both Isaac and I were wordless. We followed, stunned, as he sauntered down the stairs.

♫

Connor had disappeared by the time we entered the foyer. Trav split off from us to carry the chest back to Arlington. We offered to help, but Trav seemed determined to martyr himself. "Go home, save voice, and sleep," he ordered, already marching off with the chest, so we trudged through the snowy plains back toward the south of campus.

Our footsteps crunched. Nihal had been quiet since we'd left. I wanted to ask if he was okay, but there was no way to split up from Isaac to do it. The blank look on his face worried me.

Ahead, the theater quad peeked out of the night, dark silhouettes gilded with lamplight. I tried to steer us right, toward the street.

"Can we swing through Palmer?" Nihal said. He sounded shaky. On the verge of a breakdown. "I need to . . . um, to use the bathroom."

Isaac shot me a questioning look. I gave my head a shake as we veered toward Palmer.

We pushed inside as the bell tower boomed a solemn 11:00 p.m. Palmer's side door opened onto a hall lined with dressing rooms that snaked beneath the mainstage theater. Framed posters of student shows crowded the cinderblock walls, signed by their casts, dating back to the forties. The posters made this hall popular with visiting parents, all obsessed with picking out famous people's signatures from when they'd been our age.

Nihal sped forward, head ducked, and disappeared into the guys' bathroom. Isaac flitted from poster to poster, studying the ones with celebrities. I was restless. The sooner we got out of here, the better.

My eyes fixed on one of the girls' dressing rooms, an individual one reserved for a lead. It still had Anabel's name on the door. I could practically see her in front of the wide mirror, beneath the wide white bulbs, penning thick eyeliner in above her eyelashes. I'd always wanted one of those rooms to myself.

"You okay?"

I startled, looking over at Isaac. He leaned against the wall beside me, fiddling with the zipper on his coat.

"Yeah," I said, leaning next to him. Against him.

"Long semester," he said absentmindedly.

I glanced over at him. He looked distant. "I bet," I said. "College apps and all. You're done, right?"

He sighed. "Yeah, thank God."

"Where'd you apply?"

"Um." Isaac rubbed the back of his neck. "You're going to laugh."

"Will I?"

He glanced over at me. "I applied to sixteen schools."

"*What?*" That seemed like a terrible way to spend five hundred dollars or so.

"I know." He tilted his head back, staring at the ceiling. "I don't even know why. My parents didn't ask me to, I just—Trav was applying to fifteen, and my friends from home were doing a dozen each. So." He rubbed his forehead. "Waste of money. I just wish I knew what was happening already. It's gotten to the point where I don't even care if I get into half these places." He thought for a second. "Okay, no, I care. But I care less about getting in than just *knowing*, you know? That there's something after this that I'll be happy with."

"You think you'll miss it?" I said. "Kensington, I mean?"

Isaac laughed.

"What?"

"Nothing." He shook his head. "Just, of course I will. I had no idea who I was before I got here."

The door to the boys' bathroom swung open down the hall, and Nihal drifted through. His silence from before had turned to sluggishness. He stopped just outside the door.

"Ready to go?" Isaac called, but Nihal didn't move.

"Nihal, come on," I said.

Still nothing. Then his eyes fixed on mine, and he said in a small voice, "Julian, can I talk to you?" It barely carried down the hall.

Trading a look with Isaac, I saw my worry reflected in his eyes. I turned back to Nihal. "Yeah." I jogged down the hall to him. "What's up?" I said as I broke from my jog, ready to console him, all but ready to tell him to cry into my shoulder if he wanted. Nihal pushed back into the bathroom. I followed him in.

As the door shut behind us, Nihal swung the first stall open.

My body went cold. A poster for the monologue showcase hung on the back of the door. I remembered Ash Crawford saying, "*The best place to hang up posters . . .*"

Nihal's brown eyes brushed me up and down, and I felt an inch tall. His scrutiny turned me into a jester in my false face and bulky clothes—an actor who'd walked out into the world wearing some inappropriate costume.

"So," he said, tapping the photograph. "That's you. You're a girl?"

There was no use denying it.

I slid my glasses off and nodded.

A long moment passed. Nihal looked back at the poster, then down at the water beaded on the rubber ridges of his Bean boots. He tugged at the edge of his turban. Deep red, today.

He was waiting for me to fix it. Waiting for my apology. Back in the Prince tower, the same air of unhappy disappointment had hung over him.

What could I say? "Sorry" seemed so minuscule.

My time ran out. Nihal spoke. "I feel like an absolute idiot right now," he said, as frankly and disinterestedly as he would've said any other sentence.

I blinked fast, baffled. Everyone had bought it, not just him. He had to know that, right?

"I'm just thinking," he went on, "about the night I told you all that about me and Connor." His lips moved a bit farther than necessary to form each word, and otherwise every other muscle of his face was perfectly still. This was anger. This was what it looked like on him. My heart dropped.

"I was standing there," he said, "and I was thinking, *Thank God, someone who gets it*. I felt lucky, you know? Grateful. I'd been so nervous about telling everyone, to the point where I literally felt ill, and suddenly, oh, divine providence! Here's someone who can get why, and who can understand what it feels like. All of it. That's what I was thinking." His mouth tugged down at both corners, and I realized all at once that he was on the verge of tears.

He finally met my eyes. The firestorm of anger and hurt there made me want to hide my face behind my hands.

"And what were *you* thinking?" he said. "You must've been standing there calculating. *How do I act like I understand? How can I fool him about this, too? What an inconvenient roadblock.*"

I had no words. That was wrong, so wrong. But how could I convince him? What was the strategy here?

"I can't do this. What a cherry on top of the perfect day." Nihal drew the back of his hand over his eye, crushing back a tear before it arrived. He sucked down a huge, shaking breath.

"I wasn't trying to fool you," I said. "You have to believe me. It wasn't—it wasn't *about* you."

Hurt bled across his expression. "Of course it wasn't," he said. "I didn't say it had to be. Funny how that works. Sometimes you want people to—not even to put you *first*, or anything, but to just *think* about you a little, you know?"

His words expanded outward. This wasn't just me. This was Connor lashing out first and apologizing later. This was his parents treating him like an afterthought, gushing over his med school sister like he didn't exist. This was everything in his life, and I was the tipping point.

"I'm sorry," I said. "You deserve better."

Nihal looked so tired. The anger in the air had gotten lost somewhere.

I peeled off every layer I had. He deserved my honesty, even if it was too late. "There were a million times I was going to say something, but I kept choking, because, I guess, what if you hated me, or gave me away? I—I tried out for Sharps because of the competition; it was supposed to be simple. I just . . . got in over my head. I got scared."

Nihal sized me up with new eyes. His careful examination of me seemed complete. "I don't know what to tell you," he said in a voice stiff with formality. "Everyone's scared."

He walked out. The door drifted shut, leaving me drifting, too, out on a massive ocean. I'd floated out into the doldrums and only just realized I had no map, no oars, no compass. There was no getting back to where I'd started.

♫

It took me a long time to get ahold of myself. I came out fifteen minutes later to find an empty hall. Isaac was gone.

He must have followed Nihal. Maybe he'd tried to explain for me. Hopefully not—it wouldn't do anything except get Nihal mad at him. Not productive. Not useful.

None of this had been useful. Thirty-six hours, and I'd be slinking away with my tail between my legs, a failure whose chances had run right out. Nihal would tell the guys. That would be it.

I slipped my glasses into my pocket. The poster across the hall caught my eye: *Les Misérables*. The cast stood in double-file, military coats neatly buttoned, tattered dresses hanging off shoulders. All smiling as if they'd been invited back for a half-dozen curtain calls.

I moved down the hall, out through the hush of night, and back to Burgess. In my room, I shed my disguise.

Somebody was humming in the shower when I got there, in the stall next to me. "The Clockmaker." Over and over, as too-hot water coated the gummy flip-flops on my feet.

When I got back to my room, I packed up my life at Kensington.

Pencils and notebooks went in my backpack. The clothes I would take home barely filled my suitcase. None of the boys' clothes—I folded all that into a brown paper bag and left it on my dresser. They could do what they wanted with it when I left. Good riddance.

My desk lamp flickered, casting a blip of darkness over the room. The momentary dark reminded me how exhausted I was. Today seemed years long.

Anabel's knock came on my door. I glanced at the clock—eleven thirty, my next-to-last check-in. "Present."

Running a hand over the *Les Mis* poster by my window, I thought of the smiling Kensington cast, and a strange sense of peace washed over me. Why should I stay? What did I have to show for this place, after all? A list of failed auditions, a roll call of people I'd let down, and a fistful of rose-tinted memories.

And Isaac. For one afternoon, Isaac. I shouldn't have let him sneak up on me.

I crawled onto my bed, resisted the urge to collapse beneath the sheets. Another quick series of knocks hit the door. "I'm here, Anabel," I repeated.

The door opened, but it wasn't Anabel.

It was like he'd read my mind.

Isaac closed the door. "Hey." He crossed the room, taking in my messy suitcase, my half-opened drawers, and the makeup spread across my desk. He stopped by my bed.

"You doing okay?" Isaac said. He unbuttoned his felt coat, loosening the scarf at his neck.

"How's Nihal?" I asked.

"I don't know. He didn't say anything. We went back for check-in, and . . . yeah, nothing."

My hands were folded tight in my lap. "Right."

"How'd he find out?"

"There was a poster in Palmer for my Greek Monologue showcase."

A tight silence.

Isaac's hand landed on mine, his string-roughened fingertips a reassuring scrape. "It's okay," he said.

"But it's not," I managed. The words broke the seal. For the second time that day, my eyes burned with tears. I hadn't meant for it to be like this. I'd been thinking only of the music, and of the future.

No. You were thinking only of yourself.

I tried my best to keep my breaths quiet. It was late. Nothing worse than an inconsiderate breakdown. Nothing worse than being selfish.

"Hey," Isaac said. "Hey. Blue jay."

I managed a bit of a smile.

His hand weighed briefly on the side of my neck, still cold from outside, and then he lifted my chin. I looked into his kind, uncertain eyes. "So it's not okay," he said. "But it'll be better tomorrow. At least a little."

I wiped my eyes, avoiding the tender swollen spots.

"There's the competition, and then he has all of break to think it over," Isaac said, building up steam. "I swear, by the time we get back, start up rehearsals and everything, he'll probably think it's funny."

My throat grew tight.

"Isaac?"

"Yeah?"

"I'm not coming back."

The words sat there between us, impossibly huge. I searched his face for shock. Confusion. I didn't find it. Instead, his eyebrows drew close in determination.

"You can't quit," he said. "It doesn't matter that you're a girl. We need you there."

"No, I meant—"

"I need you there." His words rushed out. An accident.

Our eyes locked, our mouths shut. My heart went missing for a moment, wandered off between beats, leaving me with tingling fingertips.

I sank into a strange haze. For once, my head wasn't consumed with whatever might come next. The boy in front of me was a past and a present and a future. I felt outside time altogether, with him looking at me like that, knowing everything and wanting somehow to know more.

Nothing is so startling, so awakening, as when someone looks at you and you know they see you. Not just what you've polished to smoothness and perfection but the jagged edges, the rough patches, and the uncertain tangles in your center. All of you.

I rose to my knees with a creak from the bed frame and cupped my palm against the back of his neck. I leaned in and pressed my lips to the line of his eyebrow. The tip of his nose. He was perfectly still; I could tell his breath was held. I kissed his mouth deep and slow, and as he shifted against me, I closed my eyes tight and let myself vanish. I tilted my head and breathed him in, a slow inhalation through my sore nose. He was as cold as new snow. The lapels of his coat were chilly as I held them.

He drew back, his coat rustling. "Hey," he whispered, his hands curled loosely around my forearms. "We're going to figure this out, okay? I'll help with the guys—it'll work out. I know it'll—"

"Hush." I hooked one finger into the neck of his T-shirt and pulled. He slipped up onto the bed with me. I pushed his coat off his shoulders, hung it from one of the bedposts, and he kicked his winter boots off. Then his hands warmed my waist, and the rough wool of his scarf scraped up against my collarbones. I tugged it from around his neck and let my hand trace the angle of his jaw, the column of his neck, the light muscles over his bony shoulders. We keeled toward the bed and kissed, and with his back to the light on my desk, his face was shadowed and his lips were sweet, and his crooked fingers drew music out of my skin.

He touched me with the barest traces, like I was something he was imagining with his hands, some formless collection of fire or wind. I pressed closer, urging him, wanting him, until his hands closed tightly around my waist. We kissed for God knew how long. Long enough for my lips to learn the rhythms he kissed by, forceful until he turned meek, wanting until he turned fearful, the music until the quiet.

"Isaac?" I said, finally.

"Yeah?"

I swallowed my pride. It was late and dark and I didn't want to be alone. "Will you stay?"

"Sure," he murmured. "Didn't want to put my shoes back on, anyway."

A smile tugged at my lips. "Hit the light, would you?"

He leaned over to flick the desk lamp off. The sudden darkness made him tentative as he settled against me, settling one wiry arm over my waist. He dropped a kiss onto my forehead before drawing the covers over us.

"I like winding up with you," he murmured into the stillness, a breath's worth of words that ghosted across my cheek.

"I . . . yeah, you too," I whispered back, inelegant, insufficient. My voice, which had gotten me so far, gave out. My heart pulsed slow and painful and full. I moved closer, holding on tight to him, and for an instant I felt like I had it: the whole world, gathered up in my arms.

THE DAY OF THE COMPETITION, THE SUN HUNG LOW and blinding, turning buildings to ice sculptures and the stamped-down plains of snow into sheet silver. The talk in McKnight over lunch—the last school meal of the semester—was ferocious, and the glares the other groups gave me and Isaac when we walked through the Arlington doors were merciless. I'd taken concealer and foundation to my face in thick swipes this morning, covering up the creatively colored bruises that made me look like a badly conceived Jackson Pollock knockoff.

Kensington was, I decided, the worst place on earth to host any sort of competition. I expected bloodshed after the winners' announcement.

"Even if Nihal told Trav, he won't bring it up," Isaac muttered as we headed toward the greenroom, where warm-up sounds issued beneath the door, muffled cascades of lip trills and humming. "He's not going to throw the competition by dropping a bombshell."

"Fingers crossed," I muttered back. I pushed into the greenroom.

I instantly knew that Isaac was right. Trav's eyes brushed over me as if I weren't there.

Had Nihal told him?

I couldn't look at Nihal, but I felt him standing against the wall, shoulders folded in, guard up. Our awareness of each other radiated across the room, so cold with shame, I couldn't believe the guys didn't feel the chill.

After our warm-up, during sound check, I caught sight of Connor Caskey. He wore an unconcerned smirk, as if absolutely nothing of interest had happened in the last twenty-four hours, as if Trav hadn't destroyed their prized possession. The other Minuets weren't so restrained. They shot us looks that were so furious they crossed the line into being sort of comical.

We retreated to the greenroom. Soon enough, the other groups poured in alongside us to wait. We huddled up in separate corners, trading narrowed looks. As six o'clock approached, the distant whisper of the approaching crowd turned into a murmur, then into a colony's buzz of voice. Every seat in that hall would be full.

The stage manager called us out, and we filed backstage. Nobody spoke. We straightened ties, sipped water, set down water bottles, cleared throats, and adjusted cuffs. Our sound tech guys finally dropped Official Sound Guy Face, offering us a pair of smiles and a "break a leg." We waited as the lights faded and the sounds of the crowd died.

In the darkness, I curled my toes up in the ends of my uncomfortable shoes. I flexed my fingers around the barrel of my mic. The boiling water in my stomach bubbled up and up.

We walked out in the darkness, curved into formation, and

the quiet buzz of the pitch pipe rang to my right. I imagined my note, a fifth above, and cupped it in my throat, waiting.

The lights blasted on.

I made them out in the front row—a row of silhouettes with vaguely famous hairstyles. Aural Fixation. Three months ago, I'd stood alone in this exact spot, scanning seven different silhouettes. *Are you nervous?* Isaac had asked.

I wasn't nervous anymore, even with the waiting silence of a thousand people forming a thick bubble ahead. So many darkened faces in that crowd, and all I felt was impatience.

The eight of us drew breath together, lifted mics to our lips, and Erik spat the beat into life. We sang.

The familiar notes vibrated up from my chest, instinct guiding my motions. Out in the audience, one by one, the people evaporated. The distant back curves of the auditorium folded away. The spotlights became an indistinct flood, and all I could feel was the soaring pop of the tenor lines as they spun out from my lips, and the slight tremor in the back of my calf as I fell into line with the guys.

"And you asked, 'When you gonna tell the truth?' and I said, 'Never.'"

Nihal and I brushed shoulders, and my stage smile felt, all of a sudden, stretched too far. A flash of panic veiled my vision, and I snuck a deep breath between phrases.

The end of the first song approached fast, the stream-of-consciousness whirl of performance stealing time from me. I pivoted into our next formation, standing by Marcus's shoulder as he's picked up the solo. His gingery eyelashes glinted bronze when he squeezed his eyes shut. Every ounce of his awkward energy was let loose, his voice bright and sweet, his hand clenched around his mic, pale in the stage light.

Marcus handed the solo to Isaac, whose assured tenor spun up into the stratosphere and back with perfect control. Behind him, we cut out and fell back into place, punctuated silence with bursts of sound, and he hardly seemed to breathe, holding everything together single-handedly.

Seven voices dropped out at once, leaving Isaac's vibrato over voluminous silence. A cheer erupted from the crowd, the baritones slipped up into falsetto to back him, and Erik shifted into a slower beat, a steady thump-thump-thump. Chord by chord, we transitioned into the second song. Careful and measured as always. This whole discipline walked a tightrope—one flat note and everything unraveled. We had to glue ourselves together to make it through.

The others peeled back, allowing Jon Cox and me to go forward to the lip of the stage. Our voices locked together as we navigated a tight harmony.

"And your touch is heaven falling,
And your eyes say love is blind,
And your fingertips keep hauling
'Til the stars are realigned . . ."

Every time I changed expression, every time I hinted at a smile, pressure clamped over the edges of my eye sockets. My face was stiff and painful, my nose felt eight sizes too wide, and under the heat of the lights, I worried I was sweating away the foundation. I tilted my head up too far, trying not to think, and the center spotlights gazed like two white eyes into mine. In a flash of blindness, I closed my eyes and let the echoes of light pulse against the backs of my eyelids. My voice soared high. As I drew breath, feet shifted behind me, whispers of dress shoe to stage that were masked by thick harmonies. Pops of falsetto startled out of the melody; the deep, swinging pendulum of bass kept our time.

My eyes cracked open again. The world solidified, and Jon Cox and I navigated the solo toward its end.

"I fall into bed with my hands turning blue,
And my aching head
Is full of you."

The background textures faded as Jon Cox and I backed up into our cluster, Mama's chest to my back, Erik's shoulder reassuring against my arm. A second's silence sewed us together before Nihal stepped forward, bursting the seams.

I didn't want to focus on his voice, but when Nihal sang, I heard the personal care of my dad singing me a lullaby when I was younger. The words pierced too close, this time through.

"So I asked the clockmaker
How much it would break her,
Her cogs and bells and wooden ledges,
Her painted face and gilded edges,
To turn back the dial To turn back the dial
For a while."

The song rose and fell like a tide, and the sound turned wispy and sparse. Trav had abandoned his fancy cutouts and creative chord shifts for this transition. He didn't need them here, cluttering up the thread of melody.

We settled into a staggered formation, four and four, as Erik dropped the percussion into a slow hiss and scrape, like the hush of a steel brush against a cymbal. I looked between the window of Isaac and Nihal's shoulders, and I wanted to reach out to them, all of a sudden, take them and hold on, dig in my nails.

Then they shifted, and the last thoughts—the last regrets—fled my mind.

The last song arrived in unison: E major, "Halloween." We sang with tightly closed lips, humming syllables, so that I could practically hear the piano hammers striking. My freshman year song. Trav took up the solo, and his tentative delivery knocked me into remembrance, back to the start of Kensington, back to the beginning of everything, back to this: the twisted *A* of Arthur's Arch and the crows casting sharp-winged shadows as the car pulls up the drive. There I am in the back. I'm peering out of the windows up at the dappled stone, awestruck.

"A couple of weeks ago, I tried to go back
Did I tell you this before?
Back to the, back to the, back to the place
Where yours was the second drawer."

All over again, I'm sitting in my first day of class, when Reese tells us that if she hears one of us call her by her last name, she'll walk out the door and we'll just have to wait, useless, for the time to run out. I'm walking out of my first audition, exhilarated, nerves jangling, and leaning against the stone wall. I can smell the autumn air baking above Palmer's stone steps.

"I stood in the threshold,
And all of the cobwebs,
Glimmering dusty and bright,
Reminded me of the gossamer-fine
Silences we'd always tie around each other at night."

I'm staying up late one night freshman year, having a talk

with Lydia that lasts until my throat hurts, wandering through every topic that matters, faith, fear, and hope, and somehow I can't remember a single word of it a year later; I'm on a walk in the spring of my sophomore year, one of the first beautiful days that'll drag us kicking out of the cold, just me and the countryside and that massive sky sending breezes and sunlight down in patches; I'm all over this town, and in the winters it eats up my footprints with fresh snow until nothing's left.

"And it still smells like Halloween,
And the way things used to be.
Will someone take ahold of me
And promise there's something inside me
I might want to be?"

I'm leaning over Carrie's counter, trying to pull Michael back at the shoulder as he waves vigorously, *parlando Italiano*, into her gut laughter, clearing the air with it; I'm holding him by the elbows on the Palmer stage, his mouth on my neck, our legs twined, my ankles resting heavy on his calves; I'm heart-swollen at his graduation. I'm standing opposite him in my kitchen in San Francisco as he tells me there's been someone for months. There's been Alaina for months.

"A couple of years from now,
I'll stop looking back,
At least, that's what they've all implied
Back to the, back to the, back to the time
I let you come and curl up inside."

I'm in that kitchen for an eternity, imagining every time over those three months that I looked into his eyes and thought he was mine, only mine; then time's jolting onward and I'm drowning in summertime, feeling naïve and small and lost; I'm moving into Burgess alone and pinning posters to my walls alone; I'm scratching notes in black pen onto yellow college-ruled paper alone; I'm shearing off my hair and a great weight is falling from me; I am singing him away, back into my history; I am kissing someone else in a tower that pierces the sky and feeling something new; I am letting him go, I am letting him go, I am letting him go in all these tiny ways.

"I'll find in a city,
Some gray, thirsty block
A lightning-rod building that soars:
Acquiring sky, and reaching so high,
I'll leave those memories all the way down at the doors."

I have all of this to keep. Two and a half years of calls home, of bundling up against the weather, of soupy morning mists and fresh fruit every night, running lines until I know them more intimately than my own name, trying to clear my head, hoping for a nod of approval from Reese Garrison, sneaking into an abandoned cinema, sipping smooth whiskey in a field under the stars, brushing Isaac's hand in the dark, relaxing into my armchair in the Crow's Nest. It all clings to my ankles, it drags me back. It's mine.

"And it'll smell like Christmas trees,
The scent of something new and clean
But in all of my realities, I'll never forget
I'll never forget what I've seen."

There is no moment of calm before the surge of the cheering, just the audience's roar, eating up the last shreds of sound, two thousand beating hands, a thousand voices giving themselves back in appreciation.

26

THE REST OF THE COMPETITION, FROM THE OTHER groups' performances to the judges' deliberation, took about thirty years. My heart was pattering like a rabbit's by the end. Carnelian's arrangements had been so complex that I couldn't imagine what they looked like on a page, the Precautionary Measures had a set of soloists who could easily have outsung half the artists on the radio, and the Minuets may have been terrible people, but their performance, like all the best performances, made me want to sing.

Finally, the nine members of Aural Fixation took the stage to raucous applause. The other groups, also huddled back here in darkened masses of suits and dresses, fell silent. I edged closer to the curtain. I couldn't see who had taken the microphone, but I assumed it was that tenor, Watson, with the cult following.

After the applause cleared away, Watson said, "First of all, wow. Thanks for inviting us into this beautiful space. It's really an honor to visit the place that helped make our newest members into such remarkable talents." A few hands waved from the front of their group, the Kensington alums, pandering to the crowd.

Polite applause. Watson continued, "These six groups have

made our decision incredibly difficult. Please, another round of applause for the hard work everyone's put in."

The audience obliged with a short, impatient burst of clapping.

"With no further ado," he said, "we'd like to announce that the group to accompany us on our winter tour will be the Sharp-shooters."

The crowd erupted. The guys and I burst into excitement. "*Yes, yes, yes,*" Isaac was yelling, all but lost in the applause. Jon Cox jumped onto Mama's back, and Mama stabbed his fist into the air. Trav looked like he'd been clocked in the forehead with something heavy, his eyes blankly searching the darkness of the house, and I imagined his parents sitting out there in the crowd, swept away in everybody's appreciation for Trav's work.

Onstage, Aural Fixation waved us out. We ran between the curtains. Everything was bright and delirious and unreal. And then, as we came up to them to shake hands, to accept our recognition, I froze. Shock struck the smile from my face.

They'd parted. At the front of the group stood the alumni, and among them—right there, like a bad dream—stood Michael.

Michael, eyes like obsidian, copper skin burnished by stage light. Michael, tall and handsome, still himself.

My feet reacted before my thoughts, carrying me back in a rush. I made it offstage just as Watson started talking again, but the other Sharps were looking after me, and Michael hadn't stopped staring. I dashed for the greenroom. A hand—Victoria's hand, small and strong—caught my arm. "Hey. Are you okay?"

"Stage fright," I managed, which wasn't technically a lie. I darted into the greenroom, around the L-shaped room's corner, and burst through a back door, which led me into a stairwell.

My fingers clamped around the iron railing, and I levered myself to the steps, a haze settling around me, an insulating shroud of panic.

Why was he here? How could he be here like this, sprung on me like a bear trap? How couldn't I have known?

I'd imagined him in college classes, in fancy lecture halls. Or waiting tables, maybe, going to rehearsals at night in New York City or Chicago, walking fast with his coat collar up in a pair of stiff corners, his head down and hands in his pockets. Tiny in the biggest of cities. And now he was fifty steps from me. His knobbly knuckles that he cracked absentmindedly, and the blueberry smell of his aftershave, right there. The memory of him darted across my skin like referred pain.

The call during the retreat, I realized. If I'd picked up, I would have known. This must have been what he was calling about. Maybe he'd wanted to see me when he came back to campus.

And now this. We'd won. I was days from getting on a plane to Europe, days from seeing city after city that I might never see otherwise. I'd gotten all the way to the end, even as my lifelines slipped away, the guys starting to figure it out one by one.

It didn't matter. He was here now, and he knew, and that was it. I'd run out of second chances.

I shivered. This stairwell bottomed out in an exit, and cold leaked up toward me. I stood. I would grab my coat from the greenroom, run out, and that would be the last of it.

I grabbed the greenroom doorknob, slipped in, and collided with a suit-jacketed torso. Nihal reeled back from me as if burned.

The L-shaped room had filled to the brim.

Heads turned in a unanimous wave. Attention trapped me

in the threshold. Aural Fixation and the Sharps stood opposite, and—*God, why?*—Dr. Graves and Dr. Caskey had appeared beside the television monitor in the corner, near the door to the stage. Dr. Graves looked like it was physically paining him to stand so close to Dr. Caskey. Connor stood at his dad's shoulder, the button of his sport coat undone, fiddling with his red tie.

I held Isaac's eyes, the only point of reassurance in the mass of men and boys.

"Are you okay?" Marcus blurted. "What's going on?"

There was no use trying to deflect it. I stayed silent.

Michael cleared his throat. "We know each other," he said. "She's my ex-girlfriend."

Eyebrows rose. A long moment of disbelieving silence followed.

"Wh-*what*?" Trav said, his voice a rasp of shock. He peered at me as if I were a bright light.

"Yeah, I'm a girl. I'm just . . ."

"Acting," said Mama, sounding weak.

Dr. Caskey's gimlet eyes bulged. A few of the Aural Fixation guys shifted, like they would rather have been anywhere else. Dr. Graves's gash of a mouth was slightly open, and I wondered if he was reconsidering the whole *man up* suggestion.

The stares became too much. My eyes found my feet, and I studied the hard, shining lines of my shoes.

"For real, Jordan, what on earth?" said Michael's voice. The words shrank me. I got the distinct feeling that I'd had a clairvoyant nightmare about this situation.

"Wait, your name's not even Julian?" Jon Cox said. "Are you also secretly a swarm of bees wearing human skin?"

"Stop it," Isaac said.

The Sharps turned to him. Disbelief slackened Jon Cox's face. "You *knew*?"

"Yeah, but guys, this doesn't change anything." Isaac's voice strengthened. "Nothing's different, all right? We still won. We're still—it doesn't matter."

Dr. Caskey let out an incredulous laugh. "All right, excuse me," he said with icy precision. "It *matters*, Mr. Nakahara, because your group is an historic all-male society intrinsic to the culture of the academy. An unchanging part of the landscape of student life since 1937."

Isaac lifted his chin, defiant, new president clashing against the old. "Okay, sure, but what does that mean without the rhetoric? What's the actual *reason* Jordan can't sing with us? So she's a girl. So what? She's got the tenor range. She worked just as hard as the rest of us."

He shot an urgent glance at the guys for backup.

Trav cleared his throat. "Yes," he said. "True." Marcus nodded along at his shoulder.

Jon Cox and Erik shrugged simultaneously, still looking baffled. "Well, yeah," Mama said, "but technically she has a contralto range, not a tenor."

I could barely look at the seven of them. Gratitude drew my throat tight. I hoped they could read it on my face, because if I opened my mouth I thought I might be sick. Was there a chance this could still happen?

To my side, Nihal stayed quiet.

The Aural Fixation guys were murmuring. Michael was bowed into the pack. I felt disconnected from the sight of him, from the knobby crown of his head down to the neon laces of his sneakers. The shock of his appearance had worn off. Now it just felt strange not to want him.

Eventually, Watson cleared his throat. "Yeah, we don't mind if you guys are coed. The main thing is that it's weird to tour with sixteen guys and one teenage girl, but we have ladies on crew, so it might be all right, depending on whether your parents—"

Dr. Graves cleared his throat. "Hang on." He sounded a bit dazed. "Let's talk through some steps. You just—you can't do this as the group exists currently. For this tour, this . . . young lady . . . needs to be accounted for under her real name, for liability reasons among others. For her to travel as part of the group, she needs to be formally registered with the group. And for her to be allowed in, you need to get a recategorization petition from Student Life, to change the status of the organization."

"We can do that," Isaac said. "All the offices are open until the seventeenth, right? We're not supposed to fly out for a couple days, so I'll just stay and—"

Dr. Caskey shook his head, waving Isaac's words away with a confident hand. "I hate to break it to you, gentlemen, but that switch is never going to happen. Your group has a lot of influential alumni who would be diametrically opposed. Risking their relationship with the academy over this?" He clicked his tongue and shook his head. "I doubt it, guys, I really doubt it. You're not just going to need Dr. Graves's signature; you're going to need the dean's, too, and I'm afraid I'm just not going to put my name to it."

Resignation weighted my body. That was it, then. Dr. Caskey had the final say, and it was over.

Caskey finally looked to me. Something malicious was in his eyes. “Besides,” he said, “it wouldn’t be appropriate to reward this kind of behavior.”

The patronizing tone made my entire body heat up a degree. “What behavior?” I ground out, finally finding my voice.

“The Kensington motto: ‘Art through innovation, art through perseverance, and—” he raised one eyebrow,“—art through honesty. Music is nothing without honesty.”

Dr. Caskey looked around at the Sharps. His voice grew an edge. “This event has made you all representatives of Kensington to the public. This is an embarrassment.” He looked back at me. “And frankly, I’m not sure what’s more immature: the idea that you could conceivably manage an international tour under a pseudonym, or your unwillingness to accept responsibility for months of lying to your community.” His eyes narrowed. “I’ve never seen such a waste of a Kensington education.”

The sentence landed like a blow. I knew everyone felt it hitting me, because the room took on the absolute silence of held breath. In the vacuum, I tried to breathe, and tears needled my eyes. Dr. Caskey’s voice sounded like the one in the back of my mind, assuring me that I would never succeed. I was a waste. I was disposable. I was nothing.

Then a dry voice rang out to my left, clear and confident. “Actually,” Nihal said, “since she’s an acting student, I’d say this whole thing reflects pretty positively on what she’s learned.”

Chuckling broke the silence. I looked up. The Sharps were all glaring murder at Dr. Caskey, except Nihal, who was looking at me now. I met his brown eyes. One side of his mouth lifted, and I read the beginnings of forgiveness out of his expression.

Dr. Caskey's voice strained. "I can guarantee disciplinary action on this. There's a Board meeting at the turn of the year; I'll ask them what they recommend."

Dr. Graves finally broke out of his stupor. "No. That's absurd," he said flatly. "There's been no technical rule-breaking in the slightest. In fact, if she were doing this as an independent study for a sociology class, I'm sure she'd be getting high grades." He looked at me, exasperation in the grim lines of his face. "I'd be *extremely* surprised if you faced disciplinary action."

"Well," Dr. Caskey said, turning a glare on Graves, "that's a matter of opinion. We'll see."

I found myself faintly smiling. Confidence coursed through me, dissolving my guilt, rolling a weight off my back. It was strange. In so many ways, I'd failed: I couldn't tour. I would never graduate from Kensington. I had nothing on paper for these months of effort. But with the Sharps at my back, I felt a little invincible. I stood tall and clear-headed and myself, sensitive and strong, voice unhidden, a mix of everything masculine I'd stopped suppressing and everything feminine I would never let go of. This was finally me, the most perfect me I'd ever been.

"Well, I'm not sorry," I said, because tomorrow afternoon I'd be on a plane to California, and this sad middle-aged man's threats would never touch me. "I'm not going to pretend it was a mistake. I would do it again in a second."

I took a breath. I let it go. I let it all go. "I changed for this. Didn't you ever want something that much?"

Dr. Caskey looked like he'd tasted something sour. Beside him, Dr. Graves was examining me as if he'd never seen me before.

After a long silence, Dr. Caskey zipped up his coat. "I hope you all have a restful winter holiday," he said, clipped. "I'll be in touch."

He strode for the door and disappeared. Connor hurried after him, his eyes stuck to his black dress shoes.

Nobody could meet my eyes. There was nothing left to do.

"I've got to go pack," I said.

And I left.

I WEDGED THE LAST PAPERBACK IN AT THE EDGES OF the box. Its cover crumpled, and I straightened the aging card stock, grappled the box up into my arms with a grunt, and let it thud onto my empty desk.

The room smelled like Burgess always did in the winter: like the uniformly stale air from the heating vents. It was enough to give you a headache, the close, dry grip of it. I closed my eyes, trying to will away the throb of my swollen face.

I wedged a nail into my key ring and maneuvered my room key into my palm. I gripped it, the teeth bit into my fingers, and with a hard lump in my throat, I walked down the hall to Anabel's room, wig and makeup on.

"Hey," she said when I knocked, pulling the door open. "Jordan." She wore loose gray sweats, her hair in a sloppy ponytail. Cursive on her T-shirt read, *Connecticut girls do it better*. I wondered what "it" was.

Anabel played with the end of her ponytail. "Look, I went to the a cappella thing, and I heard what happened after."

My cheeks burned. After a second's silence, I pulled off my wig. "Well, that traveled fast."

"Connor's telling everyone."

"Great. Awesome."

She folded her arms, leaning against the doorframe. "I just wanted to say, everyone I've talked to thinks you're kind of a badass."

I blinked rapidly. "They what?"

"Yeah. Going undercover? Who does that? I mean, every Kensington kid wants to be that kid who breaks the mold, but this is, like, next level."

I smiled weakly and looked down at my flats, too exhausted to be relieved that the student body didn't think I was the weirdest person ever to live and breathe. After a second, I held up my key. "Should I give this to you, or . . . ?"

"Reese, probably." Her smile faltered. "She only told me this afternoon that you're leaving."

We stood in the sort of uncomfortable silence you share with people in waiting rooms, not sure whether to discuss what's next.

"Well, I'm going to—" I gestured toward Reese's room.

"Right."

"Okay." I headed down the hall.

"Jordan?" Anabel called.

I looked back over my shoulder.

"Um, good luck in California," she said. "You'll be great wherever you are."

I found a smile. "You too."

Her door closed. I let out a slow breath, turned back toward the end of the hall, and found Isaac standing there, looking into my open room, staring at the blank walls and stripped bed. When he faced me, his expression told me all I needed to know. I'd seen the same look on Michael's face at the end of last year. Goodbye looked like a crease between the eyebrows and a thinning mouth.

"You told me last night," he said. "You said—but I didn't get it. I'm an idiot. I thought you meant you were leaving the group."

"You're not an idiot."

"Why are you leaving?" He approached me.

I gripped my room key so tight, it threatened to cut. "Money."

"That's bullshit," he said.

My palms grew warm. "I mean, but it's not."

"But it's bullshit. You shouldn't have to leave."

"But I do have to, okay?" My voice rose. I couldn't keep it down. "So it's not like some unrealistic, unreasonable—it's just real life, okay? This is how it works, Isaac." I swallowed, shaking my head.

I could imagine the novel's worth of responses piling up in his head, but all he let through was, "Why didn't you tell us?"

The softness of his voice sliced through me. I heard the real question. *Why didn't you tell me?*

"I tried to," I said. "But if you don't say it out loud, sometimes it feels like it won't really happen, you know?" It was hopeless, trying to explain why denial helped, why it felt better to delay the inevitable than to move forward. "Like there's something at the last second that's going to dive in out of nowhere, and save you, and fix everything."

Isaac's hand found mine. Squeezed. "I want to."

I chuckled. It sounded horrible, a grinding little sound. "You can't."

"I know. But I want to." His voice was quiet, fierce, earnest. As if the sentiment itself could stitch everything back together. Heat coursed through me, and a second later, gratitude. Sometimes good intentions couldn't do a thing except make you feel less alone, and sometimes that was enough.

"Why're you here, anyway?" I murmured.

He tugged on my hand, leading me down the hall. "Come on."

I headed to Reese's room, slid my key under her door, and followed him.

♫

The Nest's red door creaked open, and silence took the tower's interior, a swell of a hush in the aftermath of voices. We stepped in, the door closed behind us, the flag rippled, and I leaned back against it, taking the black fabric between my thumb and forefinger.

"Hey," I said. Six pairs of eyes were riveted on my face. On my makeup, probably.

No—seven. Victoria was sitting beside her brother.

She was the first to speak. "Um, so," she said.

For a second, I didn't understand. Then I looked over at Isaac, and it clicked into place. He hadn't figured it out when he'd seen my empty room. Victoria had told them what I couldn't: that Kensington's ivory tower had grown too tall and too narrow, crowding me out.

My cheeks went hot, but I refused to feel shame.

"You're transferring back to San Francisco," Trav said, looking severe. "From a musical standpoint, it would have been helpful to know this ahead of time."

I couldn't help a bit of a smile. I could have predicted that reaction down to the word. It was sort of comforting, Trav being as unchanging as Prince Library itself.

"Look," Jon Cox said, "if we can do anything to . . . I don't know, help out—"

"You can't," I said, on gut instinct. But for some reason, I thought of Reese's eyes as she'd spoken to me in the office that day. *We can take this little by little.* And I thought, *Well, couldn't I borrow money for a plane ticket back to campus after break?* The idea of asking for a loan made a defensive instinct flare in the back of my head, but it was a start, right? Wasn't there something people could do to help?

But no. Not unless they changed my parents' minds. They'd wanted to file my transfer application since the day I'd set foot on campus.

The ensuing quiet felt like the moment of silence we took at the start of every meal, that full, reflective hush. "Thanks for having my back earlier," I said.

"Of course," Trav said.

"So . . . what's going on?"

Nihal cleared his throat and held up a sheet of paper. A fine-tipped pen hung behind his ear, casting a shadow across his eye. "I printed the recategorization petition and filled it out. I talked to Dr. Graves, and frankly, I think it would kill him if the Minuets got to tour instead of us, so he signed it. Isaac's going to visit Student Life and file it tomorrow before they close up for the semester."

I frowned, uncomprehending. "But the dean needs to sign it. Caskey needs to sign it."

"No. A cappella groups aren't discipline-exclusive, so *a dean* needs to sign it." Nihal passed me the paper. Beside Graves's slapdash pair of initials, a tight spiral of a signature was coiled up at the bottom. "So I made a visit to your housemother, who, by the way, is exactly as scary as you've claimed, and who also seems pretty interested in this whole thing. She called it *avant-garde found theater*, which sounds vaguely complimentary."

"I'm going to get this filed tomorrow," Isaac said. "I'm going to stay in the Student Life office until I see them get it done myself. We have the signatures. Caskey can't stop it from happening."

I clutched the paper for a minute, waiting for some sort of inevitable contradiction, maybe, for one of the guys to speak up. *No, we don't want you. No, no, no*. The retraction, the rejection.

All my plans had come undone. Everything was exposed. It didn't seem possible that this was where it got me.

Why was I so afraid, all of a sudden? Nervous like I hadn't been in months?

"But I—I have a flight home tomorrow," I said. "I can't cancel it."

"We talked to the Aural Fixation guys," Isaac said. "They can take care of all that. The only thing is whether you want to come with us."

My hold tightened on the corner of the flag in my hand, and I snuck the word out into the air: "Yeah." It hung there for a moment, hesitant, before settling. Then smiles started creasing faces, heads started bobbing, and the inimitable relief of crossing some sort of finish line rushed into me, cold and overwhelming.

CODA

DECEMBER 31

I JOGGED DOWNSTAIRS TO THE HOTEL LOBBY TO FIND that nightmares do come true: Isaac and Michael were leaning against the wall by the stairwell, talking. As I approached, they cracked up about something or other, Michael's nose crinkling up at the bridge, Isaac's unconcerned laugh bouncing off the metallic lobby's slopes and edges. I immediately assumed that they were comparing notes on the way I kissed and that my defects were hilarious, but I would never find out, because everybody is too polite to tell someone they're a bad kisser.

This had to happen at some point, I figured. For two weeks, they'd managed not to talk. I was lucky I'd made it this long.

Michael and I had talked the first day of tour. The talk had consisted of two parts: 1) an elaborate eight-minute apology he'd clearly scripted and figured out how to perform, which probably would have made your average audience-goer shed a tear but which left me weirdly indifferent, and 2), the realization that I had nothing to say to him, because time was the rope that hung into the pit of heartbreak and I'd finally climbed over its lip. I had no desire to look back over the edge. Some things are made to end. Storms, and winters, and hurts.

This was our last stop, the New Year's Eve show in London. Tomorrow, Aural Fixation was headed to Germany, and the Sharps were flying back to the States on a horrifically early flight. I was almost looking forward to it. At least it wouldn't have the distinct scent of urine that had permeated the back of the bus over the past few days.

Our voices were all but shot. We performed only twenty-five minutes a night, but constantly being around each other, we were talking our vocal cords into disrepair. Something about traveling, too—the bus's recycled air, maybe, or inhaling the grime of cities after the Kensington fresh air—had us all drinking hot water with lemon out of thermoses and mumbling about "saving voice," like complete caricatures of ourselves. Trav had taken to carrying around a whiteboard that read "Vocal Rest: Do Not Talk to Me," which resulted in everyone asking him increasingly insulting questions, trying to get him to crack.

"Hey, blue jay," Isaac said as I passed him and Michael. I'd been determinedly staring at my feet but couldn't stop myself from looking up at the sound of his voice. He looked like a hug feels, soft black jeans cuffed and dark sweater pushed to his elbows.

"Hey," I said, pausing midstep. With Michael's eyes fixed on me, I felt an urge to prove something, to show him how I'd moved on, to show him that this new relationship was important, too—that my entire life could still be full of important things without him. A lot of pressure for a three-second interaction.

I took a long breath and let it go. Isaac was smiling, and I smiled back. I was happy. That mattered by itself.

I walked forward, past the long stretch of welcome desk that gleamed bright purple in the light of dangling bulbs. I passed ten-foot-high panels of surrealist wall art, all incomprehensible jumbles of facial features and landscapes where seas dribbled into skies. I skirted the deep rock pool sunk into the lobby floor, which was guarded by a shin-high glass perimeter. I was convinced that this hotel's designer had been given the directions, "Imagine an acid trip that looks like it's worth eighty million dollars."

The rest of the Sharps were seated in a far corner of the lobby, where a trio of weirdly shaped sofas faced a wall-mounted TV. Jon Cox, Mama, and Erik were riveted on an American football game. Somebody in white hurtled into somebody in black. The ball popped free from his arms, and Mama let out a small, anguished wail, capsizing backward into the sofa. How had they even found a channel that played football on this side of the Atlantic?

"Hey," I said, sitting beside Nihal, who was on his phone for once. Mostly, he didn't approve of phones in public. "What are you doing?" I said, reaching over to flick at his screen.

He dodged, frowning at me. "Oh, just avoiding harassment, as always."

I grinned. "Ready for the concert?"

"I suppose you could convince me to sing tonight." He issued a belabored sigh.

"Just . . ." I waved a hand. "Just do your texting, millennial."

He obliged, looking back at his phone with a half-smile. It warmed me. The first few days of tour had consisted of superficial conversation and avoiding each other's eyes. On day four—night four, really, past midnight in Berlin—we'd given in and talked, leaning against the balcony rail outside his and Marcus's hotel room as compact cars trailed by far below. I'd unleashed an elaborate babble of apology, round two. Nihal had told me that after everything Dr. Caskey had said in the greenroom, he could understand why I'd been desperate to hide. A week out from the talk, we were beginning to find our old dynamic again.

"I see you and Isaac have detached yourselves from each other for once," he drawled.

"We're not *that* bad."

"You're pretty bad."

I sighed. To their credit, the Sharps were less insufferable about me and Isaac than they could have been. The worst thing had been when Trav very seriously sat us down and gave us a talking-to about how this could not be allowed to affect our professionalism. I'd nearly cried from trying not to laugh.

I sank into the sofa, staring up at the hotel ceiling, glad to be in a stationary location. Touring exhausted me more than I could have imagined, the cycle of boarding the bus, driving all day, checking into a new city, performing, and crashing. Wake up, rinse, repeat. It was exhilarating but intimidating, every city too huge for us to absorb much of anything before we were accelerating out of it. The entire experience was already blurring over in hindsight, becoming an indistinct black-and-white reel of dark bus seats and spotlights.

"Sharps!" called one of the Aural Fixation guys as they crowded out of the hotel restaurant. "Game time."

♫

We filed up the steps toward the stage. With the hand that wasn't holding a mic, I patted Marcus on the back—one night, the performance space had overwhelmed him so much, he'd had breathing problems and nearly blacked out halfway through a song.

We came out, blinking, into the lights, which dangled from the frame of metal scaffolding like grapes on a web of vines. The stage was smaller than most we'd performed on—unsurprisingly, New Year's Eve meant more people interested in staggering drunk through the streets than attending a singing concert—but the roar of the crowd inundated us. A semicircle of eight stools waited ahead.

We'd stripped away most of our choreography. As the opener, we needed to warm the crowd up but couldn't risk seeming like the main event. So wardrobe had us in simple matching outfits, dark jeans and heather-gray shirts, and we performed the front half of our set seated. The four songs from our competition set, plus the two we'd performed at Daylight Dance, occupied all the time they'd asked us to fill.

We took our seats, lifted eight mics, and sang. It was all muscle memory by now: the reassurance of the set going off like clockwork, and the trust hanging heavy between the eight of us.

Near the end of the set, as we were on our feet near the edge of the stage, I found myself looking around at the guys instead of playing the crowd. This was the last of the lasts I had to count: the last time I'd be performing with them.

Our voices wound around each other, chased each other up scales and down riffs in parallel. I remembered watching them perform last year: From the audience, their performances had seemed synchronized into a single machine. Here, singing among them, it was impossible not to focus instead on the harmony and the dissonance, the ways we converged and the ways we clashed, the tension and the resolution. The machine had cracked open to reveal not a collection of cogs but a multiplicity of colored threads, alive and humming. I was going to carry these colors with me a long time.

JANUARY 1

ISAAC WAS QUIET IN SLEEP, AND STILL. FOR A MOMENT I looked at him, his planes and valleys equalized, everything about his face flattened and hazed by the half-light of the opening morning. The glow snuck in through the airplane window.

"Hey," I whispered, brushing the back of his hand.

Jon Cox had been assigned the boarding pass reading *27A*, but when we'd filed down the aisle a few hours ago, he'd stood aside, waving me in beside Isaac. "All yours," he mumbled, and sat in the seat I'd been assigned, in front of us, where Isaac put his knees up on the back of his chair for three hours just to piss him off. True gratitude.

Now the guys, like everyone else on the plane, were unconscious. We'd reached the fatigue section of the flight; we'd all given up on the ambitions we'd had sitting down. I had abandoned my plan to marathon three movies in a row after finishing the first, which was discouragingly terrible. Nihal's sketchbook, meant to document the trip from top to bottom, was slipped into a seat back as he slept silently against the porthole window behind us.

Isaac stirred next to me. He pawed at one eye to wake up, a little clumsy. When he saw me he smiled. "What's up?"

"I think we should talk before we get to the airport." After we touched down in Newark, the eight of us would split, half to connecting flights, half done with the journey. For me, it was another six-hour leg to San Francisco.

"Yeah," he said, keeping his voice low. "Okay."

The drone of the plane engines hummed along. I took a deep breath. "So, I guess . . . do you want to keep this going when I'm home?"

He thought about it, and kept thinking. My thoughts began to fray, excitement into anxiety, hope into dejection. This was it. The moment he told me he didn't care, or not in the right way, or not enough. Here, again, another moment of letting go.

"How are you feeling about it?" he asked. "Do you want to stay together?"

Obviously, I thought. *This is a terrible sign*, I thought.

"I mean," I said, "I want to try."

But then relief eased his expression. "All right." He leaned forward, resting the side of his head on Jon Cox's seat. He studied me. "Then let's try."

I let out a slow breath. My hand loosened on my wrist, which I had been squeezing, afraid. But it was all right. I wouldn't have to look back on this as a hinging moment that swung the track from hope to hurt, yes to no. At least for now, we were still on the rails together.

"But you have to be honest," I whispered, after a moment.

"About what?"

"Everything. I'm serious, everything." I swallowed. "Don't keep something from me because you think I can't handle it. If something happens, or if you're not feeling it anymore. If—if there's someone else. Just tell me."

Comprehension started to settle into his face. "Jordan."

"Because I can get hurt. That's fine. But I don't want to feel stupid again. Ever."

He reached for my hand and squeezed.

"Can you do that?" I said hoarsely. "All honesty, full disclosure?"

"Can *you*?" he said.

It took me aback for a moment. Then I tightened my hand on his. "Yeah," I said. "I'm gonna try. I'm gonna always try."

♫

The coolness of the San Francisco January still felt tropical compared to the weather of the last couple months. I stepped off the bus in the early afternoon—half my day having reappeared thanks to time zones—and it growled off. The brisk wind flicked my short hair. I needed to trim the back, which was approaching mullet status.

The few blocks I walked to get home were in the middle of a serious identity crisis. My building, similar to the ones flanking it, was a mildewing brick face painted the perfect mathematical average between gray and brown. The only color was a greenish awning, which stretched over the glass doors of a shuttered business, and the snatches of muted reds behind window screens, two by two, four stories up. But from where I stood in front of our building, I saw sleek new projects in chic pastels not even a block away, with crisply trimmed bay windows and Victorian flourishes. When I was in elementary school, there'd been cheap brick housing rising high from that corner.

Everything was how I remembered it. The percussion of the passing cars blending into the groan of the outside door. The echo and faint stink in the stairwell. The cheerful barking of the lapdog on the second floor, the amused Spanish chatting of the lady in 3C. The light that caught all the dust. My front door.

I pulled my suitcase in and wedged the door shut. A bright, narrow hall stretched ahead, with old family photographs and certificates of my achievements taped to the wall at my left. Our four rooms lined up to the right: bedroom, bathroom, bedroom, kitchen. My parents' voices were bouncing around the space.

I kicked off my shoes and headed for the kitchen. The suitcase's wheels down the hall sounded like the hollowness of the highway. I stopped in the threshold, feeling the exhausted relief of a homecoming.

My father sat at the table at the far side of the room, a can of beer in front of him, crosswords and papers scattered before our ancient computer. My mother stood up from the table, her thick hair escaping its neat left part. She rushed to me, her cheeks two bubbles of restrained smile. "Give me a hug," she said, preempting this by binding me into a hug. I let my suitcase go and hugged her tightly. She'd gained weight; she threatened to spill out of my arms.

"Getting so thin again," she said. "They must not feed you anything."

She let go and looked up at me—"Your beautiful hair, *ai yah,*"—and with a single *tsk* of her tongue, turned away to fuss with my suitcase, rolling it back down the hall. I approached my dad, who wheeled his chair my way and reached out an arm. I leaned down to tuck my head over his shoulder as we hugged. "Welcome back," he said gruffly.

As we separated, I glanced over his crossword. "This one's Monaco, I think," I said, pointing. "Kelly Monaco."

Dad filled it in. "Can't ever finish them," he said. "There's always something or other. Actors, baseball players . . . I don't know how they expect me to know who these people are. Look at this—I can't get half the questions. Useless." He dropped the pen and leaned back with a sigh. I found myself smiling. I'd somehow managed to miss my father's constant dissatisfaction. Between him and my mother, I was the *least* perfectionist member of the family, which was a pretty pathetic state of affairs.

My attention shifted from the crossword to the papers scattered around it. I frowned, my eyes catching on the Kensington-Blaine logo.

I picked the top sheet up. The transfer application was only half filled in. "Mom," I called, turning around, "shouldn't you guys have mailed this in by now?"

She reappeared in the threshold of the kitchen, exchanging a long glance with my dad. It held volumes. Something in that glance, or in the air, told me there'd been a sea change between them. Maybe this wasn't just a peaceful period. Maybe it was really and truly peacetime again.

"Mom?" I repeated, after a moment.

She sighed. "We've been talking with a woman from your school. Reese Garrison, who sent us the form. She told us to wait until the New Year, so. We waited."

"And?" I said.

"And—" My mom waved her hands, a dismissive flourish. "I thought with the plays, if they didn't cast you, they didn't care. But this woman's really pushing."

Dad spoke up. "She called a couple days ago and told us about a School Board meeting they had this break. She said every year there's a motion to change the financial aid, so she brought in a petition about what you did this semester, had a list of faculty sign it, and it—" He waved at the papers. "You can read it. She sent us a copy."

I rifled through the papers and found a page-long letter with Reese's signature. I scanned it, my heart beating faster and faster. By the conclusion, I was lightheaded: ". . . *this social disguise project embodies the aggressive, real-life approach to artistic and, more specifically, theatrical applications we seek to engender in our student body. It shows a keen interest in both character study and improvisation, and from the length of the commitment, a dedication to the Kensington ideal: art through perseverance. Unfortunately, Ms. Sun's financial experience with the academy demonstrates a fundamental weakness of Kensington's current policy. She is one example of the losses we incur annually—not of funds but of exceptional academic and creative talent. We fail current students and applicants alike by using an outdated, limiting financial aid system. Luckily, the Board has the capacity to create change, and to work toward a more comprehensive, realistic network of support for low-income, often first-generation students.*"

I lowered it. God, Reese had made cutting off all my hair and cross-dressing sound like a dissertation.

"So what happened?" I asked hoarsely. "What'd she say?"

"Well, I guess they passed it," Dad said, one finger tracing the crossword absentmindedly. It occurred to me how contented he looked. "Six votes to five," he said, "starting this semester. They credited us for your flight back already."

The paper was crumpling in my hand. "And can I get on that flight?" I asked, and I knew the answer, had known it from the second my mother admitted she might have been wrong. I was going back. I could already imagine myself there. I found myself submerged in the future, again, as always. Everything flowed smoothly forward from this frozen instant: first, the rumble of hitting the runway in the Watertown airport. Then, the slow drive up to Arthur's Arch and through, that distinct sensation of slipping into a new world, as if through the wardrobe, while the Kensington winter closes me in. No longer barricaded in my room, no longer torn in two, I'm myself this time around. This time I track the Sharps down across campus just to see their faces. I am not afraid. Night falls and I walk up stone steps to a red door, laughter glowing behind it like treasure, with my hand in the grip of someone who respects me. I am honest; I am honest again. A new semester's classes break in, and I scan the collection of students arranged around the table, familiar and unfamiliar, old stirred in with new, and I feel eager and spoiled, and I think I am never going to do arm's-length again, I want everyone close. The gas-jet fire flickers in the Burgess Lounge as we scribble in silence, extracting all the scrambling thoughts from our heads, learning to line them up in order. We walk into the next audition heads up and fearless, because no matter how many times we've heard *no*, we still imagine the answer will be *yes, yes, yes*.

fin

ACKNOWLEDGMENTS

BECAUSE I AM A CHINESE GIRL WHO UNTIL VERY recently spent 90 percent of her time singing a cappella music, it's worth reiterating that all the characters in this book are entirely fictional and none of them are based on real human beings. Except two. And they're the loosest of loose adaptations. Thanks, Clara, for letting me steal approximately three of your mannerisms, and Annie, for providing my inspiration for Anabel, who actually turned out nothing like you in the end, but there we go, I guess.

I owe this novel to the people who make it possible for me to do what I love: my beyond-supportive family; my champion agent, Caryn Wiseman; my brilliant editor, Anne Heltzel; and the rest of Amulet's amazing team, especially Caitlin Miller. Thank you guys for dealing with my neuroses. Hugs and kisses also to my early readers, Mary Frame and Suzanne Payne, and the rest of my beloved Goat Posse.

A big thanks to Iori Kusano, Jackie Rayson, and Justin Martin for their invaluable insights on matters of disability, class, and trans visibility within the novel. Thanks also to the folks at

Writing in the Margins for helping to promote and facilitate authors' critical engagement with the representation within their work.

To the Kenyon College Chamber Singers, the Owl Creeks, and the ladies of Colla Voce: I love you; thank you for the mem'ries that dwell dear past supposing. Love also to my friends in Take Five, the Ransom Notes, the Stairwells, the Chasers, the Cornerstones, Mannerchör, and the Kokosingers.

Next, one of those weird, distant notes to people I don't know: thanks to the NU Nor'easters and UChicago's Voices in Your Head for making gorgeous and innovative a cappella music that I listened to nonstop while writing this novel. If you care at all about a cappella, you must listen to VIYH's cover of "We Found Love" and the Nor'easters' album *RISE* posthaste. While I'm at it, check out The Sons of Pitches, who sound the way I imagine the Sharpshooters sounding.

Lastly: the artists in this book do not exist, but the songs do. You can listen to them on my website, http://rileyredgate.com, if you're so inclined.